T0149638

Also by Mima

Fire
A Spark before the Fire
The Rock Star of Vampires
Her Name is Mariah
Different Shades of the Same Color
We're All Animals
Always be a Wolf

THE DEVIL IS SMOOTH LIKE Honey

MIMA

iUniverse®

THE DEVIL IS SMOOTH LIKE HONEY

iUniverse books may be ordered through booksellers or by contacting:

iUniverse
1663 Liberty Drive
Bloomington, IN 47403
www.iuniverse.com
1-800-Authors (1-800-288-4677)

ISBN: 978-1-5320-3211-0 (sc)
ISBN: 978-1-5320-3212-7 (e)

Library of Congress Control Number: 2017913391

Print information available on the last page.

iUniverse rev. date: 09/11/2017

ACKNOWLEDGEMENTS

Special thanks to Jean Arsenault, Mitchell Whitlock, John Howard and Jim Brown for their assistance and helpful suggestions. Special shout out to goingon.ca for the awesome ads!

Thank you to all my readers and everyone who has encouraged and supported my writing journey. It means the world to me.

CHAPTER 1

One never knows when life will give them a beautiful moment that will define their entire existence. It's that one moment when everything changes on a dime. The key is that you should always be ready for it to happen; expecting it, wanting it, dreaming of it. You can't worry about tomorrow or overthink yesterday, you must be aware so that you can fully acknowledge it's smooth and graceful presence. You must smell it, taste it and hold it close to your heart because it's that memory you will forever replay again and again, during those most difficult times when life seems unbearable and pushes you to the limit.

Jorge Hernandez had learned this lesson at an early age. Of course, there was nothing about that particular day indicating he was about to experience a beautiful moment that would change his life; quite the opposite, actually.

After getting tied up by a *perra* at airport security; a very masculine, white woman who attempted to intimidate him, holding him up just long enough to make him late at the car rental section, in turn forcing him to take some piece of shit compact, he was at his limit. Even all of this he could've tolerated, had he not arrived at his hotel to learn that the fuckers had overbooked, leaving him with some crap room that was probably designated for the cleaning staff to take a break in rather than the deluxe suite he had originally reserved.

"You gotta be fucking kidding me?" Jorge dropped his charming side, no longer presenting his infectious smile, that spark in his eye that usually made women melt had disappeared somewhere between airport security and the car rental, as another woman fucked with his day.

Jorge's warm brown eyes briefly glazed over as he tilted his head down, an upward gaze didn't hide his aggravation. "I get caught up at fucking security after sitting on a plane all day then at the car rental and now *you're* telling me I have to sleep in some broom closet. I booked this suite weeks ago. I have a meeting with business associates in the morning. What the fuck am I supposed to do? Have my meeting in the *lounge?*"

"I understand, Mr. Hernandez," The young woman behind the counter sympathized, her face a glowing shade of pink as she frantically tapped on the keyboard, while a small crowd of professionally dressed people either waited at the desk or wandered through the lobby, staring at their smartphones like mindless teenagers. Of all the times he had been to this particular hotel, Jorge never saw so many patrons in the lobby. Not that this was *his* problem.

"It looks like your usual deluxe suite was booked but someone changed it," She continued to look flushed and a quick glance at her name tag revealed she was Angela. Petit, white, young, he guessed her no older than 25, she sincerely seemed confused by what had taken place. "I don't understand."

Leaning in closer, he managed to muster the last drop of patience he had left as he calmly spoke. "Look, Angela, *señorita*, I know this isn't your fault but I gotta have my usual suite. Did anyone check into it yet?"

Angela bit her lip and shook her head as if to confide confidential information to him.

"Perfect, then I need you to get your manager or supervisor so I can sort this out." He spoke in the most gentle voice possible.

She nodded, reaching for the phone while Jorge took a deep breath and racked his brain. If every hotel in the city was booked, he wasn't about to do any better if he called around and judging from the professional looking crowd that surrounded him, he certainly wouldn't find a suite.

"Mr. Hernandez?" Angela's voice interrupted his thoughts. "Mr. Gomez will be here shortly."

A smile crept on Jorge's face. After a long day of white women making his life hell, he was finally going to talk to a *man; a Latino* man. He felt some relief.

"Thank you, Angela, your help is appreciated," He made eye contact with her and flashed the charming smile that seemed to work with most women; not airport security or the woman at the car rental place, but most women.

A tall, older gentleman appeared, his eyes immediately met with Jorge's as he approached. Wearing a gray suit that barely camouflaged his protruding stomach, he gave a professional, fake smile as he moved closer. Extending his hand, Jorge could smell a hint of cheap aftershave as he leaned forward and the two men shook hands.

"Mr. Hernandez?" His smile began to fade immediately after a brief handshake and Jorge was left wondering if he simply came out of his office to confirm what Angela had previously told him. Ignoring the reluctance he sensed, Jorge launched into his plea.

"*¡Oh, gracias a Dios! Parece que hay cierta confusión….*"

"Oh, I'm sorry," The manager immediately put his hand up in the air and Jorge didn't miss the self-conscious expression on his face as he stepped back. "I don't speak Spanish."

"Oh?" Jorge asked with a hint of surprise in his voice, raising his eyebrows, he stepped forward and purposely thickened his accent. "I'm surprised with a name like Gomez that you don't speak Spanish."

"No, unfortunately, I cannot," He halted, as if about to give further explanation and decided against it. "Would you like to step into my office for a moment so we can take a look at this situation a little more closely. I'm curious what went wrong because I'm aware that you're a regular guest with us."

"I always come here," Jorge replied as he pulled his suitcase behind him, noting that the manager didn't offer to help. It was a bit awkward between the suitcase and the laptop bag slung over his shoulder. He didn't exactly travel light.

"We definitely appreciate your business," The manager continued as he ushered him into a modest office not far from the reception area and closed the door. The room was dark, a bit dreary with no windows, not what Jorge would've expected for such an expensive hotel. "Please have a seat."

Jorge didn't reply, quietly following instructions, his eyes did a quick scan of the room; family pictures, a telephone, desktop computer, it was sparsely decorated, cluttered with boxes, the room was a mess. Showing fake compassion, Jorge decided to acknowledge this fact, knowing that sometimes it helped to get what he wanted.

"Did they move you into a dungeon?" He made a face and glanced around. "No window? Sunlight?"

Mr. Gomez took a deep breath and shook his head as he sat behind his desk. "It's temporary while they paint my office upstairs. I know, it's hardly ideal."

"Yes, speaking of hardly ideal," Hernandez decided to get right to the point as he relaxed in the chair, something his body welcomed after a long day. "I booked the deluxe suite weeks ago and I get here after flying in from Mexico and find it's no longer mine."

"Yes, that is quite unusual," Gomez replied and immediately started to tap on his keyboard. "I see here there is a Hernandez booked for the suite but not a Jorge."

Cringing at the Spanish pronunciation of his name that sounded like *Horhay*, he quickly corrected him. "I go by the English pronunciation of my name."

"Oh, really?" Gomez replied and gave another fake smile. "And here I thought I was impressing you with the one Spanish thing I did know."

Thing. Hernandez matched his fake smile and simply nodded. "I prefer the English pronunciation."

"I see here that the other Hernandez hasn't checked in yet, so I will just change it back to your name," Gomez commented as if he hadn't heard Jorge's last comment; not that he gave a fuck, as long as he got his suite and maybe something complimentary since this fuck up was the final straw of his day. "Not all the information is filled out so perhaps it was a computer glitch of some kind. Very unusual."

Jorge merely nodded, relief filled his body.

"*Perfecto.*"

After filling out the proper information and receiving a generous discount on the room, Jorge finally found himself in the familiar suite, the same one he usually stayed in while in Toronto on business. He occasionally shared it with his 10-year-old daughter Maria but he didn't like to take her out of school unless necessary. In fact, he recently had a longtime employee move into his home in order to look after Maria while he was away.

Officially, he was there as a sales rep for his father's coffee company, a popular brand, a delicacy in specialty shops that sold a premium product and not the slop that most people had grown used to drinking. It was amazing how whip cream, mountains of sugar and milk could make any *mierda* acceptable to call coffee. It was fascinating how most people settled for substandard products, substandard lives. But to him, *good enough* wasn't enough. Life was too short. He didn't want to become like his father, a man whose spirit had long died as he settled for a dull, average existence.

Jorge was very different from his parents. To him, life was about passion, impulsiveness and living on the edge as if there was no tomorrow. From that first second that his heart began to race, whether it be a result of excitement or danger, he felt his spirit soar, an intensity that could not be matched by anything else. He couldn't imagine living any other way. Once you felt that blood-rushing exhilaration, you couldn't go back.

He didn't play it safe and had it not been for Maria, he probably would've lived much more carelessly, as he had in his 20s but now a man in his 40s, his priorities had changed. Family mattered now. Loyalty was vastly more important than it had been when he was young, as was honesty. If Jorge found out anyone lied or crossed him, they were dead to him. Maria's mother had learned that the hard way.

After settling into his suite, Jorge made a quick call to his daughter followed by his business associates and finally, he went into the bathroom. Turning on the shower, he slowly removed his suit as an unexpected sadness filled his heart. Jorge's eyes were dull in the mirror, his sparkling smile had long faded with the day, a sense of gloom reflected back, his charming side merely a mask for what was beneath the surface. The truth was that he lived a secret life; no one really knew him, not his business associates nor his family because there were so many details that he could never share. It was a lonely existence and in many ways, hiding the truth weighed him down.

Glancing down at his naked body before getting in the shower, Jorge was proud that he hadn't let himself go as many men his age had, with their pot bellies and unkempt appearance. Other than a hint of gray in his hair and a few lines on his face, Jorge had a youthful appearance. However, a recent birthday was a subtle reminder that youth was fleeting and maybe one day his worst fear would come true and he would become his father; old, passionless, miserable. How did one find and keep an inner joy that others seem to have naturally? It was a question constantly on his mind.

The warm water from the shower was welcoming, soothing, as he leaned into it and allowed the stress of the day to run down the drain. Although he briefly considered watching some porn with a glass of wine after the shower, he was exhausted and instead drifted off in the king sized bed before he could even get his laptop opened or a drink poured.

Jorge was having a wonderful sleep filled with dreams of a beautiful woman fulfilling his every desire when suddenly, his eyes flew open. Now in a dark room, it took him a minute to remember where he was but what had awakened him? There was a sound. Rising from his bed, he regretfully remembered that his gun was still snug in the luggage by the door.

Pulling on his boxers, Jorge quietly made his way toward his suitcase at the entrance, led only by a dim light from a nearby lamp. It was when he was only steps away from reaching it that he could hear the click of a gun and a calm voice instructing him to stop, get on his knees and put his hands behind his head. It was a woman's voice. Why did that not surprise him?

CHAPTERS *2*

Her voice was smooth, gentle and under almost any other circumstances, it's soothing calamity would've brought Jorge a sense of comfort. His heart began to race erratically, almost as if it was about to jump out of his chest and land on the floor in front of him and yet, mixed with this intense fear was an unexpected dash of arousal. Her tone was sexy and warm, reminding him of a lover whispering in his ear just as he was about to climax. It wasn't logical but then again, weren't women a series of contradictions?

Although still a bit groggy, Jorge quickly realized that this wasn't a cop. The door hadn't been broken in, there wasn't a stream of people overtaking his room yelling commands or arresting him. The room was in fact, very still and silent, the only light coming from a small lamp he had turned on shortly after his arrival. Confused, he tried to think who had sent her.

"Ok ok, I'm on my knees, I got my hands in the air," Jorge replied, showing his willingness to cooperate, his voice relaxed despite the pounding in his chest, the adrenaline rushing through his body, he was suddenly more awake than he had been in weeks. "I'm doing everything you're asking. Can you at least tell me who you are? Why you're here? Who sent you? Are you robbing me?"

"It doesn't matter who I am," She replied with no emotion in her voice, reminding him of someone giving a meditation workshop and not preparing to kill him. He didn't have to turn around to know it was a white woman; her voice, his day, the theme suddenly felt like the

Gods were mocking him. "I'm here for Joe Romano and I think you know why."

There was a long pause before Jorge replied.

"Lady, I don't know any Joe Romano."

"I think you do."

"Look, I've made some enemies along the way but not Romano."

"Moretti, Gallo.."

"*Senorita*, I got almost no dealings with the Italians," Jorge replied, although, despite the relaxed voice, he was racking his brain to match the names with anyone from his past but he was coming up empty. The last thing he wanted to do was piss off the Italians.

When she didn't reply, he desperately continued without allowing any emotion to leak into his voice. "Look, there was a fuck up earlier today and I wasn't even supposed to be in this room, maybe you got the wrong guy." His heart raced extra fast; the longer she was silent, the more nervous he grew. This wasn't a disgruntled woman with a gun pointed at him nor was she a lightweight, everything added up to the fact that she was a professional for hire.

"Hernandez?"

"Yes, but they had some other Hernandez booked in my room," Jorge continued to keep his cool, despite the fact that there was a gun somewhere behind him, his heart continuing to race frantically. Maria's face suddenly appeared in his mind and he couldn't stop emotions from creeping into his voice as his eyes watered. "Look.... I got a little girl. She doesn't have anyone else. Whatever, whoever is paying you, I'll pay you more to walk away."

She remained silent but he could hear her backing away from him.

"My passport," He suddenly remembered the document he threw on the coffee table upon arriving in the suite. "It's on that table. Check it."

She didn't reply but he heard her shuffling.

"And even if it was a fake passport, I'm not going to have the same last name," He continued to rationalize. "Please *señorita*, whatever you want, I'll give it to you."

He thought she let out a sigh and fought the temptation to glance over his shoulder but didn't want to push his luck. Just then, a cell vibrated. It was hers.

"This isn't him," Her voice was calm. "I don't know. But this definitely is *not* him. This guy is Jorge Hernandez and he's from Mexico."

Hearing her use the Spanish pronunciation of his name, he cringed. "That's Jorge, like your English name George? If you're going to blow my head off, can you at least pronounce my name properly, *señorita*?"

He felt his heart race even faster as if to remind him that silence was necessary but he always hated the Spanish pronunciation of his name, ever since he was a child.

"*Jorge* Hernandez," She pronounced it correctly with a touch of humor in her voice. "He's sensitive to the pronunciation and...."

Her voice fell, a sexy moan came from her throat and although it clearly wasn't sexual, it still caused the blood to rush to a very inappropriate place given the predicament he was in. It was when he heard her voice moving away, that he slowly turned his head to peek over his shoulder. Her back to him, his eyes landed on her ass; a beautiful, round ass so tightly fit into her jeans that it looked like it was about to erupt from the top at the first opportunity. He attempted to see the outline of underwear through the jeans but couldn't. Did that mean she wasn't wearing any or perhaps a skimpy, little thong?

"I wasn't aware of that," She was saying and started to turn back in his direction, causing Jorge to abruptly return his attention forward while the thoughts of her ass were still prominent in his brain, he felt his dick getting hard as he listened to her smooth voice. "I see."

There was another long silence.

"Mr. Hernandez, this is very awkward but apparently, I was sent to the wrong room," She started to speak. "Right room, actually but the wrong guy. I'm putting my gun away."

"Can I stand?"

"Of course, I.. I don't know what to say," She started. "This has never happened to me before and I.."

Jorge stood up, his eyes fully focused on her face. She was a pretty blonde-not the whorish blonde he often saw when in places like

California, but the respectable shade that was flattering next to her blue eyes and pale skin. Unfortunately, those same eyes immediately were alerted to the involuntary erection that was the result of the excitement and her inspiring attributes. Chances were she wouldn't see it as a compliment.

"Oh my God," She calmly remarked and looked away, her hand rose in the air as if to block the view. "This is turning you on. You do realize I was about to kill you, right?"

Slightly dazzled by her combination of strength and softness, he didn't know how to respond to her question at first.

"I know," He finally replied, a devilish grin formed on his lips. He couldn't stop staring at her and in a way, her awkwardness brought him pleasure.

"Do you always get turned on when someone points a gun at you?" She continued to make great efforts to look away.

"Only when it's a woman with a sexy voice and an ass I'd like to sink my teeth into," Jorge suddenly felt quite brazen as he headed to the small kitchen area, turning on another lamp on his way. "Do you want a glass of wine?"

"What?" She seemed dumbfounded by his question. "Look, I gotta go. I was told *who* you are so I know that you probably aren't going to call the police and.."

"This isn't the first time I've had a gun pointed at me?" Jorge replied as he grabbed the bottle of wine he had ordered earlier that night but was too tired to drink. Placing it on the counter, he was searching through the drawers for a corkscrew. "No, but it's the first time it turned me on," He paused for a moment to glance in her direction. "I guess we learn new things about ourselves every day."

Appearing stunned, as if she was carefully evaluating the situation, she remained calm and at first, didn't reply.

"I appreciate the fact that you're so understanding.."

"I am," Jorge finally found the corkscrew and reached for some glasses and sat them on the counter. "Look, it's just business. You're clearly an assassin and obviously, a good one if you got in here and past security. There was a mistake, you didn't kill me...it's ok but if you could stay, have a quick drink with me." He stopped what he was doing and tilted his head, looking in her direction. "It'll help me relax."

With an astonished expression on her face, a small grin appeared on her lips as she glanced toward the door and then back at him. "I don't know how relaxed you think I'm going to make you, Mr. Hernandez but, I'm an assassin, not an escort."

Jorge laughed as he opened the bottle of wine. "I don't think you're an escort. I'm familiar with escorts, you're not an escort." Grabbing the bottle and glasses he walked out of the kitchen, noticing her glancing at his crotch casually, seeing he had somehow managed to calm slightly since moments earlier, he said nothing and walked toward the couch, placing the glasses and bottle on the coffee table before sitting down.

"A quick drink?" He pointed toward the glasses and she hesitantly approached and sat beside him. "Do you mind if I smoke? It also helps relax me."

She shook her head, her eyes glancing at his bare chest and he felt some pride in the fact that he worked out regularly and it showed. Reaching for his cigarettes, he felt pleasure ring through his body with that first drag and he let out an involuntary moan.

"My daughter wants me to quit but I gotta tell you," He took a second drag. "If I got to do it, I might blow my *own* fucking head off."

She looked hesitant to laugh and only did so after he did, her eyes continued to watch him. "You have a daughter?" She asked awkwardly as he poured them each a glass of wine.

"Yeah, Maria, she's ten," He replied as he pushed the glass toward her. "She's been begging me to quit and I tried, I really did but I've been smoking since I was a kid. Kinda hard to stop."

"I can imagine it would be." She cautiously reached for her glass and took a small sip.

"You got kids?"

She shook her head no.

"Actually," He leaned forward, suddenly feeling slightly self-conscious about the fact he was almost, completely naked. The rush of the previous moments suddenly falling flat, causing his emotions to rise to the surface. He took a deep breath and pushed them down. "Good thing she wasn't with me tonight."

The assassin's face actually turned whiter than it was before, her eyes grew in size.

"Again, I'm sorry," She stuttered over her words, the first hint of emotion in her voice. "As I said, I've never had this happen before, I'm very thorough. I usually observe my victims for a couple of weeks, get to know their habits but this time, there were unique circumstances."

He looked into her eyes for a long moment, feeling satisfied, he finally shrugged and rubbed his face. "*Señorita*, I've spent as much time on the other end of a gun as you probably have. You don't gotta explain anything to me. I'm not going to do anything to you. No retaliation, I promise. This isn't television. It's real life and now, I just wanna have a drink with you and maybe learn your name. I wouldn't mind finding out who you were really supposed to kill tonight."

"I don't usually talk about my work," She hesitantly took another sip of wine and seemed to change her mind. "Tonight, I was supposed to kill a religious figure who rapes children. He specifically attacks young boys, in poor, Latino communities where families are most vulnerable."

Jorge nodded slowly. "Your rates must be incredibly reasonable if poor families can afford you."

A smirk appeared on her face and she raised an eyebrow. "I assure you, my rates aren't reasonable and it wasn't the families that hired me."

"The church?" He gently asked.

She didn't reply but merely smiled. "The biggest misconception about my work is that my targets are cheating spouses and family members. It's never that simple and there's usually a lot of power behind the money I'm paid."

"So you're not catering to Mr. and Mrs. Jones Middle-class in the suburbs looking for a hitman on Kijiji?" Jorge asked quietly as he licked his lips, feeling his arousal return. He was drawn to the dangerous side of her as much as her softness. It was an unusual contradiction that made him curious and intrigued. There was a great deal of intelligence in her eyes, a set of eyes that had seen many things, he could tell. In a way, she was him.

"No," She quietly replied and appeared to relax, a small grin eased on her lips. "Organizations, politicians, powerful people, but not cheated on wives or people wanting to knock off a relative for money. It's people with a lot of resources who want a problem to go away. And it's often not the people you suspect but fortunately, I always have the option to say no if I'm not comfortable with an assignment."

"You must be good."

"Tonight's episode might prove otherwise," She let out a throaty laugh and he felt saliva increasing in his mouth, as he stared at her taking another drink of the wine. Her lips had a simple gloss, she wore little makeup and her hair was pulled back in a loose ponytail. Wearing a pair of Doc Martens, a black leather coat, and jeans, she would easily go under the radar despite her beauty.

"If I saw you walking down the street, I'd never pick you out as an assassin," His comment was almost seductive, his voice a gentle tone that didn't appear to go unnoticed. "Just the girl next door."

She let out another laugh. "Not in a neighborhood you want to live in."

He joined her and looked back down at his wine glass.

"The idea is to go unnoticed," She replied. "So no red lipstick, in fact when I'm working, I stay away from bright colors all together. No short dresses, no loud heels, not a lot of makeup, I keep things simple. The beauty of being a woman is that it doesn't take much for people to underestimate you cause most already do, so it's easy to keep under the radar."

"That's an interesting observation and I must say, simple works for you," He felt an unexpected dash of shyness and took another puff off his cigarette followed by a long drink of his wine, finishing the glass. He put out his cigarette and poured another glass of wine. "So, you must be a good shot?"

"I'm a great shot," She replied and took another sip of her wine and although her glass wasn't empty, he leaned forward to refill it. She didn't stop him. "I can shoot someone from directly behind and kill them immediately or from across the street. I can make it look like a suicide or accident, in fact, that's my specialty. That's actually the most common request."

Her voice was soft, gentle, reminding him of the original moments when she had a gun behind him and he felt his arousal grow, something that now made him feel awkward, he continued to sit forward and hoped it went unnoticed. He avoided her eyes as he took in her words and let them sink in but her voice was making it difficult to fight off his natural impulses.

"I've been hired by governments, CEOs, philanthropists, celebrities, religious figures, some of the most unexpected people but at the end of the day, are we all that different?" She continued to speak softly. "I've learned that regardless of what people attempt to show the outside world, we all have the same, basic impulses. We seek revenge, we seek retribution. It's what makes us human. We pretend to be evolved but at the end of the day, we're all just cavemen and women who are playing the same game while hiding our natural inclinations."

Jorge turned his head slowly, his eyes fixated on hers and this time, he saw something very different. This time, he knew exactly what he had to do. Easing close to her, he noted she didn't flinch or move away as his breath quickened, he no longer hid his natural inclinations when he moved in and kissed her.

CHAPTER 3

Her name was Paige Noël but this was a fact he wouldn't learn until later that night. It was after he led her to his bed, proceeded to slowly remove her clothes and finally have one of the most intense encounters of his life; one that couldn't be matched with the lack of willpower of his 20s, the monotonous relationships in his 30s or any of the cheap, lazy affairs of recent years but there was a much stronger component involved this time. It was a combination of danger, fear, and arousal mixed together that made the night beyond his expectations, surpassing anything he had experienced with another woman.

Laying in bed, his heart raced erratically as Jorge tried to catch his breath, her name flowing through his mind as he momentarily closed his eyes and enjoyed the vibrations of pleasure that continued to ring through his body. Feeling the sheets move beside him, he abruptly opened his eyes to see her begin to rise from the bed, her pale skin glistening when met with the lights creeping into the room.

"What? Where are you going?" Jorge sat up, feeling a coldness meeting his naked back. He reached out, his hand not quite reaching hers, he heard a desperation in his own voice, something that normally would've filled him with shame. "Don't leave, I want to learn more about you."

"I just thought," She hesitated before reaching for the same pair of thongs he had started to remove with his teeth earlier but ended up ripping off impatiently and throwing aside. "Maybe…look, this is a little weird, right? I mean, we can agree on that, can't we?"

"No," His answer was simple, his voice flat as he shook his head. "I agree it's hardly conventional but isn't that how all the great stories start? Plus, you hardly strike me as a conventional woman, Paige."

She seemed to respond to him saying her name and sat back down on the bed, slowly dropping the thong on the floor. Her large eyes stared at him through the darkness and he reached for her, his fingers slowly grazing over her arm sliding to reach for her hand. She silently got back under the covers and moved closer until his lips gently met with hers. It wasn't like earlier in the night when he practically devoured her but a soft, beautiful moment as he pulled her close, running his hand over her face, down her arm and pulling her even closer, he suddenly stopped.

"Who are you Paige Noël? I want to know everything," He heard his accent thicken, something he attempted to avoid when in Canada, preferring to adopt the local accent as much as possible.

"I think you already know more about me than most people," She whispered, her hot breath touched his face, causing him to reach down and squeeze her ass.

"I know you're an assassin, I know you almost accidentally killed me tonight," Jorge laughed in spite of himself as he continued to run his hands over her body. "I know I just had amazing sex with you and very recently, I learned your name. That is all."

She grinned, one of her hands rested on his chest while the other ran through his hair, something that relaxed him, causing him to fight to stay awake. An unmistakable heat grew between them, making him crave their next encounter. He wanted to make her moan, to scream and lose her mind just one more time and hope it wasn't the last but with white women, you could never be too sure. They were often fickle.

"I hardly know anything about you," She countered. "You're a Mexican man, you have a daughter and you are aroused when a gun is put to your head."

"Ok, I think I explained that one," He grinned. "That doesn't *normally* happen. It's just you. Your voice was so sexy and I turned around and saw your ass and it was over for me."

"So having a gun to your head wasn't a factor?"

"It might've turned me on a bit," He slowly admitted and thought for a moment. "There's something sexy about a powerful woman. There's something *very* sexy about a dangerous woman. I dunno, maybe I related to you."

"You think most women are weak, don't you?" She asked as if she had read his mind.

"I do, actually," Jorge admitted, surprised that she had observed him so carefully. "They make themselves weak. They choose to be weak. To be a victim. It's not something I ever understood. I make sure to not allow my daughter to be the same. I tell her every day she can do anything, there are no limits. She's powerful, she's strong and she believes it. It's hard though. She's often surrounded by women who are weak, who are soft. It's very sad."

"You know, most men prefer weak women," Paige insisted with a soothing tone. "I can promise you that. Not that I'm in the position to tell anyone what I do for a living but I've noticed that as soon as men see that I am a strong person, despite my soft voice and small stature, they often don't like it. That's why you surprise me so much. You're almost the complete opposite."

He attempted to identify her accent as she spoke. Was it Canadian? It had a flair of European and American and he guessed it was due to her travels. He assumed her line of work took her all over the world. It was elegant though, a hint of sophistication flowed through her every word, he could've listened to her all day talking about anything. Literally anything, it was as intoxicating as her perfectly round ass and huge eyes.

"I like to think I'm a little more evolved than a lot of men in some ways," Jorge admitted and shrunk back a bit. "But I'm not going to lie, there are a lot of women who've called me a sexist prick over the years."

She let out a soft laugh.

"Among other things," He continued, humored by her reaction. "I've been called a masochist at least once and a misogynist on more than one occasion. I don't hate women though it's just that, I don't know, they have a way of taking something so simple and making it so complicated. I don't understand."

She grinned and shook her head but didn't reply.

"I mean, obviously I don't hate women," He briefly stared at the ceiling. "I love my daughter more than anything or anyone in this world. I would rip my heart out for her. In fact, when you had a gun to my head tonight, that's the only thing I was thinking about. What would she do without me?"

He looked back just in time to see sadness cross over Paige's eyes and he quickly rushed in to reassure her. "But it's ok. I mean, everything was ok. I'm obviously not the fucking pedophile you were looking for tonight."

"I suspected something was off immediately," Paige gently confessed, her hand moved over his chest and he felt a spark of desire once again but he concentrated on her words. "I didn't feel like you were the right man but it didn't make sense. He came to this hotel earlier today but now, it seems like he just disappeared."

"Who changed the rooms?"

"I didn't know that they had been changed until you told me," Paige admitted. "I just received this assignment last week and clearly something was switched at the last minute. He was coming to Toronto and I was asked to shoot him execution style."

"Why didn't you just do it," Jorge felt his desires continue to build as she spoke. "Why did you even talk to me?"

"I'm often asked to tell the victim who has sent me," She took a breath as if she were about to speak and hesitated briefly. "It's very common. It comes back to the animalistic nature of people. They don't just want my assignments murdered, they also want them to know who was *responsible* for their death. They want them to know this during their last minutes on earth."

"There must be a part of you that enjoys that power," Jorge whispered as he grabbed her ass and pulled her closer. "The domination, the control, knowing you have their lives in your hands." His fingers kneaded her hip as his breath grew labored. "Does it make you feel powerful?"

"Up until a certain point, it's just a job. It's an assignment that I must fulfill, I don't think about it beyond that," She quietly responded, as his tongue ran up the side of her face then his lips reached for her ear. "But there's a moment, just as I'm about to kill them, knowing exactly why they were chosen, why I've been asked to do it that I feel untouchable, like nothing and no one could ever hurt me. It's just a split second, but it's a rush, like a drug that sends you to a place that most people never know exists."

"Ummm…. drugs, now you're in my territory, pretty lady," He whispered in her ear as a soft moan sprung from her lips. "But I'm sure you already know that?"

"I was told you're one of the best in the world and definitely Latin America," Her breath was hot against his face as he pulled her even closer. "Dangerous. Almost as dangerous as me."

He let out a little laugh. "We'll have to compare notes over breakfast tomorrow."

"It's not a very good breakfast topic."

"Maybe you can finally tell me about you instead," Jorge commented through labored breath. "Since all I know about you is your name and what you do for a living."

"I told you more."

"You told me about your assignment tonight, not about you," He replied as his fingers moved to the bottom of her hips and slowly eased between her legs. His lips moved back toward her ear, a place he noticed was highly sensitive earlier that night as his tongue moved along her lobe as she sank back and an unmistakable moan of pleasure filled the room, as his fingers moved deep inside her while his dick grew hard against her thigh. Pulling his fingers away and moving back from her ear, he focused on her eyes that were intently on his face.

"What do you want to know?" She clearly understood the game he was playing.

"How long have you been an assassin?"

"Over 10 years," She calmly replied.

"Why?"

"I was a good shot, someone recognized this in me, groomed me to be who I am today."

"A lover?"

"No."

"You aren't going to tell me who, are you?"

"No."

A grin crossed his lips. "Fair enough. Where are you from?"

"Here."

"Canada?"

"Yes, I live in Toronto."

"Married?"

"No."

"No kids, you said, was that true?"

"No kids."

He pulled her close, squeezing her ass, he slowly grinding against her, causing her to gasp in pleasure.

"There's more where that came from," He moved his lips closer to her face, his hot breath leaving a trail over her cheek, eye to eye with her, Jorge continued his gentle interrogation. "I assume you don't put professional assassin on your Facebook profile"

"I don't have a Facebook profile."

"So what do people think you do?"

"I'm a life coach."

Jorge started to laugh, perhaps a little too heartily to this information. "You're what? What the fuck is a life coach?"

"It's someone who helps you to figure out your life," She seemed to enjoy his reaction.

"You good at that?"

"I don't do it that much," She replied. "It's a front to launder my money. I'm on the Internet, I have a website."

"Facebook?"

"Yes, but it's not my profile. It's my business page."

"Ah, so you kind of lied to me."

"I didn't lie." She calmly replied. "Paige Noël doesn't have a Facebook page, her business does."

"Ok, fair enough, so you're a life coach as far as the government knows?"

"What's with all the questions, are you a cop?" She raised an eyebrow and he sensed that her desire might be fading. He certainly didn't want that.

"No, I assure you, I'm not a fucking cop," He replied. "*Señorita*, I'm anything but a cop. I'm just interested. I'm actually, fascinated."

She didn't reply but stared into his eyes and they were quiet for a moment. "If you must know, it's kind of turning me on."

"Even the life coach thing?"

"No, that shit's just funny," He grinned. "Everything else, is making me horny."

With that, he stopped asking questions and slowly slid his tongue down her body with the intention of making it the most pleasurable night of her life.

CHAPTER 4

How do you return to earth after experiencing a night that could only be described as heaven? Jorge Hernandez would hardly consider himself sentimental and although a bit of a romantic in his youth, he thought those days were long gone since the first bitter taste of love. In fact, it was only his daughter Maria that had managed to open his heart at all. After years of violent crimes against people, it never occurred to him that he still had a soft side and in a way, he wanted to push it away but mostly, it fascinated him. This feeling, this *emoción*, was as beautiful as it was frightening to him. It was like the time he almost died and saw those glorious lights that were full of warmth and color, unlike anything he had ever seen on earth; for a few, brief moments, he was in heaven. This was the closest he had experienced since that night.

It was embarrassingly encompassing. Perhaps he would even go so far as to call it distracting. For a man who prided himself on always being focused, this was not a good thing and yet, he couldn't stop thinking about Paige Noël. He felt giddy and somewhat stupid when he thought back to every second of their time together, again and again, over and over, as he prepared for his meeting to take place in less than a half hour. Was it possible to hide his jovial side or would they view it as weakness?

Sitting on the couch, head in hands, Jorge briefly closed his eyes and forced himself to refocus. They had serious business to discuss that morning and he couldn't act like a love struck teenager who just got his first hand job; he had to clear his head and think about their agenda before returning to Mexico to help his daughter with a special project for school. He had to show strength. He had to keep it together.

A soft tap on the door interrupted his thoughts. It was the food arriving; an array of sweets and coffee for his guests, meant to create a relaxed atmosphere since food had a way of bringing people together. It was a bit early for this sugary crap and he instead opted for a Canadian breakfast of bacon and eggs. The aroma of coffee quickly filled the room and although it smelled tempting, he knew that the taste would be a whole other matter.

"Oh *amigo,* I really must talk to your manager about this coffee," Jorge shook his head in despair as the young, Filipino man pushed a cart into the room leaving it between the couch and a small table. "The smell is *heavenly* but the taste, it's *despicable.*"

"I'm sorry sir," The obedient young man gave a slight smile as he hesitated for a moment. "I can pass on this message to our management if you wish?"

"Please do," Jorge replied. "But these big chains, they never listen."

"I am sorry," He apologized again.

"No need to be sorry," Jorge insisted as he grabbed a slice of bacon with his fingers and bit into it. "You work for a Latino that can't even speak Spanish, I wouldn't expect him to know good coffee either."

The Filipino man was unable to suppress his grin.

"Hey, it's great to learn about Canadian culture but don't forget where you come from, am I right?" Jorge shoved the rest of the bacon slice into his mouth.

"I agree sir," The young man nodded. "My children, they were born in Canada but we also teach them about where *we* came from, our food, our culture, our language. They can speak Tagalog along with English. It is important that they know both."

"Good man," Jorge passed him a generous tip and wished him a good day. Moments later the maid arrived and did her thing while he practically inhaling his breakfast. His night of passion had certainly left him feeling depleted but it was the kind of depleted that a man could get used to.

He also tipped the maid generously and checked his emails before his three associates arrived at 9 AM. He immediately sensed an uneasiness but Jorge was a fine actor and smiled his way through it, his usual calm, cool demeanor wasn't short of perfection, as he warmly welcomed all three into the suite and gestured toward the food on the other side of the room.

"Please, please help yourselves," He gave a generous smile and observed them approach the tray of food. Diego Silva was the first one there; prancing in wearing an Armani suit, as usual, he snatched up the one, lone strawberry tart as if he were a child who didn't want any of the others to have his favorite treat. Sinking his teeth into it, he simultaneously reaching for the coffee pot.

"Diego, you do not own all the food," His younger sister loudly chimed in, the voluptuous 40-year-old woman wore a conservative dress that wasn't exactly hiding her curves, a true Colombian woman, she was absolute perfection as she eased across the room. Reaching for a plain-looking pastry, she placed it on a small plate and moved on to the pot of coffee.

Chase Jacobs was usually the one trailing, the man who had started off as an intimidating bodyguard because of his size and strength was now as much a part of their organization as the others. Also wearing an expensive suit, his quiet presence was a welcomed relief from Diego and Jolene's constant bickering, both almost in competition to see who could speak louder, the two were at times entertaining while others, not so much. This morning was one of those times.

"Did I say I owned all the food?" Diego countered, his Colombian accent only noticeable on rare occasions when he grew deeply upset. It was something he had worked hard to lose, something that Jorge related to having worked many years in the US, he sensed that they wanted him as 'American' as possible. He played their game and became a very rich man by doing so, as had Diego.

"I did not say," Jolene replied, her accent very strong, her English lukewarm at best but that was the difference between men and women; if you were a beautiful lady, no one seemed to give a fuck if you spoke perfect English or English at all. Of course, he would never allow his

Maria to become one of those women. She spoke both English and Spanish perfectly and was about to learn French.

"You implied," Diego swung his hand around in a typical homosexual way; even though he clearly thought he hid it well, the truth was, it was obvious from a mile away. It wasn't just because Jorge had seen him with his sugar daddy many years earlier, back in California but because he attempted to hold in the truth so tightly that it always ended up leaking out. Not that Diego Silva was a closet case either it was just that he thought of himself as a man of seduction and liked to flirt with the women as well as men. As if he would know what to do with a woman if he had one.

"You run toward the food as if you were a child," Jolene countered as she stood up straighter and pushed her large breasts forward. "As if one of us might take your precious strawberry tart away. Really, Diego, why not show manners."

"I have manners but I've known Jorge forever," Diego shoved the rest of the strawberry tart in his mouth, his body twitching nervously as it always did, he attempted to make it seem as though he were shrugging but it was what he did when he felt awkward. "He don't care."

"Help yourself," Jorge commented as he closed the door and walked ahead, avoiding Jolene's intense brown eyes as they glared in his direction. "Just leave some for Chase, he's my star players these days."

Chase was silent as he approached, a small grin lifted his lips. Half indigenous, this Canadian man was probably about 24 or 25. A young man who had already lived a harsh life, he grew stronger where most would've shriveled up and died had they lost a child. If Jorge had been in the same situation as Chase the previous year, he would've lost his fucking mind and no one would've gotten out alive. The rage that filled him even thinking of it was overwhelming. Not that the man who was responsible for the little boy's death lived long after the fact. He had a lineup of people ready to take him out. The fucker was lucky it wasn't him to have done so; Jorge would've made his death torturous till the last second.

The four set down after Chase grabbed something and Diego reached for another pastry from the tray. Jorge waited until everyone finished picking out their food before pouring another cup of coffee and returning to his chair.

"So the police, they aren't snooping around anymore?" Jorge asked as he turned around, his attention on Chase as he took a large bite out of a cinnamon roll. He grabbed a napkin and wiped his mouth as he chewed quickly. "Keeping away from the club?"

"We had an event last night," Chase replied as he swallowed the last of his food and shook his head. "I didn't see anyone who looked out of place. Not unless they had a policewoman there and she was really into pussy."

Jorge laughed out loud, his head falling back. He was a major investor in Diego and Jolene's exclusive sex club that was mainly geared toward women interested in experiences with the same gender, although in the last months, they had branched out to heterosexual parties and of course, the most popular, the events for gay men. It was amazing what people paid to have such an experience, the exclusivity combined with the insidious selling of drugs made for a delightful evening. It was a secret and seductive world that people wanted to be a part of, to experience and their club presented them with the ultimate opportunity to do so in a secure environment.

"Well, I certainly can understand the temptation," Jorge raised his eyebrows and took another drink of his coffee. "So there was no one who stood out this time, that wasn't taking part?"

"I got it on my computer," Chase replied, his eyes glancing toward Jorge's laptop. "I was watching on the cameras last night and nothing was standing out."

'But we can't be too careful," Diego jumped in excitedly. "You, you might be untouchable but are we?"

Diego referred to the fact that Jorge was deeply entrenched with government officials. Most of which knew he was exporting drugs to their countries but although they played the anti-drug representatives to their constituents, the truth was that the drug business was way too lucrative to cut off at the knees. Most countries had too much to lose if they were to cut the cord, not to mention prisons full of people such as himself, people they had to use tax dollars to look after. Stopping the drug trade would only have negative repercussions on the economy. Of course everyday people, they didn't understand and the less they knew the better.

"Diego, you are safe," Jorge assured him. "We go back how long? Twenty years? Come on, my friend, we are all protected. Your Canadian government gets kickbacks from our work here, generous donations to their parties plus the taxes we pay legally. Not to mention the luxury vacations and thoughtful gifts that they've had presented to them. There's nobody who doesn't love being spoiled."

Chase listened carefully while Jolene started to awkwardly shrug.

"Yes, but this is not drugs this time," She quietly replied. "One of their people died."

"Went missing," Jorge corrected her with raised eyebrows. "Maggie Telips, she disappeared as many young women do all the time. She had that ticket to go off and meet a lover in some tropical location, wasn't it?"

Of course, that had all been staged. Maggie Telips was a lone wolf out to make a case against Jorge and the others, attempting to do so through her former friendship with Chase. The two had grown up together in a redneck Albertan community years earlier and it was her that introduced Chase to Jolene, whom he started to work for in the original makeshift office. Maggie was under the false illusion that Chase would turn his back on the two Colombians he worked for as well as Jorge Hernandez; she had been very wrong.

"Yes, but this is a distraction," Jolene spoke up and abruptly stopped. "Wait, can we talk of such things?" She pointed around to indicate the room. Of course, she was making reference to the fact that they had found listening devices in Jolene's office in the past.

"Ah, yes, I had Diego's 'cleaning' lady in earlier, just after the food was delivered. She checked and it was all clear." He gestured around the room. "Nothing here, you were saying, Jolene?"

"They will eventually find out that no one is on the other end, you know?"

"I got a girl," Jorge replied. "There's a woman who will say the two were talking online. We've created some steamy conversations between them that will look very real to the police and she will act like the jilted lover, angry, sad, all these emotions. Trust me. I got the bases covered."

"And her body?"

"Hector took care of it."

"Ah, Hector!" Diego piped up. "I haven't seen Hector in years."

"If anyone can fix a problem, it is Hector." Jorge insisted.

"But Jorge," Jolene spoke up again as she moved her plate aside. "It is not smart to kill a woman at our club. It was a bit recking."

"*Reckless*," Diego corrected her grammar, as he often did, which usually erupted into a fight and for that reason, Jorge jumped in before the two of them could start.

"Look, I agree with you, Jolene" Jorge spoke honestly. "I wasn't meaning to shoot her but I'm a passionate man, a bit impulsive at times. The woman was poison. She had to go. Not only was she investigating all of us, she was telling Chase's ex-wife that he was a dangerous man and that he shouldn't be in his children's lives. He lost one child. What kind of person tries to take a man's children away?"

Even as he spoke, Jorge felt his blood pressure rising once again. It was a sensitive topic with him, having had similar issues with Maria's mother. He hadn't realized how much anger had escaped into his voice until he saw the concern reflected in the other three sets of eyes in the room and he quickly calmed himself.

"Anyway, it does not matter now," Jorge heard a bit of his accent slip in as he took another drink of his coffee. "What is done is done. No one will ever find her. The entire bar was cleaned to perfection and we continue to monitor things very carefully until the heat is off. As of now, the police, they only know she dropped in to say *adios* to Chase and then left. They do not know anything more."

"They have no other proof? Do your connections know?"

"My connections are assuring me that all is clear," Jorge assured them. "They've been told to back off, that it is a missing person case and there is no proof of foul play."

His phone beeped and assuming it was Maria, he grabbed it.

The message was simple and sweet but it wasn't from his daughter. It was from Paige Noël. He melted.

"What is that? Your daughter?" Jolene piped up. "She is good, no?"

"What?" Jorge felt like he was coming out of a haze. "Ah, this, no this isn't my daughter." He quickly regretted telling the truth.

"Your face, it lit up like a Christmas tree," Diego observed. "Did you have someone killed this morning?"

"What? No!" Jorge grinned. "Diego, do you really think that I get pleasure out of seeing someone die?"

"I wouldn't say no to that question."

"It was a woman, wasn't it?" Jolene continued to push. "It was, I can see in your *ojos*. They went all smiling."

"Oh Jolene, your English!" Diego automatically complained and Jorge was hopeful that this would take attention away from the matter at hand.

Chase sat in silence but when Jorge looked in his direction, he merely raised an eyebrow and grinned. No words were necessary; at least, not with family.

CHAPTER 5

Although listening to the disagreements between Jolene and Diego was often entertaining, Jorge found himself growing frustrated with their antics on that particular day. He was having a difficult time staying focused in light of the night before; partly because of exhaustion but mostly because Paige Noël was distracting even when she wasn't in the room. He swore he could still smell the intoxicating scent of her hair, the gentle version of a spring flower flowing through the room as if she hadn't left at all. Her voice was soft in his ear, the warmth of her breath combined with a soothing tone that sent him to another world where he could finally be free of everything that caused him anxiety; a world where he could stay forever.

This business used to thrill him. The adventure, the violence, the challenge, the power; it had been like a fire that coursed through his veins, an aphrodisiac that made his heart beat a little faster but as time went on, it no longer had the same effect. It now filled his body with a sense of dread, a heaviness that he assumed must've been associated with old age. Was he having a midlife crisis? Wasn't he too young? Jorge hadn't even wanted to leave Mexico this time, preferring to stay with his daughter, helping her with homework and driving her to school. Perhaps, he was getting soft.

It was during a disagreement between Diego and Jolene about whether or not to increase or decrease the out of town sex parties that he finally had enough. Chomping on a piece of gum, fighting off his craving for a cigarette all morning, Jorge silently wondered why he was listening to this nonsense. They were getting too casual around him, too relaxed and acting like children and not professional business people.

"*Cállate!*" Jorge suddenly jumped from his chair and coldly stared at the two siblings sitting on the couch. "Enough! This is the kind of information you should've looked into before our meeting. Are the parties in other cities still worth it? Should we raise the prices or end them? Have them less often? These are things you two need to figure out and get back to me on."

Both stared at him in stunned silence. Jolene appearing nervous and Diego slightly pissed off, looked away. Chase remained calm, expressionless, his eyes fixated on Jorge as he began to speak.

"What about cutting down overhead and having themed private parties in people's homes? We customize the parties according to what they want in the comforts of their homes; these people invite the guests, we bring what they want? Why am I the one thinking of such things? Why aren't the two of you?"

Still standing, he shifted his attention to Chase, who ran JD Exclusive Club where most of the parties were taking place, an establishment they had opened earlier that year in order to avoid paying overhead elsewhere. "You, you got anything?"

"Yeah, I was wondering if maybe in between our parties, if we could have bands play or something like that? I mean, we can move product at those as much as the other."

Jorge felt himself calming slightly and he nodded, he stopped chomping on the gum for a moment. "Look into the expenses involved and get back to me. That's not a bad idea, Chase, I like it."

Walking across the room to pour another cup of coffee, he sensed the discomfort in the room and he felt a surge of energy flow through his body. His phone beeped again, this time it was from Maria. At that moment, he much preferred talking to his daughter than his business associates, especially considering they had been together in the hotel room for over an hour and yet, little was accomplished. It was a waste of his time.

"You all need to go sort this shit out," Jorge turned around and pointed toward the door before taking a drink of his coffee. "Go crunch some numbers, figure out details and then come back…tomorrow? I guess? This here," He pointed toward the three of them as they all hesitantly started to stand. "This shit is a waste of my time. This isn't a casual get together, it's a business meeting."

"Jorge, it's just that we are so tired," Jolene spoke up, flapping her arms in the air. "Everything since day one has been rush, rush, rush! Often in a hurry, planning, organizing, it's too much. First, we move to Toronto, then we set up, now the club, it's like nothing ever calms, you know?"

"That's business," Jorge replied. "Do you think anything ever calms with me? Look, this is all still pretty new and we're still trying to figure out what works and what doesn't. Once we do, things will be more consistent but we must be careful that we are not just a fad. We need to find a way to establish regular customers, tourists, maybe business people coming through town."

He could tell by the expressions on their faces that none of them had considered any of these things.

Shaking his head, Jorge pointed toward the door. "You guys gotta go sort this out. Come back to me tomorrow with ideas for the future, give me numbers, give me some reassurance that you're doing more than having a tea party at the office every day."

With that, he turned away and grabbed his laptop as the three of them quietly shuffled out of the room, Chase gently closed the door behind them.

Jorge immediately sat the laptop aside and removed the enormous piece of gum from his mouth. Fuck this! He needed a cigarette not gum. He would try to quit smoking again tomorrow. Maria would probably smell the tobacco on his clothes once he returned to Mexico but he would eventually quit, someday. There was too much stress, too many things on his mind to quit smoking at this time.

Walking toward the balcony, he lit up his first smoke since the evening before and inhaled. He immediately felt a sense of relaxation, as if he could carry on with his day and finally think clearly. It didn't make sense that such a disgusting habit could actually bring clarity to his thoughts but it somehow did. Perhaps it was something he just wanted to tell himself but it gave him comfort that he didn't always feel and yet, didn't people rely on him to be the voice of reason and reassurance? It was a power that he once thrived on but now it felt more like an extra weight on his shoulders.

Taking out his phone, he texted his daughter back. She asked if it was 'a good time' to call him; he grinned at her politeness, such a little elegant lady, even at the age of 10, she was considerate of his time. He called her instead.

"Aren't you supposed to be in class, *pequeña dama?*" Jorge spoke gently into the phone. His words were met with sniffling. She was crying. "Oh no, not this again?"

It had started months earlier. Around the same time that Jorge took over as the full time parent, Maria began having issues in school; problems with teachers, other students and most recently, a group of girls started bullying her. For a man who felt powerful in many areas in his life, this was the one place he felt powerless and conflicted on how to resolve it.

"I want to go to another school," Maria sniffed. "The other girls, they hate me."

"Calm down, Maria, tell me what happened," Jorge quickly moved the phone away from his face to puff on his cigarette. His heart raced in anxiety, with nervousness in his stomach, a chill ran up his spine as a dark cloud moved in overhead. He walked back inside.

"We were in gym class," She sniffed and Jorge immediately pictured his daughter in her gym outfit, one provided by the school, that accented her thin, frail figure. "We were playing soccer and the girls kept shoving me on the ground. I was so dirty with grass stains and mud all over my clothes and when I went to change after class, my other clothes were gone! Somebody stole them and all the girls were laughing at me."

Her sobs became louder now as she moaned in the phone. "And I didn't want to get in trouble, so I went to class in my gym clothes and the teacher, she embarrassed me in front of everyone telling me that I had plenty of time to change. She wouldn't even listen to me. She said she was tired of hearing my excuses."

"Oh sweetheart, I'm sorry," Jorge felt anger pulsate through his veins.

"Papa, I need to go to a new school. Please," Maria begged. "The teachers, they hate me and the kids are so mean."

"We will think of something," Jorge felt helpless and pathetic, unsure of what to say to his little girl. To be so far away and hear the pain in her voice was heartbreaking. "Where are you now?"

"Home, Juliana picked me up," Maria replied referring to his housekeeper. "I don't want to go back tomorrow, Papa. Please don't make me!"

"You have to go back, Maria," Jorge felt it was necessary to say. "These kids, you can't let them get the best of you. You are a strong, smart little girl and you must learn to stand up to these children. There is nothing bullies hate more than when you stand up to them. They are usually cowards and they slink away."

"Can I go to school in Canada?" Her question shocked him even though it wasn't the first time he had heard it. "You do business there. Maybe I can stay with Chase."

Jorge grinned. Chase Jacobs had a brief stint as a babysitter with his daughter a few months earlier and she immediately took a liking to the man who most found intimidating. She talked nonstop about their few times together as if he were her best friend, something that warmed his heart and rose his opinion of Chase to a whole other level. His daughter was smart, sensitive and insightful for such a young age and he wondered if that was why she had such difficulty relating to other kids. Very ladylike, she often wore dresses and carried a purse with her to school, along with her schoolbag. She asked a lot of questions, was always curious and had interests that were beyond her tender age of ten. Although he felt these were positive traits, he could see why it made her unable to fit in with other children.

"Maria, we cannot ask Chase to take on such responsibilities, he's a very busy man," Jorge reminded her. "Let me give this some thought and I will see what I can do. I think I should call your principal?"

"Papa, do not bother," Maria insisted. "She does not care for me. This is something I already know. Can I come to Canada with you? I will do my homework there."

"I'm returning to Mexico soon," He insisted and bit his bottom lip. Unsure of what to say, what to do, Jorge helplessly ended the call and glanced at his phone to see the message from Paige earlier that morning. He had replied asking her to dinner that evening but she hadn't responded. This day had started on such a beautiful note and was going downhill fast. He usually didn't allow things to upset him but lately, he was constantly anxious; trying to quit smoking, dealing with his daughter's issues at school, the impromptu business issues that seemed to continually crop up, it was starting to feel like a dark spirit was telling him that his life was completely off track and all he could do was surrender. For once, he was powerless in many areas of his life. For a man who was always in control, this was not good.

He ended up taking a brief nap only to wake an hour later with several more text messages; work and otherwise. The school contacted him to speak of his daughter's 'insubordination', Diego contacted him about the time of the next morning's meeting and his insistence that Jolene was 'burnt out' and needed a break and finally a picture of his daughter's freshly painted fingernails. The photo had been taken outside by the pool so clearly, she was finding ways to comfort herself after a terrible day at school.

Papa, I am fine. You are right, I must learn to look after myself. I must stand up for myself or the girls will only bully me more and more.

Her text included kissing and heart emoticons. It should've given him a sense of comfort but for some reason, it didn't. Was she telling him what he wanted to hear? What if she got hurt? Maria wasn't shy to express herself and he feared she would say too much. Maybe he could hire another local kid to beat up her bullies so they would leave Maria alone?

Feeling sad and lonely, frustrated with his day, he sent Paige another text and noticed she didn't reply. Perhaps she was out looking for the man she was supposed to kill the previous night? Perhaps the thoughtful text earlier that morning was simply a reflection of Canadian politeness and not a shared affection? What if she only thought of him as a fling? Perhaps after all the times he had treated other women as flings, he deserved it but at that moment, he needed something *good* in his life. Had he never met her it would've been different but thinking of the previous night, there was no way he could move on and not investigate.

Realizing that these torturous feelings were only fucking with his mind, he decided to go for lunch. Grabbing the rental car keys and pulling on his leather jacket, he swung open the door to find a startled man on the other side.

CHAPTER 6

It only took a split second to realize that it was Gomez, the hotel manager, on the other side of the door and beside him stood the Filipino man from earlier that morning, holding an enormous fruit basket. Confused, Jorge glanced from one man to another but remained silent.

"Mr. Hernandez, you must once again accept our apologies over the mix-up from last night and of course, Marco told me that you didn't find our coffee up to your standards this morning. I would be more than happy to sit down with you at some time and we can discuss what you feel is a more acceptable option. We pride ourselves on listening to our customers and please, always feel you can bring any of your concerns to me personally."

Before Jorge had a chance to reply, Gomez reached into his pocket and pulled out a business card and handed it to him.

"This is my direct line as well as my cell number, please feel free to contact me at any time with your concerns or maybe, suggestions," Gomez said the last word in a slightly altered tone from the other words and this told Jorge he was nervous.

"Thank you for this," Jorge finally spoke, quickly flashing his engaging smile, pointing first at the card and than the fruit basket that appeared to be almost as big as Marco. "Too bad my daughter isn't with me this trip, she would devour that entire basket." He attempted to ignore the uneasiness between him and Gomez.

The three men walked into the suite and Marco immediately rushed across the room and sat the oversized basket on a counter in the kitchen area and turned back to Jorge, who was still slightly stunned by this impromptu visit.

"Is this ok here, Mr. Hernandez?" Marco asked as he pointed at the basket.

"Yes, of course," Jorge shot him an awkward smile and turned on his heels to look back at Gomez.

"Clearly you were on your way out earlier, so we should leave you to your business, Mr. Hernandez," Gomez nodded and pointed toward the food tray that was still there from earlier that morning. "If you have finished with that, I can have Marco take it away for you?"

"Ah, you know, I might grab a couple of things off it for later," Jorge replied with uncertainty and glanced back at Marco. "Then he is welcome to take it away."

"Very good," Gomez nodded and started toward the door while Marco eased toward the cart. "I shall leave you to enjoy your day and as I said, please do not hesitate to contact me if there are any issues in the future."

"Thank you," Jorge replied and watched him walk out of the door, closing it behind him.

Turning back to Marco, he raised an eyebrow. "What the hell just happened here?"

"I mentioned to Mr. Gomez that you were unhappy with the coffee and he immediately ordered this fruit basket for you," Marco pointed toward the enormous gift. "He said your comfort was of great concern to him."

Jorge glanced at the basket briefly and wondered if there was a hidden camera or listening device in it. This was very unusual.

"Wow, well that's very thoughtful of you Marco but this seems kind of...extreme," He gestured toward the basket. "Does Gomez usually do this for his customers?"

"I have never seen him do this kind of thing before," Marco admitted. "I assume you are very important to him to make a personal visit. Usually, when he has an unhappy customer, he sends me with a complimentary bottle of wine."

"I kind of admit," Jorge started to grin. "I would've rather the wine."

"No, sir," Marco shook his head and glanced toward the door as if his boss was still standing there. "I assure you, most usually leave it in the rooms or leave it barely touched. This basket is of greater value."

"You must be a very powerful man in your country," Marco continued as he glanced toward the cart brought in earlier that morning. His eyes fixated on a donut that had been left. "My boss, he seemed quite concerned with pleasing you."

Jorge followed the Filipino's eyes and gestured toward it. "Please, Marco, if there is anything that you want on that cart, have it."

"Oh sir, we are not allowed to eat the customer's food."

"Take it," Jorge commented with a smooth grin on his face. "If your boss is concerned with pleasing me then nothing would please me more than if you take whatever is left on that cart for yourself."

Marco smiled and nodded before reaching for the donut and carefully wrapping it in a napkin. "I shall have this with my lunch."

"Please, do help yourself," Jorge commented as Marco glanced over the cart again and took another donut and wrapped it in another napkin. "If you like fruit, you might have lots to take home for your kids in a day or two."

Marco laughed as he pushed the cart across the floor. Just as they reached the door, Jorge caught up to the Filipino and handed him some cash on his way out the door.

"Have a good day, Mr. Hernandez," Marco nodded with an infectious smile as he left the room and headed down the hallway.

Alone in the room, Jorge hesitated briefly and grinned to himself just as his phone vibrated. He hoped it was a text from Paige but it was Chase. He quickly responded.

I was on my way to see you. I'll bring lunch.

A half hour later, he was unlocking the club door with a bag of food in hand. The empty club was silent as he walked through, only dimly lit in the main area, he crossed the floor to Chase's office. He was on the phone, his face expressionless as he simply said an occasional 'Yup' or 'Ok' until ending the conversation and sitting his iPhone aside.

"That smells good," He commented as he glanced at the styrofoam tray placed in front of him. Jorge was already inhaling the large burger with great gusto as he watched Chase slowly open his own package.

"I got you the salad instead of the fries," Jorge talked with his mouth full. "I know you're all healthy. Me, I can only eat this stuff when I'm away from Maria or she lectures me about healthy eating."

Chase laughed and nodded. "Maria is very concerned over your health. No smoking, no junk food, does she make you exercise too?"

"Actually, I'm pretty good with that one. I have a gym at home," Jorge swallowed his food and reached for a fry. "The women, they don't like fat men."

Chase grinned and reached for his own burger, taking a generous bite, he immediately lifted his eyebrows and nodded. "This is good."

"Little family restaurant near the hotel," Jorge pointed toward the bag. "I go there every time I'm in the city."

Nodding in silence, Chase suddenly widened his eyes. "Thank you for this, Jorge."

"No problem," He replied and pointed toward the laptop. "So what you got for me?"

"Well, I've been doing some research on costs and it's looking like we should have some bands come in because they can pull in a huge crowd. I'm also thinking of getting a sign at the door emphasizing the fact that we are a drug-free zone and don't condone such behaviors in our club. Maybe even stating that we have the right to kick people out if we think they are under the influence."

Jorge laughed when considering the irony. "Ah, very nice, my friend, very nice."

The sex parties that usually took place through Diego and Jolene's company required patrons to agree to a contract stating drugs weren't allowed on the premises, along with many other frivolous stipulations that in the end, were only meant to protect their company from a legal standpoint. Drugs were the true essence of their company and vigorously flowed through events with carefully placed dealers, trained on how to approach potential clients without appearing to be pushers but as a thoughtful peer who felt they were doing a public service and not selling a product. In actuality, it was common for them to make more money from the drugs sold at the party than they ever did from the parties themselves; and that was saying a lot considering how pricey it was to even walk through the door.

"If we were ever questioned by the police, all we have to do is to point at the sign and remind them that we take a strong stand when it comes to drugs. Unless they can trace them any other way, we're covered," Chase replied as he dug into his salad, the smell of garlic and lemon filled the room. "Can we help what other choose to do while here?"

"You learn fast, my friend, you learn fast," Jorge commented even though it was redundant to even comment. Chase had been with the group since they were working out of a small office in Calgary. In the end, Diego insisted that Toronto was more of a hot spot and the group uprooted to Ontario. As it turned out, he had made the right decision. Their business had steadily increased ever since.

"Anyway, we will talk about it more at the meeting tomorrow but I have some ideas on how to make this place even more lucrative," Chase inspected his burger before taking a bite. "A little at a time."

"Very good," Jorge replied and suddenly felt uninterested in discussing business. His phone vibrated and he grabbed it out of his pocket, again disappointed that it wasn't Paige. As the day moved on, he couldn't help but fear that her passion for him was limited. Perhaps she had someone else? Then suddenly, he had a thought. "Hey Chase, can I borrow your laptop?"

Chase nodded and gestured toward it. Sitting his food container on a nearby chair, Jorge wiped his hands on a napkin and did a quick Google search. Hadn't she said something about doing life coaching? He immediately felt himself light up with all the results found, recognizing her face in the YouTube videos, images and of course, her name associated with a website that boasted that it could change your life.

Clicking on a video, he was watching and listening to a very different woman than the one he met the previous night. Bubbly, friendly, the woman speaking of 'making your life better' and 'immediate results that will make you excited to wake up each morning' she didn't even have the same tone in her voice, she wore bright, business attire and he noted, red lipstick. The polar opposite of the woman who made a living killing people, *this* Paige Noël was all smiles and assurances, offering people the option to 'be your best self' and 'make every day the best one ever.'

He couldn't help but break out in laughter. Clapping his hands together, his head fell back and noting the stunned expression on Chase's face, only caused him to laugh even harder. A tear trickled down his face; wiping it away he finally calmed down. Chase stared at him intently and although he opened his mouth to say something, he stopped and waited for Jorge to comment.

"This woman," Jorge turned the laptop around and pointed at the frozen image of Paige Noël with her mouth open ajar. "Do you know her?"

Chase studied the image on the screen and shook his head. "I don't think so. Should I know her? Isn't she one of those self-help people like Tony Robbins?"

"Oh this here," Jorge's voice lowered to an almost seductive tone. "This is no Tony Robbins."

"Is she not good at this kind of thing?" Chase continued to look confused.

"This woman, here," Jorge pointed at her again and reached for his burger, he took a big bite while the two of them studied her image. "Wait…. has the *cleaning lady* been in lately?"

Chase appeared confused. "Diego's cleaning lady? Yup, she was in just after I got back today, we're good. No devices here. Why, who's this lady?"

"This here," Jorge pointed with the hand holding a burger. "This self-help, make your life better lady, is nothing like this in person."

"I assume most people online aren't the same in person."

"No," Jorge continued to speak while he ate. "No, I mean, she's not really a self-help, life coach *whatever*. She's an assassin."

"What?!" Chase's eyes widened and he looked back at the screen. "This chick, the life coach lady is an assassin? Are you sure? How the fuck do you know this?"

"Cause she had a gun to my head last night," Jorge continued to speak while he ate, noting the stunned expression on Chase's face. "Long story, wrong room, mix up at the desk when I got in last night, anyway, she ended up in my room with a gun to my head."

"What?" Chase's eyes doubled in size and he stopped eating. "Is she, I mean, did you have to call Hector again?"

"No no," Jorge shook his head and swallowed his food. "Professional courtesy. Once she found out it was the wrong Hernandez, she was quite dignified about it. It could happen to anyone."

Chase didn't respond. His eyes fixated on Jorge for a long moment he finally commented. "You *didn't* kill her? I mean, after she had a gun to your head, you didn't kill her?"

"No, she was harmless," He shrugged. "Well, *not* harmless but she was just doing her job. It's fine."

"I just assumed if anyone ever had a gun to your head that you would kill them," Chase replied and slowly started to pick at his food again. "Are you sure we don't have to watch out for her?"

"No, she won't hurt me," Jorge replied. "She's one of us. After all the confusion was settled, we had a very...enjoyable evening."

"Oh yeah," Chase settled back in his chair. "How enjoyable are we talking?"

Jorge didn't reply, just lifted his eyebrows and popped the last piece of burger in his mouth.

CHAPTER 7

All was calm when he returned to the hotel but Jorge continued to feel unsettled over the previous night's mix up. It wasn't that no one had ever tried to kill him before but for some reason, he always felt a false sense of security while visiting Canada. In truth, his enemies could appear anywhere at any time and Paige had proven that such risks didn't stop at the Mexican border. He hoped that when they spoke again she could reveal more details on what happened. Perhaps she had learned some new information.

Not that she had got back to him since early that same morning.

Regardless, he wouldn't admit defeat. It simply wasn't in his nature. Jorge Hernandez was always in control of things no matter how relaxed he appeared, regardless of the insanity going on around him, people relied on him to show strength and to stay calm. It's the reason why they respected him and listened to his reasoning; had he shown even the slightest doubt, they would doubt him too. That was just human nature. People didn't want to admit it but they grasp at any sense of security that they could find during moments of fear and those who defeated it was often made into an idol. That's why completely despicable people were the rulers of countries; it wasn't that they knew what the fuck they were doing but their fearless exterior that people flocked to, much like moths to light.

Jorge had either met or spoken to a few of these leaders over time; although some of them were careful not to show association with him, especially in Mexico where many suspected him of having a seedy underground business but other countries were much more liberal and their leaders thought nothing of inviting him to their overpriced charity events and campaign fundraisers. Of course, he always accepted. Many powerful people knew Jorge on a first name basis. He wondered if many knew Paige in these same circles.

There were so many questions he wanted to ask her, so many things he wanted to know about Paige Noël and yet, what if she had no interest in being in his life? It would be such a tragedy considering that she was the first woman he could be fully honest with and he suspected, this was something she struggled with too. When you did their kind of work, it wasn't as if you could trust just anyone. Perhaps, to a certain degree, it was that detail that made him feel such an immediate connection to her. It was as if a part of him was thinking that finally, here was someone who could see who he really was and not just a small part. There were so few people in this world that can see all of us with complete acceptance.

The gigantic fruit basket had an ominous presence in the hotel suite that he briefly considered having Diego's cleaning lady return to check it but changed his mind; she would be back in the morning before the meeting anyway, he would leave it till then. It wasn't looking as if he had much on the agenda that night if Paige didn't get back to him. He attempted to call her again but there was no answer just as there hadn't been a reply to his texts all day long.

Disappointed, he decided to call his daughter to check in. He could hear the television in the background.

"*Qué estás haciendo,*" Jorge asked before saying hello and even more so before she could deny that she was viewing a violent, American program. "What is it you are watching, Maria? I told you that you're too young to watch those shows."

"Papa, it was just a bit and I was about to turn it off," She insisted and their connection suddenly became silent. "I did all my homework."

"That is good, so tomorrow at school…"

"If anyone picks on me, I will stand up to them because they are bullies and bullies don't like being stood up to," Maria insisted. "Papa, I want to go to another school. I don't like this one. You're in Canada, can you look into some of the private schools there? I was online today doing research and…"

"Maria, I can't have you that far away from me, you know that," Jorge spoke softly into the phone.

"But *Papa*, you're *always* in Canada working, so you would see me lots," Maria continued to plead her case. "I will send you some information on the schools. You will see, it will be a good thing."

"Maria, I.."

"You want me to improve my English and learn French, Canada is the perfect place to do both!" She continued to plead. "There's so much I could learn there. I've got all I can out of Mexico, to be honest."

Her last comment made him laugh and Jorge was about to reply when he heard a tap on the door. Assuming it was either Marco or Gomez with another elaborate gift, he went to answer it while continuing to speak.

"This is true but," He opened the door to find Paige on the other side wearing a short, red dress. It was flowing, classy but yet the material was so thin that he wondered if it would become transparent under the right light. She wore a white cardigan over it. "Listen *cariño*, I gotta go. We'll talk about this more when I get home."

"Ok," Maria didn't sound convinced. "Make sure you check your emails about the schools and let me know what you think."

"I will, I will," He assured her. "*Te amo*, good night."

"*Te amo, Papa!*"

Disconnecting the call, he gave Paige another once over before he said anything. "I didn't know we had a date?"

She hesitated for a moment. "I think it was here," Reaching into her purse, she pulled out an iPhone and studied it. "In one of your like, 50 messages that we should have dinner tonight."

He grinned in spite of himself and gave her upward gaze that only seemed to humor her. "You mean one of the 50 messages you did not reply to? I just assume you were trying to tell me something when you weren't answering my messages." Although he meant to challenge her, Jorge moved aside and allowed her in the door.

"What's with the giant fruit basket?" She immediately pointed at the cumbersome object across the room. "You might want to make sure that it's not ticking. Fruit baskets have been known to be delivered for some very sinister reasons."

"If it's ticking, it's been a long time. The hotel manager delivered it this morning," He replied as she approached and carefully inspected it. "Something over the mix up last night and a subtle complaint I made about the coffee."

"Hmmm…." She turned it around, her fingers tracing over the clear wrap that covered it. Jorge approached her, his eyes fixated on her ass, he instinctively wrapped his hands around her waist while she seemed more preoccupied with the basket than him. She quickly untied the ribbon on the top and reached in. "Well, this might be a problem."

She passed a yellow apple to him while her other hand grasped the plastic wrap together at the top. "There may be more *wormy* apples if you keep looking."

Jorge moved away from her and looked at the tiny camera neatly placed in the stem. Feeling slightly stupid, he suddenly felt his heart race as his eyes landed on the basket. Although he certainly had considered it a possibility, perhaps he was being too casual and inattentive.

"Fuck, do you think there's more?" He quietly asked as she turned the basket around slowly, studying it.

"I'm not seeing anything so far but a basket this size, it's always a little suspicious, don't you think," Paige continued to turn it around before stopping and reaching in again, this time to capture a pear, grasping the top of the plastic wrap again while passing the piece of fruit to him. "Maybe you should give this thing to someone?"

"Shit."

"Maybe sit it on the floor behind the counter," She suggested. "Or we can get rid of it now?"

"I have someone who comes in and checks the place before our meetings. She's coming in the morning," Jorge replied as he glanced at the camera in the pear.

"In the meanwhile," She pointed toward the camera. "They flush well."

Following the instructions, he adjusted his tie while in the bathroom and inspected his face briefly before returning to find her sitting on the couch, staring at the basket. Grabbing his leather jacket, he felt nerves creep up on him that he hadn't expected. "Are you ready?"

She turned and with a simple smile, nodded before standing up.

"Anywhere, in particular, you want to go?" He gently asked.

"No, it doesn't matter," She replied. "I've had a busy day and haven't had time to eat so preferably somewhere that is close by and doesn't require a long time to wait."

"McDonald's?" He joked and she grinned and shrugged.

'If you wish," She calmly replied.

"I was teasing," He reached for her hand as they approached the door and on impulse stopped and gave her a quick kiss. Her lips were soft and warm and although he instinctively wanted to lead her back to his bed and tear her clothes off, a shyness crept in and he opened the door instead.

"The food here at the hotel isn't bad," He considered. "Would that be of interest to you or would you prefer somewhere else?"

"It's fine," Her words were soft, gentle as his defenses slipped away. He felt at ease with her, as if all was right with the world despite the cameras hidden in fruit, despite the issues his daughter was having at school and despite the unsuccessful business meeting he had that morning. All of that was irrelevant while he was with her.

In the lobby and on their way to the restaurant, Jorge spotted Marco and gestured for him to come over.

"Yes, Mr. Hernandez, I was on my way out but I will certainly help you if I can," He spoke kindly.

"Hey, umm, that fruit basket, what do you know about it?" He asked casually and Paige squeezed his hand. He would have to choose his words carefully. "Where did it come from? Who put it together? I would like to thank them personally but I wasn't sure who to go to."

"I do not know, Mr. Hernandez," Marco replied. "I was asked to get it from Mr. Gomez's office and carry it upstairs to your room. I do not know the details. I assume it was to apologize for the room mix up he said you had?"

"And you said, they usually bring wine in a case like that?"

"I do not see a lot of those cases," Marco paused and shook his head. "It does not happen often but yes, usually when there is an error, they send wine. Not good wine, though."

Paige grinned but didn't say anything.

"Oh, well, I guess I will have to talk to Gomez," Jorge glanced at Paige who nodded and she squeezed his hand again. "Thanks again, Marco. Actually, I might give you the basket in the morning, if you want it. I gotta go back to Mexico soon and that's a lot of fucking fruit."

Marco let out a hearty laugh as he started to walk away. "Yes, Mr. Hernandez, I would be happy to take the basket. My children, they love fruit."

"Perfect, I will see you in the morning," Jorge replied with his usual charisma before turning to Paige who raised one eyebrow.

"He doesn't know anything," She confirmed his suspicion. "But this Gomez guy, he might be trouble."

Jorge briefly considered his behavior that morning before nodding. "He might."

She merely smiled as he led her into the restaurant.

CHAPTER 8

Once seated in the near empty restaurant, Paige casually glanced around and returned her gaze to Jorge. "So, you say the food is good here?"

Following her eyes, his response was to grin, an unexpected trace of self-consciousness struck him and he looked away. Unsure if her question was out of interest or a subtle way to make a point, he was hesitant to respond.

"Well, I like it," His eyes finally met hers and he noted a touch of humor in her expression and recognized she was teasing him. As much as he felt connected to her, the truth was that he still didn't know Paige Noël at all. He placed blind faith in her, something he rarely attempted even with people he had known for years.

"I'm sure it's fine," She calmly replied and opened the menu while Jorge did the same.

He barely had time to glance over the choices when a loud, booming voice suddenly interrupted them, causing him to jump. An overweight, white woman wearing a blue dress was standing by their table, her gaze fixated on Jorge's date.

"Paige Noël!" She enthusiastically clapped her hands together. "I can't believe it's you! I watch *all* your videos online. You inspire me so much."

"Oh, thank you," Paige replied with a smile. "I'm glad you find them...helpful..."

"I'm trying to lose some weight and your *You Must Do It Now* video really connected with me the most," The stranger placed her hand just below her neck, her expression grew solemn and she slowly shook her head. "It's just so damn hard."

"I know it is," Paige nodded in understanding, her expression full of compassion. "But every day is a fresh start."

"Anyway, I don't want to interrupt your dinner," The excited woman glanced toward Jorge who flashed his movie star smile, before returning her gaze to Paige. "I recognized you from across the room and had to tell you that I so, *so* appreciate all the work you do. Are you still working on the book?"

"I didn't start it yet," Paige calmly replied. "I'm still doing some research."

"Well, I can't wait till it's out," The woman replied, clapping her hands together. "I just know it's gonna be a bestseller."

"Thank you," Paige cordially replied as the woman started to turn away but then hesitated.

"Would I be able to bother you for a hug, Ms. Noël?"

Although she appeared a bit hesitant, Paige slowly rose from her chair and was immediately pulled into a bear hug, causing the few people in the restaurant to look in their direction. When the woman finally let go, Jorge noted that Paige's fan had tears in her eyes before saying a quick 'thank you' and walking toward the exit.

Unable to suppress his grin, Jorge cleared his throat and looked down at his menu as Paige returned to her seat. "Wow, you have a real fan there."

"She smelled of alcohol and sweat," Paige replied as she continued to fake a smile.

"Does this happen a lot?"

"Actually, it almost never happens," Paige said as her eyes scanned the restaurant exit.

"I didn't realize you had such a huge fan base," Jorge closed his menu and sat it aside as he looked into her eyes. "Or that you were writing a book? An authoress at my table, I feel smarter just being here."

"I'm not writing a book," She quietly replied. "Although I kick myself for suggesting it now because I can see people really are hoping for it."

"Why did you say it then?"

"Cause all these self-help people either go out on speaking tours or they're writing books, so it would seem suspicious if I wasn't doing one or both," Paige confirmed as the waitress approached the table. An older woman wearing glasses, her hair in a bun, Jorge noted that she looked tired.

"Were you ready to order?" She forced a smile and glanced toward Paige than Jorge. "Or do you need a few more minutes?"

"I'm going to have Fettuccine Alfredo," Paige said with a slight smile on her face, returned her menu to the waitress while Jorge took one last glance at his and shrugged.

"I guess I'll have the same, thanks."

"To drink?"

Jorge ordered a bottle of white wine that was known to be superior in quality, glancing at Paige, he was disappointed when she had no reaction. After the waitress left, he stared at her in silence for a long moment. She returned his gaze and seemed to lean in.

"I.. um…. saw your website today," He commented as the waitress returned with their wine and two glasses. After pouring them each one, she asked if they needed anything else before rushing away.

"So you saw my website?" Her eyes lit up slightly, a smooth grin slipped on her lips as she reached for her glass. "I'm impressed. You would be surprised how many people don't even look me up even though they know I'm online."

"I did," Jorge proudly responded and felt his heart pick up in pace, he hid his discomfort by reaching for his glass and took a long drink. "So, tell me something, how does that work? People pay for appointments with you?"

"Essentially, yes," Paige nodded. "Although, most of the appointments are fake. It's a terrific way to justify my livelihood."

He slowly nodded in understanding. This was something he knew well. He had thought of many clever ways to explain his finances over the years. Most of it, however, was locked away in several safe locations.

"I spend most of my time creating fake fans to contact me through my site and social media, making fake appointments and bringing in payments. It's actually a lot of work but I have time. My real job only requires me to work a handful of days a year although lately, demand is increasing."

"So you were saying the other night," Jorge said as he finished his wine and poured more into his glass. "You can pick the ones you want? You don't have to necessarily do the jobs you're asked."

"I have someone who contacts me with the potential jobs," She replied as her fingers slid up and down the wine glass. "He's the person that the interested parties reach out to and it's up to him to figure out the best person for the job."

"How many of you…do your work?" Jorge chose his words carefully.

"Well in our team," She quietly replied. "Not many, I think there's four of us. I don't actually know the others."

"Are you the only woman?"

"I think so."

"I might know your boss," Jorge commented. "I know a guy, you can contact if there's a problem…."

"I'm sure you do," She nodded. "In your line of work, I'm sure you may have used our services at some time."

"I usually do my own work," Jorge confirmed. "Although I was looking into it at one time for a personal situation."

"Right." She quietly commented, her voice was consistently relaxed. "And did you end up hiring someone."

"Not at that time," he cleared his throat and thought briefly of Maria's mother. "I decided to go a different route."

Paige nodded and glanced toward their waitress who was approaching them with two plates of steaming pasta, the aroma caused his stomach to rumble. After she left the food and walking away, Jorge continued his thoughts.

"So, I guess it's safe to say that no one knows it's you who takes care of things?"

"No one knows," Paige replied. "It's a secret *who* does the work and really, no one cares, as long as it's done properly with no traces coming back to us or the client."

Jorge nodded and dug into the Fettuccine, as his mind put everything together. Taking that first bite, the rich flavor caused him to moan in pleasure.

"That is fucking good," He commented. "I see why people get fat when they quit smoking. Everything tastes so much better."

"I hadn't realized you quit?"

"Well, I have cut back and already," He swallowed his food. "I'm seeing a difference. I did quit for a few weeks but sometimes, I just gotta have a smoke."

"In fairness, last night, you had a pretty good excuse," Paige was picking at her food as the steam rose from it. "I can attest to that."

"Not every day that someone tries to kill you," Jorge replied as he reached for his wine glass. "The last time, I snorted a bunch of coke, drank too much tequila and in a moment of not great decision-making, had sex with a crazy woman. Nine months later my little girl was born."

Paige let out a little cough, appearing to almost choke on her food. "So, having someone try to kill you is an aphrodisiac?"

"Well, no," Jorge felt his face warm up and he took another long drink of wine. "I mean, that time was a little different. The aphrodisiac that night was the cocaine more than it was having a gun to my head."

"The tequila probably helped too?" Paige added as she chewed on her food, her hand covering her mouth as she spoke.

"It probably was a pretty big factor, yes," Jorge replied. "Not that I regret my daughter. I regret the mother but not the daughter. Had I not been so fucked out of my mind, I probably would've been more proactive about condoms that night."

"These things happen," Paige confirmed and took another sip of her wine while Jorge poured another glass for himself, then filling up hers.

"Slow down, I don't want to have to carry you back to the room later," Paige teased and gave him a quick eyebrow flash.

"I can handle my wine," Jorge felt lighter and more at ease and he looked away. "So, tell me more about your work."

Looking back up at him, she continued to eat and gave a slight shrug. "What did you want to know?"

"This guy calls you and you choose if you want the job?"

"Yes."

"You don't have to do it?"

"I don't have to, no."

"So you won't do petty things, like say something domestic?"

"No, I stick to the people who I feel deserve it."

"How do you decide that?"

"I guess it's a matter of opinion."

"And the guy you were looking for last night?' Jorge tilted his head down, his eyes swooped into an upward gaze. "Did you find him?"

"I found him."

"And?"

"He's out of the picture," She confirmed and offered little in the way of details. "In a slightly different way than originally requested but we had to do something that was fast and yet, didn't look suspicious."

"And?"

"I think he had a heart attack at the airport."

Jorge stopped and stared.

"There's more than one way to skin a cat," She replied without him asking. "If you're aware of someone's medical history, it sometimes isn't all that difficult."

That was all she was going to say and Jorge understood. People always assumed an assassin used a gun or knife to do their work but in reality, there are many weapons that are much more subtle. At the end of the day, it was about getting the job done. It didn't matter how it happened. The results were the same.

"So you can make that happen," Jorge was in awe and noted that her eyes showed no signs of remorse as she nodded casually, as if they were discussing an average job.

"I can make it happen," She replied. "It takes skill and research. The smartest way is to know your target but unfortunately, things were quite rushed with this one. He's usually well guarded and protected, so when an opportunity arose at the last minute, we had to throw things together fast."

Jorge stopped eating and stared into her eyes. There was a tranquility about her that seemed completely unexpected considering the topic of conversation and yet, it filled him with a gentle smooth energy that made him feel safe, even though logically, he should've felt the complete opposite in her company. There was an unmistakable power, a strength that was unlike what he usually saw in women and it was what intrigued and aroused him.

"And that's my life," She forced a smile. "You have to be ready for anything and act accordingly."

"So like, last night," Jorge suddenly felt vulnerable; what if she had acted 'accordingly' with him as a way to ease over her mistake. "When you found out I was the wrong person?"

"Yes, I'm curious why the rooms were switched at the last minute," She missed his point completely.

"I.. umm.. booked the room ahead after my last visit," Jorge replied but felt preoccupied. "When I got here, I was told it was booked to another Hernandez and when I spoke to Gomez, he claimed that the information wasn't even filled out correctly and just gave me back my room."

"Hmm,.. maybe someone hacked the system."

"So where was he?"

"He wasn't even in this hotel," Paige commented and calmly ate her food. "That was the weird part but I guess it was meant to throw me off track at the last minute. Someone must've suspected something was up."

"Do you think they know it was you?"

"No," She confirmed. "I was dressed like an employee at the airport and was talking to him in the lounge area. If you had been there, you wouldn't have even known me."

Jorge grinned and reached for his wine again. "Do you think Gomez knew?"

"I think, if anything, he was following instructions," Paige replied and wiped her mouth with a napkin. "I guess that remains to be seen."

"But the fruit basket?"

"Also some instructions," Paige replied. "I would suggest that your next visit, you maybe go somewhere else."

"Maybe I should check out tonight."

"You don't want anyone to get the impression that you're suspicious."

"Removing the cameras might do it."

"All they know is that the cameras went black, they don't necessarily know how or why. Maybe you put the fruit in a grocery bag?"

"True," Jorge finished another glass of wine. He noticed Paige watching him carefully, her eyes disarming, and he felt his original inhibitions falling away as if they no longer mattered and all that he could think about were his fears that were floating to the surface.

Looking away, his heart began to race and emotions crept up on him, something he hadn't expected and normally, wouldn't have welcomed. His arms felt heavy and his body was weak, causing him to lean against the table as he bit his lower lip. When he finally did speak, even he was surprised by the words that came out of his mouth.

"How do you feel about marriage?"

CHAPTER 9

She didn't reply right away but Jorge couldn't help but notice that her usual calm exterior disappeared. Emotions crept into her eyes, followed by the rest of her face; it was as if Paige Noël's body relaxed, her shoulders softened, perhaps her head drooped slightly and although she opened her mouth to speak, she remained silent. There was a definite shift in that moment that was unmistakable. It was unexpected; but then again, Jorge Hernandez bringing up the subject of marriage wasn't exactly an everyday occurrence either. In fact, had a woman ever brought it up to him in the past, it would've signaled the end of their relationship.

But this time was different and had anyone suggested such a thing a week earlier, Jorge wouldn't have believed it. He would've laughed, casually lit up a cigarette and laughed some more at such a preposterous notion. Even when Maria asked if he ever planned to marry her mother, he had to bite his lip in order not to erupt into laughter; as if he would marry that *puta* coke whore, a woman who made a lot of promises that she could not keep. Of course, he simply told his daughter that it wasn't the 'right time' and that her mother 'was ill' and it was better to wait until she recovered. Not that she did.

So if this change of heart made him the fool, so be it. He would be the fool. There was no shame in changing one's mind and perhaps, it showed some maturity on his behalf. Maybe this proved that he had a soul after all and was not *el diablo,* as Maria's mother often called him while in the midst of a heated argument. It was an accusation he wasn't always sure he could deny.

When Paige didn't say anything at first, Jorge felt his heart sinking.

He was 16 again and pouring his feelings out to his first girlfriend; vulnerable, a passionate moment of excitement that quickly started to deflate upon sensing that her feelings weren't mutual. She was an older woman and in fact, much too old for him but to a young man in love, there weren't any consequences. Once again, he felt himself deflate with every silent second, the room suddenly seemed louder than before, as a rush of people came in all at once and yet, they were alone as he stared into her eyes. He didn't even blink for fear he would miss something; even a clue to what she was thinking as his words started to have a life of their own. They were so powerful and yet, left him completely powerless. But he refused to break eye contact.

"Marriage?" She finally asked. "What do I think of marriage?"

"Yes," Jorge said as he welcomed the break in silence, suddenly wishing they were somewhere alone and not in the middle of a restaurant. "How do you feel about it? Have you ever been married?"

"No," She barely whispered her reply, her face turned a light shade of pink and she shook her head, finally breaking eye contact. "In my profession, it's…"

"I know," He reached forward and touched her hand. "Nobody knows that better than me."

A crowd was swooping past them and Jorge glanced around the room, feeling as though his own personal dream had been interrupted by the brutal sound of an alarm, as he let go of her hand quickly grabbed his glass of wine and knocked it back. Glancing at the empty bottle, he noticed Paige was no longer eating, her body language softening once again making her seem so small in the chair across from him. Was that what he was doing to her? Was he making her weak?

"Do you want to go upstairs?" He asked as the people continued to rush in and she quickly nodded and stood up. After paying for the meal, Jorge silently led her back to the elevator, where the two waited in silence as they returned to his floor and finally, the suite. Once inside, an awkward silence filled the room as he reached out for her hand.

Looking into her eyes, Jorge was about to speak but instead leaned forward and kissed her. What started off as a gentle, loving gesture, quickly exploded into yet another passionate encounter that shared the intensity of the others but this time was a little different, there was something extra that filled the bedroom that night. It was a beauty that he had never witnessed before, something he hadn't known existed and left him feeling exposed, emotional in a way he hadn't thought possible. It was a weakened state that pulled him down to a level he spent most of his life running from for fear that in such a gentle condition, someone or something would rush in and destroy him but instead he discovered something completely different. He was content, relaxed and felt free.

Jorge Hernandez had been called a soulless monster, a heartless killer and the devil by more people than he could count; many feared him and yet, here he was in the dead of the night, tears pouring out of his eyes while the woman he had barely met, barely knew, held his naked body against hers and gently ran her hand over his back.

"What the fuck is wrong with me? Jorge abruptly wiped his eyes as if silently demanding the tears to stop but they didn't. Paige ran her hand over his arm as she studied his face. "This isn't me. I'm a drug dealer. I'm a killer. I am dangerous."

"I think it *is* you," She whispered and ran her fingers over his face. Her eyes were huge in the dark, studying his face. "And it's a part I love."

Both the emotional and physical experiences of the night soon drained him and for the first time in years, Jorge Hernandez fell into a peaceful sleep. He dreamt of his childhood, a time when his parents didn't hate one another, before his younger brother died and life was beautiful, peaceful; but could it ever be that way again, if not in heaven?

Jorge awoke to his iPhone alarm and for a few brief seconds, a sense of dread filled him as memories from the previous night came swooping in. As Paige stirred beside him, he wondered if he should deny his emotions or blame it on the alcohol but as soon as she looked into his eyes, he knew he couldn't do it. He couldn't lie to her.

"Good morning," Her voice was soft, gentle as she embraced him, her fingers grazing his shoulders as she reached across his body and her lips softly touched his cheek. Turning to her, neither said a word, their silence encompassed them both like a protective cocoon that he never wanted to leave. It was as if getting out of bed would somehow break the magical spell.

"What I said last night," He slowly began and her rich, blue eyes widened as she listened. "I want to marry you. I know that…." He hesitated and wasn't sure how to end his sentence. This was *not* Jorge Hernandez. Had he lost his mind?

"No, this," He started to say, as if to argue with himself but instead, he continued with his original thought. "I mean, yes, this is what I want to do. Nothing has ever felt so amazing and fucking scary at the same time but I want to marry you Paige Noël. Like, today, now…." He sputtered and he anxiously glanced at a nearby clock. "Maybe not right now cause I have a meeting but after that, tonight, tomorrow?"

Her eyes searched his face as if trying to keep up with all his crazy, random thoughts, a small smile crept on her lips. "Are you sure about this? You seemed upset last night and…"

"No, it's just," Jorge glanced up at the ceiling for a moment as he collected his thoughts. "I've never had anyone, ever that I could talk to about everything." His dark eyes looked into hers, he moved in closer so that their faces were barely apart and he felt her hot breath falling on his cheek. "This huge part of my life, I could never tell anyone about because no one else could know. And if I had, they would've thought I was a monster. They wouldn't understand. But you understand. You know. You know this life. You know me without even having to say a word. It's the most amazing, beautiful thing I've ever experienced."

Her eyes widened in surprise and she opened her mouth to say something but he interrupted before she could speak.

"No, I'm saying this wrong," He immediately closed his eyes and wished he was better with words. His heart was racing erratically and he felt tongue-tied and stupid. To a woman who appeared to always be in control, he must've seemed like nothing more than a fucking moron that couldn't communicate. Wasn't that what women thought of men? That they were hopeless apes who weren't able to articulate their emotions, express themselves with nothing more than a dictionary of simple words and expressions; drivel they saw in movies and thought women wanted to hear but so out of touch, they couldn't say anything with meaning. He had to prove to her that he wasn't like the fucking *gringos* that she usually dated.

"You're fucking beautiful and amazing and perfect and you're powerful and strong and fearless and all the things women should be," He spoke so fast that his words almost stuck together but he couldn't stop once he started, his heart pounding excitedly, his breath heavy as he continued to speak. "No one can ever understand you like I do and no one can understand me like you do. We're perfect. This happened so we could meet. This insane fucking mix up, it was fate...whatever you call it. It was supposed to happen. It was... I don't know..."

She started to giggle and for a second, he felt crestfallen until she reached out and touched his face, her eyes full of kindness, he felt safe and began to relax. "I love you too."

Without a second's hesitation, his lips immediately reached for hers and he glanced over her shoulder and suddenly realized the time and stopped.

"Oh fuck me!" Jorge ran a hand through his hair as he moved away from her. "Fuck, I have a meeting here soon... shit," He looked back in her face, relieved he didn't see any anger. "I'm so sorry, this is... this is totally not how I wanted to do this or... this isn't me.."

"Impulsive, passionate, crazy?" Paige calmly asked. "I'm not so sure about that." She grinned and he knew everything was okay.

"I promise, I'll make this up to you," He started to get out of bed.

"I don't want you to make up anything, everything is perfect," She continued to watch him as he frantically grabbed his phone. "If you have a meeting, you should go get ready."

"Yeah, I'm sorry, I got to shower," He sat his phone down and anxiously glanced around the room. "Unless, or do you..."

"I think you should take a shower first," She calmly replied and sat up in the bed. "Then I will."

"Ok," He felt swept up in her calmness and walked toward the bathroom. "Are you sure?"

"Yes."

"You aren't going to leave while I'm in there?"

She shook her head no.

When on the other side of the bathroom door, his heart began to race again as his brain quickly took inventory of the previous night.

His hands shaking, he was dying for a cigarette. Jorge didn't care if he had done well to avoid one for, what, how many hours had it been? His anxiety was over the edge and yet, there was a gleeful excitement behind it that was undeniable. He felt weak and yet safe like the world was caving in but he was protected. By the time he got out of the shower, a tranquility took over as he slowly dressed; underwear, shirt, pants.... fuck the tie. He didn't need it today.

He excitedly burst into the room to find Paige wearing his shirt from the day before, sitting with her legs crossed under her; both palms pointed toward the heavens, her eyes suddenly sprang open and he stopped in his tracks.

"Were you…"

"Meditating," She replied and uncrossed her legs and sat on the edge of the bed. "It centers me."

"You need to be centered?" He was confused. "Cause of me?"

"No," Her smile was calm, relaxed, easing across her face while love flowed from her eyes. Love. He was sure that was love. "From life. Everyday stuff. In my line of work, I have to always be thinking on my feet and I can't get into a panic or upset, I need to be as centered as possible because anything can happen…as you know," She gestured toward the next room. "So, I need to meditate to make sure I can think clearly."

"Wow," Jorge was both stunned and impressed by this revelation. "Does it help?"

"Yes, it does." She replied. "You should try it sometime. It might help you with the smoking thing too, you never know."

"Oh fuck, I need a smoke," He spoke apologetically. "I'm sorry."

"Don't apologize to me," She insisted.

"I know but it's a disgusting habit," He spoke honestly as she rose from her seat and moved in to give him a brief, chaste kiss and he felt his heart melt. "It's fine. Do what you have to do. I'm going to take a shower."

After she went into the bathroom, he sat on the edge of the bed for a moment, feeling swept up in pleasurable sensations of euphoria as he heard the shower turn on in the bathroom. He slowly rose from the bed and went into the next room to look for his cigarettes. It was just then that there was a knock at the door. Glancing at his phone, Jorge realized it was breakfast.

Marco was on the other side with a bright smile, he nodded. "Good morning, Mr. Hernandez! I hope all is well this morning."

"It is, thank you, Marco," He spoke with a certain amount of insincerity, thinking of the cameras in the fruit and feeling slightly betrayed, even though chances were good that the Filipino had no idea that they even existed. He watched him roll the cart across the room, the smell of fresh coffee filled the room.

After placing the cart near the couch and small table, he turned back around and glanced at Jorge. "Is there anything else I can get for you, Mr. Hernandez?"

"No, that's fine, thank you," Jorge hesitated and suddenly remembered the fruit basket. "Oh yes, did you want that basket, Marco? I have to leave soon and I can't possibly eat it all."

"I do thank you," Marco nodded. "If you are sure? I have to get back to work now but maybe later, after breakfast? Please, do eat all you want though first."

"I have a meeting here shortly, maybe after that?"

"Very good," Marco nodded and headed toward the door. "If you need anything else, please let me know."

After thanking him and closing the door, Jorge glanced at the phone as another knock interrupted his thoughts. This time it was Diego Silva's cleaning lady; the older Latino woman who was able to find any hidden listening devices or cameras, making her invaluable. After a few brief words about the basket, she went right to work and searched the room carefully, including the food cart brought in moments earlier and each piece of fruit and the basket itself. She found one more camera but fortunately, it was pointed away from the door.

It was just as she was finishing up that Paige walked out of the bedroom; in a walk of shame, she wore the previous night's clothing, her purse in hand, her wet hair pulled up in a bun, creating a more professional image as if she were a woman on her way to work, she didn't skip a beat when she saw Diego's cleaning lady in the next room. For a brief second, when their eyes met, Jorge feared they were about to have a negative reaction toward one another.

"Paige!" The Latino woman excitedly ran across the room with open arms. *"No te he visto en mucho tiempo!"*

"Clara! ¡Oh Dios mío! ¡Buenos días!"

Confused, Jorge watched the two women as they excitedly embraced.

"Qué? What is going on here?" He shook his head and looked at the two women as they moved away from one another. "You two know one another?"

"Qué?" The cleaning lady asked.

"Preguntó si nos conocíamos," Paige responded to her question. "Yes, we know one another. *Trabajamos juntos en el pasado."*

"You worked together," Jorge was stunned by this coincidence. "You speak Spanish?"

"Si, Yo hablo español, francés," She replied and shared another smile with the cleaning lady. "English, obviously and some Mandarin but… not as much as I should. Work requirements."

The two women started to speak in Spanish again and Jorge, who normally took everything in stride, felt like the earth was about to cave in beneath him. Reaching for his cigarettes, he calmly walked toward the balcony and lit one up. The first drag immediately relaxed him as he looked down at the city. With each puff, he found some comfort until he heard someone approached from behind and turned to see Paige.

"Do you feel better?" She asked as her hand reached out to gently touch his arm.

"Kind of," He replied and stared into her eyes. "You speak Spanish? You didn't tell me that?"

"I didn't want to seem like I was… bragging I guess," She shyly replied. "People tend to sometimes take it the wrong way if you show off what you know."

"But come on, *yo hablo español,* you might've wanted to share this with me," He grinned and took one last drag off his cigarette and blew the smoke away from her.

"Everything just.. happened so fast, I felt like I wasn't able to catch up," She confessed as he butted out his cigarette. "It crossed my mind a few times and we would be talking about something else...."

"Then in bed," He whispered as he glanced toward the next room to see if they were alone. "Okay, fair enough. It just proves what I said earlier. You're perfect."

"I'm not perfect."

"I think so," Jorge gave her a rushed kiss as the phone in his pocket buzzed. "That might be my meeting people."

He pulled the phone out and glanced at it. "Yes, they're on their way, is..... the lady..."

"Clara? She's gone."

"Is that her name?"

"You don't even know her name?" Paige's eyes widened and she began to laugh.

"No, I only know her as Diego's cleaning lady. He told me not to talk to her, just let her do her work or she gets mad."

Paige started to laugh. "She thinks you're very secretive and that's why she doesn't talk to you. The woman's a genius, her capabilities are well beyond finding cameras and listening devices, you should know that."

"Really?"

"Oh yes," Paige nodded and gave him a quick kiss before moving away. "That woman is amazing."

"When did you meet?" Jorge asked as he followed her back into the suite. Approaching the basket of fruit, now opened and spread out on the counter, Paige grabbed a dark, red apple and made her way to the sink, where she washed it off.

Turning around she took a bite and shrugged. "We met ages ago. Like maybe ten years."

"How? Why?"

Shyly, she shrugged and hesitated before replying. "I saved her life."

CHAPTER *10*

Much to his relief, Jorge's meeting went smoothly. Unlike the previous morning, Diego, Jolene, and Chase were more organized, their usual erratic energy replaced by a rare sense of professionalism. In fact, there wasn't even any bickering and if there was a day that Jorge appreciated all of this, it was that one. Still feeling uneasy about his morning, he was slightly preoccupied even though he appeared focused when everyone spoke.

"This is a huge improvement over yesterday," Jorge commented as he slowly took a drink of his coffee. It actually tasted good. Perhaps it was love that colored his judgment; did the sun not also seem brighter? The peacefulness of the morning more beautiful? Jorge had somehow become the person he once laughed at and yet, he couldn't deny it. Who knew that one person could have such an impact on his life?

"We will keep doing the same thing but we put limits on where the parties can go for now," Jolene continued while Diego sat back, his beady black eyes watching Jorge in silence and Chase merely nodded, both allowing Jolene to take over the meeting. Dressed to perfection, as she always was, her beauty was so easy to get lost in and yet, Jolene was a strong business woman. "We only have a few larger cities where we do parties and will review things in the future. I know there are demands in other places but it's expensive if we must fly someone there to organize it and all that…. too much."

She made a face and took another drink of coffee, barely touching the croissant on her plate as if it were merely her treat after speaking. Breaking off a small piece, her bright red nails seemed to shine as she carefully picked at the fluffy pastry. Jorge listened and nodded but felt distracted, he scratched his face and looked away.

"Great, everything sounds great," Jorge finally replied and tried to recall what else he wanted to discuss. What had they talked about the previous morning? It felt like weeks had gone by although, it wasn't even 24 hours and yet, in that short time, his entire life had changed dramatically. Jorge was flying by the seat of his pants and wasn't sure where he would land.

"So, yes," Jolene continued after nibbling on a small piece of croissant. "Everything is good. We will mainly try to focus on Toronto, on the club and whatever Chase, he has planned there," Jolene gestured toward the young man who sat at the edge of his chair, his attention fully focused on every word spoken. Only in his 20s, Chase Jacobs was very efficient and reliable, although it was clear he didn't have a stomach for violence like the rest of them did. There was a gullible side to him that they all seemed to protect and yet, his loyalty was strong, his character solid. If anyone ever needed anything, he was there.

"I looked into the cost if we hired some bands," Chase jumped right in, his eyes bright and wide, reminding Jorge of his 10-year-old daughter when she launched into a story. "It seems to depend on their popularity, obviously the more recognized ones want more money but at the end of the day, I think it will be cheaper than hosting a sex party."

Everyone's ears suddenly perked up.

"Really?" Diego finally spoke and turned his attention toward Chase. "But would it draw the crowd, *amigo?*"

"It can," Chase continued. "I was talking to Gracie from the office cause she's a little more in touch with local bands and she gave me a rundown of what grabs the most attention. I also went online and looked at events at other bars to see what seems to draw the crowds. Between the Facebook event interests and pictures posted on their social media after bands play, I'm getting a feel for what might draw the crowd in and in turn, we can sell them as much product as we could at a sex party. Who knows? Maybe even more?"

"We must be careful," Jorge pointed out. "These events aren't exclusive so we have no control over who comes in or what happens."

"What if they were exclusive?" Chase offered and everyone was silent, exchanging looks, Jolene's eyes widened. "What if we had exclusive events that maybe had something extra and required you to get a ticket in advance? Maybe a smaller, more intimate event. That way we're assured of money in the bank and can plan accordingly."

"I like how you think," Jorge replied and nodded. "We need to set up the scene that makes people want the drugs. The sex parties are easy because people are a little nervous, it takes the edge off, enhances the experience. What about this?"

"To celebrate? To have fun?" Diego offered.

"Can't they do that with alcohol?" Jorge countered.

"Nah, it's not the same," Diego replied, his lips twisted into a smug look of defiance. "Too much liquor makes you sick and half the time, it won't do the trick. Drugs are more effective."

"So what makes people do drugs at these kinds of shows?"

"I think same as at sex parties," Jolene commented, her Colombian accent thicker than usual. "A pretty lady, a handsome man encouraging someone might help. I also think a private VIP room where we have a blind eye helps. We place people there to sell the best stuff. Have the beautiful people go out and give special invites to the people they sense might be interested."

"But will they know?"

"I can watch the camera in the office and recommend who to target," Chase offered. "I can usually tell."

Jorge grinned and nodded. Chase was exceptionally perceptive and his observations at these parties were pretty accurate. He could pick out the lost and lonely in a crowd, the woman who was sad or the guy who was feeling self-conscious and hesitant to talk to anyone; a keen eye, Chase Jacobs was invaluable during these parties. His job mainly consisted of being the 'big brother' eye, he was their research development, behavioral psychiatrist and marketer all rolled up in one.

"I'm liking what I'm hearing this morning," Jorge nodded and finished his coffee, he ignored his craving for a cigarette. "I wonder if people who listen to specific types of music are more prone to certain products. If so, of course, we must invite the corresponding musicians to play at the club."

"I will get on it," Chase commented. "I wonder if there is a way I can find out from Gracie without tipping her off."

"Just pretend you're concerned that the 'wrong' bands will bring in too many of the drug crowd," Jolene suggested, her perfectly arched eyebrow rose a little higher and a small grin formed on her lips. "Then after she tells you the information, act dismissive as if you do not care."

Jorge silently nodded.

"I feel so manipulative and devious," Diego commented in his gruff voice as he made a face and crossed his legs, his right hand adjusting his tie. "This must be how Big Pharma feels every day."

"Our competition, unfortunately," Jorge grinned and rose from his chair to get another cup of coffee, holding out the pot to offer some to the others; only Chase accepted. After refilling both of their cups, he returned to his chair. "Of course, they have the advantage of being able to legally sell their poison and no one blinks an eye."

"And if someone dies from their drugs, they blame the victim," Diego muttered. "But if someone overdoses on coke, it's our fault cause we're pushers?" He made a face.

"But this country has a very liberal view on marijuana," Jorge commented and took another drink of his coffee, which now seemed bitter in comparison to earlier. Setting his cup down, he pointed toward the window. "I was in contact with someone from British Columbia, I believe the largest producer in that province and I want to bring their product here to sell. I think I have mentioned before that maybe we could open one of these medicinal marijuana stores. If we do, I would like the most superior product we can get."

He noticed everyone nodding and only Chase spoke up.

"Bc Bud, you don't get any better."

"Ideally, we could do so close to the club," Jorge continued. "You know what they say, location, location, location and my understanding, it's relatively easy to get special permission allowing you to legally purchase pot. I would like one of you to look into what is required to open one of these stores so I can also figure out which of my contacts I need to have a conversation with to get the wheels in motion."

"We would need someone to run it," Jolene commented. "Who do we trust to do so?"

No one replied.

"I have a few ideas," Jorge commented.

There was a sense of excitement when the meeting ended and Jorge felt lifted from a rather heavy, emotional morning to feel light once again. It was after everyone was gone that he glanced toward the fruit basket, some of which, his guests dug into before leaving but there was still a hell of a lot of fruit left. Approaching it, he gingerly started to place the dismantled basket back together again, feeling calm and relaxed, a knock at the door alerted him. Perhaps it was Paige? Glancing at his phone, she hadn't sent a message but then again, it wasn't unlike her to just arrive.

However, it was Marco on the other side of the door and Jorge welcomed him in.

"I was just trying to put this basket back together for you," He pointed toward the other side of the room and upon noticing Marco's hesitant expression, he closed the door and immediately addressed his concern. "You look ill at ease, my friend, a difficult morning?"

Marco hesitated, his eyes showing a clear sign of worry.

"Mr. Hernandez, I'm not sure how much I should say," He started slowly. "I need my job so I do not want to be disloyal to my employer but there is something I feel I should share with you."

"Please, come sit," Jorge grew serious and touched his arm while gesturing toward the couch. "Marco, you must know that whatever you share with me, stays with us. I will not put you in the middle of anything. Now, what concerns you?"

"This morning," Marco began as he gingerly sat on the edge of the seat, almost as if he didn't feel he deserved to be comfortable. "I was asked to take some food to Mr. Gomez's office and when I did, there were two men there with him. I didn't think anything of it but as I left, I did overhear your name."

"My name?" Jorge asked casually. "Are you sure?"

"Yes, sir," Marco replied, his eyes widened in a way that implied a trusting nature. "I do not know who they were but I heard Mr. Gomez say to them, 'Jorge Hernandez is still with us. I took him the fruit basket.' I am afraid that is all I could hear before I left and I felt that you should know. I knew you had some concerns about him…"

"Thank you," Jorge quickly cut in. "I do appreciate you making me aware of this information. As you probably could tell, I was feeling a little apprehensive toward your boss."

"I know, sir, after I spoke with you last evening, I went home and started to think about it," Marco spoke candidly and he seemed to relax. "And you know, I don't recall Mr. Gomez ever doing something so elaborate in the past. In honesty, he is usually…not a nice man."

Jorge nodded and gave a compassionate smile.

"I do not think he has ever done such a thing before over a room mix up or a complaint," Marco continued and glanced at the slightly dismantled basket on the counter. "And then today, I heard this conversation and I felt uncomfortable with it."

"Would you be able to identify the men if I had a picture?" Jorge wondered. "Did you get a good look at them?"

"Yes, we are encouraged to always make eye contact and smile at everyone," Marco replied, his eyes seem to widen as he spoke. "This is in a training manual."

"Gomez is a hard ass with the stuff?"

Marco let out a little laugh. "Yes, sir, he is insistent we follow all rules to the letter. In fact, for that reason, I am not allowed to accept this basket you offer me. That is against our rules too."

"Do you have a car, Marco?"

"Yes sir, it is in the employee section."

"So if I choose to take this out and put it in your car, would you get in trouble?"

Marco thought about it for a moment. "I do have a break shortly."

Twenty minutes later, Jorge was placing the oversized basket into Marco's car and after handing him a generous tip, he headed back into the hotel. While in the elevator, Jorge was on the phone with a contact who investigated everyone he ever worked with or was suspicious of; he used him to research Chase, Jolene and even Diego, despite their long history as friends. This man could find out anything about anyone; and he did.

"I got a name for you," He glanced down at a piece of paper with a number scribbled beside it. "Marco Rodel Cruz. Find out everything you can about him and get back to me."

CHAPTER *11*

It didn't take long for Jorge to receive the information he sought on Marco Rodel Cruz. A family man, he had three kids, a wife and although he looked quite young, turned out he was closer to 40 than he was 30, which led Jorge to believe that something kept him youthful and if that were the case, it certainly wasn't brought on by financial comfort. How he survived on so little money was unbelievable. His income at the hotel was modest but certainly not enough to provide for a family of 5 in a city like Toronto.

The Cruz family had immigrated from the Philippines a few years earlier and led a very quiet life; the kids were relatively young, didn't get in trouble and his wife worked in the kitchen of the same hotel as Marco. They were definitely struggling.

He was clean; no criminal record or connections. This was further confirmed when Jorge took a drive through his neighborhood to check the address where he lived. It was a shitty end of the city and his building was in great need of repair, his landlord was known as a slumlord in Toronto and somehow the useless fucker got away with it. Probably because his buildings were full of low income Canadians who had little to no resources to get ahead in life and no other options.

It certainly wasn't for a lack of ability. Both Marco and his wife were well-educated; she was a teacher in the Philippines and he was in IT and from what Jorge could understand, he was somewhat of an expert. He knew computers and the Internet in a way that would give a hacker a hard on and in fact, just before they moved, Marco had started to teach various classes in technology; everything from helping seniors figure out their cell phone to classes that were well over Jorge's head.

And now both Marco and his wife worked at a hotel cleaning dirty dishes and serving people; with a smile, no complaints, both had a perfect work record. Neither had as much as missed a day.

Marco was also involved in a martial arts called Kali. Jorge looked up a competition the Filipino man had taken part in before moving to Canada and was impressed by his ability to smoothly combine the swift actions of fighting along with the quick wit of using a weapon; in this case, a knife. This man certainly could be a huge asset. In fact, Marco would be a perfect addition to the Toronto crew; but would he be interested?

By noon, Jorge felt satisfied that he had a productive morning and was once again thinking about Paige. Not that she was ever far from his thoughts but he had to be careful to not allow her to drift into his mind when it was necessary to concentrate on work, otherwise, he would be lost in a sensual and beautiful world that was quite distracting.

He sheepishly asked his source about her while on the phone. For that, the research wasn't necessary because Paige Noël was well-known in the underground world; an assassin who covered her tracks well and in fact, most people really believed her to be a self-help guru. Her reviews were generous and plentiful.

Paige's intellect and ability to have her finger on the pulse of what was going on caused a surprise visit to his hotel early that afternoon. Jorge felt his heart lift when he saw her on the other side of the door; until he noticed the displeased expression on her face as she entered his suite. After closing the door, he turned to see her stop as if her feet were nailed to the ground, with no interest in going further into the room.

"You checked up on me?" She crossed her arms over her chest. Her blue eyes turned a dark shade of gray. Hurt was clearly brimming from every inch of her face. Jorge immediately felt his heart sink and a sudden lurch of panic filled him. It looked like he didn't trust her.

"I was looking into someone else and I," He hesitated and wasn't sure on how to explain his impulsive move. "Look, I've always researched everyone in my life for as long as I can remember. I did it automatically. I... you, I..."

"What the hell did you think?" She continued to speak in an even tone even though her face was full of hurt. "That I would make up this whole story? Seriously, Jorge, if I was really assigned to kill you, you would've been dead that night."

She thought he didn't trust her and knowing how it felt on the other side of that situation, as he had been most of his life, Jorge felt shameful and immediately glanced down at his feet as his heart raced. If someone had done a check on him, he would've raked them over the coals. He wanted to talk but felt frozen, unable to speak.

"I thought you trusted me but I was wrong," Paige continued and he looked up just in time to see her pass him and reach for the door. A sense of panic filled him and he heard his own voice speak in desperation.

"No, please don't go."

His words were vulnerable, sincerity flowed from his lips and rather than grab her arm, pulling her back as he wanted, Jorge instead found himself unable to move. It was a fear much deeper than the one he felt when she had a gun to his head.

Something stopped her. She hesitated and slowly turned around. Their eyes met and he shook his head slowly, his throat dry, he finally found his voice.

"I swear that's not it at all," Jorge continued. "You're right. If I were in your shoes, I'd be pissed too. In fact, I would be hurt but I wouldn't admit it cause I'm an asshole."

For a moment, he thought she was going to smile but her face remained stoic. But she also didn't leave.

"Look, I.... I'm like you. I can't trust anyone," Jorge spoke honestly and his throat tightened as if someone were trying to strangle him. "I'm 44 fucking years old and I never had anything like this happen to me and I've had a *lot* of things happen to me in life. But nothing like this. I never, in my wildest dreams, thought I would meet someone who I would propose to let alone right after we met. It wasn't even a possibility. I still feel like I'm dreaming and someone is going to slap me in the face and tell me to wake up cause life, it's not this good."

Paige listened, her eyes watching him carefully, she barely blinked as her face softened and she gently tilted her head to the left, her lips parted as if she wanted to speak but she said nothing, so he continued.

"You know what my biggest fear was?" Jorge asked as he felt the tension easing from his body. "That I would find out that *this* wasn't real. I know someone wants me dead, someone usually does. I know that life, it is not fair but I'm not used to feeling a connection with anybody. Our world, it is so small. We live in secret. What are the chances of two people connecting in it? It felt too good to be true."

She glanced down, pulling her leather jacket closer to her as if the room was suddenly chilly, when in fact it was not.

"You're right," Paige admitted and she looked into his eyes as sincerity flowed between them. "When I heard you were asking about me, it was like a slap in the face."

Jorge felt a bout of vulnerability and posed the question that had lurked in his mind since that night. "Why didn't you shoot me? Why did you hesitate that night? You're an assassin. Most would have. In fact, there are a few that would've paid you generously after the fact."

"I couldn't do it," She shook her head and her eyes filled with regret and she looked away. "I immediately felt you weren't the right guy, that I had been tricked. Then I saw your passport and…I can't explain it, I just couldn't do it. I had never been in a situation like that before, I've never made a mistake with my work."

"You have a perfect record," He said and cleared his throat, slowly reaching for her hand. "You were tricked. But you figured it out, right? Must be that meditating thing you do. You're more connected to God or something."

She let out a short laugh. "I somehow don't think God helps assassins."

A smile curved his lips and he squeezed her hand. "I'm sorry, I shouldn't have done a background check it's just second nature to me. I've researched every business associate I've ever worked with, fuck, I even researched the guy who brought the fruit basket."

"Gomez?"

"No, the guy working with him," Jorge suddenly felt stupid "Fuck! Why didn't I check into Gomez?"

"You looked into me but not Gomez?" A hint of humor was in her voice as she let go of his hand and walked toward the couch. "I see your enormous basket is gone. Was the Easter bunny back earlier today?"

"Marco the Easter bunny," Jorge followed Paige and sat beside her on the couch. "I sent it home to his family."

"Then did a background check on him?" She looked puzzled.

Jorge already had his phone out and was texting his connection who researched everyone for him, relaying another name only with no instructions. He knew what to do.

"Ah," Jorge replied and for a moment forgot the question. Sliding his phone back in his pocket, he suddenly didn't want to talk about any of this at all. Watching her remove her jacket, his hormones were raging as if he were 17 years old again, as if sex were his preoccupation and not power and money. "What?"

"I asked you about your basket and why you didn't look into Gomez?" She spoke in her usual calm voice, her eyes studying him. He was getting hard.

"I… yeah, I just sent a message about him to my guy…" His voice faded and he leaned in to kiss her. Within seconds, Paige's breath became labored as he slid his hand under her blouse and she leaned forward as their kiss grew more hungry. It was as if they couldn't get their clothes off fast enough, as she started to unbutton his shirt. He felt his phone buzz.

Frustrated, he grabbed his phone from his pocket and was about to throw it on the nearby table until he noticed the number and his eyes widened. "It's my daughter, sorry, I will just be a second."

Paige nodded and immediately pulled back, her eyes watching him carefully as he answered.

'Hi Maria, I'm in ah… meeting right now, can we…"

She was crying and he immediately felt guilty for being so overwhelmed with desire that he wanted to postpone their conversation.

Watching Paige unbuttoning her blouse while glancing at his

erection, it was difficult to concentrate on the conversation until he heard the word 'knife' followed by 'suspended'.

"Wait, what?" Jorge asked as Paige immediately stopped unbuttoning her blouse. Closing his eyes, it took some effort to come back to their conversation. "You took a knife to school?"

"Papa you said I had to stand up to bullies," Maria cried in the phone. "Juliana said I must tell you myself before the principal calls you."

That's when he heard his phone beep with a second call and sure enough, it was the school.

Fuck!

"Oh, *ninita* no, you cannot do that," Jorge replied in a gentle voice as he closed his eyes again and ran a hand over his face.

"But Papa, they were scaring me," Maria insisted. "I had to protect myself."

"But you cannot take a weapon to school," Jorge spoke sternly. "When I said stand up for yourself, I meant in words, not action. Violence is *not* the answer."

His eyes automatically flew open and Paige was giving him a wide-eyed looked, to which he merely shrugged.

She grinned and looked away.

"But Papa, they are bigger than me," Maria whined into the phone. "There is nothing I can say that will make them leave me alone."

"Look, Maria," He felt his desire wane slightly although not completely. "I got to talk to your school, they are calling. I will call you back."

"Ok," she sounded disappointed. "I think I should go to school in Canada."

"That might not be so easy now that it's on record that you brought a knife to school," Jorge's stern remarks were met with silence. "I will call you back."

He ended the call and threw the phone aside.

"Fuck me! My daughter, why must she be like Verónic?" He felt defeated as he compared the child to her mother. Paige's eyes met were full of curiosity as she moved away.

"Do you want me to go?" She asked hesitantly.

79

"No," His reply was strong, as he stared into her eyes and reached for her hand. "In a few minutes, I gotta call Maria's school and calmly try to explain to them why she brought one of my switchblades to school. Do you have any suggestions on how to relax me?" He slowly eased Paige closer, her hand automatically reached into his pants causing him to moan as his hips rose slightly from the couch as waves of pleasure flowed through his groin.

"I have a few ideas," Her voice was small, gentle as she moved closer, her breath hot against his face. "But I'm always open to suggestions."

CHAPTER 12

The principal was not understanding. Although he was perhaps a little paranoid and bias, Jorge couldn't help but feel that the school was ready to throw his little girl in prison without asking why she brought a knife to school in the first place. In fact, the principal even admitted that she hadn't actually pointed it at anyone but merely pulled the switchblade out of her purse to prove that she could defend herself. Although Jorge was hardly condoning her behavior, he wasn't about to admit defeat and was insistent that he had no knowledge of her possession of the weapon.

It was when the principal decided that the phone wasn't the place to hold this conversation but that they should meet in her office, that things started to take a narrow turn. Specifically when Jorge admitted to not being in the country.

"La madre?"

Fuck!

"Su madre también está fuera del país."

There was a hesitation on the other end of the line. Unfortunately, this wasn't the first time he had received a call from the school's principal and it always seemed to happen when he was out of the country. Unfortunately, he couldn't tell her where Maria's mother was so he merely said she was also not in Mexico. There was a pattern and the principal was seeing it and it was this assumption that caused Jorge to start to lose his composure. Glancing at Paige as she made coffee, his eyes silently begged her for strength as he started to fall apart.

It began with an accusation. Why was his daughter constantly being bullied in school? Why had she felt the need to bring a weapon to defend herself? Why weren't they doing their job? The emotion was clear in his voice and by the third question, he started to slowly lose grip, his body craving that cigarette, his heart racing erratically as he sat on the couch only wearing his boxers, feeling as emotionally exposed and vulnerable as he had with Paige only minutes earlier.

The principal grew defensive. She accused him of being out of touch with his daughter which was like hitting an invisible rage button inside of him. He felt fury racing through his body like the most toxic drug shooting through his veins; it was a vile poison that threw all logic out the door, his tongue would soon catch up as outrage took over. All bets were off.

"*Mira señora, pago mucho dinero a tu escuela ...*"

Across the room, Paige's eyes were bulging out and she quickly flew to Jorge's side and grabbed the phone out of his hand.

"*Hola! Esta es la madre de María ...*"

Stunned, Jorge's hand that had held the phone slowly dropped to his side and he listened as Paige spoke in perfect Spanish, attempting to defuse the situation. She explained that Maria was very frightened and although Jorge had attempted to encourage his daughter to stand up to the bullies, he certainly didn't condone violence. She went on to apologize and asked if there was a way they could resolve this situation in a reasonable way. By the time the conversation was over, Jorge was in awe of her negotiating skills.

"Your principal," Paige calmly pointed toward the phone shortly after ending the call, as she sat beside him on the couch. "She would still like to meet with you as soon a possible but feels that Maria needs to be punished."

"I never said she didn't," Jorge spoke evenly but frustration began to creep back in his voice. "I feel as though she's judging me as a father."

"This isn't about you," Paige pointed out. "It's about Maria and even though she's young, she's obviously her own person. Do you think it's a coincidence that these things happen when you're out of the country?"

"But I have to leave the country to conduct business," Jorge insisted as his body craved a cigarette, so much so that he was almost unable to concentrate on their conversation. Fidgeting, he felt like a crackhead coming off drugs. His emotions were on the surface as he shuffled uncomfortably on the couch, finally jumping up, he started to pace the room. "I don't know what to do. I don't want to be *my* father and I want to bring up Maria the right way but how do I do that?"

Paige didn't reply but quietly listened.

"I want her to be responsible, strong but I don't want her to turn out like her mother or me," Jorge stopped and gestured around the suite. "I want better. I want her to be educated and to have a great job and perfect life, you know? I don't want her to ever know who I really am or what I do but sometimes, I feel like everything is slowly starting to fall apart. She's asking a lot of questions about her mother lately and what I do for a living, why I'm always going away? She wants to come to Canada and go to school here. I just don't know what to do."

He hesitated for a minute and collapsed on the couch and started to cry.

"Hey," Paige's soothing voice brought him comfort as her hand gently rubbed his back. "It's fine, Jorge. Her life isn't ruined because she took the knife to school and it sounds like her principal is willing to be reasonable. But maybe you should listen to your daughter. Really have a conversation with her."

Feeling humiliated by his emotional response, Jorge shook his head and refused to look Paige in the eye. He didn't speak.

"You don't have to tell her what you do," She continued as her fingers worked their way up to his shoulders and stayed there. "You tell everyone you're in the coffee business, right? I mean, it's not unreasonable that as a salesperson you would travel a lot. You work for your father, does he know what you do?"

"Kind of," Jorge's voice was small. "We have a don't ask, don't tell kind of relationship."

Facing his embarrassment, he finally looked up into Paige's eyes and she gave him a hesitant smile, as if unsure of the best response. He wiped his face with the back of his hand.

"But he knows," Jorge continued, his voice once again calmed as he sat up straighter. "Everyone knows in Mexico. I'm scared my daughter already knows and if she doesn't, someone will tell her. She can't know who I really am. It would kill me."

"Then maybe you have to consider her wishes to go to school here or somewhere else," Paige calmly suggested. "I mean, I'm not her parent, so I'm not in the place to tell you what to do, it just seems like that might help to resolve that specific problem. No one here knows who you are here and those who do, probably aren't going to say anything. Your bases are covered, right?"

"Yes, they are," Jorge was lost in thought for a moment and suddenly shifted his attention back to Paige. "Thank you, by the way. Pretending to be Maria's mother, that was perfect."

"I could see you were starting to have a meltdown," Paige replied as her hand ran across his shoulder and down his arm. "You're surprisingly quite emotional for a gangster."

Jorge laughed. "This is true."

"It's almost like you get to that breaking point at record speed," Paige observed."

"I never used to be like that either," Jorge confessed. "I was pretty calm, actually. I mean, not as calm as you, but I wasn't exactly having outbursts of anger or crying like I do now."

"Everything is coming to the surface," She suggested. "Things always do, eventually. Your whole life that you tried to avoid has a way of exploding in your face around our age. It's like the first act is finished and you're suddenly looking at the reviews."

"I don't want to think about my reviews," Jorge shook his head and sighed. "It hasn't exactly been a smooth ride."

"Can I ask you something?" Paige asked as she moved closer to him. "Where *is* Maria's mother?"

Jorge hesitated for a moment, unsure of how to explain.

"Maria's mother, she was always very unhinged," Jorge replied and took a deep breath. This wasn't exactly a topic he wanted to deal with today. "Verónic came into my life during a rough period. I was living the high life on coke, drinking, with no cares in the world. She was trying to straighten out her life when she found out she was pregnant with Maria and I tried but I didn't stop. Then after my daughter was born, I didn't want to do that shit anymore, you know?"

He turned toward Paige and she nodded in understanding.

"But Verónic couldn't handle her life or the baby or me. I guess when I stopped, she started again," Jorge continued, his body feeling exhausted even telling the story as if he were reliving every second all over again. "In and out of rehab for short amounts of time, fighting, screaming, terrible fucking years. Not a happy moment after Maria was born. We both fucked around on each other. Then she got knocked up by some other guy..."

He turned and saw Paige was patiently listening but he stopped. Shifting uncomfortably in his seat, he felt like collapsing on the floor and sinking into the ground. He couldn't tell her this story.

"So, what happened?" Paige asked.

Jorge didn't reply at first but stared into space, avoiding her eyes.

"I can't talk about this," He shut down and grabbed a package of cigarettes from the nearby table.

"Was that when she...disappeared?" Paige asked, showing no judgment. "Jorge, you know you can trust me. I'm hardly in line to become the next Mother Teresa."

Jorge laughed in spite of himself as he took out a cigarette and stared at it.

"I trust you, Paige," He gently replied and looked back into her face, quickly realizing that she was prepared for anything. "But I can't talk about this, you'll just have to understand. It's not a side of me that I want you to see."

"That's part of a relationship, Jorge," She quietly commented as he put a cigarette in his mouth and lit it up. Pleasure ran through his body with that first puff, even though he knew it was poison, perhaps that is what he deserved. "I can handle the truth. I kill people for a living. There's nothing that you *can't* tell me."

"Wait, no," He shook his head. "I didn't kill her."

"Okay, then what happened?"

"I cannot," He felt his heart racing. "This is bad, Paige."

She didn't reply but continued to listen.

"You'll never look at me the same if I tell you the truth."

"Did you ever consider that if I told you some things from my past that maybe you wouldn't look at me the same?" She quietly asked.

He stared into her eyes for a long, silent moment, while the cigarette burned down, the ashes falling to the floor. Quickly grabbing a nearby cup, he put it out.

"There's nothing you could say that would change how I feel about you," Jorge barely spoke above a whisper. "Unless you hurt my daughter or me, there's nothing."

"I'm a killer, Jorge," She softly replied. "An assassin sounds very clinical, professional, acceptable but I'm a killer. People, mainly corporations, and highly influential people pay me a lot of money to get rid of another human life. And I have no conscience about it."

"Paige, I've killed people too," Jorge replied as he reached out and touched her arm. Slightly more modest than him, she was dressed five minutes after their encounter earlier, because he had no qualms about walking around either naked or in his boxers. "I've beaten people, badly. I've threatened people, their families…. their *children*. I'm a monster and I'm scared that the more you see that side of me, the less you will want me as a part of your life."

Her eyes watered and she quickly blinked away these emotions and a forced smile appeared on her lips. "You're not a monster to me."

"And I never would be," He assured her. "Please, no matter what I've done in the past, please don't ever think I would hurt you."

"What did you do to Verónic?" Paige asked as her hand ran over his arm and she stared into his eyes without judgement and his heart broke as he started to speak again.

"When she told me she was pregnant for this other guy," He began to confess and his eyes watered immediately as shame filled his body. "I grabbed her. I was so furious, I couldn't control myself. I screamed at her and shook her. Maria was thankfully asleep, she was about 7 at the time."

He stopped and shook his head. Sighing, his heart raced and he wiped his eyes.

"Did you beat her?" Paige asked. "Jorge you have to tell me. This is obviously eating you up, what happened?"

"We fought," Jorge continued. "Argued, she was hitting me and screaming. Things accelerated and I shoved her and called her a whore, even though I was no better. But her being pregnant, that just was too much. I told her that she was getting an abortion if I had to tie her down and do it myself."

For the first time, Paige looked slightly alarmed. "You... you didn't.."

"No," Jorge shook his head, somewhat relieved that the story was going in a different direction. "No, that was just something stupid I said in a rage. I can't lie. I wanted to hurt her."

"She ran into the kitchen and grabbed a knife," Jorge continued and he saw the instant connection that Paige was making to that day's events. "Said she would make sure I couldn't knock up some 'dirty white whore' when I was in America doing business. We struggled and I finally got the knife away from her but I was furious and I hit her. I hit her hard, Paige. She fell on the floor."

"Did she lose the baby?" Paige asked.

"Not right away," Jorge confirmed. "It was a couple of days later."

"Is that when you broke up?"

"I would've sent her away but she threatened to take Maria with her," Jorge confessed. "I was scared to leave my daughter alone with a cokehead. I mean the last few years, she was increasingly worse. At one point, she left Maria alone in a mall. Forgot where she left her! I wanted to murder her!"

"That's understandable," Paige replied. "So.... where is she now?"

"She kept doing coke and more drugs and making accusations about my life and threatened to take Maria away, to tell everyone what I did for a living, to have someone murder me," He raised his eyebrows, recognizing the instant recognition in Paige's eyes. "I had to get her out of the picture and away from us. So I sent her on a vacation."

Paige raised an eyebrow.

"With pure heroin," He continued as Paige moved closer to him, the room suddenly so silent that he thought she could almost hear his heart as it pounded furiously, his body suddenly feeling stronger. "She thought it was coke, which is exactly what I wanted her to think."

"She overdosed?"

"I'm not sure. She disappeared months ago. I have people trying to find her."

"And Maria?"

"She doesn't know her mother's missing," He whispered. "I wanted to tell her so many times but I can't. I try but God…it's going to break her heart. I just say she's on vacation."

"You can't hide it from her. You have to prepare her…"

"I know," Jorge admitted. "But she's her mother. A terrible mother but a mother. I mean, my baby brought herself up. That's why she's 10 going on 30 but there was nothing I could do. I sent Verónic to rehab but she wouldn't stay, I wanted to separate but then she would take Maria with her and I worried she would overdose or neglect our daughter. And if I went to the authorities, my shit would come out along with hers and I would die if I lost my baby girl. I couldn't chance it. I might be a terrible person, I might be 'el diablo' as she would always tell me but I love my daughter. I would do anything for her."

"You need to tell her the truth about her mother," Paige insisted in a soft, nurturing voice. "Tell her that her mother was sick, that she had a problem, that you tried to help her but you couldn't. You can't hide it from her. You can't protect her from everything."

"I know," His eyes searched hers and he tried to read her thoughts but was uncertain. "I didn't want to tell you any of this…I don't want you to think I'm this maniac. I'm not proud of many of my decisions, especially with Maria's mother. As for the coke, I haven't done it in years. It made me crazy. That's another reason I couldn't look at Verónic, she was a reminder of who I used to be."

"A lot of things were going on back then," Paige considered. "Everything fed off the other."

"It did," Jorge spoke honestly, perhaps the most honest he had ever been in his life. "Look, that was just the tip of the iceberg. Every day with her was crazy. Fighting, screaming, always fighting, pure insanity and the drugs fuelled it. Always scared of what would happen next, always on high adrenaline and then one day I told myself it had to stop. Sometimes I think she wanted to push me over the edge. I really do. I felt like I was playing the role of calm Jorge Hernandez in business and with my daughter and then walking into my own personal hell every night."

Paige didn't reply.

"And that's the story of Maria's mother," Jorge confessed. "I didn't kill her but I set her up to die. Except now she's missing and her family, of course, they blame me."

"Do you think her family wanted to have you killed?" Paige asked, her eyes widening.

"It crossed my mind," Jorge bit his lip and finally shook his head. "But I don't think her family would have the resources."

"So," His eyes stared into hers as he reached for her hand. "Hopefully this doesn't scare you away. I can't say I would blame you if it did. Sometimes I want to run away from me too."

A smile lit up her face and she shook her head. He felt an enormous sense of relief when she pulled him into a silent hug. It was the unconditional love that flowed through his body like a soothing brook that brought him a sense of calamity that he hadn't known existed and if he did, he had long forgotten it was even possible. Tomorrow, he would buy her the most beautiful, perfect, engagement ring ever; after he returned to Mexico and talked to his daughter. Big changes were around the corner. Big, big changes. His life, it would never be the same again.

CHAPTER 13

Mexico wasn't fun. Dealing with the principal was pretty much the hell he expected; she suspended Maria for a week and insisted that she apologize to the girls that she threatened before returning to school, despite the fact that these children were bullying his Maria. It was those words that made Jorge consider, for the first time, granting his daughter's wish and looking at the possibility of transferring her to a Canadian school. It wasn't such a bad idea, especially now that he was planning to marry Paige and also, he had a lot of business in the country. Although he loved Mexico and would still have to travel back, perhaps it was time to move. He would make some calls to his big shot government friends in Canada about pushing the immigration process along. They had a way of helping him when he needed it.

But it was the conversation after they returned home from the school that was the most difficult of all. Feeling an intense craving for a cigarette, he attempted to ignore it as he and Maria made their way into the living room and sat down. His daughter automatically grabbed a pillow from the couch and hugged it, something she did when sensing something was wrong. He sat in a chair across from her.

"Papa, I don't understand," Maria automatically began to whine. "How come these girls can bully me and call me names but I cannot defend myself?"

"A knife is a weapon, *princesa,* you cannot bring weapons to school," Jorge attempted to explain and felt like a hypocrite doing so; if his daughter was older and chose to carry a weapon for her safety, he would've bought it for her himself. The world, it was a dangerous place.

"But I didn't hurt them, I barely took it out of my purse," Maria insisted, her innocent eyes grew in size as she spoke. "I wanted to let them know that I wasn't scared of them anymore."

"I know, Maria, I do, but it's not acceptable to have it with you in school," He attempted to explain the other side of things to her. "There have been many incidents where children have brought weapons to schools and hurt their classmates and therefore, the school has to have a strong stand on this matter."

"But why aren't they helping me with the bullies?"

Good fucking question! Jorge had to look away from his daughter and he made a face.

"Did you talk to your teacher or principal about them?"

"Yes."

Although he wouldn't put it past his daughter to lie, he also knew she wasn't shy to express herself, so had little doubt that Maria would think nothing of talking to the teacher about the bullies.

"And?"

"They talked to the girls who say that they didn't do it."

"Do what?"

"They gather around me and call me names," Maria replied. "Sometimes they push me."

She looked away and he automatically knew she wasn't telling him everything.

"Is there anything else?"

She was hesitant and finally shook her head and said no. There was more but she didn't want to share it. Had they made a reference to him? He wasn't sure how or what to ask.

"Papa, where is *mi madre?*" Her eyes were studying his face carefully and he noted that she pulled the pillow closer. Fuck! He wanted a cigarette so bad and promised himself one if he could get through this conversation.

"This is something we should talk about," He quietly acknowledged and rose from his seat and sat beside her on the couch. Her eyes grew in size as she watched him. "Look, Maria, I've been avoiding having this conversation with you but we must talk about it now."

"She's dead, isn't she?" Maria asked as she pulled the pillow closer. "That's why she hasn't come back."

"The truth is, I don't know," Jorge spoke honestly as he sat sideways on the couch facing his daughter, he leaned against his arm. "Baby, your mom, she's very sick."

"She takes drugs, doesn't she?" Maria asked in a little voice that reminded him that she was still a child even though, she often acted more like an adult. Her chin pushed against the pillow, her eyes looked up at him.

"Yes," He spoke honestly. "How did you know?"

"I saw her."

His heart started to pound and he bit back his anger. Thinking about how Paige always stayed so calm, he attempted to emulate her in this situation. "You saw her?"

"Yes," Maria nodded and seemed hesitant to reply. "She was snorting something with her friend."

"What?" Jorge asked and forced himself to relax. "When did you see this? Who's her friend?"

"I don't know, some man," Maria replied. "You were away at the time, it was before she went away. They were snorting it on that table." She pointed toward the small table in front of them.

"I'm sorry you had to see that," Jorge spoke honestly and leaned in closer. "You should never have seen that. She was wrong to do that especially in the house while you were here."

"You're angry," Maria observed. "Papa, I already knew. She was always acting funny."

"How did you know?"

"I watch American television," She replied. "I see how the people in those shows act when they take drugs. Mama acted weird so I already suspected that was what she did. But daddy, I do not agree. She is not sick. She could stop."

"It's an addiction, baby, it's not that easy," Jorge spoke evenly when he thought back to the days when he was doing coke. "I agree, it was her decision to do so and I tried to help her but it's not easy."

"Like you smoking?"

"Like me smoking," He replied. "But it's much worse."

"So do you think she's in rehab?" His daughter seemed to relax.

"No, I don't know where she is," He answered honestly. "I wanted her to go to rehab but she wouldn't. She wanted to go on vacation and that is the last I know."

He checked Maria's response before going on.

"I have someone looking for her," Jorge continued and reached out to touch her face. "I wanted to tell you this before but I didn't want to scare you but I was wrong, I should've been honest and I am sorry."

"It's ok," She replied in a little voice and dropping the pillow, Maria reached out to hug him. Relief flowed through his body and he gave her a quick kiss on the cheek and she moved away again.

"Papa, can I ask you something?"

He said yes, assuming that anything would be a piece of cake after the conversation they had just had but he was wrong.

"Do you miss her?"

He almost said yes. He almost told her the answer that he knew she would expect in this circumstance but something stopped him. If he lied to her now, she would never trust him again.

"Maria, my relationship with your mother really should've ended a long time ago," He replied and saw her eyes widen in surprise. "I don't condone her decision to take drugs. I don't like that she was doing them around you and to be honest, it scares me. I'm sorry if that sounds harsh but I'm not going to lie to you. You might be 10 but you're a smart young lady and telling you a lie is only going to hurt you."

She nodded and seemed to take it in with ease.

"Thank you, Papa I understand," She replied in an adult voice. "I used to be scared when she was acting funny."

"And you shouldn't have felt that way and I'm sorry that I wasn't handling it better," He insisted. "I really am."

"Papa, I was scared but I feel better when I'm here with Juliana," Maria referred to the hired lady as her hand tracing the outline of the same pillow she had held. "She takes good care of me when you aren't here."

"That's good," Jorge replied and shared a sincere smile with his daughter. "You know, baby, you ever want to talk to me about anything, I'm always here and if you need to talk to someone else…"

"I don't need a psychiatrist," His daughter giggled and forcefully pushed the pillow toward him.

"I know," Jorge grinned. "But you have had to deal with a lot for such a young lady."

"I'm resilient," She insisted.

"That's good," Jorge replied and decided to deliver some good news. "Since you've been kicked out of school, how would you feel about coming to Canada with me for a few days?"

"Yes!!" Her eyes lit up. "I can see Chase, we can look at schools…"

"Hey now," Jorge replied and put his hand up. "I didn't say yes to transferring schools but yes, we will *consider* it. It's looking like I'll be spending much more time in Canada now and so, it mightn't be a bad idea."

"Oh, Papa! If you allow me to go to a Canadian school, I will do so much better," Her eyes lit up as she spoke. "I promise, I will be good. I won't take knives to school and my grades will improve. It will be the best thing ever."

Jorge couldn't help but grin. "Ok, we will talk about it later."

"You have been there a lot lately," Maria observed. "Maybe it would be better if you move there too and we can start a new life in a new country! Wouldn't that be exciting?"

"Yes, yes it would," Jorge answered and hesitated for a moment. Should he tell her about Paige? After considering it a moment, he figured he might as well put all his cards on the table. "Look, Maria, there is one more thing I do have to tell you."

"What?"

"There's someone in my life, a lady friend who is very special to me," He was hesitant to share this news especially in light of everything else. "I would like you to meet her when we go to Toronto."

The smile disappeared from her face and she appeared frightened. He decided to continue regardless.

"She's very nice, I think you will like her," He added. "She speaks Spanish too."

"Is she white?"

"Yes," He wasn't sure how to interpret her question. "Why do you ask?"

"I didn't think you liked white people," She innocently replied. "And I noticed there's a lot of white people in Canada."

"Maria, I never said I didn't like white people," He quickly corrected her while his mind raced through the many times when she might have gotten that impression. "And Canada has many ethnicities, people from all over the world."

"I know, Papa, it's a multicultural country that is why I want to go to school there," She insisted. "And you did say you didn't like white people, I heard you."

"Sweetheart, I don't know what you heard but you clearly misunderstood," He replied and even as he said it, he knew that he was kind of lying to her. Not that he didn't like white people it was more that he didn't trust them. He had a lot of reasons to feel that way too. "In this family, we do not judge people based on their color, that would not be right."

"Mommy used to say that the men here preferred white women," Maria continued. "She said that once a Mexican man got rich, he married a white woman."

Fuck!

"Maria, it's not like that," He struggled with his emotions. How could her mother say such a thing? Was she trying to put her own daughter down or was it a way to get back at him, since she always suggested he was chasing after 'white American ass' when he was traveling? Not that he hadn't although, in fairness, a beautiful woman was a beautiful woman. "Your mother, she had some negative ideas. The fact that this woman is white is a coincidence. Love, it has no color."

"So, if I married a white man, you wouldn't care?"

"You're ten," He began to laugh. "If you married anyone at this point, I would be a little upset." He teased and started to rise from the couch.

"Are you marrying the white lady?" His daughter coaxed. "Is she pretty? What's her name? Does she like children?"

Sitting back down, he looked into his daughter's face. "I would like to marry her, yes. But not because she's white but because I love her. And yes, I think she's very pretty and her name is Paige. Of course, she likes children."

"Does she have any children?" Maria continued to question him. "Are you going to have babies with her? Is she pregnant now? Is that why you are marrying?"

"No," He replied slightly more sternly now. "None of that has even been discussed. There are no plans to have children."

"Are you sharing a bed?" Maria asked. "Because if you are, there could be babies. I know, Juliana explained this to me."

Fuck.

"Juliana, what?" Jorge was confused. Had she given his daughter 'the talk' without his knowledge?

"She told me about sex and how babies are made."

Stunned, Jorge couldn't speak. His daughter was ten!

"What??"

"I asked her and she explained everything to me."

Everything?

"You are too young for these things."

"I just wanted to know," Maria said and shrugged. "I was curious about stuff and she explained it to me."

Jorge wasn't sure how he felt about any of this and suddenly his need for a cigarette greatly increased.

"Did someone do something to you?" He asked and panic filled his heart. Who the fuck did her mother have in the house when he wasn't around? What if one of these vile coked out men tried something with his daughter? He would kill them.

"No, daddy, nothing like that," She answered much to his relief. "I just asked her when I would get my period and why, that kind of thing."

Jorge was too stunned to talk.

"That is why, if you are sharing a bed with this Paige, you might make her pregnant."

"Ok, *niñita,* it is not proper to talk about people's private or intimate issues."

"I asked Juliana if she did these things with her boyfriend and she said yes."

"Oh baby," Jorge covered his eyes and shook his head. "You cannot ask such things. That's very *very* private."

"Do you think that's why Chase had so many babies, because…"

"You do not ask Chase such things," Jorge spoke sternly with his daughter, although still in shock over where their conversation led. He was expecting rebellion over his new girlfriend but not this topic. "Or anyone."

"I already did and he didn't answer," Maria replied gestured toward her phone. "I didn't know it was improper. On American TV…"

"Let's not base our lives on the television shows you watch," Jorge calmly explained even though his heart was racing. "They are made that way to be entertaining. You are too young for this and you are *not* to ask anyone personal questions and you certainly are *not* to do anything intimate with anyone till you are much, *much* older. Do you understand?"

She nodded. "I wasn't going to, I just was curious."

"Ok, good."

"Like when I'm 12?"

Jorge thought he was going to have a heart attack on the spot. "*Twelve?*" He felt his emotions building up and he placed his hand over his face as if to hold back his emotions. "*Niñita,* no! When you are an *adult* woman but not while you are still a child. Twelve is a child. And if I find out you are doing such things, I will send you to an all girls school."

Maria appeared crestfallen. "Papa, I don't mean I will be promiscuous. Is that the word?"

Jorge stared at her and didn't respond.

"It will be someone I love," She insisted. "And…"

"That's it!" Jorge stood up and put his hand up in the air. "No more of this! You are ten years old, Maria, none of this! You are too young!

If I even see a boy try to hold your hand, you will be sent to an all girls school until you're 18. Do you understand?"

"Papa?" She hesitantly started. "There's this all girls school in Canada…."

He should've known his daughter had an angle.

CHAPTER 14

Jorge had a bodyguard in Mexico. To his daughter, the large, burly Mexican was merely an 'associate' that took care of security but in fact, Jesús was one of the most valuable people who worked for him. While in Canada, he chose to leave this trusted employee to watch his daughter but things were getting dicey and it was starting to look like he might need to reconsider this decision.

"Usted no es seguro en Canadá," Jesús insisted with an expressionless face after hearing a very brief version of the hotel mix up. Jorge shook his head no as he reached into his desk for a pack of cigarettes and quickly placed one between his lips. "Maria say you quit, what's with the cigarette?"

"Tell you the truth, after the conversation I just had with my daughter, I think I might actually start smoking more," Jorge admitted and shook his head as he leaned back in his leather chair, the one he had so carefully picked even though he rarely spent time in his home office. The dreary little room was small, cramped and in fact, hidden from the rest of the house. A secret room seemed to be necessary in his line of business because there were some things you didn't want anyone to know about and there were times, he wanted to hide from the world. This was one of them.

"I guess I wanted to believe I was somehow safer in Canada," Jorge admitted as he took long, welcomed puffs off the first cigarette he had since leaving Toronto. He felt his body instantly relax. "No one knows who the fuck I am there. At least, they didn't."

"Maybe it is your own people," Jesús suggested as he reached for one of Jorge's cigarettes, his voice was always slow as if he had a battery installed in his back and it was starting to die. "Do you think?"

"No," Jorge spoke honestly. "I'm scared this somehow might be related to Verónic, the woman always wanted me dead."

"Everything, it is not always about the heart," Jesús replied, pointing at his chest. "This is more likely business. You are making a lot of money in Toronto, there are perhaps people there who want you out."

Jorge considered this for a moment as he inhaled the cigarette, blowing out a huge puff of smoke.

"I gotta be honest with you, this is all wearing me down, Jesús," He admitted and shook his head. "I'm thinking more about the pot business in Canada. They have some fucking awesome pot there and it sells like crazy. Everyone from teenagers smoking up between classes to sick grandmas do this stuff. Coke? Not so much. It's a rich man's drug, you know?"

"Hmmm…. I have heard this about Canadian pot, tell me, is it true?" He continued to speak slowly, puffing on his cigarette and looking as if he was about to nod off in the chair.

"I can do better," Jorge grinned and reached into his pocket and pulled out a joint. "I got some."

"Oh, I cannot say no to that," Jesús grinned, his eyes widened as Jorge put out his cigarette and lit up the joint and inhaled it before passing it to his bodyguard. It didn't take long for him to react. A huge smile spread across his face and he enthusiastically nodded.

"Yes, this is good, this is *very* good," He genuinely looked impressed and took a couple more drags. "This is from Canada."

"British Columbia," Jorge commented as Jesús handed the joint back to him. "I'm working with these people. They got ways to do it legally in Canada and with my connections, I can make sure that if there's a shop raided, it ain't gonna be mine but my competition, they may not be so happy with me."

"Very nice," Jesús nodded and started to cough. "Wow, that is some good shit. So why not sell the cocaine and this at the same time?"

"I'm getting too fucking old, Jesús, too old for this," Jorge replied and took another puff and shook his head. "I had a huge reality check this week. Having a gun put to my head, falling in love, learning that my daughter took a switchblade to school and knows that her mother was a cokehead and now she's talking to me about sex! She's fucking 10. What the fuck is going on, Jesús?"

He was about to hand the joint back to the bodyguard but hesitated. Jesús was frozen, barely blinking, it was clear that he was slowly taking in the words as his lips fell open but he didn't speak.

"Ah, see what I mean, you are *so* stoned, my friend," Jorge let out a hearty laugh and finished off the joint and lit up another cigarette. Talking about Canada reminded him of Paige. Glancing at his phone, he noticed she hadn't text since earlier in the day. He would call her after this meeting.

"Wait," Jesús spoke slowly, his eyelids were drooping as if he was about to pass out. "What? You fell in love and Maria, she took a switchblade to school. And sex talk? I don't understand?"

Jorge laughed and took another puff of his cigarette. The weed was making him giddy, his worries were slipping away and he suddenly didn't care about anything. This was perfect.

"I don't know," He finally replied. "The woman who came to kill me, the one who had the wrong room, she was hot, man. *"Culo,"* He shook his head and put his hand up as if to grab an ass. *"Perfecto.* The perfect woman, not like the others. Independent, smart, calm… so calm and she *gets* me. No one ever gets me."

"I get you," Jesús corrected.

"Yes, but I don't want you sucking my dick" Jorge commented with a straight face and then he joined Jesús in a hearty laugh that was beyond the real humor of the comment and suddenly, Jesús stopped and looked at Jorge as if attempting to understand the situation.

"So, this woman, she comes to kill you and you end up…"

"All night."

"What? I don't understand," Jesús appeared to struggle with the idea. "How does that happen? You're going to have to tell me the whole story."

"It was a mistake," Jorge answered and reached into the mini-fridge beside the desk and pulled out two Coronas. Opening both, he pushed one across the desk. "Big fuck up. I got to the hotel that day and they had no room for me, this was after a bunch of other fuck-ups at the airport and car rental place. I was ready to lose my fucking mind. I find out that they had the room switched to another Hernandez, who apparently was her target and after I made a fuss, they switched it back. Next thing I know, I'm on my knees with a gun to the back of my head."

"Fuck!"

"I know," Jorge took a long drink of his beer. "But I noticed the woman talking to me has a very calm, sexy voice and I'm trying to tell her, you got the wrong guy. She's naming off some Italians that sent her and I'm like, *what the fuck?* I got nothing going on with the Italians unless I'm on their territory but then she figured out she had the wrong guy and that was that."

"She didn't kill you anyway?"

"Wasn't paid to kill me," Jorge shrugged and leaned back in his chair. "She was on the phone to someone who apparently told her *who* I was and she backed off immediately, was going to leave and I was like, '*bonita,* why don't you stay awhile, you know?" He raised an eyebrow and Jesús nodded.

"She's an assassin?"

"Yes."

"You're dating an assassin?"

"Yes."

"What's the name?"

"Paige Noël."

"Fuck off!" Jesus leaned in, his mouth hanging open. "*You're dating Paige Noël?* She's the top fucking assassin in the world."

"Really?" Jorge was slightly surprised. "Seriously?"

"The fact you sit here now, with me and tell me this, I am surprised," Jesus commented. "Paige Noël, she does not leave witnesses. You do not piss off this lady, *senoir,* she is a cold-blooded killer."

"*I'm* a cold-blooded killer."

"Not like this one," Jesús shook his head and pushed his body further back in the chair. "You, you have met your match in this *señorita*."

"Well, I agree with you on that point," Jorge admitted, slightly surprised by this revelation. "Do you know that she does this whole self-help thing on the Internet as a cover up?"

"Yes," Jesús let out a laugh. "Yes, she is a clever lady. I do admit this about her."

They shared a silence and suddenly Jesús spoke up again.

"And Maria, what is going on that she took a switchblade to school?"

"Bullies."

"Bullies?" Jesús made a face. "Your little girl, she must learn self-defense. I will look into classes for her."

"Don't bother, I think I might put her in a private school in Canada," Jorge admitted. "She will always be judged while in Mexico, as soon as the teachers learn that I am her father. She is begging me to go to Canada to study and with work and Paige, I think maybe it is the best decision for now but don't worry, my friend, I will continue to have work for you."

"Ok, yes," Jesús nodded. "I do understand."

Jorge's phone rang and he barely moved, feeling too stoned to bother, he quickly changed his mind upon seeing the number. It was Paige.

"Hey," His voice automatically softened and from across the desk, he noted that Jesús looked like he was about to start drooling, he was so baked. "I miss you."

"I miss you too," Her response gentle and he immediately felt warmth blanketing his body, a slight stirring in his pants he gestured for Jesús to leave. After he was out of the room, Jorge continued to speak in a seductive voice. "I can't wait to see you again tomorrow. I'm going to lick every inch of your body and.."

His phone beeped.

"Just a sec," He glanced at it to see that Maria was texting asking where he was, which he chose to ignore. She didn't know about the secret room. "I'm back." His breath was slightly labored. "Hey, do you want to move this conversation to Skype, I want to show you something."

"I'm afraid this isn't a great time for me," She admitted with a gentle laugh. "I'm actually at one of the private schools that you mentioned to me, for Maria? It's quite nice."

"Really? Wow!" Jorge felt his tone immediately change. "You know, you didn't have to do that."

"It's fine," She replied and he could hear the sound of people talking and traffic behind her. "I'm doing a little more in-depth research than most people do though, finding out the real deal on these schools. Would you believe one of them is owned by some old perv that was actually arrested for child porn once?"

"What!?" Jorge suddenly was jolted from his warm place of comfort and stimulation to a cold, sharp reality. "What? You're fucking kidding right?"

"Nope," Paige insisted. "He was arrested in the 90s and again a few years ago for child porn of young girls and he now owns a school for girls."

"I'm...I'm shocked!"

"I'm not," Paige insisted. "These fucking creeps always find a way to get around kids and they throw a lot of money around so they go under the radar."

"But, wait," Jorge thought for a moment. "Wouldn't there be a group of investors that own the school?"

"Yes, but the primary owner is a fucking pedo who hides behind these other guys," She replied. "So, like, his picture isn't on the wall with the others who are supposedly concerned with the education of young girls. But he's apparently around a lot."

"Wow, I think I am going to be sick."

"It's fine, I'm checking another place and it's looking good. No big scandals. The girls have been known to occasionally sneak in boys and pot but so far, that's the worst I'm finding out."

"I do thank you, Paige, with my heart," Jorge commented, realizing that he never would've thought to look so closely at the schools. The assumption is that something like that couldn't get through the cracks and yet, it apparently did.

"It was no trouble," She insisted and the noise seemed to disappear. "I'm going to have to let you go, I have a meeting. What time is your flight coming in tomorrow?"

"I believe noon your time but I will get back to you," Jorge felt his heart racing again. "Unless my daughter, she decides to give me a heart attack between now and then."

"Oh no, what happened?"

"I…. I don't even know how to explain the conversation I had with her earlier," Jorge confessed. "I feel so out of touch. I thought I knew my daughter but I couldn't believe what she said to me. I'm ashamed of my ignorance."

"That sounds like every parent ever," Paige gently assured him. "She's testing you. She wants a reaction."

"I think I died a bit after our conversation, my heart," Jorge reached for his chest as he spoke. "She talked about sex! She's ten years old!"

"Like I said, she's testing you," Paige assured him.

"I do not think I can pass this test," Jorge confessed.

"You will be fine," Paige assured him. "I will talk to you later tonight."

"I like the sounds of that," He replied and licked his lips. "I will be waiting for your call."

With a heavy heart, he ended the conversation and glanced at the phone. His daughter was looking for him. He just hoped she had no more bombshells. The week had already been much more than he could handle. But things weren't about to slow down. They were only going to move faster.

CHAPTER 15

The rest of the afternoon went smoothly. He enjoyed a pleasant meal with Maria while she told him everything she planned to do during their visit to Canada. He did smoke a lot though and for that, his daughter reprimanded him. He simply kissed the top of her head and smiled. She was a child but felt it was her job to look after *him*. How badly had Verónic messed up their little girl? It was sinful but he truly hoped to never see that vile woman again. He put a phone call in to a police officer that he had in his pocket to see if they could do a more thorough search in the area where Verónic went on 'vacation'. Where would an addict most likely be found?

Although his people had searched the area for weeks, in the end, it was the police that found her body. Relieved that he had listened to Paige's advice to prepare his daughter in advance, Jorge hadn't expected that he would be telling her this dark news so quickly after the fact. It was late at night when he received the report from his informant. He dreaded delivering the news to Maria and decided that perhaps it would be best to wait until after returning to Toronto the next day. Then again, was there ever a good time to deliver such news?

Verónic's death added no weight to his heart. The woman was truly evil from his perspective. An addict, a despicable woman, a terrible mother, she had no value. The fact that she was found naked in some dirty rented room with needles, drugs and used condoms on the floor seemed to be a perfect reflection of her life; she was a dirty fucking whore with no soul. He had been stupid enough to get involved with her years earlier and granted, Jorge had a beautiful daughter but he deeply regretted that of all women to have a child with, it was her.

Oh, Maria! How do you break such terrible news to a little girl? She had lived through enough already and he certainly took responsibility for not always being around but it was the past, he could only focus on the future and how to give her the best life possible. A move to Canada might be perfect, he decided, a new start, in a different country that had no idea who Jorge Hernandez was or of his crimes. She would be given a fair shot and that's all any parent wanted for their child.

Although a part of him wanted to put it off, Jorge felt it was necessary to tell her the truth as soon as they arrived in Toronto; a suite in a different hotel than before, a place where the staff weren't familiar with him and hopefully, he wasn't being watched.

The difficult conversation with his daughter went a bit smoother than he expected. In fact, he was a little concerned with her lack of emotion when he delivered the news. Maria didn't cry but her analytical mind took over and she asked a million questions; Where was she? What happened? How did she die? Who found her? He answered everything carefully, gently, his hand placed on her shoulder as the two sat on the couch and with each answer, he could see her slowly deflate. Little by little she broke down until suddenly, she burst into tears.

He did his best to comfort her regardless of his limited feelings toward Verónic. It broke his heart to see his daughter in such despair and at a certain point, he wasn't even sure what to say or how to make things better. Eventually, he accepted that he couldn't. There were no words. He had no conscience about sending Maria's mother off with pure heroin, the same drug that put her on a path to her death because, in his mind, she had no soul; she was already dead.

Exhausted from her tears, his daughter eventually decided to take a nap and he used this time to text Paige with the news and call her a few minutes later.

"An overdose?" Paige asked almost immediately. "How do you explain that to a child?"

"You don't know my daughter," Jorge insisted. "This child can understand some pretty complex situations. She asked a lot of questions.

I did my best to comfort her but I am afraid that maybe I wasn't much of a help."

"There's nothing you can say in these circumstances that will fix everything," Paige insisted. "You can just show your support and I'm sure you did. It's going to be a rough few days for her."

"I did tell her we were looking into schools for her so that might help."

"*We?*" Paige teased.

"Ok, I should say *you*," Jorge grinned on the other end of the phone. "I misspoke. Forgive me."

"I'll think about it," She replied with humor in her voice. "I think I found a good school. Of course, this isn't the ideal time to talk about it but when she's ready, maybe you can bring it up."

Much to Jorge's surprise, when Maria awoke from her nap, it was the first thing she inquired about and the second thing was when they would return to Mexico for the funeral.

"I don't know *bonita*, it depends on your grandparents," He spoke earnestly. What he didn't tell her was that they were furious with him. Regardless of the fact that their daughter had willingly taken drugs long before he had even met her, they continued to blame him for her disastrous life and now, her death. "They never got back to me with the arrangements."

"They probably aren't made yet," Maria gloomily replied and glanced down at her hands. "They don't like me anyway."

"Baby! Of course, they *like* you!" Jorge insisted, automatically kissing the top of her head. "Don't be silly, they are your grandparents, they *love* you"

"They love their other grandchildren," Maria corrected him and her piercing eyes met her father's and she shrugged. "They do not care for me. The other grandchildren are perfect and me, they don't care. They feel obligated to talk to me, that is all."

"Oh Maria! Where do you get these ideas?" Jorge shook his head. "That's not true."

"Papa, it is true," She insisted and tilted her head. "Sometimes you are a little naïve."

Stunned, yet again by a statement made by his daughter, he didn't respond.

Of course, he had noticed their lack of attention toward Maria but he certainly didn't want her to see it. The fact that they cherry picked the grandchildren who were significant in their lives repulsed him and for a moment, he welcomed their current suffering. No wonder Verónic had no soul, her parents had brought her up to be that way. He worried, wondered if he was doing the same to his daughter.

Taking a deep breath, he finally managed a smile.

"How could anyone not love my Maria?" He insisted with a smile.

"Papa, you're being naïve again." She insisted in a very adult voice that was hard to ignore.

He simply replied with a smile and didn't continue with the topic.

Jorge had cleared his schedule to spend the day with his daughter, to be there for her if she needed comfort or someone to talk to but it appeared that she had other plans. A knock at the door later that afternoon sent Maria running and before Jorge could stop her, she swung it open; fortunately, it was only Chase Jacobs on the other side.

"Chase!" She immediately put her arms up to show she wanted a hug. The two had bonded earlier that year when Verónic first went 'missing' and Jorge brought Maria to Canada during a business trip and needed someone to look after her a couple of times.

"Chase? I didn't expect you today," Jorge was pleased yet surprised by his visit. He approached the two as they hugged. Wearing a suit and tie, it was clear that Chase had left work at the club he managed to visit. He let go of Maria and affectionately touched her arm.

"Maria sent me a text about her mother," He glanced hesitantly toward the child. "I thought I would drop in to pay my respects. I'm sorry for your loss."

"Oh Maria, you shouldn't have taken Chase away from his work," Jorge gently commented and she merely shrugged.

"He's my friend, I had to tell him about this terrible event in my life."

Jorge made a face over her clinical analysis of the situation, almost as if she were a doctor talking about a patient but he didn't say anything as he invited Chase in and closed the door.

"I learned of the news last night after Maria was asleep and wanted to wait to tell her when we arrived here," Jorge commented as the three walked toward the couch. Chase and Maria sat side by side while Jorge picked a nearby chair. "Can I offer you something, Chase? I can have some food brought to the room?"

"Daddy, Chase and I have a dinner date."

"Ah…. you have a dinner *date?*"

"Yes, I text him and suggested we go for a nice meal and catch up," Maria commented and pointed toward her pink dress. "That's why I'm dressed up, for our *date.*"

Jorge managed to keep a straight face and merely nodded. It was not unusual for his daughter to change several times a day so he hadn't thought anything of it.

"Yes, of course."

"Well," Chase cut in at this point with a grin on his face. "I thought maybe I would take you *both* out for dinner and we could *all* catch up."

Maria made a face.

"No no, that is fine," Jorge said and winked at Chase when his daughter glanced down at her phone. "You two go catch up on your… *date* and your old Papa will stay here and catch up on some work."

"Papa, don't be a martyr, you can always go see your new lover."

Jorge cringed at the word while Chase looked slightly horrified.

"She is my girlfriend, Maria, please, can we choose our words a little more carefully?" He remained calm even though his heart was racing. Across from him, Chase studied his face as if he wasn't certain of what to do. "If Chase has time and would like to have dinner with you, I suggest the two of you do so and I will run some errands while you are out. Does that sound good? Perhaps text me when you have finished and I can pick you up."

"I can bring her back."

"Don't worry, Papa, I will text you," Maria spoke earnestly. "That way if you and your *girlfriend* are doing something sexual, it will give you time to stop."

Chase looked completely horrified at this point, his eyes doubled in size while his mouth fell open slightly, he awkwardly rose from his chair.

"Maria!" Jorge felt as though he was on his last nerve, his voice expressing more anger than he wished. "That is enough from you! My lady friend is someone special to me and I will not have you speak of her in such a manner. This is not appropriate especially when she is going to a lot of trouble to look into private schools for you. Do not be rude!"

"I'm sorry, Papa," Maria replied, her face turned a bright shade of pink, her eyes looking down. "I was joking."

"That is not funny, Maria and jokes," Jorge spoke angrily, "they are meant to be funny not mean."

Grabbing her purse from the couch, she didn't say anything but glanced at Chase shamefully as the awkward moment sunk in.

"Now, the two of you go to dinner, I will take care of some things," Jorge spoke evenly as he watched them leave, Chase turning around for a second and shrugging as Maria led the way toward the door, talking a mile a minute. Hadn't she just learned that her mother was dead? Wasn't she being a little too…casual?

Of course, his daughter hadn't been completely wrong. She was barely out of the door when he text Paige and she, in turn, was barely in the suite when the two of them were in bed, naked. He devoured her body, clinging to her as if she were his last hope of sanity as pleasure ran through him and for a few minutes, he forgot all his problems. His daughter wasn't growing up into a defiant teenager a few years ahead of schedule, no one was trying to kill him, his ex wasn't dead, her parents weren't attempting to blame him and there weren't a million things he had to line up to start this new pot shop. For a few, beautiful moments, his life was perfect.

Glancing at his phone, he suddenly felt hopeless again. Beside him, Paige cuddled up closer, her hand running over his bare chest. "Is she on the way back?"

"No, are you kidding, she probably will have Chase running all over the city for the rest of the night and he's too kind to tell her no. I already text him to say that if he had work to just tell her but he said it's fine. They are heading to the mall."

"Maybe she needs the distraction. It's been a tough day."

"It's been a tough week. You're the only thing that is keeping me sane at this moment and I'm not even too sure about that anymore," Jorge confessed. "My daughter is a fucking mess. Her mother used to do drugs in front of her. I just found out. She neglected her and now my 10 years old thinks she's already an adult. She's talking about sex. She's ten. You know what I was thinking about at ten? Nothing! I was playing with toys and pretending to shoot things with a toy gun."

"I don't remember what I was doing at ten," Paige confessed, her blue eyes dreamily staring into space. "I would have to say playing with Barbie dolls, maybe? I don't remember. I certainly wasn't having adult conversations."

"I don't know what to do anymore," He admitted.

"Maybe a new school, a new country will be exactly what she needs," Paige offered. "This one place that I was zeroing in on yesterday seems to have a lot of extra activities for the children and it sounds like that's what she needs, to keep busy and make some new friends."

"Yeah, she loves Chase," Jorge considered. "Maybe spending time with him will help. Maybe she will listen to him. She seems to be growing defiant of me. I actually snapped at her before she left today."

"That mightn't be a bad thing," Paige muttered. "Perhaps she needs boundaries. Maybe she didn't have a lot with her mother? I don't know. I'm guessing."

"No, you're right. I was away for business so often that I didn't realize," Jorge nodded. "I have to get tough with her now or she could get off track."

"Sometimes, we need a little...discipline," She eased closer to him, her hand sliding down his chest while her lips grazed his and he felt his breath immediately increase. The smell of vanilla filled his lungs and he tasted mint on her lips as pleasure began to flow through his body once again. Throwing his phone on the nightstand, the problems, they would wait.

CHAPTER *16*

"A Fentanyl overdose," Jorge said as he reached for his glass of wine. Across the table from him, Paige appeared sympathetic although hesitant, as if words were on the tip of her tongue but she wasn't ready to say them. Instead, she quietly listened. "Verónic did street drugs for years and survived. She does a fucking pharmaceutical and is dead. Yet, people look at me like *I'm* the devil? Big Pharma is getting away with murder and those fuckers are legally filling their bank accounts. I mean, they blame it on the black market shit but *come on!*"

He hesitated when the waitress appeared with their food; an enticing aroma filled the air as she approached, his stomach growled at the site of the pasta dishes; his being a hearty piece of lasagna while Paige had ordered spaghetti, the aroma of garlic filled the air and immediately gave him comfort. Food was a natural sedative that calmed him in a way even a cigarette never had. There was nothing more beautiful than sharing a meal with someone you cared about, a business associate you wished to bond with or even a stranger in the right situation.

After the waitress left, they ate in silence but it didn't stop Jorge's brain from running in circles as he considered the irony of the entire situation. Verónic survived the heroin that he sent her off with weeks ago and yet, it was a *legal* drug that killed her. Of course, it wasn't legal for her to possess for recreational purposes but regardless of the killing spree Fentanyl had already had in this country alone, it still seemed to get on the streets with relative ease. And no one was at fault. The manufacturers, the doctors, the pharmacists, they certainly weren't getting raided by the fucking police.

"You know the irony of all of this," Jorge complained between bites, no longer content to simply think about the topic quietly over dinner. "The police, they could show up at my door and arrest me for trafficking and yet, who is arresting the CEOs of big Pharma? They're just as much a drug dealer as me and yet, it's ok, you know? They act as if they have no idea how their drugs get on the street? Which both you and I know, is fucking bullshit, they count on their drugs getting out there and people becoming addicted but the police, they don't put them behind bars. If I didn't have the right connections, I would be in a prison somewhere. But them, it's ok."

Paige nodded and cleared her throat.

"I understand what you're saying," She spoke thoughtfully for a moment. "But some would argue that a lot of people die because of drug cartels."

"True," Jorge considered and took a hearty bite of his garlic bread and chewed. "But, do not tell me no one dies at the hands of the Big Pharma and I'm not talking just the addicts."

Paige nodded.

"You're right," She paused for a moment. "One of the jobs I took on years ago, one of the ones I actually regret was for a pharmaceutical company. I don't know all the details of course, but apparently someone was causing waves that was costing them too much money and there was a hit put on them. I had to make it look like a suicide."

Jorge froze and stared into her eyes and then slowly nodded.

"This does not surprise me," He replied. "I'm sure there are many others before and since."

"Money has a disturbing effect on people and moreover, the thought of possibly losing it," Paige observed between bites. Jorge appreciated a woman who actually *ate;* there was nothing more frustrating than being out to dinner with a woman who picked at her food like a child would, as if it were poison on a plate and talked about diets and all that nonsense.

"Me, I never did it for money," Jorge confessed and saw a hint of surprise in Paige's eyes as she tilted her head slightly and listened. "I mean, yes, in the beginning, but not now. It was about the challenge, the power, the excitement but the money? Not so much. I have so much money now. What do I need for?"

"It was about," He started and glanced around the room as he finished his food. "In the beginning, it was becoming successful and becoming rich in a white man's world. Proving that I was capable of surpassing them with a product they lusted after and knowing I had that power. Showing my father that I wasn't the *mierda estúpida* that he insisted I was. Then, I started to do the drugs myself and it was about supporting my habit and lifestyle and that, of course, is when Verónic showed up, just like a vulture. Now, it's not the same. I don't feel the need to prove myself anymore."

"So you don't want to do it anymore?" Paige asked as she took a drink of her wine.

"You know, I'm looking into marijuana now," Jorge replied and relaxed in his chair and glanced around the quiet restaurant. "It's about to blow up like crazy, I can see it. Not to suggest it wasn't already all over the place but its acceptance is increasing. There are benefits for health as well as recreational. Now that's something I can sink my teeth into here in Canada."

Paige held her wine glass and silently watched him. "Things are definitely changing," She hesitated, a grin formed on her face when he stuck a toothpick in his mouth and rolled it between his lips, his body craved a cigarette but he had made a promise, once again, to his daughter.

"I have a boss that I work for in Mexico," Jorge commented. "He's the kingpin, not I. He can find someone younger, stronger, hungry and he will not care. I will still be involved but separated to a degree. That is my preference now. The thrill, it's gone."

"Just like that?"

"Well, it's slightly more complicated but that is what I wish to do," Jorge admitted. "He knows that I prefer to focus on pot and to him, that means more money. My life, it has taken a different turn. If I don't start paying attention to my daughter, she might get off track and I wouldn't be able to live with myself."

"Very noble," She gently commented.

"It is what I must do," Jorge commented and finished his glass of wine. "Her behavior is a concern to me. Since Juliana is here to help us, I told her to pay close attention to Maria."

"If she starts her new school here, maybe it will be better," Paige suggested and took another sip of her wine. "It will be a big change."

"I'm not sure," Jorge admitted with a loud sigh. "I did not tell her about the Fentanyl or the circumstance in which the police found her mother, but she does know Verónic was an addict and that can't be easy for her. She can't have closure either since Verónic's parents are not allowing her to attend the funeral."

"What?" Paige didn't hide her shock to this news. "Are you serious?"

"Well, they officially," Jorge said with a lopsided grin, his eyes looking up as his head tilted down. "They say that the heartache of her death is too much and that they are embarrassed so, there will be no funeral proceedings. But for me, I believe they are having a private one and do not wish Maria to be there."

"That's pretty cold," Paige made a face. "Who does that?"

"These people, that is who," Jorge replied and gestured for the waitress and pointed at his wine glass. "They have no souls."

"How did Maria take it?" Paige gently asked as the waitress approached with two glasses of wine and asked if they wanted anything else. After Jorge said no with his charming smile, he then returned to his original brooding nature as the waitress walked away.

"She did not take it well," Jorge replied and took a long drink. "She was more emotional than she when learning her mother had died. She cried like I had not seen her cry in years. My heart, it broke for her but what can I do? And to tell you the truth, I wasn't looking forward to taking her to see that side of the family. I feel they look down at her because of her mother's reputation as well as mine."

"But to hold it against their own grandchild?" Paige appeared stunned by this news.

"You do not know these people," Jorge replied, feeling the warmth of the wine filling him, his body relaxing. "They are cold as ice."

"That's terrible."

"But Maria, she will come around," Jorge insisted. "I see her feeling better today and the idea of trying a new school is exciting, so this is good. And of course, I thank you for your help researching everything."

"It was my pleasure," Paige insisted as she stared into his eyes.

"It was a big help," Jorge commented and reached out to briefly touch her hand. "And of course, Maria would like to thank you in person. She wants to meet you and I think this would be a good time."

"Sure," Paige hesitated. "But maybe it is too soon with everything?"

"Actually, I believe the opposite is true," Jorge commented. "I think it is necessary to introduce a positive role model in her life now."

"I'm not sure how positive I would be," She replied with a grin.

"Nonsense! You're a woman of the world, an entrepreneur, a self-help guru," Jorge teased. "What more could she want as a role model?"

Paige laughed and raised one eyebrow.

"Whatever you think."

"So, my baby, she will be starting this new school on Monday and going for a half day before that," Jorge commented thoughtfully. "And I am looking into us becoming citizens. My business associates here in Toronto are from Colombia and recently became citizens, courtesy of my contacts so I am thinking my ordeal shouldn't be too difficult either. And you and I, we can marry and buy a house in suburbs or whatever it is you Canadians do."

Paige giggled. "You have our futures planned out."

"Planned? Not so much," Jorge said with a shrug. "Plans have a way of falling apart. These are my dreams."

"It's happening so quickly," Paige commented and moved forward in her chair. "We just met and it's so new and at the same time, it almost feels like you've been in my life forever."

"That's what you get with a ready-made family," Jorge teased. "But seriously, you know how I feel. I want to marry you and it is my hope you feel the same way. I will miss Mexico but everything is pointing me in this direction and so, who am I to question fate? It has sent me here for a reason just as it has sent you to me. Plus my instincts, they tell me that things are getting a little too hot in Mexico. I feel my daughter and me are safer here."

"You're forgetting how we met," Paige commented as a smile spread across her lips. "You may not be so safe here. Clearly, someone is watching you."

"I have a meeting tomorrow with Marco, the Filipino that you met?" Jorge quietly commented as he finished his glass of wine. "He is apparently quite talented when it comes to computers. I want to see if he can find out who hacked the hotel computer to change the room, that will hopefully give us some answers. Perhaps you wish to join us for the meeting?"

"Perhaps I will," Paige agreed. "Once we know who was behind this, we can hopefully resolve the problem. I don't exactly appreciate being tricked."

Jorge laughed. "Imagine how I feel."

Paige glanced away and her face became flushed. "I almost made a huge mistake that night. What if I had killed you?"

"But you didn't," Jorge reassured her, moving forward in his seat. "So let's not worry about it."

"But it, it haunts me," Paige admitted, her eyes full of unexpected vulnerability. "What if I had?"

A heaviness encompassed the table and although Jorge attempted to give her a reassuring smile, the power of the moment quickly extinguished that gesture and instead, he reached for her hand.

"The 'what if' game," Jorge shook his head, his voice barely a whisper. "It is a dangerous game to play. What if you had killed me? What if you hadn't been sent to the wrong room? What if Verónic wasn't dead? What if my daughter got along with others in her old school? What if I hadn't got mixed up with Verónic years ago? What if I didn't have a daughter? What if I never got involved in drugs? There are so many 'what ifs' and at the end of the day, where would we be if we thought about them so much? I have long forgiven you for this mistake. Why do you not forgive yourself?'

And for the first time since meeting her, he saw Paige Noël cry.

CHAPTER 17

"Today, my love, you will meet some people," Jorge announced as he met Paige at the door of her apartment. Looking around as he walked in, it was the first time he had been to her place and it caught him off guard; it was quite small for a woman who could afford something much more luxurious. Cramped, to be exact. But it was cute, simple and when he considered that she perhaps hadn't planned to keep it long-term, he didn't ask questions. "This place, it is nice."

"Not really," Paige replied followed by a laugh as she closed the door behind him and they shared a quick kiss before she led him to a two-person couch in the middle of the room, where they both sat down. She wore a pair of black jeans and a simple t-shirt but still looked spectacular. "I was kind of off the grid for many years and so when I returned to Canada, it would've looked suspicious if I bought a large house or something expensive. Actually, it was a good thing I kept things modest since the CRA audited my business last year and it would've been suspicious if I had a larger place."

"Clever," Jorge commented and continued to look around. The ambiance was bright, relaxed with soft yellow walls, some pink ornaments in the corner of the living room; he recognized it as the place where she recorded her life coach videos. "Yes, the government! They must always be looking in our lives and trying to 'catch' us doing something wrong."

"It sure feels that way," Paige muttered and shook her head. "So, you want me to meet some people today? Should I change?" She gestured toward his shirt and tie ensemble and he shook his head.

"No, you're fine but grab a coat," He commented as he adjusted his own leather jacket while standing up, pointing toward the window. "The sun, it's deceiving. Fall is definitely in the air."

Twenty minutes later they were in downtown Toronto and entering a building after being buzzed in by Diego Silva. Although Jorge had been there in the past to drop off or pick up someone, he never actually had stepped foot inside the luxurious building before that day. Although owning a house was his preference, there was something to be said for condos despite the fact that they were the box store version of a home. Tradition, it seems, was slowly being thrown out the door for a cold existence.

Glancing at Paige as they got off the elevator, he sensed she was slightly nervous about the meeting and figured that was probably normal. Things had happened quickly between them and perhaps she worried his associates wouldn't approve of her. Reaching out, he gave her hand a quick squeeze when they arrived at the door. Almost immediately, he could hear Diego's loud voice booming from the other side.

Abruptly swinging the door opened, it was clear he was in the middle of another conversation when he suddenly halted, his eyes fixated on Paige Noël. His eyes jumped back and forth between the two of them until Jorge felt himself grow frustrated by the dramatics and snapped at him.

"Diego, do you think maybe we can go inside or would you prefer to conduct this meeting in the hallway?" His voice was sharp but that was sometimes required when dealing with Diego. The two went way back to their youth in California when Jorge did a lot of business with the man who was, at that time, the sugar daddy to the Colombian. Their relationship had always been awkward but then again, everything with Diego was awkward. He was an anxious man with the attention span of a hummingbird.

"Come in, come in!" He moved aside, allowing them to walk into the room. Diego's younger sister Jolene sat on the couch, wearing a professional blouse and skirt combo, her curvy figure accented perfectly while next to her sat Chase Jacobs, always in a suit and tie, he was holding a cup of coffee in his hand. Jorge turned back to see Paige standing aside, appearing awkward. He assumed it was Diego's erratic energy that was making her uncomfortable and shot him a dirty look.

"Can I get you a coffee, either of you?" Diego asked, his eyes jumped between his two guests as if ready for one of them to lurch forward and attack him. This entire scene was making Jorge frustrated and uncomfortable.

"Not for me," Jorge suddenly wished for this meeting to be over so he could leave. "Paige?"

"No, I'm fine," Her voice was calm even though her face still carried a trace of discomfort.

"I shall introduce you to my associates," He pointed first toward an antsy Diego. "This nincompoop here is Diego Silva, the co-owner of Diego and Jolene Inc. I was telling you about their company on the way here," He ignored the dirty look shot in his direction. "Diego, this is Paige Noël."

"Nice to meet you," Diego's face immediately lit up as he approached and the two shook hands. He stared at Paige like he was a lovesick puppy, which seemed rather odd for a homosexual man but then again, Diego had a habit of flirting with women despite his disinterest. It was confusing. "I love your jacket!"

Paige was wearing a red leather jacket that she grabbed on their way out the door. Jorge grinned at her and she merely smiled at Diego and thanked him.

"This is your home, right? It's really nice. Much nicer than mine," She politely commented.

"Nicer than Jorge's place in Mexico?" Diego shot back, his big creepy eyes widened and Jorge grew frustrated again.

"No," Jorge replied to the question despite the fact that it had been directed at Paige, who was shrugging. "Now can we move on with this, Diego. We only have a few minutes."

"Of course! I will go grab another chair," He pointed to the two loan chairs across from the couch and rushed away while Jorge turned toward Paige, attempting to give her a reassuring smile as they walked toward the couch. "This here is Diego's sister, Jolene Silva the other owner of Diego and Jolene Inc. for which I invest in. Don't worry, she is not crazy like him."

The two women appeared awkward with one another, almost as if they weren't sure whether to shake hands.

"It is nice to meet you...Paige?" Jolene spoke slowly, she reached out and the two shook hands while giving each other a long stare.

"Yes, it's nice to meet you as well, Jolene," Paige replied as the two women continued to communicate through their eyes, something Jorge interpreted as jealousy. Of course! Paige was intimidated by the voluptuous Colombian and perhaps, Jolene was a little jealous of Paige. After all, he suspected she had a crush on him but he didn't like to mix business with pleasure...usually. Although the two had managed to convince her brother Diego that they were having an affair once during a business...mission, which was hilarious since it rattled his cage.

Jorge then introduced her to Chase, adding that he was the manager of JD Exclusive Club. Their introduction seemed to go more smoothly as they shook hands and Paige quietly repeated, "Chase Jacobs, nice to meet you."

A loud noise from the balcony grabbed their attention as Diego dragged in a large chair from outside. "Sorry, I didn't expect another person." He apologized and pulled the chair close to the one where Paige stood, he gave her another infatuated smile and Jorge glared at him.

"Ok, we must start, Paige and I," He gestured toward her as the three of them sat down. "We must go soon."

"Go ahead," Diego insisted and Jorge was about to start talking when his attention was pulled across the room to a huge tree.

"Diego, is that a lime tree?" Jorge tilted his head slightly to look behind Jolene, who sat across from him. "You have a lime tree in your condo?"

"I like limes," Diego insisted stubbornly. "The ones at the store, they aren't good." He made a face and Jorge rolled his eyes.

"Anyway, back to business at hand," He continued "Diego, your cleaning lady, was she in?"

"Clara," Paige spoke up.

"Yes, thank you, was Clara in today?" He asked and watched Diego nod.

"She just left."

"Perfect, this information is of a sensitive nature," Jorge continued and turned in his chair. "There was a situation recently where it seems that someone might have tried to have me killed. At first, it appeared to be an error but we aren't completely sure that it wasn't organized in such a fashion to look that way. For this reason, I felt that it was necessary to let you know so you can be vigilant."

"Who try to kill you? Was it in Mexico?" Jolene's eyes grew in size, she briefly glanced at Paige and back at him. "Was it here?"

"It was here in Toronto," Jorge replied calmly. "The point is that we are looking into it further and plan to find out who was behind it. You all may have nothing to worry about but just in case, keep your eyes opened and be prepared for anything. We are making a lot of money here in Toronto and that could be pissing off some people. I don't know. It could be so many things and I don't wish to speculate."

"Don't you have that bodyguard?" Diego piped up as he crossed his legs, his foot anxiously bouncing in the air. "You know, that big, rugged man?"

"Jesús? Yes, but he was in Mexico at the time watching my daughter. I never had problems in Canada before so I assumed I was fine here."

"How did it happen?" Jolene prompted and Chase grinned and scratched his neck and rubbed his face in attempts to hide his reaction.

"It doesn't matter," Jorge replied and immediately moved on. "I brought Paige with me today because she is somewhat of an...expert in this area and she might have some thoughts to share?"

Although they had discussed this in the SUV on their way, she still appeared surprised by his question.

"Yes, well...."

"*Why* are you an expert" Diego cut her off, putting a loud emphasize on the 'why' that Jolene jumped slightly. "Aren't you Jorge's girlfriend? I thought you were Jorge's girlfriend? Chase, didn't you say Jorge had a girlfriend named Paige?"

"I.. um...." Chase looked apologetically.

"You gossip like schoolgirls," Jorge complained and glanced toward Paige. "Yes, she is actually my fiancée, if you must know but she's also…a professional…. you know, never mind. We should go."

Irritated with Diego, Jorge jumped from his seat and glared at him.

"It's fine," Paige calmly took over, her eyes appeared to be observing his face and he immediately took a deep breath and sat back down. "It's ok, I got this."

Glancing around, he quickly noted the look of shock on everyone's face.

Fuck!

"Ok, so, I don't think we need to get into a lot of details here," Paige started, her hand in the air as if in defense and calmly explained it again. "As Jorge was saying, he might be in danger and so there's a slight chance everyone here might be too. I would recommend more vigilance than usual if you have a gun you might want to have it close at hand. If you notice anything suspicious, let Jorge know."

There was a brief silence. Not surprisingly, it was Diego that broke it.

"Why are you an expert?" He asked and twisted around in his chair. "You're not a cop are you?"

Paige laughed at that question and turned her attention to Jorge, as if not sure how to answer his question.

"Come on, we're all family here," Diego insisted. "Tell us."

"Family?" Jorge snorted. "Really, Diego?"

"The point is she can trust us," Diego insisted, his huge eyes focusing in on Paige again. "Are you like a dirty cop?"

"No," Paige hesitated for a moment and glanced at each of their faces. "I'm an assassin."

Diego looked the most surprised by the news and practically jumped into a jumbled rush of questions.

"Oh my God! How did you get into that? Like how many people have you killed? Anyone famous? No, no, don't tell me. Yes, actually, yes, do tell me! Did you kill Kurt Cobain?"

Paige appeared calm despite Diego's insane outburst and Jorge wanted to strangle him as he rambled on like an idiot.

"Diego, I wasn't in this line of work in the 90s," She calmly replied. "And I'm not sure we have any reason to believe he was murdered."

"Yeah, right!" Diego sniffed. "You people can make it look like a suicide. I *know* things."

"Ok, Diego, you need to calm the fuck down," Jorge interrupted. "She didn't kill Kurt Cobain."

"No, I didn't mean *you* did," Diego replied turning toward Paige while on the edge of his seat. "I'm just saying, someone could've made it look like a suicide. It happens. Am I right?"

"Yes, Diego, you are correct," Paige replied. "It *does* happen, however, I don't know about that specific circumstance. I've never heard anything in my circles suggesting he was murdered."

"Ok, enough!" Jorge snapped. "Diego, let it go! It's been over 20 years. Can we get back on point here?"

Everyone fell silent.

"Jorge, I don't mean to imply," Jolene suddenly spoke up, her voice boisterous. "But could this not be...personal too? Could it have nothing to do with us, here?"

"It's possible."

"Like your ex-wife?" Diego jumped in.

"We weren't married, Diego," Jorge replied and took a deep breath. "Also, she recently died."

The room was silent.

"She overdosed," Jorge felt the need to add. "So don't you all look at me like that."

Diego gave Paige a suspicious look.

"I had nothing to do with this one either," Paige replied without looking directly at Diego.

"Yes, Diego," Jorge spoke up. "She did *not* kill your Kurt Cobain and she did not kill my ex-girlfriend, not a wife, *girlfriend*."

"Oh, Maria, how is she?" Jolene spoke up.

"We're working on it," Jorge felt like what was meant to be a short meeting had gone completely off track. "Look, guys, we must go soon. I know I've given you a lot to think about but what can I say? It has been a busy few days."

With that he stood up and Paige did the same.

"We will let you know when *we* know more," Jorge insisted and he noted they all appeared stunned by the news but when his eyes met with Paige's, a smile erupted on his lips and she did the same.

CHAPTER *18*

"So, let me get this straight," Paige calmly asked after they got in the empty elevator and the door closed behind them. "Jolene and Diego own this sex party business you were telling me about and Chase runs a club, where you have most of the parties? You invest in all of this?"

"Yes," Jorge confirmed everything as he hit the elevator button and glanced back to catch her reaction. She appeared to be processing all the information that she learned at the chaotic meeting. "And I am sorry for that back there. Diego, he's a little ADD at times, nervous guy, just talks and thinks later."

"Oh, no that's fine, Diego didn't bother me," She shook her head. "So you're an investor plus you sell at the club."

"And launder the money, yes," Jorge quietly replied with a sniff as the elevator hummed behind them and he reached for her hand. "They started off small and when things took off, the business grew. Then we opened the club so we wouldn't be paying out to someone else for a venue. It is a great place to sell all kinds of things."

She grinned and nodded, reading the message indicated. "So, are you *into* this kind of thing? Sex clubs?"

Jorge let out a boisterous laugh. "No, *bella dama*, I'm into making money. Think about it, it's the ideal place to sell my product."

She nodded as the elevator stopped and the door slid open. It wasn't until they were back in the SUV that either spoke.

"Again, I'm sorry for that meeting," Jorge commented before turning on the ignition. "Diego, he can be *loco* and I just really wanted to get in and out of there. I hope I didn't put you on the spot, I thought you were prepared to talk about what you did…I may not have understood?"

"No, it's fine," Paige replied and looked out the window on the passenger side as they got back on the road. "I wasn't clear on how much they knew or how much I should say. I'm not exactly used to telling people what I do."

"They are trustworthy," Jorge insisted as if reading her next thought. "I promise you, these people, they are no angels. Everyone in that room has either killed someone or been somehow involved. Diego, he seems harmless but he, he can be dangerous. Jolene also and by the way, there is nothing to worry about." He stopped and glanced toward Paige. "Her and I, we never had anything, so do not worry."

"What?" Paige appeared sincerely lost.

"You know, we never got together," Jorge clarified as they drove through the downtown streets. "I know that was what you were thinking. We pretended once for business and to freak out Diego a bit but we never had an affair."

"I actually hadn't thought about it," Paige flatly commented.

"Oh come on," Jorge grinned at her when they stopped at a red light. "I could tell when you met her that there was a little jealously. I mean, Jolene is a very attractive woman, very sexy but I do not mix business and pleasure. I learned that lesson many, many years ago."

"I honestly didn't assume that," Paige replied and began to laugh. "Why did you think I did?"

"You were acting weird around her so, come on, you can admit this to me," Jorge replied, feeling very generous in his comments. "I know women."

"You think women are always jealous?" Paige asked, her eyes watching Jorge.

"Yes, of course, women are always jealous of one another," Jorge commented with some arrogance and reached for his cigarettes. "I see it all the time. Especially where there is a man involved. Every woman wants to think every man wants her and *only* her and therefore you are very jealous of one another."

Their eyes met briefly before the traffic started to move again and suddenly he wasn't so sure. "Right?"

Paige shook her head no.

"Ok, then why did you two act weird around one another?"

"I'm not sure that we did," Paige replied, her eyes fixated on him.

"I thought so."

"I noticed that everyone in the room seemed to think you might've killed Verónic," She changed the subject. "Why is that?"

"Because of how much I hated her but they didn't know why," Jorge replied. "The woman was a drug addict but I didn't necessarily share that information. I don't believe in telling people too much of my personal life or problems."

"Makes sense," She quietly replied.

"I do not normally kill for personal reasons," He insisted while parallel parking with ease in front of a trendy coffee shop. "Always business. I made that rule for myself a long time ago. I know my temper and if I allowed myself to attack people when they angered me, half the world would be gone."

She laughed. "So, do you have guidelines or rules when it comes to this kind of thing?"

"Instinct," Jorge replied as he shifted into park. "For example, the last was a girl working with the RCMP and had already attempted to spy on us when the office was in Calgary. She also was doing a lot of behind the scenes investigating, was attempting to get Chase to flip on us, which he wouldn't."

Jorge turned toward Paige. "That man back there, Chase? I think I told you that he lost one of his small children. A hunter shot him by mistake so we took care of him. This bitch was snooping into all of this plus telling Chase's ex-wife that we were criminals and encouraging her to pull his other two kids out of his life. That, to me, was a bit personal. It was business too but it was very personal. It hit a nerve."

Paige nodded, her lips curving slightly into a sympathetic smile.

Jorge leaned in and gave her a quick kiss before they both got out of the SUV and together, entered the coffee shop. They immediately spotted Marco next to the window and fortunately, away from anyone else. Only a few people with laptops sat around and to that, Jorge rolled his eyes. Why the fuck would anyone want to work in a noisy coffee shop? Music, the clatter of dishes, chatter, it was distracting to him.

After getting a coffee for him and Paige, the two joined Marco at his table.

"*Buenos dias*," Jorge commented as he sat across from Marco and Paige said hello as she sat beside Jorge. "I'm not sure if I introduced you to Paige, my fiancée?"

"I don't think so," Marco replied and with a smile on his face, reached across the table to shake her hand. He returned his attention to Jorge. "Thank you for meeting me. Did you receive my résumé, Mr. Hernandez?

"Yes!" Jorge nodded enthusiastically. "Very impressive work history. I might be able to use you in the future if you're interested. Either with side projects or full-time, whichever your preference is but, for now, I wanted to ask about your IT skills."

"Yes, of course, I have listed my experience and training, were there further questions?" Marco asked as his brown eyes grew in size.

"Yes, actually," Jorge settled back into his chair and glanced around before continuing. "Can you hack into someone's system. Let's say, the hotel where you work?"

Although there was some hesitation, Marco finally nodded. "Yes, I believe I can. But sir, I did not mix up the rooms…"

"I didn't think that was you, Marco," Jorge commented and noted the relief on his face. "You're too smart. You work at the hotel and know that all the information would have to be filled in correctly to not raise suspicion. The person who did this only changed the name and left most of the information blank, it was done hastily. That is not my concern. I am hoping, however, you might be able to figure out who could've done this, if it was from within the hotel, outside, who, when, anything. If you can find out some information, I am willing to offer you a very generous gift in exchange."

Marco took this in and slowly nodded. "I cannot promise but I will certainly try."

"If you are nervous about doing it on your own computer, I can provide you with whatever you need," Jorge added. "We need to find out who did this because I have reason to believe that it was done to put me in a dangerous position."

Marco mouthed the word 'Wow' and shook his head. "I haven't heard anything more from Mr. Gomez. He has been away on business this week."

"What about emails," Paige jumped in as she leaned forward. "Can you get into his emails? Maybe something around that time frame? That would be perfect."

"I will try," Marco insisted. "I cannot promise anything but I will definitely try."

"*Perfecto*," Jorge commented and nodded. "I will get back to you with the details later and as I said, I am willing to reward you generously and possibly give you some future work, if you're interested."

"Yes, sir, I would be interested," Marco replied and seemed hesitant to continue. "You said danger? Would I be in danger for doing this?"

"Not at all," Jorge insisted. "And if you think you ever are, then you tell me. We'll take care of your safety concerns."

Marco nodded to show understanding. Although his résumé was clean, something told Jorge that this man was far from innocent. Perhaps it took one to know one? Glancing at Paige, he could tell that she trusted him too. He was in.

They left the shop shortly afterward, each with a coffee in hand, they headed to the SUV and once inside, Jorge pulled on his sunglasses as the sun suddenly burst through the clouds, after what had been a hazy morning. At first, neither spoke as Jorge turned the ignition.

"I think he could be helpful," Paige said as they pulled back on the street. "I see that in him. He's someone who reads between the lines but doesn't ask a lot of questions."

"Here's hoping," Jorge spoke wearily suddenly feeling exhausted despite the large coffee in his hand. "If we can find out even where the system was hacked, we can figure out everything else too."

"I bet it was Gomez himself," Paige commented airily as they drove through thick traffic and she glanced out the window. "Just a feeling I have."

"This is possible," Jorge yawned. "We have one more person for you to meet. If it is ok with you, I would like to introduce you to my daughter today."

"Are you sure that's a good idea?" Paige asked with some hesitation. But to that, Jorge merely shrugged.

"I think it is time," He commented as they sat in traffic. "She has had time to process everything and today she went to the school to *try* it. They allow children to go and sit in, see what the classes are like, mix with the other students, get a private tour and see the facilities. It's a nice idea. It is a half day so she is about to finish. I must go pick her up."

"Ok," Paige replied. "If you feel it is a good time then I do too."

"She is resilient, my daughter," Jorge insisted as traffic slowly moved. "I told her that you went to a lot of effort to find this school for her so I think she will be appreciative of your thoughtfulness."

Although he said it, he wasn't so sure himself and hoped his daughter wasn't defiant or rude when Paige met her but at the same time, he knew it was unavoidable. In order for their relationship to move forward, it was necessary for the two to meet. He feared Maria would say something inappropriate and embarrass both him and Paige. She seemed to have the need to shock people and he wasn't sure where that came from at all. Rebellion, perhaps? He didn't understand. He was a man who prided himself on being professional, a gentleman, smooth and yet, his daughter was becoming very crass and rude.

The school was in a nice area of town, pricey buildings sat around it while a large fence surrounded the property. He learned that this was for privacy since some of the girls were daughters of very rich and successful people, some of which were in the public eye; government, CEOs of larger companies and of course, children of celebrities.

Getting on the grounds required a pass under normal circumstances but for that day, he was allowed when he told both his name and answered a few questions about Maria before entering the property.

"It feels like a prison," Jorge observed as they drove forward on the property to the visitor parking area. "Then again, my daughter, she might need that now."

Paige let out a small laugh as he parked the SUV. "I doubt she's that bad."

"You might take those words back when you meet her," Jorge insisted as they got out and headed toward the school.

Inside, they met another line of security that required them to walk through a metal detector. A quick glance at Paige indicated that she didn't have a gun with her, much to his relief because he had almost brought his with him. After successfully reaching the other side, he saw a young, plain-looking woman standing with Maria. As soon as his daughter spotted Jorge, she ran toward him.

"Oh Papa! I love it here!" Her eyes were immediately focused on Paige and much to his surprise, her reaction was one of conformity rather than defiance. That was unusual. "Is this her? Paige?"

"Yes," Jorge spoke hesitantly, nervously glancing at Maria then Paige. "Maria, I would like you to meet Paige Noël."

Much to his surprise, his daughter curtsied and then reached out her hand. "It's a pleasure to make your acquaintance."

Paige smiled and quietly replied, "It's nice to meet you, Maria, I've heard so much about you."

Jorge was a bit stunned and wondered for a moment if he had accidentally stumbled on the wrong child. Of all the reactions he expected from Maria, this wasn't one of them.

"Well, I…I'm very happy you've finally met," Jorge spoke hesitantly as he glanced toward the plain-looking woman who was approaching him with a bright smile on her face.

"Mr. Hernandez, what a pleasure to have your daughter with us for the morning," Her comment was honest, no sarcasm, which delighted him.

"Yes, well, she was really looking forward to…spending the morning here with you," He commented in disbelief. "Thank you for having her."

"She was a delight," The strange woman insisted while beside him, Maria started to chat with Paige. Slightly hesitant to leave his daughter and fiancée in order to talk to the principal, he followed her toward the office with hopes that Maria would continue to behave while he was out of earshot.

It was a crapshoot at best.

CHAPTER 19

"Do you believe in miracles?" He whispered to Paige in the dead of the night as he reached out and pulled her closer to his body.

"What?" Paige spoke softly, her voice faint as if half asleep. She turned toward him and cleared her throat. The air conditioner was on after an Indian summer had taken over Canada's largest city causing residents to talk non-stop about the crippling heat.

"Miracles?" He repeated and paused. It was well after midnight and Jorge was wide awake, his thoughts racing like a freight train that was about to crash. A late night text indicated that Marco finally had some information for him and they were to meet in the morning.

'Yes, like you came into my life and everything changed overnight," He commented as she turned to face him. Naked, he reluctantly had one thin sheet covering half his body out of fake modesty, sensing that Canadians were slightly conservative in nature. "Everything is so different now. I want to leave Mexico. I *never* thought about leaving Mexico despite all the work I did here and in the US. Never occurred to me that I would ever feel this way."

"Is that necessarily a miracle?" She whispered, her voice now clearer, her eyes watched him carefully, her long eyelashes flickered gently and her hand traveled up his arm. "Your life just took a turn, wouldn't you say?"

"But it's a good turn. I hadn't realized that Mexico, it is over for me," He commented and took a deep breath. "Perhaps I didn't want to see it. But my daughter, she wasn't thriving, Verónic's death just further proves that our time there has concluded. I hadn't seen it and then you

136

came into my life and everything was in focus, it was so clear. To me, that is a miracle."

"I think you might've come to that conclusion without me," Paige pointed out. "I don't know that I had such an impact."

"Oh, believe me, Paige, you have much to do with this," Jorge gave her a quick kiss and sat up slowly getting out of bed. "Our life together will be beautiful, here in Canada, a new start for my daughter, a new start for me. I don't even feel like the same person anymore. As I said, I don't even want to be involved in cocaine anymore. I *never* thought I would say that either."

"Is it something you can get out of?" Paige asked pointedly. "I'm not an expert on these things but my assumption is that it's not exactly something you can give your letter of resignation for and move on."

"My boss," Jorge started to speak but paused for a long moment as he pulled on his boxers and sat back down. "I've done a lot of work for him over the years and he knows how I feel about the pot industry. I know you're worried but you have no need to be."

"I hope you're right," Paige sat up, pulling the sheet close to her chest and he grinned and looked away. "I'm in no position to lecture you on your career choices but I feel like I can walk away from what I do but you, I don't know if it is that easy."

Jorge didn't reply at first. "Have you ever considered giving up what you do?"

"All the time," Paige admitted, her eyes were huge in the dark.

Jorge returned to his quiet hotel suite and went directly into his room, where he sat on the edge of the bed. Juliana and Maria were obviously asleep and he enjoyed the peacefulness. Soon, they would be returning to Mexico and he would have to deal with, among other things, Maria's old school. Her new school agreed to work with her online while she away and at the same time, he would have a million other things to deal with including his boss. Although they had already, briefly discussed getting into the pot business, he hoped that this could be his primary focus after moving.

The next morning, he woke up with a stiff neck, his body welcomed a hot shower before Juliana and Maria got out of bed. Although he still felt terrible when Maria popped into the kitchen for breakfast, he threw a smile on his face and acted as if everything was normal.

"Papa, when we come back to Canada after Mexico, are we moving in with Paige?" Maria asked as she picked up a muffin while he scanned the news on his laptop. Juliana was in the shower and had agreed to take Maria to school. Unfamiliar with the city, Jorge had asked Chase Jacobs to drive them and make sure everything went smoothly; he assumed it would but knew Maria would take comfort in having her 'one Canadian friend' with her.

"Not yet, Maria," Jorge spoke evenly but was relieved that she was even considering the possibility. "Her apartment is quite small, there simply wouldn't be room for all of us."

"She doesn't have two bedrooms?" Maria asked as she picked at the blueberries in her muffin.

"No, there is only one bedroom at her place," Jorge commented. "As I said, it is quite small. We will be renting a place until we find something permanent for the three of us. I have someone looking for me."

"Paige?" She asked.

"No, a real estate agent," Jorge replied and shut his laptop. "I know this is a lot of changes very quickly, Maria. I hope you don't find it too much."

Shaking her head no, Jorge realized that in fact, it was him that was having a hard time adjusting, not the other way around. Perhaps it was age, he decided. At one time, any change didn't phase him in the least but now, it seemed like every decision had a thousand factors to consider. Maria being the biggest of all factors.

"But it is a big move," Jorge reminded her and searched her eyes but she continued to show no reaction. "A new country, a new school, Papa is getting married, you just lost your mother. *Bonita,* that's a lot."

She merely shrugged. "Papa, I wanted to leave my old school, so this move is a good thing to me. I like Paige, did you think I wouldn't?"

Jorge answered with a smile.

"Everything is fine," She attempted to reassure him but he wasn't necessarily believing it. She was quieter for the last few days, unusually subdued as if she were processing a million thoughts but not revealing any of them. It was unlike his daughter and he wondered if the school had a counselling program that he should look into. Then again, maybe he should look outside the school? He would talk to Paige. For not being a parent, in many ways, he felt she was a better one than him.

"You are quiet," He observed.

"I'm tired."

"Are you sleeping well."

Maria shrugged.

"If you want to talk about anything…"

"I have nothing to talk about," Maria insisted defiantly. "The only thing I wanted for was to go to school in Canada and it has been arranged. This is what I dreamed of for so long. Why would I be unhappy?"

Jorge didn't reply. He wasn't so certain. But when he brought up his concerns to Paige later that morning, she gave her usual, relaxed smile and shrugged.

"It's her first day of school," She gently commented. "Maria is probably nervous so that might explain why she was quiet. Don't you remember your first day of school?"

"Oh, my love, I haven't had a first day of school in *many* years," Jorge replied and immediately began to laugh as he drove toward the same coffee shop where he had last met up with Marco. "I didn't think of it as such a big deal though if I recall."

"Maybe it's different for girls," Paige insisted. "I remember being nervous on the first day of school every year. Worried about teachers, if I would make friends, if I would fit in, I think that's normal. This is a whole new country to her. You've spent a lot of time here but from the sounds of it, Maria hasn't, so she's probably scared of fitting in especially since she begged you to make this switch."

"God, I hope she gets along ok," Jorge suddenly considered the possibility that she wouldn't. "I hope the kids aren't a bunch of rich snobs."

Paige laughed. "Jorge, we are talking about a girl who brought a switchblade to school when she was in Mexico, I don't think she is easily intimidated by anyone."

A grin quickly changed to laughter as they pulled into a parking space near the coffee shop where Marco could be seen sitting next to the window. He immediately waved as they got out of the SUV and walked toward the entrance.

"On top of everything, I have to finally buy a vehicle when I move here," Jorge commented as he hit the remote to lock the SUV. "Moving is stressful."

"Just take it one thing at a time," She commented as he checked his buzzing phone and grinned.

"Chase sent me a picture of Maria," He smirked and pointed the phone toward Paige. Standing in her uniform, a bright smile on her face, the picture somehow gave the boost of contentment that he needed that morning. Sliding the iPhone back into his pocket, he welcomed the shot of air conditioning as he walked into the coffee shop. Unlike most days, he wore a Beatles t-shirt and jeans and not a shirt and tie. It was probably the most casual outfit Paige had ever seen him in.

She wore a slinky strapped top that looked dignified with her petite figure, a flowing skirt that accented her ass and a pair of flip-flops. Walking ahead of him, his attention focused on her body, he suddenly wondered if anyone else was noticing the same thing. He quickly scanned the room to see if any other men's eyes were on Paige. One man was definitely checking her out and he felt his anger build up just as she turned and asked what he wanted.

"No no, *mi amor,* I will pay," He immediately slid his arm around her waist, noting the wallet she held in her hand, his attention switched to the lady behind the counter. "I will have the largest coffee you have. Do you have sandwiches or something?"

After getting a ready-made ham and cheese sandwich, he walked toward the table with that in one hand, coffee in the other. Paige opted for a latte.

"Good morning, Marco," Jorge said as they approached, a smile on his face, he place the food on the table before sitting down. "I like this shop. Coffee's good."

"My cousin, he works here, that is how I know about it," Marco insisted with wide eyes. "The food is very good although, a bit expensive."

"Everything seems to be in these places," Jorge agreed as Paige sat beside him. "I must have the gang here for a business meeting someday. It's a nice atmosphere. The coffee might actually meet the standards of my associate, Diego."

"Diego is fussy about coffee?" Paige asked with a glowing smile, as the sunlight flowed into the room and touched her face.

"Diego, he's fussy about *everything,*" Jorge insisted and took a hearty bite of his sandwich.

"I know you are particular about coffee as well if I remember correctly," Marco grinned. "That is why I chose this place so carefully."

Jorge thought back to his original meeting with Marco at the hotel and laughed. "This is true."

"So, were you able to find anything?" Paige quietly asked Marco, her eyes fixated on him as Jorge continued to eat his sandwich in large bites.

"I was, unfortunately, maybe not as much as you were probably hoping," Marco looked regretful. "I was able to see that the change was definitely made within the hotel but I cannot tell by who yet. See, it was done at one of the main computers at the check in desk and although the clerks all have their own login information, it is not uncommon for someone else to jump on when things get busy or if they have to excuse themselves to go to the washroom, that kind of thing."

"Who are you getting so far?" Jorge asked. "Who's number is it?"

"It is the same young woman who works most evenings, she was probably working at the desk the day you arrived. Her name is Angela."

"Hmm...." Jorge thought back to the woman who originally tried to check him on that disastrous day when his room had been switched to another Hernandez. "I do remember her but she seemed harmless."

"That is the thing," Marco commented. "I have seen other people take over her computer to change something, including Mr. Gomez."

Jorge and Paige exchanged glances.

"Anything else come up?" Jorge asked patiently.

"Yes, I have found a series of emails that from around that timeframe," Marco commented and pulled out his phone and began to tap at it. "I can, of course, send them to you but in one, there is a suggestion that someone was asking about you. They do not say your name but it was around the time you arrived and he refers to your suite number, that is what stood out to me."

"Really?" Jorge sat down his sandwich and wiped his hands on a napkin before taking Marco's phone and glancing over the email. It was vague-clearly on purpose-referring to his suite during the same time of his visit.

"See the problem here is," Jorge pointed at it while Paige read it over his shoulder, causing him to pass her the phone. "It could be referring to the other guy who was supposed to have the room cause he had the same last name. I mean, after the rooms were switched."

"See that is it," Marco commented with a shrug. "I do not know but maybe you will read the emails, you may see something that I do not."

"This email was sent earlier on the same day," Paige commented. "I recognize the date. I kind of get the feeling that it is about the other guy but I would have to see the emails leading up to this one." She seemed to be scanning through his phone and once satisfied returned it to Marco. "You can send these to Jorge?"

"Of course, there are a lot and some probably have nothing to do with you, if any," Marco's eyes flickered from Paige to Jorge. "I do not know. If you see something you want me to look at further, please let me know. I will continue to investigate who was on that computer. I have a friend in security. Maybe he can help."

Jorge raised an eyebrow. He liked this guy.

CHAPTER 20

It wasn't until after they got back into the SUV and Jorge turned on the ignition that either spoke.

"He's clean," Paige insisted with certainty in her voice as she glanced out the passenger window and toward the coffee shop before returning her attention to Jorge. Fastening her seatbelt and rubbing her lips together, Paige's eyes shifted to his face as she turned in her seat. "I gave his phone a quick search to make sure and nothing alerted me."

Unsure of what to say, it suddenly hit him that Paige was extremely crafty; which led him to wonder if she had also researched him? Did she scan through his phone or computer when he was in the shower? Did she do a background check on him even though she scolded him for doing the same to her? He trusted her with all his heart. Perhaps it was rash to assume she felt the same for him. Words were on the tip of his tongue but he didn't say them. It was the first time he held back from her.

They drove in silence to her building. Once arriving, she started to unfasten her seatbelt and then suddenly stopped and looked in his direction. "Aren't you coming in?" Her eyes jumped to his face and she hesitated. "Is something wrong?"

"No," He took a breath and ran a hand over his face. "I'm just thinking. Maybe I should go back to the hotel and look through these emails."

"You can look at it here," Paige commented and gestured toward her building. "We both can."

"You know what," Jorge shook his head. "Who cares?"

"What do you mean who cares?" She turned toward him, her hand clutching her purse. "This could tell us who set things up at the hotel. Maybe there's someone out there that wants to kill you. Don't you want to know?"

"Tell you the truth," Jorge confessed and reached for the pack of cigarettes and took one out. "I'm sick of this. This would've been exciting to me 20 years ago, but now? I don't have it in me anymore. No matter what you have in this world, someone is trying to take it away or at least, wants to."

"What are you talking about?" Paige calmly asked and shook her head. "Where is this coming from? I don't understand. You were fine at the coffee shop."

Taking a deep breath, Jorge glanced out the window and watched a young woman push a stroller down the street.

"Money, my daughter, my life," Jorge replied and continued to avoid looking in her direction as he spoke, feeling slightly pathetic as if this confession somehow showed his weakness. "You. It doesn't matter what I have, there's always a fear of losing it."

"I just want to live my life," Jorge continued as he lit his cigarette and blew smoke out the window before looking back in her direction. "We work hard to have everything only to fight to keep it. People are always lined up wanting money. My ex threatened to take Maria away from me every day we were together. Now someone wants to take my life and granted, it's not the first time," He hesitated and flicked the ashes out the window while glancing in the rearview mirror. "But the other times, I knew who I was dealing with and I knew why. I saw it almost like an adventure, like playing a video game and rushing to kill them before they killed me. But this time, I don't know who my enemy is or why."

Paige reached out and touched his arm.

"We'll find the answers," She gently insisted. "Until we do, we can't figure out whether it was even intended for you. Information is powerful but we need to get it to sort this out and we *will* sort it out."

"What if they hurt Maria?" Jorge replied and heard the vulnerability in his voice. "What if they do something to get to me?"

"That's not going to happen," Paige insisted. "We will get to them first."

"I would die," He shook his head, having ignored what she was saying. "Chase, he lost his child but me, I couldn't continue to live. It would be the end of me if anything happened to Maria."

"*Nothing* is going to happen to either of you," Paige continued to insist and turned more toward him. "Come inside, we'll talk about it more in there."

Apathetic and tired, he reluctantly followed her into the building. Once inside her apartment, he collapsed on her couch and stretched. "This is very comfortable," he commented with a yawn. "I could fall asleep right here."

"You can if you want," Paige suggested as she headed toward the kitchen, where she threw her purse on the counter and poured them each a glass of water. "Maybe that's what you need."

"Can I ask you something?" Jorge asked with some reluctance. "How much do you know about me?"

Paige hesitated for a moment. "You've been very forthcoming."

"No, no that's not what I mean," Jorge commented and ran a hand through his hair. "I mean, other than what I tell you. What have you heard? That night you came to my hotel room, you talked to someone, what did that person say? And today, you were looking through Marco's phone to make sure he was ok. You must've done research on me."

Had Paige been offended by his question, she didn't show it. Approaching with the glasses in hand, she calmly sat both on the small table before joining him on the couch. "I'm not going through your phone, if you're asking," She appeared humored by the question.

Grabbing it out of his pocket, he quickly hit a few digits and passed it to her.

"Go ahead," He grinned.

She hesitantly took it and glanced toward her purse.

"Do you want to look on my phone?"

"No."

"Are you sure?"

"Positive."

"I don't want to look on your phone either."

"You can," Jorge insisted and gave a tired shrug. "I don't have anything to hide."

She handed the phone back to him.

"I've never checked your phone," She spoke with an even tone. "And as for the night we met, I was just told you were the wrong person…"

She suddenly stopped talking and turned away.

"What?" Jorge quietly asked as he watched the recognition on her face.

"We are looking at this the wrong way," Paige commented and fell silent for another moment. "What if this isn't about you? What if this is about saving the other guy, as opposed to killing you? If you were marked then I would know. No one would feel the need to hide it or trick anyone."

"Not necessarily," Jorge insisted. "Maybe it was a way to keep it quiet. If someone wanted to kill me and the right people knew, *I* would know too."

Paige considered his words. "Can you send me those emails? I want to look at them."

"Sure," Jorge shrugged and picked up his phone, forwarding the document Marco sent him to her.

"You look exhausted," She commented. "Why don't you take a nap?"

Rubbing his eyes, Jorge felt like he couldn't keep awake for another moment if he tried. He had barely slept the night before and suddenly the weight of the day was too much. Following her instructions, he removed his shoes and grabbed a nearby pillow before plunking down on the couch.

He drifted off immediately and awoke later, feeling groggy and for a moment, disoriented. Remembering he was at Paige's, he glanced around with blurry eye and finally sat up and looked around. Where was she? Taking out his phone, he checked the time only to realize his nap lasted almost three hours.

Standing, he listened for some sound indicating where she was and slowly started to walk around. Not at her desk or in the kitchen, he headed toward her bedroom and glanced in. She wasn't there nor was she in the bathroom. Walking back toward Paige's desk, he noted that her laptop was still opened but the screen was locked. Reaching into his pocket for his phone, he texted her. Maybe she ran out to get something?

Wandering around the apartment some more, he attempted to figure out where Paige may have gone to but was seeing no sign. Unsure of whether or not to leave or to stay, he sat back down on the couch and glanced around. The entire place was so perfect. So clean, so organized. A small shelf contained books on meditation and natural healing, something you wouldn't expect to find in an assassin's apartment but then again, why not? Did being spiritually connected necessarily mean you were a saint too?

He was just about to make some coffee when the door opened and Paige quietly walked in. When she saw him sitting on the couch, a smile spread across her lips. "I was afraid I would wake you."

"No, I just woke actually," He commented. "Any luck?"

"A little bit," She commented while shutting the door then walking toward him. "Remember you said that Marco overheard your name in a meeting between Gomez and some men? It was the police and they were just clarifying that you were here in the room that was supposed to belong to the other Hernandez, the guy I was assigned to kill. They were trying to put together a timeline to figure out why he switched hotels at the last minute. The investigation is officially closed now."

This brought him some relief and he nodded. "Good, right? That's good?"

"Yes, the other Hernandez was rushed away at the last minute," Paige commented as she stood in the middle of the floor. "I met with a friend who knows more about these religious figures and he said it's not unusual for them to have a sudden change in routine just in case someone has them marked. That's what I kind of suspected but I wasn't sure."

"Having said that," Paige continued as she walked over and sat beside him. "We're not out of the woods yet. Although my sources tell me you aren't marked, we still don't know who sent that fruit basket with the cameras. It's looking like Gomez just followed instructions but who's instructions, I'm not sure."

Jorge nodded as he took it all in. He felt stronger than he had earlier that day, more prepared to take on whatever was around the corner.

"All this," Jorge couldn't help but grin. "And here I was, sleeping."

Paige simply leaned in and kissed him.

CHAPTER *21*

It was the rule of the jungle; kill or be killed. If someone stuck a gun to your head and you survived, it was assumed that they wouldn't. When someone pulled out a gun, it was rare that both parties walked away. In fact, it made him laugh when he saw such a thing happen on television, as if criminals had a sudden change of heart; as if they had a heart at all. Then again, Hollywood had a way of making everything look prettier than it actually was, his kind depicted as being sexy, tough, yet vulnerable. No vulnerable criminal survived.

It was for this reason that he had been a cold-hearted prick for most of his life. It was the birth of his daughter that chipped away at his heartless nature and at first, he admittedly resented it. However, as years passed, he began to understand that it was not only the love of a child but the beauty of the feminine. They balanced the earth. Had it not been for women, men would be complete savages but it was the feminine that brought a softness, a warmth and certain beauty to the world, something that was a mystery to men but they needed it; even gay men like Diego were appreciative of a beautiful woman, the way she lit up a room with her smile like nothing else; no sunrise, no flower, no drug. He even wondered if that was why so many homosexual men strived to be more feminine. They wanted to tap into some of that beauty but it was impossible. Only women possessed this special gift and he both loved and despised this about them.

The vulnerability that he avoided for years chipped away even further when he met Paige. It wasn't days after, as he grew to know her, it was mere seconds upon looking into her eyes. He was obsessed.

It wasn't just her beauty or his many lustful thoughts that pulled him to her, it was a fascination on how she was able to lower his defenses when holding a gun to his head. You couldn't be weak when someone was threatening to kill you and he had been fearless when faced with a loaded gun in the past, but this time was different. It wasn't just because she was a woman or a beautiful, it was because there was something in her voice that immediately lowered his defenses. There was a calamity that was more powerful than any threat, the loudest voice or the most aggressive hands. It was disarming. It made him weak. It was the recipe for the perfect assassin because it was instinctual to relax when you heard the soothing, soft voice that reminded you of your mother when you were a child. It was the voice that took you to a safe place when in reality, you weren't safe at all when Paige Noël was hired to kill you.

"Why didn't you kill me that day?" Jorge asked the question that he had asked before and yet, had she ever really answered? Now as he sat beside her on the couch, after the dust settled regarding the night they met, it was the one fact that still didn't make sense. As Jesús pointed out, she was known to leave no witnesses.

Paige parted her lips as if she wanted to reply but then stopped. Finally, she shook her head. "Logically, I've been telling myself that it was because you had a daughter or that you were part of the cartel, something I swore I would never get mixed up in. But it was more than that. When my boss told me who you were, I suddenly felt this strong connection. Our world is a small one that most people would never understand. It's like being in the middle of a country where no one else speaks the same language and when you finally find someone who does, it's the most powerful connection."

"But what if I had turned on you?" Jorge couldn't help but pose the question. "What if I had walked over, grabbed a gun and killed you?"

"Don't think it hadn't crossed my mind," Paige confessed with downcast eyes, her eyelashes flickered quickly and she lifted her head with renewed confidence. "I was ready for anything for that first few minutes but I had the sense that I was fine, that I was safe."

"Really?" His voice was soft as he eased closer to her while looking into her eyes.

"Well, the fact that you appeared quite excited did tend to instill some confidence in me," She gently replied as he leaned in and kissed her. Moving closer, his hand on her thigh, the sound of his phone ringing abruptly stopped him. It was Chase. Glancing at a nearby clock, he realized that Maria was finishing school for the day. He quickly answered.

"Chase, is everything okay with Maria?" He asked without bothering with any of the usual formalities.

"Maria's fine," Chase immediately reassured him. "She loves her new school, talked about it all the way home but there is a slight problem."

"What is it?" Jorge asked and glanced at Paige, who silently watched him.

"The principal reported that she's apparently talking about her mother's death a lot with classmates," Chase attempted to be tactful but Jorge was already cringing. "Telling people how she was a drug addict, probably a little more detail than she should."

"*Any* detail is more than she should share," Jorge confirmed and shook his head. "How much is she telling classmates? Should I be concerned?"

"She said that she had watched her snorting cocaine," Chase broke the news calmly, as carefully as he possibly could have, all things considered. "And that she went away, overdosed and her grandparents hate her so she wasn't allowed to go to the funeral."

"Oh fuck!" Jorge shook his head and noted the alarmed look in Paige's eyes. "Is there more? Please tell me there is no more."

"Not that I am aware of," Chase replied. "Look, the principal thinks she's making it all up to get attention with the other kids, she doesn't even think it's true. She knows Maria's mother recently died but she assumes that the rest is the result of an overactive imagination. She's not in any kind of trouble but the teacher who overheard was concerned and took her aside to ask a few questions but even *she* thinks Maria just has a strong imagination."

"Fuck!" Jorge repeated. "Ok, I thank you, Chase. You are a good friend."

"No problem, please let me know if there is anything I can do."

"No, thank you, but Maria and I will be returning to Mexico tomorrow and hopefully, we can sort out everything so when she comes back, she will stop this nonsense."

"Good luck with that," Chase attempted to joke and although Jorge understood the humor in it, he was tense after ending the call.

Shaking his head, he looked at Paige.

"That child, she will be the death of me yet," He sighed loudly. "She's giving me gray hairs just like her mother did."

"That's because she's exactly like you," Paige teased. "I saw it right away."

"No," Jorge shook his head. "I would not tell the world my life's story like she did."

"I don't mean that," Paige corrected him. "I mean she's strong-willed, determined, she tries to hide her emotions but then they come flying out all at once. That is you too."

"You think that is me?" Humored by her analysis, Jorge briefly considered the comparison. "Yes, this is all true, but the more you get to know Maria, the more you will see it. She can be manipulative and that is like her mother. I fear I left them alone together too much and now, I must remove everything that Verónic taught her."

"I gather Maria is being too chatty at school?" Paige asked as a grin curved her lips. "And they think she's making things up?"

"God, I hope so!" Jorge groaned and closed his eyes.

"They do," Paige quietly confirmed. "When I originally met with the principal to learn about the school, she was asking about Maria's life and it occurred to me that perhaps it was best to keep her on a need-to-know basis. It also occurred to me that if she was asking *me* a lot of questions, she might do the same with Maria so I suggested that she had an active imagination."

Jorge was in awe. He never would've thought of such a thing! It was brilliant!

"I figured," Paige continued, "that way if she said a little too much, it would be written off as her imagination and not reality. They're used to the wealthy élite going to this school. Things like drugs and dramatic deaths are stuff that they watch on television so they assumed that it is pretty distant from their own lives, so it would be natural for them to believe her stories are the result of an overactive imagination."

"Even though we are Mexican?" Jorge challenged her with a smile.

"That would be racist," Paige reminded him with a smirk on her face. "The last thing a school wants is to be labeled that way. Not in a multicultural country where some of the richest parents are minorities."

Jorge let out a hearty laugh. "Yes, this is true."

"Also," Paige continued, "I pointed out that Maria had a habit of watching some very violent television on the sly, shows that sometimes depict Mexicans in a less than stellar light, so perhaps she would mix fantasy and reality."

"And the principal?"

"She was very understanding," Paige commented with a serious face before her smile returned and Jorge laughed again.

"Brilliant! *Mi amor*, brilliant!"

Although relieved that Paige had prepared for this potential fire, it still gave him little comfort that his daughter was so quick to share so many personal details about her life. It was as if she had no idea on what things were private and what things you could share with others. Then again, how would she learn with a cokehead mother?

Once again feeling guilty for his lack of parenting in the early days, Jorge felt a heaviness in his heart when he sat down to talk to his daughter that night. It was when she was ready for bed that he broached the subject. He had been careful not to bring it up when first arriving home, as Maria talked excitedly about her first day 'as a real Canadian student'. Relieved that she was finally happy to go to school, he focused on that and decided to discuss his concerns later.

"So, Maria, we must talk about something," Jorge commented as his daughter crawled under the covers of her bed that night. "Today at school, you were discussing your mother's death and I feel you probably shared too much information with the other children. It is not appropriate to share too many things from our personal life with others, especially when we don't know them very well."

"But they asked about my parents," Maria spoke innocently. "I said my *Papa* worked for a coffee company that my *abuelo* owns and travels a lot for work and when they asked about my mother, I said she died."

"That," Jorge started a little more sharply than he intended, causing him to stop. "That is where you should have ended your story. You should not have told anything else."

"But they asked how," Maria insisted and sat forward, her brown eyes growing in size. "I couldn't lie. You always say not to lie."

"You do not have to lie," Jorge confirmed. "But you also did not have to share that much information. People do not have to know she was involved in drugs, that is a personal, family matter, only to stay within the family or to be shared with *very* close friends."

"Oh," Maria appeared slightly defeated. "I just wanted them to like me and they seemed interested in my story."

"I do realize that but you must be careful," Jorge insisted. "We are trying to fit in this country and the best way is to be nice, to be polite but not overshare our personal information. That is not appropriate."

"I'm sorry," Maria spoke regretfully. "Do you think the other kids won't like me now?"

"No," Jorge replied but wasn't so sure. What if these kids went home and repeated these stories to their parents? Would they tell their kids to avoid the new, Mexican girl?

"Keep in mind," Jorge continued. "We are new here. We must try to fit in and stories about drugs and death, these are things people don't want to hear about, do you understand?"

Their conversation ended with a hug and a kiss before he turned off the light and closed the bedroom door.

He needed a drink.

Pouring himself a small glass of bourbon, he drank it quickly before sitting on the couch, alone with his thoughts.

In Mexico, he would have to deal with Maria's former school, not a task that he looked forward to in light of the fact that he had pulled her out without any notice. He also wanted to deal with Verónic's parents to see if there was some way Maria could pay respects to her mother but he already knew the answer. He also had to deal with his own parents, his father, who already was reluctant to hide Jorge's real activities with his 'job' as a salesperson for the Canadian division; luckily, it was an easy sell and someone else was doing the work. So many loose ends to tie up.

And yet, that was just Mexico, the Canadian side of his new life was even more stressful. Luckily he had Paige to deal with finding an apartment, looking into marriage procedures and he had already reached out to his contacts about pushing forward the immigration process. The ordeal normally took a great deal of time but there were ways around that, as there are ways around everything and Jorge never had qualms about pushing to the front of the line.

A text from Paige interrupted his thoughts.

Is everything ok?

Grinning, he thought of the many daunting tasks and all the stressful conversations he would have while in Mexico, not to mention the many things he had to sort out once returning. He thought of the life he was about to leave behind and what it meant to move ahead. He thought of the endless checklist of things that required his attention, a list that had no end in sight.

His fingers brushed over the phone.

Everything is perfecto.

CHAPTER 22

The next few days were like a whirlwind in Jorge's life; assuming, of course, that whirlwinds took place in hell. There was definitely something to be said about the belief 'you can never go home again' and somehow, Jorge had managed to slip into that zone somewhere between Verónic's death and enrolling Maria into a new school. This bothered some people in Mexico more than others.

Despite the fact that Verónic's family had no relationship with Maria, they seemed the most opposed to her attending school in another country. In fact, when he contacted them to see if they could have a ceremony for Maria's mother to give his daughter a sense of closure, they seemed more concerned with the fact that he was taking their grandchild out of the country.

"*Ella pertenece a Mexico!*"

"No," Jorge was quick to disagree and stood his ground. "She belongs wherever she can get the best education."

The reality was that he didn't know for a fact that Canada had a better educational system but felt it was a more suitable argument than the truth; that Maria was bullied by her classmates, took a switchblade to school and got kicked out or that it suited his own, personal life since he was about to marry a Canadian woman. It wasn't necessary to dip into that information. Verónic's parents were on a need to know basis. The worst part was that she was dead and yet, he was still dealing with these *pendejos*.

The argument went back and forth, however, when it became clear that Jorge's original request was ignored, he ended the conversation. It was a waste of his time and time wasn't something he had a lot of while in Mexico.

His own family seemed less concerned with Maria going to school in Canada. His father apathetic, very old school in his twisted beliefs that male children were of more significance, his ignorance on the matter was an embarrassment to Jorge. Fortunately, his daughter didn't seem to pick up on this mentality because she loved her grandfather despite his lukewarm reception to her. Jorge's mother was more affectionate and yet, she seemed to show little concern that the two of them were about to leave the country. His father, in fact, didn't even hide his relief.

"I am selling the business," His father immediately announced, almost as if he hadn't heard anything Jorge said about his move, his daughter's education or his plans to marry in Canada. "This would be a perfect time. I have looked over my shoulder for years in fear that your dirty business would catch up with both of us, that the government would start asking too many questions, now I can rest and enjoy my last days."

His father! Always expecting to drop dead at any minute, a natural reaction after losing Jorge's brother when he was a child, he talked about death as if it were merely waiting around the corner and wouldn't allow him to ever enjoy his time on earth. He spent most of his life in misery, looking for trouble where it didn't exist and yet, he would probably outlive them all.

Choosing to ignore this remark, knowing that it was an argument that he couldn't win, Jorge took a deep breath and thought about the pack of cigarettes in his SUV. Glancing toward the garden, he spotted his mother with Maria, a fake smile on her face as his daughter spoke enthusiastically about her new school and her 'one Canadian friend' as if the older woman was truly interested. Her favorite son had died and took her heart with him because her love for either Jorge or grandchild was never anywhere close to what it had been with Miguel, the one she declared was closest to God, just as he had been on earth.

Taking a deep breath, Jorge contemplated how to respond and simply shrugged. The old man's eyes stared through him with the same cold, cruelty that had always been there except now, they looked slightly weaker. His face wrinkled, his skin darker than Jorge's, while his stature less prominent, his shoulders leaned forward after spending so many years crouched over a desk, staring at numbers, as if nothing else mattered. Both his parent's lives had ended with Miguel's and in many ways, Jorge was nothing more than an afterthought. It was a bitter pill to swallow but being angry about it hadn't served him well either so all he could do was let it go.

"Ok then," Jorge stood up from his chair and let the words flow past him, the hurt intended rolled away as he glanced back toward Maria in the garden, who suddenly looked up. The two made eye contact and Jorge nodded. The little girl leaned in and gave her grandmother a quick hug before rushing back into the house. It wasn't until they were in the SUV that she spoke again.

"Why is it that she does not seem interested in my life?"

Her question was innocent enough but still pulled at his heart. Managing to bite back his anger, Jorge continued to focus on the road ahead and stiffly shrugged.

"She's old, Maria," He commented and paused for a moment. "She's not well, don't mind her. It does not matter what she thinks anyway, does it?"

"No, I guess not," Maria reluctantly agreed. "It's just weird."

"This is true," Jorge agreed but bit his tongue, holding in his emotions until talking on the phone with Paige later that night.

"They are cold people," Jorge complained, pausing only to inhale his cigarette. "After my brother died, their emotions turned off forever."

"Really?"

"Yes, Miguel was their favorite child and the fact that I survived and he did not, was very bittersweet."

"I'm sure that's not the case," Paige insisted on the other end of the line while Jorge leaned back and closed his eyes. "You probably just thought that at the time."

"No, I could feel it," Jorge insisted, his eyes opening again. "A kid knows these things, they are very intuitive."

"I'm sure it was just because they appeared so upset about losing your brother," Paige continued to insist. "Were you wearing helmets?"

Jorge let out a bitter laugh when he thought back to the day when he and Miguel found their cousin's dirt bike and decided to go for a ride. He had been plucky back then, much in the same way that Maria was now, Jorge assumed that the few lessons their cousin gave him was enough to prepare him to drive solo. Of course, his 10-year-old brother was reluctant, but Jorge had insisted he jump on the bike too.

"It was the 80s baby, no one wore helmets," He stared at his cigarette and thought back to the horrific day. Everything happened so fast, how quickly he had lost control of the bike, much in the same way that he had lost control of his own life so many times as an adult. It wasn't until he had a spiritual awakening years later that he realized his former drug use was intimately connected to that horrible moment in his childhood that clung to his heart ever since. Not that it ever fully went away but there came a point when he forgave himself, although it was clear no one else in his family had.

"I'm sorry, this can't be easy to talk about," She calmly remarked and paused for a moment. "We're impulsive as kids, we do things and don't see the danger."

"I don't think much has changed since those days," He let out a laugh and finished his cigarette. "I'm still impulsive and don't think of the danger; although, admittedly, I have improved."

"If you say so," She teased.

"I do," He laughed, welcoming a break from the tension. It had not been a good day. "Now tomorrow, I have more fun activities which include talking to the school. Apparently, they have some 'concerns' about Maria switching to another school. Most likely because it means they will no longer get my money. In fact, I would like to be reimbursed for this year since she was has learned nothing and wasn't protected from these bullies. Everything with that school is an uphill battle."

"You'll be back in Canada soon."

"It's too bad you couldn't have come here with me," Jorge commented as he opened his cigarette pack again then, deciding against it, "I could've shown you Mexico."

"I've been to Mexico."

"Nah, not the tourist traps, I mean *my* Mexico," His comment was seductive. "It is a whole other world."

"I actually was never there as a tourist, at least, not officially," She replied. "I was working."

"Ahh...yes! Of course."

"So I didn't have an opportunity to see much."

"You will, *bonita dama*, you will." Jorge thought for a moment. "I was going to sell the house but I may keep it. I'm conflicted. So many terrible memories and yet, my daughter grew up here."

"Maybe you should see how Maria feels about it," Paige suggested. "I think it would be good to let her weigh in."

"Yes, you are right. It is too soon to sell," Jorge glanced around his house. "But, you know me, I want a fresh start."

"Well, I found an apartment and you might be able to move in soon," Paige commented. "It's not perfect but since it is temporary, I think it will be fine."

"Oh, this is good," Jorge perked up with the news. "What about your place?"

"That's the problem, I had to give a month's notice so I figured it might be good so I can make a slow transition to move in with you and Maria," Paige considered but sounded unconcerned. "Needless to say, I have to start packing."

"*You* have to start packing," Jorge shook his head. "Thankfully, we left Canada with almost empty suitcases because they will be full again going back. The rest, I will leave here for now. I would ship my belongings but who knows if they would ever make it there. Try telling that to a child with so many clothes and possessions, it is not easy."

Paige laughed. "It might be easier to buy new here."

"Maria's in her room now, going through her clothing," Jorge glanced at the ceiling. Even from the kitchen, he could hear his daughter dancing around on the floor, her pop music on, as she sorted her possessions. "I told her, some we will keep, some we will donate to poor children, so she is on a mission."

"Good idea."

"She has so much stuff," Jorge yawned and made his way outside. "So my father is selling the business, this is good. Everyone will have a new beginning now."

"In Canada, you're an investor," Paige commented. "Your family business is being sold and now you're weighing your options."

"That's exactly what I will say," Jorge agreed. "My story, it will check out."

The next day started off smoother than the first. Jorge was pleasantly surprised when his daughter was happy to part with three large bags of clothes and old toys from her childhood. She carefully considered all her clothing and decided on the items she would bring and the rest, she would leave for now. Jorge discussed the possibility of selling the house and to this, she seemed unsure.

"*Papa*, not yet," She wiggled uncomfortably in her seat. "Paige needs to see the house first."

"Of course!" He agreed, relieved that his daughter actually liked his fiancée. He hadn't expected that but as usual, Maria was full of surprises.

The visit to the school also went well, with little hassle, the principal seemed content that Maria was moving on to a more 'suitable' environment and it was a toss-up which one of them was more excited to walk out of that building for the last time; him or Maria. Carrying her belongings to the SUV, which included the switchblade that she brought to school on that last day, she suddenly stopped in her tracks and defiantly looked back toward the school.

"What is it?" Jorge halted in his steps and glanced toward the school. Three little girls were looking out at Maria, they appeared to be giggling. His heart sank as he turned to his daughter to offer her comfort, only to discover that Maria was giving them the middle finger.

"Oh Maria! You cannot do that," Jorge quickly rushed her into the vehicle.

"Like hell, I can't!" Marie spoke defiantly, attempting to turn back around.

"No no no!" Jorge insisted and fought off this impulse to laugh as they got in the SUV. "That is very rude."

"They were rude to me!"

"Two wrongs, don't make a right."

"Neither does saying I was permanently kicked out of school."

"You know," Jorge attempted to rack his brain to figure out how to deal with this situation. "You cannot do this in Canada if you get angry with any of the other children."

"I won't," Maria assured him. "Mexican girls are way meaner than Canadian girls."

"Maria, you know that isn't true," Jorge insisted.

"It is true!" Maria insisted. "These kids were mean, mama, she was not nice, my *abeulas*, they are uncaring."

Feeling unable to prove his point, Jorge racked his brain as he started the SUV.

"Juliana, you don't think she is mean, do you?"

"No, but she can't come to Canada with us."

"She can, but only temporarily."

"She does not want to stay. Her boyfriend is here."

"Yes, that is true."

"Is she returning to Canada with us this time?"

"No, not this time."

"Is Jesús?"

"I'm not sure," Jorge admitted. He had a meeting with him that night.

"Papa," Maria turned toward him, her eyes large and innocent. "I will not miss living in Mexico."

As much as he understood where the child was coming from since so many terrible events had taken place in this country, it also broke his heart.

CHAPTER 23

"I will kill them both with my bare hands before I let them take Maria!" Jorge fumed during what was supposed to be his last night in Mexico. Locked away in the hidden room of his house, he sat across from Jesús as the two of them smoked cigars and contemplated the most recent issue to crop up. Jorge was always ready to deal with complications and he certainly was no pussy but his patience for people who got in his way was growing weak. Tolerance had a breaking point and he had just about met it.

"Wait, so Verónic's parents, they want to take Maria?" Jesús spoke slowly, his eyes squinting with each word. "I do not understand. Where is this coming from?"

"It's coming from the fact that their daughter is dead and they want to blame someone, so they choose me," Jorge spoke bluntly as he tapped his cigar in the ashtray before taking another puff and momentarily closing his eyes. Although he sat casually in his chair, his heart was pounding erratically, as blood shot through his veins with the same intensity as someone who thought they were about to die. Except, of course, it wasn't *him* that was to die.

"But you are the father, they can't take her away," Jesús said with a shrug, he continued to make a face. "That does not make sense."

"They claim they know things about me," Jorge replied calmly while puckering his lips together momentarily as he glanced at his hand. "They claim that it is time for everyone to admit what Mexicans all know and it is that I'm in the cartel and that their precious, *princesa* never took a drug in her life until she met me."

"Ouff!" Jesús didn't attempt to hide his shock with this comment as he shook his bald head. "You tell me, that they think Verónic never did drugs before the night she met you? She was high *on* the night she met you, was she not? I think I know the party."

At first, Jorge didn't say anything, simply nodded while his eyes glared at his phone, the same one he had the infuriating conversation with Verónic's parents earlier that day. The temptation to pick it up and throw it against the wall was strong but it was senseless; it would simply require him to purchase a new phone. Of course, the temptation to go to their house and throw them both against the wall was even stronger at the moment.

"It is what it is," Jorge finally commented. "They believe what they choose to believe and that is fine," He stopped speaking for a moment, taking another puff of his cigar, his eyes darted toward Jesús and a slight grin appeared on his lips. "After all, they are old, how many days do you think they have left on this earth? Let them live in a fantasy world for that short, *short* time."

Jesús nodded and shared a similar expression and let out a short laugh.

"There's been a lot of house fires in recent weeks," His comment was quick, his eyes suddenly wide open as he looked at his boss. "The weather, it is so dry and homes have been known to spread quickly."

"I was thinking a murder-suicide," Jorge replied casually, suddenly feeling better as his expression formed into mock compassion. "You know, they just lost their daughter and did not take it well. They couldn't even have a funeral, they were so overcome with despair." His eyes full of innocence that was not lost on Jesús as he started to choke on his cigar and quickly reached for his bottle of beer that had, until that point, been untouched.

"But I do not wish either of us to do this one," His comment was thoughtful as he peered again at his phone. "I have someone else in mind. You will be here attending a small going away party for Maria. I think that would be nice for her. I feel that she's had so many sad experiences in the last few weeks that perhaps this is exactly what she needs. I will extend my stay in hopes of cheering her up. It would be nice, no?"

"That would be nice," Jesús agreed. "If you are sure, boss?"

"I think I got it taken care of," He reached for his phone. "I got the perfect person."

Paige answered the phone after the first ring.

"How soon can you come to Mexico, *bonita*?" His question was gentle, smooth as if her visit were an answer to his lonely heart and not on official business. "We are having a party for Maria, a going away celebration and I wish for you to be here."

There was a pause. "I thought you were coming back tomorrow?"

"Yes, well things, they change and there's been some difficulty here so I thought a nice party might cheer up my niñita and perhaps, we could finally have some...resolution? Is that the word?" He spoke awkwardly as if his English were lacking. "Oh excuse, I mean it may help her with the grieving process for her mother. This is a very difficult time for her. The grandparents, they do not allow her to have a final goodbye and I worry. They just don't seem to *understand* that sometimes, you must let things go."

"I will schedule a flight right away and text you the details," Paige calmly replied before a brief pause and the sound of keys tapping could be heard. "People aren't always rational when they are grieving. Just be patient. Is there anything I can bring?"

"Just yourself, baby, I got everything you need here," He spoke seductively before hanging up and turning toward Jesús who continued to smoke his cigar. "It will be taken care of soon."

"So the party?"

"Tomorrow night," Jorge thought out loud. "Nothing fancy, just food, drink, that kind of thing. Very small get together. You, of course, will be here. I will invite the grandparents but having never stepped foot in my home, I am doubtful that this invitation will be accepted. My parents might but I don't really care. The point is that we are having a party for my daughter."

Maria learned of the news the following morning when he snuck in her room early to tell her that she could sleep in, their trip was postponed for a few days.

"We are having a small get together tonight," He whispered. "I will invite your grandparents, Jesús will be here and, Paige is also coming to see us."

"Really?" Her eyes lit up. "Can she bring Chase?"

"Baby, it is too short of notice to have Chase come here," He commented with some regret. "I spoke with Paige late last night when I decided and she made arrangements right away. In fact, she is already on her way."

"That's cool too," Maria yawned.

"You, go back to sleep," Jorge commented and gave her a quick kiss on the forehead before leaving his sleepy daughter. Checking his phone in the hallway, he was unsure if he should tell Maria of their death when it happened or wait. Although she acted tough, he knew the loss of her mother was still weighing heavily on her. He could see it in her face and that was the one and only reason he regretted Verónic's death. He would see that she talk to someone about it when they returned to Canada. Although, he was wary of psychiatrists, what if his daughter said too much, as she often did?

A problem for later, he returned to his morning routine, calmly checking emails while drinking coffee. He had to postpone a meeting with Diego, Jolene and Chase for the following day, which he was sure would be met with relief. His demands for the business had increased recently and were about to get higher now that he was leaving Mexico and had to justify his income and sudden move to the Canadian government. His connections could only do so much but it was up to him to appear legit. They should do as much too with all the money he was about to bring to the country especially if he got involved in the pot industry. With the resources to expand the business, he was looking at British Columbia; there would be a lot of money added to the economy.

Jorge had a brief meeting with his boss in the midst of the insanity and explained his plan to move to Canada. Much to his surprise, this was not met with any discouragement but was instead seen as a bigger opportunity, especially if they were to get involved in the very lucrative marijuana industry in Canada. Although he would continue to be involved in cocaine and other drugs, it was agreed that his focus should be on pot. As laws continued to loosen when it came to marijuana, it was just a matter of time before it would be commonplace for people to have it in their home, much in the same as they would with liquor, so this was the time to get on the ground level so they would be able to profit off it.

Jorge was smart, savvy, he knew how to present this in such a way that made him an asset to keep around-and alive-without having the ties to the cartel that were as strong and dangerous. At the end of the day, perhaps his boss would realize that this change was necessary for the future. Hernandez had many connections within the Canadian government and this would allow him to take over the pot industry before the others had the opportunity. On the outside, they would, of course, do things legitimately but behind the scenes, there were ways to get around the rules when necessary. It just took a creative thinker and Jorge was exceptionally talented when it came to working around problems.

Of course, his first problem was Verónic's parents and that had to be taken care of immediately. Although they perhaps had no proof of his crimes, it was a certainty that his ex would've shown no vocal restraint especially when high. Of course, to the average person, she was a junkie spewing nonsense but to her parents, who never trusted him, it would be suspicious. He refused to allow the possibility of this train leaving the station, it was necessary to take care of them before they caused problems. Nothing and no one would take Maria from him unless it was death itself. Verónic's parents were about to reunite with their daughter in hell, where they all belonged.

The day was a busy one as Juliana and he planned a party for that evening, a small get together with some delicious food, a few adult beverages and of course, a few friends. Juliana would bring her boyfriend, Maria invited a couple of school friends-*boys*, which Jorge wasn't very happy with and of course, Jesús would be there too. The grandparents were all invited. Verónic's parents declined.

"I do not understand," Jorge innocently commented. "You want custody of your granddaughter but yet, you don't take every opportunity to see her?"

"I will see her plenty when we get custody," The old man grumbled in the phone. "No judge would let someone as dangerous as you keep a child."

Knowing the man's fate, Jorge merely laughed as if they were all involved in a joke.

"Ah, you always did make me laugh," He commented with not a hint of stress in his voice. "However you know that this will never happen."

"I'm meeting with a lawyer tomorrow," The old man insisted. "That is when your smugness will disappear."

"We will see," Jorge replied and laughed. "I believe the joke will be on you when you talk to that lawyer."

Maria suddenly walked in the room.

"Yes, and you have a good evening as well," Jorge quickly commented, cutting off the old man before he could reply, he hung up the phone.

"They aren't coming, are they?" Maria asked as a gentle flame burned in her eyes and Jorge recognized it as being the same one he had after Miguel died years earlier. He regretted to see it there, as she was only a child of 10 and yet, he couldn't deny his daughter's maturity because to do so, would be ignorant.

"No, *cariño* and for that, I am sorry," He paused and thought for a moment. "And I will admit to you, that this is because of me, not you. Your grandparents do love you very much but me, they do not like. They never have."

"I don't understand why not," She approached him and gave him an impromptu hug. "Why do they not like you, Papa?"

"It's natural," He attempted to explain. "Parents are often suspicious of the man who takes their little girl away as I will, one day, be suspicious of any man in your life. It's just being overprotective."

"Do they blame you for *her* death," Maria's question was sharp, causing his eyes to widen as he processed the bitterness in his daughter's voice and for a moment, wasn't sure of how to reply.

"I do not know," Jorge commented but upon looking in his daughter's eyes, his defenses fell. "Yes, they do. I am sorry you have to learn this but I cannot lie."

"It's ok, I kind of figured that since mama, she blamed you for so much," Maria spoke tenderly and leaned against her father. "*Madre*, she was weak?"

"Yes," Jorge spoke regretfully. "I am afraid your mother, she was weak. The drugs, they are never a solution to a problem and unfortunately, she felt they were."

"Papa, did you ever take drugs?" She asked innocently and although his first instinct was to lie, he knew it would be a mistake.

"Yes, Maria, regretfully, I have taken drugs," Jorge admitted, putting his arm around her, he gave her a squeeze. "But no more, that was a long time ago. I was stupid back then and now, I know it is very bad to do. You must never do drugs either."

"I won't," She shook her head. "They make you do things you regret."

"They do."

"I don't want to be like mama."

"You will never be like her," Jorge assured her. "You are stronger now, at 10 years than she ever was."

It was true and he wasn't certain that this was a good thing but overall, it did give him some comfort. His daughter, she was very much a Hernandez and that filled him with pride.

By the end of the night, Verónic's parents would no longer be a part of her life. Not that they ever really were in the first place. Paige was on her way and he had no doubt that she could take care of this situation like no one else. Although he had regrets about getting her involved, he also knew that she was the perfect person for the job. He was too close to it, his emotions too strong to take care of this kind of situation in a rational way, his fantasy was to butcher than both and make their last breath as painful and miserable as possible. Paige would do it quickly, easily and it would look like a murder/suicide. This was her specialty and although a part of him felt shame for asking his fiancée for help, another side of him was highly attracted to this side of her personality.

The danger, the darkness in her eyes when she spoke of death, it was provocative how she was so strong and gentle at the same time, much like a dominatrix who degraded you then slowly licked honey off your balls. Perhaps it was perverse but he wasn't one to question what gave him pleasure.

Fortunately, neither did Paige.

When Jorge Hernandez returned to Canada in a few days, he would own the world. He'd be unstoppable. He would send a message to those in Mexico who ever questioned his power. No one ever threatened to take anything from Jorge Hernandez and lived to talk about it.

CHAPTER 24

Paige took care of it. Perhaps this is pointing out the obvious but it happened during the celebration that Jorge had for Maria, the same one that Verónic's parents chose to snub, that they died in their bed. An illegal gun would later be found on the scene and with everything pointing to a murder/suicide, few questions would be asked. Few, but some were to follow protocol. This occurred a couple of days after the bodies were discovered.

"And you were at home that night?" The first of the two officers asked Jorge; he hadn't paid attention to their names because it was irrelevant but it was the skinny kid who looked as though he just graduated from high school, that was speaking. "This can be verified?"

"Yes," Jorge spoke confidently, attempting to throw a touch of sadness into his voice to keep himself from bursting into laughter. "We, in fact, had a small party here for my daughter, Maria," He made a point of turning her framed photo around on his desk to show them. "Oh poor Maria, to lose her mother and now her grandparents so tragically."

The older, fatter *policía* took over at this point, ignoring Jorge's comment. "You had guests here that can verify you were here?"

"Yes."

He nodded and jotted something down in his notebook. Jorge felt like reaching across the desk and ripping the fucking notebook out of his hand and reminding him that it was a *murder/suicide* and that you don't harass family members during this mourning period; but alas, sometimes you had to play nice even though it's not in your nature. Rubbing a hand over his face, he noted that the skinny kid was watching him and so he quickly placed his hands back on the desk. The officer was perhaps reading body language as taught during his hours of useless training in classes. Jorge sent a warning glance in his direction and the young man quickly looked away.

"And you say they were invited to this party?" The fat one glanced up from his notebook. "And did not show?"

"Yes, I invited them and thought they would like to see their granddaughter before we both go to Canada but unfortunately, they showed no interest," Jorge commented with a trickle of innocence in his voice. "I was confused but thought perhaps because they are still mourning their daughter, maybe it wasn't a good time for a party and perhaps it was in bad taste but it was for my daughter. So much grief, so many changes lately, I felt that it would be nice to have a small get together with her friends and some family to celebrate life, to say goodbye before she returns to her Canadian school."

"Canada?" The fat officer nodded and jotted something down. "Lucky girl! I wish I had been able to go to school in Canada."

"Have you ever been there?"

"No," The fat one replied.

"Ahhh! Well, you must go!" Jorge spoke with enthusiasm. "Such a beautiful country, beautiful women, welcoming people, so many opportunities."

The young one perked up.

"I don't think we have anything else to ask," The fat one commented and closed his notebook. "It was clearly a murder/suicide but we still have to investigate."

"Of course you do," Jorge spoke solemnly. "Their grief was strong, there's nothing worst than the death of a child. I lost my younger brother, Miguel as a child and I saw what that did to my parents. I would never wish that kind of misery on anyone."

The younger one looked skeptical, if only for a moment, before smiling and nodding while the fat one stood up and the kid quickly followed his lead.

"It is very tragic but we sometimes don't think clearly when we are mourning," The fat one replied.

"This is true! I do appreciate you looking into this though. To show my gratitude, I would like to offer you both a quick drink or a cigar before you leave," Jorge reached into the box of cigars placed on what he called his 'public desk' as opposed to the one in the hidden room. As if he would ever show the *policia* that one!

The fat one looked intrigued and glanced at the young one, who appeared nervous.

"We are due for a break soon," The fat one commented and the younger one quickly nodded in agreement.

"Yes, this is true," The kid replied and looked at the fat one as if wanting permission.

"It is good," The fat one assured him. "We must make the public feel that we are approachable, no?"

Jorge faked a smile and nodded as he stood up.

"Please! You serve us, the public and keep us safe," He said the words like any fine actor while on the inside, he was laughing at their stupidity. Almost gleeful that Paige had done such an extraordinary job covering her tracks and yet, she still managed to make the party. "And everybody," Jorge pointed at each of them as they took turns reaching for a cigar. "We all need a break sometimes, am I right?"

Both nodded enthusiastically before following him outside to the pool where Maria was swimming. Perhaps this wasn't a good idea. What if she were to say something incriminating? Of course, she knew nothing but one never knew with his daughter. However, she simply continued to swim, peering toward the two uniformed men on occasion but for the most part, unconcerned with her father's company. She had been quiet since learning of her grandparent's death but almost seemed more depressed when Paige had to return to Canada early.

"Such a beautiful day," Jorge commented as he lit the two officer's cigars then his own. "Please have a seat, I will get us a drink. A beer? Tequila? What would you like?"

"A beer," The fat one nodded and the younger one did the same.

The kid inside of Jorge momentarily giggled when he walked to the fridge to retrieve the three Coronas, opening each, he would've loved to poison their beer but it was always nice to stay friendly to the imbeciles that called themselves *policia.*

"Here you go, gentlemen," He passed them each a bottle, noting that they were pretty relaxed in their chairs, both enjoying their cigars while commenting on the beautiful home in which Jorge lived.

"This place is spectacular," The fat one commented. "You obviously don't work for the police to get something so nice." He glanced at the younger one and they both laughed. "Our money definitely isn't this good."

"Well, I have a lot of investments along with working for my father's company," Jorge commented. "Here in Mexico, as well as other countries, including Canada."

Although Jorge's home was quite impressive, it wasn't as elaborate as he could actually afford. He preferred to keep low-key when it came to guests such as these two police officers.

The visit was, fortunately, a short one, the three laughed and joked, the conversation remained light, neither seemed too concerned that they were being unprofessional but the key was to make them feel more like friends than an authority figure. It was important to always keep everyone in their place, this is what Jorge Hernandez believed.

Maria didn't get out of the pool until after the police left. Sauntering into the kitchen with a curious look on her face, she poured water from a nearby cooler and drank it fast then suddenly stopped.

"What were *they* doing here?"

Shit.

"They were here to ask a few questions," Jorge spoke honestly and finished his beer while he thought about the best way to handle this situation. Setting the empty bottle on the nearby table, he noticed his daughter giving him a look. How many times had he told her to put her empty dishes and soda cans with the recyclable? Knowing her stern eyes were watching, he retrieved it and walked toward the specific garbage can. She followed.

"About?"

"Your grandparents."

"Oh," Maria commented with a hint of sadness in her voice. "It is so sad. *Papa,* if I die before you, please do not do what they did."

"Maria!" Jorge felt a surge of anger fill him at the very suggestion of her death. "Do *not* speak that way!"

"But Papa, it could happen!" She was equally defiant. "Kids die all the time."

"We do not talk about such things," Jorge felt his heart race at the thought. "This will never happen to you, not while you are a little girl. Now please, please don't talk about it."

"It could," She was insistent, her eyes widened. "Chase, he had a son die. He was *distraught* when it happened. So, I do understand but I keep playing it in my head and…"

"Maria, do not do that," Jorge was shocked by these comments. When did his daughter become so morbid? Was it from spending too much time with her mother that caused Maria to be this way? It alarmed him that they were even having this conversation.

"What happened, it was very sad but you must *not* overthink it. It is not healthy to do so. People react when they are grieving and sometimes, they are not rational. Perhaps this is one of those times."

"Were they on antidepressants, I have watched a video that said they can have the opposite effect sometimes," Maria spoke honestly, leaving Jorge stunned and unsure of what to say; it was as if his tongue was frozen and he just shook his head.

"It's fine, Papa, I guess you wouldn't know," Maria continued. "I promise not to overthink it if you promise that if anything were to happen to me, you wouldn't do something like that too."

"Maria, I would not…" He couldn't even finish the sentence. Perhaps this was karma for him being behind their murders but he resented his consciousness for presenting him with the possibility. "Maria, you are not going to die and if you did, heaven help me because a part of me would die with you but I promise, I would not do anything to hurt myself."

It was possibly a lie. He wasn't sure what he would do if anything were to happen to either her or Paige. He did know, however, what would happen if anyone was at fault. He would mutilate them in the most torturous way possible, making them suffer for the last minutes of their pathetic life.

Taking a deep breath, he placed his hand on her shoulder and looked into her eyes. "Maria, I am sorry about your grandparents but we must not talk about death anymore. There has been too much lately and we must instead focus on the future and our lives. OK?"

"Yes," Maria nodded and reached up to give him a tight hug, followed by two sloppy kisses before letting go and running upstairs.

His heart raced for the entire conversation. Originally, his worst fear was that she would ask questions about the police being there and having a very casual visit with him or be depressed over the death of her grandparents. It hadn't occurred to him that she would, instead, focus on her own potential death. It wasn't something he had considered when preparing for the death of either her mother or grandparents. It never occurred to him that a child thought in such a way. Then again, most children her age probably didn't.

Reaching for the pack of cigarettes, he ignored the Post-it note from Maria stuck to it, reminding him to chew gum instead. Fuck, he hated gum. It was disgusting. He needed a cigarette. Taking one from the pack, he returned to his seat beside the pool, pulling his phone from his pocket.

He dialed Paige.

"Hello," She answered in her usual, soft voice that always made him relax, if not a little horny at times but at that moment, he was too distraught to consider the latter.

"I think I might lose my mind with this daughter of mine," Jorge commented and glanced over his shoulder to make sure she hadn't returned and took a deep breath. Inhaling his cigarette, he felt instant relief and closed his eyes, as the sun touched his face.

"Oh no," Paige spoke gently and let out a laugh. "What did she do now?"

"Give her *Papa* another small heart attack," He grinned and felt warmth fill him. "Like I needed another one."

"Tell me a story," Paige commented.

"I will tell you a story," Jorge relaxed in his chair and enjoyed the moment for everything it was and everything it wasn't.

Chapter 25

As much as Jorge saw his child as being rambunctious, he was actually quite lucky. There were many little girls who let the world rule them and not the other way around. These were the children who grew up staring in the mirror, looking for faults in their appearance, their eyes always searching, begging for someone to compliment them to feel that they were somehow, in the smallest way, an acceptable person in the world. It was that kind of little girl that he had to worry about not someone like Maria Hernandez.

The child was full of spunk and as much as Jorge didn't see it, she was very much his daughter. She looked like him. She talked as he did. She carried his mannerisms in her every movement, even the condescending look she gave when someone made a remark that was ridiculous. When he called Paige with claims of being shocked by her latest remark or action, it was quite often not so different from something that he would do or say himself and at the end of the day, wasn't that what *really* shocked him? Perhaps seeing himself in a different mirror was as much a rude awakening than the fact that his daughter was growing up.

Once upon a time, Paige Noël was that little girl. She had never been one that fit in with the other children, her mind always racing ahead to adulthood with only a mild interest in playing with dolls and no interest in dreaming of Prince Charming. She had watched her mother and older sisters fall into this pattern of pleasing others and didn't much like how it ended. Even to that day, her mother was probably still waiting on Paige's father, her sisters chasing after children, catering to their husbands, having no or little time for themselves. Their worlds revolved around everyone else and somewhere along the way, they had lost themselves. That's usually when bitterness sprung and well, nothing ever went well from that point on.

Paige had briefly feared that she was becoming that same woman when first meeting Jorge. After all, she had helped find Maria's school, assassinated Verónic's parents and was always there for him when he needed her. Perhaps she was becoming a slightly altered version of her mother and sisters? She finally decided that this wasn't the case at all. He would do anything for her but the problem was that first, she would have to admit needing help, something that she rarely did. It had never been an option in the past.

Assassins seemed like everyday people, living among society but unlike most people, they had a huge secret life that they could never reveal. They carried on as if they were like everyone else but deep down, they knew they were nothing like anyone else. They carried a tremendous secret that grew heavier and heavier over the years until eventually, it would explode. Some made errors, perhaps in hopes of getting caught so they could finally confess the many people they had slaughtered during their career. Others had heart attacks because the stress of carrying such a tremendous secret was often something that most couldn't handle for long. Then, of course, there were those people who simply snapped and committed suicide. It wasn't a profession for the faint of heart.

Of course, Paige Noël was the rare exception. Her health, both physically and mentally, was tremendous. In fact, if her last check up was any indication, she was in better shape than most 20-year-olds. The secret was that she meditated every morning and although she killed people for a living, she did so with great consideration. Regardless of the amount of money offered, she only chose the jobs she felt were justified. Pedophiles were at the top of her list of people she enjoyed killing. Like Jorge, she hated anyone who hurt a child and thought nothing of bringing them to the only justice they would ever truly receive; cause let's face it, the legal system wasn't equipped to protect the vulnerable and any claims of otherwise were usually nothing more than lip service, giving people an unrealistic sense of safety.

One such pedophile was the Hernandez that she had agreed to kill on the night she met Jorge. It was a pretty unsavory way to meet your future husband but then again, what was the normal way? Online dating? An app for criminals wanting to hook up? Most men met Paige Noël, the fictional character that was a life coach and wanted to make people, specifically other women, have the best life possible. It didn't take long for the intelligent ones to sense that she was actually a very different person than her online reputation. It was impossible for a relationship built on lies to last.

Fortunately, she had never lied to Jorge about anything. There were a few secrets lingering in the dark corners but nothing too serious and she assumed that eventually, they would come out too. One step at a time. It had been years since she revealed so much truth about herself to anyone else it was the freedom of doing so that was a bit overwhelming at first. It was almost like escaping a prison of the mind and being plunked in the middle of the largest city in the world. The freedom was exciting and intimidating at the same time. Where do you start? What do you do first and is it ok to proceed? These were the questions she had asked herself from day one.

She had learned long ago that when life presented you with a situation, you abide it and see where it leads. That is exactly what she did that first night. Logically, she shouldn't have stayed. He could've killed her and felt justified in doing so; had she been a man, he probably would've. Hadn't a part of her feared he would? Watching his every move carefully, waiting for him to pull out a gun, break a glass and slit her throat, perhaps stabbing her with a knife hidden in a drawer beside his bed.

It was his eyes that told her something very different. It was the way he looked at her that sent waves of tranquility through her body, unlike anything she had experienced before, unlike anything she thought was even possible. She felt unbelievably safe, something that up until it happened, Paige would've deemed impossible, just some fluff you found in a cheap, romance novel or a terrible Saturday afternoon movie on television. It was the most intense feeling she had ever felt and yet, to put it into words was impossible. There were no words.

There was nothing like having your world open up beyond the limits you previously assumed existed. Most often these limits were only created in our minds and we chose to believe them, however, logically, telling someone you killed for a living was hardly something you could confess most of the time. That was, of course, unless the person you confess to had also murdered.

Jorge Hernandez, as it turns out, had a reputation that preceded him. Her boss had briefly informed her of this on the night that she had a gun to his head, letting her know that he was a ruthless criminal and to proceed with extreme caution. He had killed people; men, women, he didn't care. If you were left with a threat and unharmed or alive, it was a rarity and those people, they didn't talk. No police would ever be involved. If there were, it wouldn't matter because he would get away with it. Everyone knew about him and yet, he was untouchable.

This didn't surprise Paige because being untouchable was the name of the game and went both ways. There were some leaders in business and politics that always had a huge price tag on their head; if anyone could get to them, they would be set for life. The best assassins could do so without getting caught or in a really underhanded move, find someone with known mental issues to take the blame. That had happened before although, she hadn't personally done it. No one had ever been accused of her crimes. The investigations usually ended quickly. It was clean.

Quite surprisingly, Jorge didn't have a price tag on his head. No one, that she could find, wanted him dead. Most seemed to feel that if they were to ever do so that the world would collapse on them with an almighty thud. He almost had celebrity status in the underground world; the George Clooney of ruthless criminals. It made her wonder who his boss was; that was a bit of mystery but it wasn't one she felt inclined to investigate. Perhaps because she wouldn't want him to investigate hers either. That was one of the secrets she couldn't tell him yet.

Not that you really had a 'boss' when you were an assassin but it was more like an agent. Someone who approached you about jobs and you decided whether to take them. There was no pressure but simply an offer. In essence, Paige was a freelance assassin.

She was growing tired of it though. The thrill was gone. It was too easy. This was the point when most assassins would've either gone crazy or attempted to find bigger targets but for Paige, it wasn't something she felt inclined to do. Maybe she would retire and focus on her fake website although, that seemed kind of boring too. Jorge had spoken along the same lines, tired of the drug cartel but she feared that it wouldn't be so easy to get out of regardless of what he thought. Then again, perhaps someone younger would be more suitable to his boss since Jorge's attention was diverted. His idea to get into pot was probably ideal. Although he even seemed iffy on that idea lately, she somehow doubted he would ever live a quiet, suburban life either.

She could though. There was something to be said for the simple life. It wasn't something she had thought would exist for her. Paige had assumed her life would be a string of meaningless affairs, childless and free, a lone wolf wandering the world, discovering where it would take her. She never thought it would take her to this place. It was something she would've once dreaded and yet, perhaps she had fooled herself that she didn't want to be 'normal'; if that was even a thing.

Now, she couldn't picture her life any other way. Wasn't it interesting how much we can change in such a short period? Life, it was full of surprises. This had been a good one.

It was late in the evening when Jorge arrived at her door. Just in from his trip to Mexico, his eyes bloodshot, dark circles below them, the deeply vulnerable look he gave her somehow said everything, even though he, himself, said nothing. Pulling her into a gentle hug, he seemed powerless in her arms, unlike the many times before, he appeared weak as if he was in the state of shell shock. It was something she hadn't expected and for a moment, she feared something terrible had happened.

"Maria?" Paige managed to say, her heart now racing erratically for fear something had happened to his child.

"She's with Juliana," He barely whispered and Paige slowly let go of him, looking again into his eyes, a small smile barely formed on his lips before it drifted away again as she let him into the apartment, closing the door behind them. Taking his hand, she led him to the couch, continuing to feel anxious as they sat down. She waited in silence, fear continued to grip her as he glanced around her apartment, his eyes avoiding hers until he finally spoke.

"I can't do this anymore," He barely whispered and shook his head.

"What?" Paige squeezed his hand and he tilted his head forward.

"This life," he continued while shaking his head. "My daughter, I think she knows what I am."

Although her first instinct was to insist that this wasn't true, instead Paige decided to explore where this thought process was coming from because this was not the man she met; the night he boldly insisted she stay in his hotel suite, when he ravished her in bed and captivated her in ways she thought weren't possible. It was as if a part of him got lost along the way and she had to figure out how to get it back.

"Why would you say that?"

"I just," He continued to shake his head. "I feel it. The way she looks at me. The way she talks about death and her grandparents, her mother, she's so cold about them all. I realize that I'm one to talk but her, I don't want her to be like me. I don't want her to be heartless and cold."

"You aren't heartless and cold," Paige insisted. "And neither is she."

"I'm not so sure," Jorge leaned against the back of her couch. "She doesn't care that they died. She shrugs it off as if it's nothing, that's not a good thing. Maria's only 10, she acts like an old bitter woman. What has her mother done to her? What have *I* done to her? Why is she like this? It's not normal."

"Maybe she's acting stronger than she actually feels," Paige attempted to console him. "She had no relationship with her grandparents and her mother, I suspect she saw this coming long ago. She sees you as being strong and she's trying to emulate it. I don't think she's cold or heartless."

"I hope not," Jorge insisted. "This has been a very eye-opening trip to Mexico. It certainly wasn't an easy one. My country, it has so many bad memories."

"Leave it behind," Paige advised as she moved closer to him, she leaned against his body, his arm slowly curled around her waist and he looked into her eyes.

"Do you think I'm a monster? A psychopath" He asked bluntly his eyes softened. "That's what she use to say, Verónic, that is also what her parents have said about me too."

"As I've told you before," Paige reminded him. "You are no more a monster or psychopath than I am."

"You're perfect," He quietly insisted as he pulled her closer into a hug. "You and Maria, you're my whole world. I could leave this all behind if it would make my daughter not be like me."

"She doesn't have to be," Paige insisted. "Her world is very different now and it's going to change even more when I move into the apartment and we get married. A new school, new country, new friends, this is a new life for her. She has left the darkness behind. Maybe we all have?"

"If only it were that easy," Jorge commented as his hand massaged her arm and he closed his eyes. Together on the couch, they were just a normal couple. One that met unexpectedly through work, him fresh out of a bad relationship, his former girlfriend having died tragically, a daughter that was having normal problems that children dealt with and yet, they weren't normal at all. As much as they pretended to be or regardless of what kind of story they would tell others about their lives in the future, the truth was that few others would really ever know them. Then again, maybe it was that secret that held them closer together.

CHAPTER 26

Life was good. Jorge was back in Canada and away from all the nightmares he had to deal with in Mexico. He would miss it; his former home was a beautiful country but at the same time, he couldn't imagine being anywhere else at that point in his life. Paige was in Canada. His daughter insisted on going to school in Toronto and most of his key business contacts were in this country. This was meant to be.

The apartment that Paige found was sufficient however, he couldn't wait to finally find a new home. He had lived in a house for his entire life but in Toronto, it felt like he was going to be pushed into a condo. Everyone he knew in the city lived in a building but the idea of sharing a living space with a group of strangers made him feel claustrophobic. It was a little too close for comfort. Someone had suggested that he could consider moving a bit out of the city but Jorge wasn't sure. He left it up to Paige. Whatever made her happy, would make him happy and fortunately, real estate was something that appealed to her.

Having sorted out some issues along the way, he finally was able to meet with Jolene, Diego, and Chase to discuss business. The four planned to meet at a restaurant for dinner however upon arriving, he discovered a text from the Diego stating that it was closed for a private party and that they instead were in a nearby bar. Locating the sketchy little dive, Jorge went inside to see the three sitting near the back of the room. Diego immediately caught his eye and rushed over.

"Did you bring *Paige?*" He said her name with great emphasis, his menacing eyes bugged out like a cartoon character as he glanced about as if she was about to make a surprise appearance.

"It's a business meeting, Diego," Jorge reminded him and pointed toward the others as they both walked toward their booth, where Jolene and Chase were talking. "Why would I bring her to *our* business meeting?"

Diego made a face and slid back into the booth, immediately reaching for a red, feminine looking drink while his hand dramatically waved in the air. "I just thought it would be nice, you know, to get to know her better."

"Do you have some kind of weird crush on my fiancée, Diego?" Jorge grinned while attempting to hide his bitterness on the subject; he was starting to resent the male attention that Paige gathered when they were out. He certainly understood it but it made him feel uneasy.

"Oh he, he likes Paige," Jolene suddenly spoke up, waving her hand in the air, she appeared to be a little drunk. "Paige, Paige, Paige, that is all we hear about lately. She's like his…how do you say? Gay icon?"

"I like her, ok, is that such a crime?" Diego retorted and returned his attention to Jorge. "I think she's cool and I want her to be my friend."

"Chase, isn't he your friend?" Jorge casually commented as he grabbed a nearby menu that displayed their list of drinks, his eyes were suddenly diverted to across the room where someone was setting up a microphone. "How many friends do you need, Diego?"

"You can never have too many friends," Diego insisted and shrugged, sniffed and scrunched up his face. "And let's face it, every woman, they need a gay boyfriend who likes to do things their boyfriend doesn't want to do?"

Jorge laughed and shook his head. "A gay boyfriend, Diego? What the fuck is that?"

"You know, like a guy friend who is gay," Diego made a face as if it were the most obvious thing in the world. "A lot of women have 'girlfriends' that they do things with, I'm the male version of that. I'm the one that she goes shopping with, watches chick flicks with or say, I don't know, goes to a Katy Perry concert with."

"Oh, ok," Chase suddenly spoke up. "So, the next girlfriend I have, can you be her gay boyfriend cause I don't wanna do any of that stuff."

Jolene let out a loud laugh and Jorge couldn't help doing the same, especially after looking back at Diego's super serious face.

"I don't know if Paige is big on any of those things either but what I can do is pass her a note during Science class later," Jorge mocked him and glanced up at the waitress approaching them as Jolene and Chase continued to laugh.

"Ok, you know, you don't have to be a jerk, Jorge, I was admiring your girlfriend and I think we would be good friends," Diego said as he leaned in, his big eyes bugging out as he did, only causing Jorge to laugh more as he looked up at the waitress, now standing by their table.

"Can I get you anything?" She asked as a loud squeal from the microphone interrupted her, causing Jorge to point toward the makeshift stage near the bar.

"What's going on there?"

"Open mic night," She replied and raised her eyebrow in a way that suggested she wasn't happy about it for some reason. "It starts at 6."

Jorge nodded. "All right then, I shall get a Corona and ah…. anyone want to join me for a shot of tequila?"

Chase shook his head no, while Jolene and Diego said yes.

"Ok, I guess that makes it three shots of tequila," Jorge replied and after she left, he turned his attention to Chase.

"No tequila?"

"I'm not much of a drinker," He shook his head just as the man in the background started to sing; and badly.

"Sure about that, Chase?" Jorge grinned and glanced toward the stage but the music was suddenly so loud, it occurred to him that perhaps it was time to find another establishment to do business. This wasn't going to work, plus he was hungry. Bar food always seemed unsanitary.

Chase merely shrugged and grinned. He was a man of few words but unfortunately, Diego was not.

"So Jorge, when are you and Paige getting married?" He continued to lean in, his eyes piercing.

"I don't know, Diego," Jorge replied, relieved to look up and see the waitress approaching with his order. He thanked her and gave her cash, leaving her a reasonable tip. She thanked him and walked away while the terrible singer continued in the background. Jorge made a face while he tapped shot glasses with Jolene and Diego, quickly sinking his shot, the bitterness hit the spot as a warmth filled his chest. This was exactly what he needed.

They barely had finished the shot when Diego had to go to the bathroom, meaning that Jorge had to move out of the booth to let him out. It was once they were both standing that Diego gave him an evil grin. "Wait till you see this."

Not responding, Jorge noted that Diego was stopping at the bar to talk to the waitress. He then walked away with a self-satisfied smile on his face. Jorge attempted to ignore him, he slid back into the booth and started to drink his Corona, while listening to the conversation between Jolene and Chase. She was definitely drunk and that wasn't like her. She was usually the dependable one in the group, the person who always kept it together, her secret world so carefully hidden and yet, it almost appeared that she was hitting on Chase.

Deciding that he didn't care and just wanted to take this meeting elsewhere, preferably somewhere with food, he quickly checked his phone before glancing up to see Diego's dark eyes piercing into him. Without saying anything, he stood up from the booth, allowing him back inside. Turning is attention toward the Colombian, he shook his head and sat back down. "We're gonna have to go somewhere else, this fucking noise," He gestured toward the singer, who didn't seem to be winding down, "I can't hear myself think."

"Just wait five minutes," Diego's face lit up. "You're going to want to see this."

At first, Jorge didn't realize what he was talking about but decided to finish his beer then put a fire under the rest of them to go somewhere else. It was probably a few seconds into the next song before he recognized the poorly sung version of 'Jolene' ringing through the room. It was terrible. His eyes drifted toward Jolene Silva and it was clear by the look of utter disgust on her face, that she was horrified.

"What is this?" She spoke as the dark clouds gathered over her as she wrinkled her forehead. "What is this? Diego, did you put them up to this?" She glared in his direction.

"What?" Diego played innocent. "I don't know what you are talking about?"

His words came out just as the chorus of "Jolene' was being pelted out from the stage, causing everyone at the table to cringe or make a face of some kind. Jorge decided to play along, giving a casual shrug.

"What? Did I miss something?"

"The *song!*" Jolene continued to make a face. "It is terrible. Do you not hear, it is my name?"

"Ha?" Jorge gave a disinterested shrug. "I don't know, I hadn't noticed."

"Oh come on!" Jolene continued to fume and turned her attention back to Diego. "This was *you!* I know this was *you,* Diego! You asked him to sing this!"

"Jolene, the entire world, it does not revolve around you," Diego shot back, dramatically waving his arms in the air. Beside Jolene, Chase appeared to be suppressing a grin while Jorge continued to show no reaction as he took a drink of his beer.

"You did this, I know you!" She was so angry that tears began to form in her eyes. "You know I hate this song and you asked this terrible singer to butcher it on purpose."

Jorge broke out into a laugh and everyone quickly followed; except of course, for Jolene.

"Oh come on," Diego teased. "In fairness Jolene, he probably butchers every song he sings."

Watching everyone laughing at her expense, Jolene practically pushed Chase out of the booth as she staggered to her feet and with her head held high, made her way toward the door.

"Ok, you guys really pissed her off," Chase observed but continued to laugh as he sat back down.

"Hey hey," Jorge put his hands up in the air. "I got nothing to do with this one."

"No, it was all me," Diego replied as the singer on the makeshift stage continued to destroy the song.

"You know, she's going to kill you, right?" Chase directed his comment at an unconcerned Diego.

"No, she's my sister, she *loves* me."

"We should follow her," Jorge gestured toward the door. "She looked kind of drunk. What the fuck's with that, anyway?"

"Don't ask!" Diego replied before removing the straws from his drink and knocking it back. "It's been one of those weeks."

"Ok, how about this," Jorge said as he stood up from his seat, quickly grabbing his beer to take one more drink before leaving. "I don't fucking care but we gotta go finish this meeting."

Sinking most of the bottle, he followed the other two out the door and wandered into the dense, Toronto air as people walked past them in every direction. Glancing around, he didn't see Jolene until Diego spotted her across the street. She was sitting on a bench, her arms crossed over her breasts.

Glancing back toward Chase, he noted a concerned look on his face that made Jorge wonder, once again if the two of them were hooking up. There was something going on but he couldn't pinpoint it. Diego, of course, seemed blissfully ignorant. Jorge would have to meet with Chase later in the week and sound him out on the subject. Not that he was one to get caught up on gossip but if he was fucking Jolene…. wow, he had to hear about it.

Across the street, she still fumed over the practical joke, taking it a bit too seriously, Jorge grew frustrated with the childish arguments between the two Silvas and as another one began, he quickly cut them off.

"*Suficiente*!" Jorge put his hand up in the air while reaching into his pocket for his cigarettes; all he had was fucking gum.

"Ok, that's it, you guys," He shot both of them a look. "We got work to do."

Acting like scolded children, they both fell quiet as Jorge pointed down the street. "That restaurant down there, the one with the chicken, let's go there and get some food," He then looked at Jolene. "Maybe a cup of coffee?"

Diego regained his composure and walked toward the restaurant. "Let's go."

Jolene staggered behind.

Jorge turned toward Chase as they got out of earshot and shook his head. "And you," He pointed toward him as he chomped on his gum and dug in his leather jacket for his sunglasses. "You gotta fuck one of them so this miserable bickering will stop."

He watched as Chase's mouth fell open in stunned disbelief as Jorge casually pulled on his sunglasses and walked behind the others.

CHAPTER 27

"So what's the big emergency, Jolene?" Jorge didn't attempt to hide his irritation when she opened her apartment door. It was shortly before midnight and Jorge certainly would've preferred to be anywhere doing almost anything than dealing with the dramatics between Diego and his sister and yet, that's exactly what he was doing.

Walking inside the apartment, Jorge immediately sensed the cloud of fury floating over Diego's head. Sitting at the far end of the couch with his legs crossed, one foot bouncing around erratically, he avoided eye contact with both his sister and Jorge but instead leaned against his hand, his black eyes shooting arrows across the room. He was unusually silent.

Jorge looked from Diego to Jolene and shook his head. "What the fuck is going on here?"

"He is mad at me," Jolene muttered and pointed toward a chair across from the couch, indicating that she wanted him to sit.

"Really?" Jorge raised his eyebrows while sarcasm rang through his voice. "I had not notice."

Diego grunted from the couch and continued to avoid eye contact.

Jorge showed some hesitation but finally sat down. Yawning, he ran a hand over the stubble on his face and shrugged. "Can we get on with this? I wanna go home, maybe get laid and get some fucking sleep. So, what you got your panties in a knot about, Diego?"

"Ask her," Diego snapped and continued to not look at either.

Taking a deep breath, Jorge turned and glared at Jolene. "What the fuck's going on? I don't got all night."

"I was a little drunk earlier," Jolene quietly started, her fingers nervously played with her hair as she sat on the other end of the couch from Diego.

"Yeah, I notice," Jorge didn't bother to hide his annoyance. "And what? You fucked Chase and Diego is mad at you?"

"What?!" Diego was suddenly making eye contact with each of them, his eyes bouncing from one to the other as he turned his body toward them. Still wearing the same suit from earlier, he quickly brushed out a wrinkle in his pants while attempting to hide the hurt in his eyes. "Are you hiding this from me too, Jolene?"

"I did not sleep with, Chase, no," Jolene was quick to snap back at him. "Not that it would be any of your business if I did."

"I told Chase tonight to fuck the misery out of one of you, I didn't care which one," Jorge shrugged and reached in his leather jacket and found gum. Hesitantly, he took one from the package and put it in his mouth. "I'm sick of listening to you both bickering all the time. I figured one of you needed to get laid."

It was a toss-up which of the two looked more disturbed by his comments, something that caused him no shame as he ignored it, quickly changing the topic.

"So if you didn't fuck Chase, what the hell did you do since we ended our meeting," Jorge pulled out his phone and glanced at it. "I dunno, like four hours ago."

"Talked!" Diego's comment was so loud, so abrupt that it caused Jorge to jump and give him his full attention. "About things that she shouldn't have talked about."

"What things?" Jorge shrugged with disinterest.

Jolene suddenly appeared very small, leaned over she appeared shameful before even speaking. "I tell him everything about his son."

The room fell silent.

"About the kid that was shot?" Jorge asked. "What did you tell him?"

"Everything!" Diego answered for her. "We said we'd never tell Chase anything about what happened. That the case was closed."

Jorge thought about the frantic call he received from Diego the previous year. It was when Chase's four-year-old son had been shot and the killer appeared to be getting away with his crime. Not that this surprised Jorge, he was familiar with how useless the legal system was; it didn't seem to matter which country he went to because it was generally a safe bet. Diego and Jolene sought some justice; real justice and asked Jorge for his help. Once he heard the entire story and met Chase, he didn't even hesitate.

"Ok, so, let's just start from the beginning here," Jorge attempted to put the facts together. "What exactly happened, Jolene?"

"I was a little drunk," She started again, her face was dark, lines formed around her eyes and lips as she recalled her evening. "Chase, he brought me home and we start to talk. I had forgotten but it was around this time of year when his son was shot. And we talk about that and how sad it was and I just, I felt bad for him..."

"So she told him everything!" Diego cut in.

Putting his hand up in the air, Jorge gave him a warning glance and returned his attention to Jolene.

"I tell him that Diego reached out to you because of what happened to his little boy," Jolene appeared to be on the verge of tears. "And that you said we would take care of it."

"By the way," Diego cut in again, his comments directed at Jorge. "Thanks for lying to *me* for all this time. I really appreciate how you tried to make me feel stupid."

"How did I make you feel stupid?" Jorge asked, slightly lost in the conversation.

"You led me to believe the two of you were having an affair," Diego referred to their cover story at the time. Supposedly the two of them were going on a romantic getaway to Whistler, a story created for Chase but Jolene thought it would be funny to mislead Diego as well since he was so easy to provoke. "No one ever told me otherwise."

"Come on, Diego, clearly it was part of our story," Jorge grinned. "Don't tell me you really believed that?"

"Yes, why wouldn't I? In California, you used to sleep with everyone, why not my sister?" Diego snapped.

"Let's not talk about my youth," Jorge glared at Diego. "If I recall correctly, neither of us were exactly careful about what we put our dick in back then."

Diego looked away again, his mouth tightened into a frustrated pout.

"So you told Chase that didn't happen?" Jorge turned his attention back to Jolene. "That we were really going to kill his son's killer?"

"Yes," Jolene admitted.

"Come on, this isn't a big deal," Jorge moved forward in his chair and angrily chomped on his gum. "Let's face it, he probably already figured it out."

"Oh, but there's more," Diego insisted.

"There is more," Jolene appeared hesitant. "I tell him that we went to his town, I decided to pay respects to his ex-wife."

"Which I told you not to do," Jorge reminded her, "that was a stupid idea."

"I know but I feel sad for her and plus," Jolene continued. "I thought maybe I could learn more about this Luke Prince man, the man who shot her baby."

"We didn't have to know anything else," Jorge reminded her. "I had someone watching him, I knew his routine, we were going to get him in the wooded area when he was out shooting. That was it. Then we were going to come back to Toronto as if nothing happened. Like we were spending a weekend in the hot tub at Whistler."

"So did you guys even go to Whistler?" Diego spoke up.

"We stop to check in and then leave again," Jolene replied. "Then went for 'a drive' to Hennessey. That is when I meet with Chase's ex-wife, Audrey. I say that I am Chase's boss and want to pay my respect and she confront us, say she heard from Maggie that we were dangerous."

Jorge rolled his eyes when he thought of the former employee who attempted to give them trouble.

"Anyway," Jolene turned toward Diego, who was just learning this story. "Jorge threw on his charming smile and tried to cover up but as it turn out, she didn't care about what we do, she wanted our help."

Jorge decided to take over the story at that point.

"Diego, she knew what we were but didn't care," Jorge spoke honestly and shrugged. "She *asked* us to kill this Luke Prince guy. Of course, we didn't actually tell her that was why we were in Hennessey. We gave her the romantic vacation story and she seemed to believe it."

"Not that she care," Jolene cut in. "She just want Luke Prince dead. She said she would pay us, anything."

"I was suspicious," Jorge continued. "Maybe she was working for the cops too, who knows? Until she asked us if we would help *her* shoot him herself."

"She wanted to kill him herself, she was so sad," Jolene spoke with emotion in her voice. "I could not blame her, me, I would do the same."

"I said no because I felt she was too close to the situation and it was clear, she would've shot everything in that woods except for Luke Prince."

"I say, I do it for her," Jolene spoke with confidence this time. "But she continued to insist she do it. I say no, I will."

"Then, I got called back to Mexico because Maria was nervous with how her deranged mother was acting," Jorge said and suddenly stopped. "So Jolene said she could take care of things herself. Which, she obviously did, since the man is now dead and it was a perfect shot, right?"

Jorge turned his attention back to Jolene while Diego let out a disgruntled snort from the other side of the couch. He hadn't known most of the details but it was really not something either Jorge or Jolene felt was necessary to get into at the time. Diego was very close to Chase and the last thing they wanted was for him to break under the pressure if asked any questions. At the time, Chase had approached each of them to find out more information but neither of them would tell him the truth. They all agreed it was for his own good to know as little as possible. It was too close to his heart and unlike the rest of them, he wasn't a seasoned criminal with murder and mayhem in his past.

"Well, not really," Jolene muttered and Diego shot Jorge a frustrated look and shook his head. "There is more."

"Jolene, how much more can there be?" Jorge shot back at her. "You killed the fucker, you left no evidence, right?"

"No no evidence," Jolene reassured him.

"And Chase's ex, she will keep her mouth shut?"

"Definitely, she wanted this," Jolene gave him a wide-eyed look and dramatically told the story. "She beg us and she collapsed in tears after it was done, she practically kiss my feet, she was so grateful."

"So, that's it," Jorge rose from his chair. "Did we really have to rehash all this in the middle of the night? I don't like the fact that Chase knows but whatever, time has passed, I guess it's ok now. I'm going home."

He started toward the door but Diego told him to wait, "There's more and you're gonna want to hear this."

Turning around, not attempting to hide his irritation, Jorge tilted his head and continued to chew on his gum. "Look, guys, it's after midnight, I want a smoke and get some sleep. What the fuck do I have to know? What's so urgent?"

"I did not shoot him," Jolene said in a small voice, her forehead wrinkled. "I wanted to but the more I talk to Audrey, I just, I cry with her, it so break my heart." Tears welled up in her eyes. "I cannot even begin to imagine such a terrible thing happening to her."

"That's why I told you to *not* talk to her," Jorge reminded Jolene and she shamefully looked away. "Don't tell me she went out and killed him? Seriously? Come on! Who really did it?"

"I call Hector," Jolene sniffed. "I tell him that I wanted to do it but was not sure if I could come through because it upset me for Audrey, it upset me for Chase, it break my heart when I see that little boy's pictures and when she talk about seeing the little boy after he was shot…"

"Ok, I got it," Jorge snapped, tired of the dramatics between the two Colombians, although he noted that Diego now appeared apprehensive as his sister continued the story. "You called Hector and he sent someone else? It's done. Ok? It's fine, Jolene, that's fine."

"But you do not know who it was that did it," Diego took over and glanced toward Jolene as she sobbed beside him. "It was Paige."

The room fell silent.

"What?" Jorge finally asked in disbelief.

"It was your Paige," Diego shuffled uncomfortably in his seat. "Hector asked Paige to do it. That's why it was a perfect shot and blabbermouth over here went and told all this to Chase. *We* didn't even know but she told Chase."

Stunned, Jorge wasn't sure what to say. As the news settled, he realized it wasn't Paige's involvement that bothered him but why hadn't she told him? What else was she not telling him?

"Chase, he's upset," Diego quietly added as he rose from the couch and approached Jorge. "He never gets upset but obviously, he feels shocked."

"He wasn't angry," Jolene sniffed from the couch. "He was upset, I think because he was already feeling emotional about his son and this all came as a surprise to him."

"I text him but he's not replying," Diego shoved both hands in his pockets. "We should've all been open with one another when it happened. Too many secrets."

Jorge was still trying to process everything and felt weak, as he turned and walked out the door.

Chapter 28

By the time he got in the SUV, Jorge felt as if he was about to pass out. His arms and legs were weak as he sat behind the wheel and for a long time, he just stared into space. His mind swirled with all the new details as the feeling of deception was strong, even though he knew that Paige likely wasn't in the place to tell him the truth in the matter, it still created fear in his heart. What if there were more secrets? He trusted her in a way he had never trusted anyone else in his life; but maybe, she didn't trust him.

Exhausted, Jorge couldn't think straight and decided to drive back to confront her on this matter. Finding one lone cigarette in his dash, he gratefully lit it up and got on the road. He replayed the conversation with Jolene and Diego in his head and slowly started to shift his anger; it was Jolene that had been lying to him all along. True, Paige should've told him the truth but it was Jolene that had been the most deceitful. She had always been a very secretive woman and secretive people made his suspicious. He felt some compassion for Diego because regardless of his frustrating ways, at least he was always straightforward and didn't hide much when it came to business. He, unlike his sister, was an opened book.

Things slowly came together and Jorge began to calm with the cigarette, as he drove through the dark streets and allowed everything to settle. When he later stood over Paige and watched her sleep, he just stared at her for the longest time and wondered what he should do. Maybe it was better to not bring up this topic but then again, he still felt she should've told him the truth. Was she trying to protect him?

Jolene? Perhaps she didn't want to get in the middle of a dicey situation, knowing that Jorge would be pissed at Jolene.

It was too late at night to worry about it. Although he did wonder about Chase. Grabbing his phone, he sent him a quick message.

I just talked to Jolene and Diego. Some of this was news to me too. Let me know if you are ok.

Jorge felt it was necessary to at least reach out but he was surprised when he received a reply seconds later.

It's fine. I appreciate all you've done for me.

Then moments later, he sent another message.

I'm a little drunk.

Jorge grimaced knowing his earlier insistence that he rarely drank.

Be safe, my friend. Message Diego. He's worried.

Exhaling, it suddenly occurred to Jorge that the five of them were tightly woven together because of this situation. They were all involved in helping Chase after his son's death. Although he had gone to great lengths to separate business and personal matters, it was no longer possible to do so. As Diego would say, they were all family now. They were as connected to one another as they would be by blood. It was somewhat relieving but at the same time, Jorge had mixed feelings about it. He didn't like to combine business with pleasure. It never seemed like a good idea to him.

Paige stirred and Jorge turned to see her slowly open her eyes and with that mere glance, all his apprehension drifted away.

"You're just getting home?" Paige slowly sat up, still wearing her clothes from earlier. "I should get going. It's late and if Maria wakes up and I'm still here…"

"It's fine, Paige," He reassured her. "Plus it's late, you shouldn't be out."

Paige let out a laugh. "You're forgetting that I carry a gun, I'm probably the safest person out there at nighttime."

"I know but you're tired," Jorge turned toward her and looked into her eyes. She immediately woke up as she studied his face.

"What's wrong? Did something happen in your meeting?" She asked and eased closer to him. "You look upset."

"I guess you could say that," Jorge replied, his heart began to race and he decided to get right to the point, rather than retelling the entire story. "I found out that you shot Luke Prince tonight. Why didn't you tell me?"

Paige backed away slightly, as if not sure how to respond. "It's not that I wanted to keep it from you but I didn't want to get into the middle of things with you and the others. I knew you didn't know."

Jorge slowly nodded. He could understand where she was coming from and he reached out for her hand and took a deep breath.

"I understand but it's important that we don't hide things like this from one another," He insisted.

"I'm sorry, Jorge, I just knew…" Her voice trailed off and suddenly she looked like an animal trapped in the cage. "Jolene didn't want you to know the truth."

"I know," Jorge took a deep breath and ran his hand up her inner arm. Her skin was so soft, so inviting and he wanted nothing more than to devour her but this was working too heavily on his mind. He had to get it out of the way. "I do understand. I'm not angry with you, I'm shocked."

"I'm sorry."

"Don't be," He leaned in and kissed her gently on the lips and leaned back on the bed. "Just tell me the truth, is there anything else I should know?"

"I will tell you anything," Paige replied and leaned forward, "everything."

"Jolene said that she couldn't do it and called Hector," He replayed the story in his mind. "That Hector sent you and that you killed Luke Prince because she was too emotional and feared she couldn't do it."

Paige eased back and studied Jorge's face.

"Tell me," Jorge insisted. "Your loyalty is with me, right?"

"Of course!" Paige said and backed off a little more "Why would you ever think otherwise?"

"Then tell me," Jorge insisted. "If that's not what really happened, I want to know. I don't have to necessarily go into it with Jolene, I want the truth from you."

Paige's defenses seem to drop, her usual calm voice returned. "She called me directly, she only called Hector to get my number."

"So you knew each other before?"

"Yes, Jolene and I met many years ago."

"How?"

"I did a job for her a long time ago," Paige slowly replied. "There was a man in Colombia that she had me kill for her."

"An old boyfriend? A lover?" Jorge shook his head and studied Paige's face. She was clearly apprehensive to say too much. "You can tell me. I won't tell her that we had this conversation. As long as it doesn't affect my business, then I don't care."

"It doesn't affect your business," Paige assured him. "It has nothing to do with you. She probably didn't even know you back then."

"But she knew you?"

"Not really," Paige confirmed and looked away. "Look, back when I started out, I spent a lot of time in South America doing work. That's why my Spanish is pretty good, I was there all the time."

"And you were in Colombia?"

"Yes, Hector and my boss are quite close," She started slowly but it was clear she didn't want to talk about whatever had happened.

"This was many years ago," Jorge insisted. "You can tell me anything."

"It's not that I'm hesitant to tell you this," Paige insisted. "It's that this is very personal to Jolene and I don't want you to look at her differently. I feel like I'm somehow betraying her by telling you anything at all. It's no one's business."

"Me, I won't say a word," Jorge insisted and moved closer to her, his hand running over her thigh. "I won't even pretend to know the truth. It stays with us."

Licking her lips, her eyes briefly looked away and she took a deep breath and continued. "Jolene knew Hector because she had done some work for him. I'm not sure of the details but they were quite close."

"Drugs?" Jorge guessed.

"Honestly, I don't know," Paige quietly replied. "But she got involved with a man who turned out to be with the police. She had no idea. He knew all about her though and used that information to basically control her. He said if she didn't do what he wanted that he would turn her over, put her in prison. He beat her and raped her and he made it clear she couldn't leave without repercussions."

"Oh my God!" Jorge was genuinely shocked by this story. "You mean to tell me that anyone *ever* made Jolene do anything she didn't want to? Why didn't she just kill him?"

"He was a very dangerous man," Paige insisted. "She was scared. He had her so paranoid that she thought if she did anything, it would immediately come back to her. It had to look like an accident."

Jorge wasn't sure what to say. The fact that Jolene had this kind of past was shocking to him and he was a man who was rarely shocked. It did explain many things about her. Why she was so closed off and secretive about her life. It also explained why she now carried a gun and was well aware of how to use it effectively. It was in response to her past that made her what she was today. Then again, were any of them so different?

"I had no idea," Jorge finally spoke.

"No one does," Paige replied. "That's why she seemed awkward around me at the meeting recently. I think she was scared that I would tell you about her past in Colombia. I also knew she lied to you about shooting Luke Prince."

"I don't get it," Jorge shook his head, suddenly exhausted. "Why didn't she tell me the truth?"

"Pride, I would guess," Paige spoke evenly. "At the time, she feared that you would get angry since obviously, you didn't even want her to meet with Audrey, which you were right. She shouldn't have. Although, I certainly had no issue killing Luke Prince. The man deserved it."

Jorge felt the weight of everyone's secrets and without saying another word, he sighed and stared at the ceiling. The pillow felt like heaven underneath his head as he contemplated everything he had just learned.

"I'm sorry, Jorge," Paige said with some apprehension. "But I promise you, that's it. I don't have any secrets and if there is anything you want to ask, I will tell you the truth. I didn't feel it was my secret to tell."

Jorge didn't reply but reached out and took her hand, moving Paige closer. Without speaking, she laid down beside him as he leaned into her chest and closed his eyes.

CHAPTER 29

He despised the idea of being there. After a restless night followed by an early morning, Jorge sat across the boardroom table from Jolene and Chase, at the office of Diego and Jolene inc. To his left was Paige, dressed professionally in a tight, cherry red skirt and white blouse, a slight distraction from the tension in the room. Not that this bothered Jorge all that much as he bit into a gooey maple flavored donut, the only one taken from a box that sat on the table.

In attempts to ignore the awkwardness in the room, he glanced outside at the dark, dreary day as rain pounded against the window pane causing a blurring effect. He then looked the other way, toward the glass doors as a few staff drifted by, casually glancing in. He was certain they knew of the 'big investor' coming to visit that day and were naturally curious. He would've preferred they hadn't known anything about him but it was immediately clear by their fake smiles and stiff disposition that they were aware of his relevance to the company.

Diego suddenly rushed into the room carrying a tray of coffee, cream and sugar and without saying a word, sat it in the middle of the table. The aroma filled the room and without any hesitation, Jorge reached for a cup and Paige did the same. Grabbing a napkin, Jorge wiped the sugary crap from his fingers and before pouring cream in his cup and taking a drink. His eyes widened in surprise and he nodded.

"Fuck Diego, this is pretty good," Jorge took a second drink.

"It's your company's coffee," Diego replied in an unusually calm voice as he sat at the head of the table, his shoulder twitched in a nervous shrug. "You know, I'm picky about my coffee."

"Ah, not my company anymore," Jorge continued to ignore the discomfort in the room, his focus on Diego. "I'm finished with them and my father is selling it and retiring."

"Really?" Diego appeared sincerely interested.

"Yes," Jorge reached for his donut and took another bite and pointed toward the coffee again. "But this is good, Diego, I hate to admit it but you make a good fucking cup of coffee."

Diego gave a satisfied smile, taking pride in this compliment as he glanced toward Jolene and Chase, each was reaching for cup of coffee while Paige took her first drink, having finally settled on a donut.

"This is good, Diego," She agreed and his face immediately lit up from the praise.

"Thank you, Paige, I will tell you my secret later," His big eyes pounced on her as he leaned forward as if to further engage and Jorge bit his tongue.

"Please do," She calmly replied and took a bite of her donut.

Across the table, the tension remained while Chase seemed more melancholy than anything else, it was Jorge that took control of the meeting.

"Ok guys," He swallowed a mouthful of donut and wiped his fingers on the napkin while all eyes were on him. "Look, I don't wanna be here. Probably none of you do but Diego was right, we do have to talk about this *revelation* that Jolene brought to our attention last night."

"Wait," Diego interrupted and reached for a donut while glancing at Jolene. "Was the cleaning lady in this morning?"

"Clara," Paige interjected.

"Yeah, that one," Diego replied before taking a huge bite out of a chocolate donut while tilting his head toward the door.

"Yes, she was in first thing and this door, I had it locked until we start the meeting," Jolene spoke for the first time since they arrived in the room. "We are fine here."

Diego appeared satisfied as he sat back and took a drink of his coffee.

"Anyway," Jorge continued as he loosened his tie slightly and glanced toward Paige. "Look, I don't want to go through all this shit again but the point is that we all might've had a few surprises last night, at least, *most* of us," He glanced at Chase who had a deer in headlights expression on his face. "And I'm not pissed off at anyone. I understand why everyone kept the secrets that they did and whatever, it's fucking done."

"Luke Prince is dead," Jorge continued and thought for a moment. "That was the right thing to do and Chase, if it hadn't been Paige, it would've been me. And if it hadn't been me, it would've been Diego." He glanced at the head of the table and watched Diego nod as he chewed. "And if Jolene hadn't been an emotional mess, it would've been her." He shot her a dark look and noted that she avoided his eyes. "The point is that he's gone, *muerto,* burning in hell where he belongs."

"I guess I always knew it was one of you," Chase finally found his voice, although barely as he stopped to clear his throat. His eyes red, as if he hadn't slept a wink and although dressed in a suit and tie, he still appeared somewhat disheveled in appearance. His dark stare focused on Paige and with sincerity in his voice, he said, "Thank you."

Paige opened her mouth as if to reply but hesitated for a long moment and finally nodded as if she couldn't speak without getting choked up.

Jorge touched her leg under the table and gave it a quick squeeze before he turned back to face Chase.

"As I said," he spoke gently. "If it had not been her, it would've been one of us and that, I can promise you. He killed your son. There was no get out of jail free card for him."

Chase looked down at his coffee and didn't reply.

Taking a deep breath, Jorge loosened his tie again and quickly realized that it wasn't the snugness of it around his neck that was making him uncomfortable.

"Look, as much as I hate to admit it," Jorge started again and relaxed in his chair, his eyes turning toward Diego since he seemed the most attentive. "We're all connected. Until now, I wanted to keep my personal and business life separated and only introduced you to Paige in attempts to explain the possible danger we might've been in at the time…"

"Are we still?" Diego shot the question before Jorge could even finish his sentence, causing more tension in the room.

"It's looking less so," Paige's voice was gentle when she spoke before taking another sip of her coffee.

"Diego," Jorge put his hand in the air. "Just settle down and don't worry, ok? We will get to that."

"As I was saying," Jorge took a deep breath and wondered how to get back on his original train of thought. His mind was elsewhere, his eyes glancing at the nearby clock, he just wanted this awkward meeting to be over. "We must keep the lines of communication open. This is very important. We have less power when we have less knowledge."

No one replied. Diego reached for another donut but appeared engrossed in the conversation.

Feeling as though he was wading through quicksand, Jorge decided that perhaps the best way to deal with all of this was to address each one individually.

"Diego, you were blind to what was going on, at least, for the most part," Jorge spoke thoughtfully. "But now you know everything. I know you're angry that your sister kept it from you, from all of us, but it's fine."

"Same to you, Jolene," Jorge continued and her face softened as he spoke. "This is finished. I don't think you should've called Hector at the time, I wish you would've told me but it's fine. It was taken care of and let's move on."

"Chase," Jorge shook his head. "Chase, all of us, our hearts went out to you. No one should ever have to lose a child, a baby." He hesitated and shook his head. "I just knew that when Diego came to me with this, especially after I met you, I had no hesitation to go after this guy. It was not something that I had a doubt about and we did it and we did it for you."

Across from him, Chase remained silent but nodded in understanding.

"Now, there is some more that we must share with you," Jorge leaned back in his chair, his left hand massaging his right as he looked up at the ceiling and finally back at Chase. "Your ex-wife, she wanted him dead too. She had heard from our *friend* Maggie that we were criminals and made it clear that if we were in fact as dangerous as she had been told, that she needed our help."

Chase was wide-eyed as he listened while beside him, Jolene made a face.

"I won't get into the whole story with you," Jorge continued as he thought back to that day and the unexpected conversation that took place between Jolene and Audrey, as the grieving mother begged them to help her kill Luke Prince. *Begged.* What had started off as a supposedly thoughtful visit from Chase's business associates ended on a very unexpected and emotional note causing him to later berate Jolene for her decision to visit in the first place.

"Needless to say, it was not my decision to visit her," He glanced toward Jolene and she shrunk back in her chair. "But since we did and since Maggie decided to share all her theories on us with Audrey, we found ourselves in a rather awkward situation. It's one that I still wish we had avoided, however, since it was too late at that point, we made it clear to Audrey that if something were to happen to Luke Prince, she was to keep her mouth shut. Nothing that Maggie told her was to ever reach the police or anyone else, for that matter."

What he wasn't saying was that he threatened Audrey. Speaking with her privately, he made it clear that she could never share this conversation with anyone; her fiancé, the police, Chase, no one. If she did, someone else in her life could die. It was a simple comment but it was powerful. To threaten the grieving mother herself would've been senseless, she was so deeply entrenched in misery that she would've gladly welcomed death but what she couldn't handle, was to bury another family member. Of course, he hadn't suggested it would be one of her remaining children because that would make him no better than Luke Prince however, it was his sudden interest in a photograph of her mother that caused the color to drain from her face.

"She, of course, agreed," Jorge continued and watched Chase's reaction closely and noted that he showed no signs of distrust. "She wanted to do it herself and we said no." He glanced at Jolene with a brief, if not intense look, he assumed she was also recalling the grieving mother as she fell to the floor in tears, begging to be the one to pull the trigger. Could they show her how? Could they help her? "It was not right…for so many reasons."

Under the table, he felt Paige's hand on his thigh and rather than the comfort he assumed she was attempting to transmit between them, he instead felt desire lurch through his groin. Attempting to regain his composure as her hand moved away, while his lust continued to linger, he finished his story.

"Maggie Telips, she was causing a great deal of difficulty," Jorge confessed as he reached for his coffee again, his body craving a cigarette. "More than I led you to believe at the time."

Chase watched Jorge attentively but there was so much vulnerability in his eyes. After all, this was a woman he had once loved even though the feelings were never reciprocated. Maggie Telips was a user and she didn't care who she hurt. It was time for Chase to learn the cold reality of this situation.

"My sources, they told me she was going to see you that day," Jorge spoke directly to Chase about the day when he shot Maggie, his eyes fixated on the man across the table. "That is why I was at the club. I wasn't even supposed to be in town. Granted, I was quite jet-lagged and that probably did not help my disposition."

He looked away briefly as he recalled that morning. The poisonous woman who attempted to slither back into Chase's life as if she were trying to help him when in reality, she was about to throw him under the bus with the rest of them. He didn't have the heart to tell him about her coldness but he also didn't have the heart to lie.

"Her plan was to get you to talk," Jorge continued, his eyes once again on Chase, who stared back with many emotions crowded on his face. "She would've tried to reach and pull out those feelings from the past, maybe put her tits in your face but somehow, she was determined to get to you that day. That's why I was there. To stop her."

"I know this," Jorge continued, answering a question he was certain was crossing Chase's mind. "Because our lovely cleaning lady, Clara," He turned toward Paige and received an appreciative nod. "She put a listening device in her apartment. She was going to get you to confess everything and offer you a reduced sentence of some kind to put me, Diego and Jolene behind bars."

"I would never do that," Chase spoke with emotion in his voice.

"I know that," Jorge replied and gestured around the table. "*We* know that and that is why I was there. She was giving us much trouble and this actually came out after Audrey attempted to get you to sign those papers. Remember the ones giving custody to her new man, Albert?" He watched and Chase nodded, his face in shock. "That was not her idea, it was Maggie's. When I contacted Audrey to find out what the fuck was going on, she told me that Maggie was hanging around, asking a lot of questions and insisted that if she shared her concern that you were linked to crime, she would be happy to disconnect the children from your life."

A darkness hovered over Chase as his face tightened with this news but he said nothing.

"I didn't want to share it with you at the time because of course, that would imply that we had met Audrey, that we had something to do with Luke Prince dying and so I gave you as little facts as I could. But now you know, this is the whole story."

Chase nodded slowly, his eyes looking away only briefly before returning to Jorge's face. "Everything makes much more sense now."

"Audrey, she is not a bad woman," Jorge continued. "She wants peace. And the rest of us, it is time that we leave it behind us and move forward. We must continue to work together and see this as a way of showing our loyalties to each other as opposed to focusing on the secrets." He glanced toward Diego, then Jolene and finally, Paige, whom he reached out and touched, if only briefly before returning his attention to Chase. "Every secret that was kept was to protect each others but no more, after today, no more secrets."

Serenity followed but one person didn't appear completely relaxed despite Jorge's speech but Jolene, she was always the secretive one. Her actions were making him increasingly nervous and as the truth slowly came out, his curiosity continued to pique and this, it was not a good thing.

CHAPTER 30

"Fuck, I've never been so happy to end a meeting in my life," Jorge commented to both Paige and Chase in the elevator. He immediately relaxed once leaving the office of Diego and Jolene Inc. and although it occurred to him that it was Chase that he should've felt the most discomfort around, this wasn't the case. As the young man stood beside him in the elevator, Jorge was completely relaxed as he reached out to hit the button taking them to the underground parking. "And I've had a fucking gun on me during one of them."

"Just one?" Paige teased as she seductively raised one eyebrow and he quickly moved in to give her a quick kiss.

"Who's counting?" Jorge shrugged and turned his attention to Chase. "And you, what are you thinking about now?"

"That I'm incredibly naïve," Chase attempted to joke but there was some unmistakable sadness in his eyes.

"Naïve? How could you be naïve?" Jorge asked as he dug into his pocket for his cigarettes as the elevator door opened. "You didn't know. It's not like I even knew about Paige or that I shared information with you. We wanted to protect you."

Shoving an unlit cigarette in his mouth, they walked through the parking garage and toward his SUV. Reaching into his other pocket, Jorge pulled out his lighter, preparing to start smoking as soon as he got to his vehicle.

"I know and believe me," Chase directed his comment at Paige, "I really do appreciate it." He then returned his attention to Jorge. "It's a lot to process."

"For all of us," Jorge glanced at Paige and she gave him a nod. "Look, Chase, you wanna get something to eat? A drink?"

"Oh God no," Chase shook his head. "I had enough to drink last night."

"That's not like you," Jorge observed. "Drinking, no?"

"I don't even know why I did it, a lot on my mind," Chase commented evasively and pointed to his right. "My car is over here."

"Ok, well, take care my friend," Jorge replied as he watched Chase walk away before sharing a silent look with Paige before getting into the SUV. It wasn't until once they were inside and he lit his cigarette, that he turned and they made eye contact. Searching her eyes, he didn't say anything at first. "You think something's up too, don't you?"

Paige thought for a moment and Jorge turned the ignition. "At the risk of seeming paranoid, yes, I do feel like something is…off."

Jorge took a drag off his cigarette as he drove out of the parking garage, ignoring the man walking out of the nearby door, glaring at Jorge as he casually blew smoke out of the window before pulling onto the street. He thought it was interesting on how society frowned upon him smoking a cigarette as if it were ungodly and horrifying and yet, big corporation casually polluted the air every day.

"Off?" Jorge repeated as his mind drifted to a completely different place. "Speaking of things being off, do you think Chase fucked Jolene?"

"What?" Paige began to laugh. "After everything that came out since yesterday, that's what's on your mind now?"

"Well no, it's not the primary thing," Jorge joined her with laughter. "It's just, I can't say that in the meeting."

"Really, you seem pretty comfortable saying anything else to them," Paige observed. "Are you sure you should be?"

Jorge ran his tongue over his front teeth and sniffed before taking another puff of his cigarette. "I don't know. I trust Diego, we go back like 20 years and Chase…."

"Jolene?" Paige asked and when he didn't respond, she quickly continued. "Don't let what I told you last night make you judge her."

"It's not that I'm judging her," Jorge casually replied as they stopped at a light. "I don't know, I got a weird feeling about her today. Something about her story isn't adding up."

"With her calling me about Luke Prince, you mean?"

"Yes, but, I don't know," Jorge shook his head. "Jolene doesn't strike me as someone who would be too emotional to shoot someone, you know?"

"Yes, that kind of crossed my mind too," Paige commented as the SUV started to move again. "Not at the time because my only experience with her was when she was younger, so I couldn't compare it."

"Like, if say, someone were to break into her place tonight," Jorge considered and took another drag off his cigarette. "I don't think she would have trouble shooting them."

"Different situation," Paige commented and shrugged.

"Yeah but, I don't know," Jorge commented. "Everything isn't adding up with her."

"Should we be watching her more closely?" Paige asked as they drove along. "But what other reason would she have to not shoot this Prince guy?"

Jorge thought for a moment. "That's just it, I don't know."

"Perhaps we are underestimating her," Paige considered as she looked out the side window. "Maybe we are making something out of nothing. It's possible that she was too upset and didn't know if she could do the job."

"Maybe," Jorge was suddenly bored with the topic. "Regardless, something feels…off about her."

"What if Jolene and Chase are closer than we think," Paige considered and turned her attention back to Jorge. "It would be too emotional for her or perhaps, too important to not get right?"

Jorge shared a quick, intense look with Paige and nodded. "That would, actually, make sense but I'm not sure. I'm not getting that from them, you know?"

"Maybe it hasn't happened yet?" Paige considered. "Not all relationships are like ours."

"You mean, everyone doesn't meet and decide to get married within a week?" Jorge teased as he kept his eyes on the road. "Sounds boring."

"Maybe it's a slow flirtation," She commented. There was something about the way she said flirtation that caused his eyes to jump toward her, drifting over her body before returning to the traffic around him.

"Slow is overrated," He spoke in a low, smooth voice, the same one he used when attempting to seduce her. "If you ask me, fast is the only way to go."

"But not everyone can handle fast," She spoke in a softer voice than usual as she leaned in closer just as he stopped at another traffic light, her hand gently sat on his thigh and slowly moved up, barely touching the fabric but still causing him to shift in his seat. Her lips moved close to his ear, her hot breath touched his earlobe as his heart begin to race as her fingers reached up a little higher. "Not like you can."

The light changed and she moved away and sat forward in her seat leaving him feeling aroused and with the challenge of figuring out how much longer it would be until they reached her place. He was already visualizing what he would do to her, his hands gripping the steering wheel, his eyes fixated on the road ahead as she continued to talk.

"I bet she's trying to slowly seduce him so that when they finally do hook up," Paige commented in her usual, calm voice as if they were merely discussing the weather or local gossip. "It will be explosive. She will completely ravish him. Chase won't know what hit him."

He wouldn't admit it to Paige but visions of Jolene naked, her large breasts and full hips, riding Chase wasn't exactly reducing his state of arousal. Then again, glancing toward the passenger side at Paige, wearing that skin-tight skirt and blouse, the first few buttons opened, wasn't helping either. He wanted her to go on but didn't want to seem too intrigued by the fantasy of Jolene and Chase, so he did so carefully.

"Maybe she's not interested," Jorge calmly commented, his breathing labored.

"Maybe she's into women."

This wasn't helping. Visions of Jolene with another woman filled his head and he had to turn and look away.

"Maybe her and Chase were having a secret affair all along," She spoke thoughtfully as they arrived at her apartment. "She's very secretive so it's not like she'd tell anyone."

As soon as he parked the SUV, he ripped off his seatbelt, pushed back the seat and reached for her, his mouth covering hers, he pulled her closer. His hand automatically slid inside her blouse, squeezing her breast causing a moan to come from the back of her throat as she managed to maneuver around the steering wheel to climb on his lap, pulling her skirt up as she did. Quickly unbuttoning his pants, her lips moved to his ear as his eyes did a quick scan through her parking garage. It was small, no cameras and fortunately, no people. Not that he gave a fuck right about then, his state of arousal made him unconcerned with any outside factors as he moved inside her with an immediate gasp of relief as she moved on top of him, he grasped her hips and pulling her closer as she wiggled so fast that he thought he was going to lose his mind. Closing his eyes, it wasn't until he heard her animal like moans of pleasure as she wiggled around uncontrollably that he finally let go as an intense orgasm ripped through his body and pleasure filled him.

Fortunately, her parking garage was quiet during the day. As they both quickly pulled themselves together, Jorge zipped up his pants, his heart still sending a triumph of satisfaction throughout his body, he slowly eased out of the SUV at the same time as her and they walked toward the elevator as she straightened her skirt.

"You're definitely are the woman of my dreams," He whispered as they got inside and hit the button to her floor. "And that's not something I've ever said before."

She gave a shy smile causing him to smile back.

"When are we doing it, by the way?" He continued. "Why are we waiting? Let's get married."

"I like the sounds of that," She moved closer and kissed him. "But we have to do the paperwork, although that sounds relatively easy."

"Then let's do it," Jorge commented. "Let's get married. Tomorrow? The next day? I don't care."

"Maybe not tomorrow," Paige commented as they arrived at her floor, she gave him a brief kiss and lead him out of the elevator. "But soon, I agree."

"*Te amos,*" His comment was gentle as they arrived at her door, his hand on her back. "Anytime, anywhere. I got to get our rings and I didn't even get your engagement ring…"

"It's not a big deal," She pointed toward her hand. "It's just a ring."

"It's not *just* a ring," He commented as she led him inside her apartment and locked the door behind them. "It's more significant than that."

"I know," She thought for a moment. "I'm not a big wedding person. I find big weddings, big rings, big dresses, it's ridiculous what people spend on a wedding, as if the more they spend, the more significant their relationship is, you know?"

"Yes, I do," Jorge laughed. "I knew a guy when I was in my 20s, he spent a fucking ton of money on a wedding and six months later, he was still paying for it when he was getting divorced."

"Exactly," Paige commented.

"Not that we are getting divorced," He quickly added. "I don't marry casually, so if I'm doing it, I'm doing it right. Divorce isn't an option."

"Strict Catholic?" Paige grinned.

"No, I don't think people should be looking for a way out just cause things get off track at times," Jorge commented as he headed toward her kitchen to make coffee, loosening and removing his tie on the way. "Call me old-fashioned but that's what I believe."

"I don't think anyone who has sex in a parking garage or is part of a drug cartel is what I would refer to as being *old-fashioned,*" She spoke slowly, emphasizing the last words as Jorge turned the coffee maker on and returned to the living room, where she stood in the middle of the floor.

Without saying a word, he began to kiss her again, slowly, gently this time. Stopping, he stared into her eyes for a moment before smiling. "Tomorrow we can look at rings and decide on when we want to get married."

"Maria will have to be there," Paige commented. "We also have to talk to her about all this."

"She knows we are getting married."

"She knows we are getting married *sometime,*" Paige corrected him. "Not in the near future."

"I'll talk to her."

"It might be too much too soon."

"We gotta live our lives," Jorge commented as the aroma of coffee filled the room, his hand sliding up and down her back. "Just be ready, there will be a lot of questions."

"I figured that."

"That's why I gotta tell her myself," Jorge commented calmly, fearing his daughter's response. And to his relief, Paige agreed. Not that he looked forward to the conversation but if there was one thing he couldn't deny, it was love.

CHAPTER 31

Not that Jorge had many opportunities to talk to Maria about the wedding or anything else. He managed to pull some strings to move into their apartment early and that combined with his daughter's extra curricular activities made it almost impossible to catch her during waking hours. It appeared that her new school believed that children should always be busy and he wasn't sure if it was to prepare them for a bright future or simply to keep them out of trouble. Of course, volunteering was important, as were sports and other things that appeared to be required of them but at the same time, couldn't a kid just be a kid? What happened to the days when children went on little adventures with their friends? Didn't little girls play with dolls and have tea parties or things of that nature? Apparently, not so much anymore and to him, it was sad. Perhaps he was a child in much more innocent times.

When he finally had time to discuss the wedding with her, Maria took everything in with ease and showed no emotion. She didn't even ask questions, invasive or otherwise but merely nodded and yawned as if he were keeping her away from something much more important.

"So is this," He wasn't sure of how to word the question and cleared his throat and shrugged. "Is this all ok with you? Are we fine here?"

"Yes," Her answer was simple as her brown eyes studied his face. "When is Paige moving in?"

"Soon, the place she rents, she had to give a month's notice," Jorge confirmed. "She's been slowly bringing her stuff here and of course, we are looking for something more permanent than this apartment."

"Ok, Papa," Maria's answer was simple as she rose from the couch, pulling her backpack up from the floor and swinging it over her shoulder. "Sounds good."

"Well, ok…" Jorge stumbled, feeling that this conversation was way too easy as his daughter turned and walked away, still wearing her school uniform. She went into her room and closed the door.

Unsure of what else to do, he sent a quick text to Paige expressing his concern over Maria's apathy toward the situation. Her response was quick.

Give it time to sink in. Leave her with it for now. She will come around.

Unfortunately, she didn't. Maria seemed to live at the school, swallowed up by various activities, always seeking permission to join her class to tour a museum, volunteer to pick up trash at a local park or work behind the scenes for a school production. He was starting to question if this was normal but with no other parents in his life, he wasn't sure whom to ask. In Mexico, she was busy with school but not to this extreme. He finally decided to contact Marco. He had children and Jorge also wanted to touch base with him about the hacking.

"I've been so busy," Jorge admitted over the phone. "Moving, new school, there is so much to do for these things."

"Yes, this is true," Marco agreed. "I remember moving to this country and it is a lot of things you must know and do, I understand."

"Marco, can I ask you something?" Jorge hesitated and looked around his empty apartment. He was waiting for Paige to arrive and Maria was already in school for the day. "Do your children, do they seem to be in school or doing projects all the time? I never see my daughter, the school has her doing so many things, you know?"

"Yes, my children are involved in many activities, much more than when we were their age," Marco confirmed and let out a little laugh. "It is nice but sometimes exhausting to keep up with their schedule."

"When I was a child, there were no extra curricular activities other than sports," Jorge commented with a sigh. "Oh my, but how things have changed."

"This is correct," Marco kindly confirmed. "It is so much more different from our childhood and also, we live in Canada now, children here seem to be involved in many things here."

"My daughter was involved in a few things in Mexico," Jorge replied and thought for a moment. "But she seemed to be home more, you know?"

Marco let out a laugh. "Yes, perhaps it is good, no? It will help her in the future?"

"Maybe so," Jorge reluctantly agreed and shifted gears. "Anyway, we haven't talked in a while, have you learned anything new? Should we meet?"

"Unfortunately no," Marco spoke with regret in his voice. "I would be just guessing to say who made these changes. There are certain protocols that staff is required to follow regarding passwords and such but it seems, no one here follows these rules. I have watched and to be honest, I think anyone could go in and change arrangements at any time."

"Wow, an expensive hotel like that one," Jorge was somewhat surprised, although he shouldn't have been. "I would expect more security. There are credit cards and personal information involved."

"Yes, I know, that is what I say," Marco spoke with regret in his voice. "I do not know why they are like this."

"Ok, well keep me posted," Jorge commented. "Also, I may be in touch soon, I'm working on a new project and may have an opportunity for you if you're interested."

"Oh yes, thank you," Marco continued to show enthusiasm. "I will welcome a new opportunity."

"We will be in touch," Jorge ended the call and remembered that he still hadn't looked at the emails forwarded to him weeks earlier. Paige was constantly reminding him but he was pretty sure there was nothing important. He kept telling her that he would look at them but unfortunately, he never had the chance.

That morning was no exception. Jorge was expecting Diego, Jolene and Chase to arrive for a meeting. They had so much to discuss; their new pot connection in British Columbia, the increase in business at the nightclub, including some of the bands that Chase had recently hired to perform. The staff were requesting to hire extra help but he wasn't sure. Many things would be changing now that he was less involved in the Mexican side of importing drugs and he worried that they might be taking too much of a gamble. Another side of him had a disinterest in all his business transactions lately and he wasn't sure why. It no longer excited him as it once had and it was difficult to deny, however, what else would he do? This was the only life he knew.

The door suddenly opened and Paige walked in carrying a huge box. Jorge rushed over and grabbed it from her hands.

"*Mi amor*, why did you not tell me you were here," Jorge gently chided her. "I would've come down to your car to get the box."

"It's not heavy," Paige insisted as he took it from her arms and saw what she meant. "Just more clothes."

"Good," Jorge commented as he placed the box on the floor. "I hope that means you will soon be moving in. I need you here with me."

Leaning in to kiss her, he felt himself pulling her close, his breath increasing as his hands slid under her jacket to touch her naked back, a soft moan escaped from the back of his throat as the buzzer rang, indicating someone was at the door.

He moved away from her and sighed. It was Chase and Diego downstairs. Buzzing them in, he swooped in to give Paige another quick kiss. "We have a meeting, you should stay."

"I was actually thinking of doing some more packing," Paige calmly replied and glanced toward the box on the floor. "Are you sure?"

"Yes, I'm sure," Jorge insisted. "You are my family, I would like you to stay although," He hesitated when he heard a soft knock at the door. "I would like to see you also move in quickly, my bed, your Canadian falls, they are *so* cold."

She joined him in laughter as he opened the door, letting both Chase and Diego inside. Chase was carrying coffee while Diego had a box of donuts.

"Jolene's on her way," Diego commented as if Jorge had asked, quickly handing him the donuts, his eyes lit up when he saw Paige. Rushing toward her as if the two hadn't seen each other in years, he swooped her up in a hug causing Jorge's fiancée to let out an awkward laugh. "Paige, it's so good to see you."

Chase's eyes widened in surprise while Jorge glared in Diego's direction as he watched their hug dissolve. Paige appearing amused as Diego started to ask her a million questions-when was she moving in? When was the wedding? Did she have any 'assignments' lately? Paige answered each question with ease; she would be moving in soon, nothing was decided yet for the wedding and no, she had not recently accepted any assignments.

"Accepted?" Diego asked as he sat on the couch while Paige continued to stand nearby. "Is that how it works? You have offers and you choose the ones you wish to do?"

"Something like that," Paige confirmed and glanced toward Jorge who was shaking his head.

"Diego, we must start our meeting now," He quickly changed the topic as he rushed ahead and placed the donuts on the coffee table. Chase followed, removing each coffee and handing it to the specific person it was for and then he hesitated when the last one sat in the tray, his eyes immediately looked in Paige's direction.

"You can have mine, Paige," He commented as he held the tray toward her. "I...I don't need this."

She gracefully declined. "I probably should go. I just stopped in to drop off some clothes."

"Are you sure?" Chase appeared a bit nervous in her presence while Diego looked enamored, as he gazed at Paige.

"Oh Paige, you should stay!" Diego insisted.

"Yes, Paige, do stay." Jorge continued to insist.

"I...I guess," She slowly commented as she glanced toward Chase, who was attempting to wiggle the last coffee out of the holder when the cover suddenly loosened and a huge splash lurched toward his white shirt.

Immediately dropping the cup holder, Chase attempted to pull the piping hot liquid away from his body, as he sat the cup down and hastily unbuttoned his shirt, ripping it out of his pants and taking it off. Regardless of the fact that they all cringed at the sight of hot coffee against his skin, Paige rushing into the kitchen for a paper towel, everyone was slightly transfixed by his muscular chest. The man had the 6, 9, 12 pack-Jorge wasn't even sure but he couldn't help but stare with admiration following by jealousy, as Paige rushed over with cold paper towels while grabbing his shirt.

"I will get this out for you," She made a beeline into the bathroom. The water started to run and Diego asked if he was ok. Before he could answer, Paige sang out from the bathroom.

"I got the stain out, I can throw it in the washing machine for you," She stuck her head out of the bathroom door, pointing toward the shirt.

"Nah, that's fine," Chase appeared slightly embarrassed while Diego stared at him with lustful eyes.

Jorge watched as Paige approached Chase with the shirt in her hand, jealousy continued to creep up on him and he looked for his cigarettes but changed his mind. He offered Chase a t-shirt to put on while the patch of wet material dried but he declined.

"Is this," Jorge pointed at Chase as he put his shirt back on, "is this what a 20-year-old body looks like now? I feel old and out of shape."

"I assure you," Diego quickly answered his question. "Most 20-year-old bodies, they don't look *this* good." His eyes widened. "Chase is a rarity."

"Yeah, that's like Brad Pitt in *Fight Club* kind of body," Paige commented as she casually joined Diego on the couch while Jorge sat on a chair across from them, reaching for a donut, although feeling guilty doing so, his eyes returned to Chase.

"Oh yes!" Diego commented. "I forgot about that movie."

"*Fight Club?*" Chase looked confused. "I never heard of it."

"One of the best movies from the 90s," Jorge commented as he bit into his donut. Fuck it, he was in good enough shape. "You never heard of it? Seriously?"

"Twenty-somethings have never heard of anything in pop culture before now," Paige spoke evenly. "Music, movies, television, they are very much in the present."

"Oh, come on!" Jorge spoke with his mouth full of donut. "Maria knows what *Fight Club* is, how do you not, Chase?"

"Maria watches a lot of shows that aren't age appropriate," Paige calmly remarked, a grin on her face, she also reached for a donut.

"My love, you aren't telling me something I don't know," Jorge replied, he took a drink of his coffee. "I was unaware she recently started to watch the show *Weeds*. A few days ago she asked if there was a tunnel between Mexico and the US to import drugs."

Everyone laughed.

"I say, Maria, this is all imaginary," He pointed toward a nearby laptop. "This is not true."

"Is there a tunnel?" Chase shyly asked.

Jorge shrugged with a grin on his face. "I don't know, perhaps. Not for me. When I show up at the US border, they just look at me and say, "Good morning Mr. Hernandez" and wave me through."

No one replied. Everyone knew.

"So *Fight Club*," Chase awkwardly asked, taking a sip of the rest of his coffee. Fortunately, not much spilled. "I assume it's about boxing."

"Actually, it is about consumerism and how big corporations, they own us. They tell us what we need to be happy," Jorge replied as he finished his donut and grabbed a napkin. "We work jobs we hate, to make money to buy all this stuff to impress people who we hate even more. To keep up with the Jones' as you say."

"See I thought it was about good versus evil" Paige replied as she slowly chewed. "Like how our dark side is always there and if we attempt to separate ourselves from that side of our personality, it will come back with ferociously, stronger than ever before."

"No no," Diego quickly cut in and dramatically waved his hand in the air. "You both got it wrong. The movie is about the brutality. How we, as humans, we're all animals by nature but we feel the need to hide it from the world because it's considered unacceptable so we keep it underground, thus the underground fight club."

"I think, Diego," Jorge commented as he fixated his gaze across the room. "It is safe to say we might all be right. There are a lot of messages inside this movie, unlike the movies of today, our generation used art to express something. Now it is just all tits and ass, some guns thrown in and poorly done comedy. I do not enjoy the movies anymore."

"The key to *Fight Club* though," Paige directed her comment to Chase, who was taking in all their comments. "You have to watch it very carefully because the ending, it's not at all what you expect."

"And that," Jorge raised one eyebrow, his eyes slide from person to person and returned to Paige. "That is something I think we all can agree on. The best endings, you never see them coming."

CHAPTER *32*

Despite how the meeting started, they eventually were able to get back on track shortly after Jolene's arrival. Although the others discussed more plans for the future, all Jorge heard were numbers. If the numbers were good, he was happy. Everything else wasn't relevant to him, his mind drifting off slightly as Diego and Jolene talked about some holiday themed parties for Christmas, Jorge instead glanced at Paige, their eyes meeting briefly as she returned her attention to Jolene. In fact, for most of the meeting, his fiancée had been carefully watching the other woman in the room with ease, as if merely interested in her words as opposed to observing her due to any suspicions.

The meeting started to drag on as they discussed bands playing at the club on 'off' nights when sex parties weren't taking place; all Jorge heard from this conversation was the bottom line of the night. He already knew that he was actually selling as many drugs at these events as he was at the sex parties, which made him wonder how the pot business would play out between the two. Now, the parties mainly sold cocaine but they also had some other drugs available where pot was actually more of a new domain for him.

"So," Jorge cut in with hopes of wrapping things up before the entire morning was gone, "I want to get that convenience store next to the club and open a dispensary. It's perfect because we can insist on a prescription at the store and for those who don't have one, someone will be around to sell them some outside the store. Also, we're right beside the club which means, we can attract customers from there and sell within as well."

"When are you doing this?" Chase inquired as he quickly glanced at his phone.

"I already spoke to the man who owns it," Jorge spoke evenly. "He doesn't seem interested in selling but I have a feeling he's about to change his mind."

Everyone knew what that meant.

"After that, we just have to throw it together and my people in BC are more than happy to work with us."

"But aren't these dispensaries always being raided?" Diego asked and made a face.

"So?" Jorge shrugged. "We close the door for the day and open it the next one. Like I give a fuck."

"Don't you have connections?" Paige referred to the people he paid off in government. "A way that your dispensary will be overlooked."

"My goal is to have the others shut often and mine left open so that we get all the business," Jorge commented with a smooth grin. "Of course, every once in a while, we will have to be raided also to keep up with appearances."

"So, someone else is doing your old job with the cocaine?" Jolene appeared confused and Jorge hesitated to answer her. He weighed his words carefully and finally nodded without giving her any further information.

"But do not worry," Jorge insisted while his eyes sized her up. "Nothing will change on your end. You will see no difference. Everything, it will run as usual."

There was an awkward silence and Jolene merely nodded.

Jorge glanced toward Paige briefly and noting that Jolene was watching him, he quickly covered.

"We still have that appointment this afternoon, Paige?"

Playing along, she silently nodded.

"Wedding stuff," He casually commented and stretched and stood up. "I don't think there's anything else for today. We will meet once I have more information on the store and Chase," He turned his attention to the youngest person in the room, who was also standing up. "I may need your help this week when I go to speak with that store owner. We must have that place."

Chase nodded and didn't say anything. Jolene was standing awkwardly and Diego jumped up hastily.

"Wedding stuff?" He glanced toward Paige and back at Jorge. "Can I help with your wedding stuff?"

"Not unless you are also getting married," Jorge joked and Paige grinned.

"It's fine, Diego, thank you though," Paige commented and he lit up like a Christmas tree.

"Paige, we should spend some time together soon," Diego commented enthusiastically as his eyes bugged out. "Maybe shopping or something?"

"I'm not much of a shopper," Paige admitted. "Perhaps we can have a cup of coffee."

Diego appeared satisfied with this answer and quickly told her his number and watched Paige add it to her contacts.

It wasn't until everyone left that Jorge collapsed on the couch and closed his eyes.

"What an exhausting group of people," He commented and opened his eyes to see Paige carrying the box she had brought earlier into the bedroom. "I could've got that for you.

"I'm fine," She sang out before he heard a soft thud of the package dropping to the floor, she returned to the living room. "I think Diego is so adorable."

"Ugghhh, really?" Jorge commented as he sat back up on the couch. "I find *him* exhausting. He's like a crackhead on the highest settings. He never stops moving or twitching."

"He's a very nervous, anxious person," Paige attempted to analysis him as she sat beside Jorge as he rubbed his face. "I like him though. I love his energy."

"What do you think of Jolene's energy?" Jorge leaned up against his hand and watched her expression change. "What did you think of her today?"

"I don't know," Paige thought for a moment, her eyes drifted across the room. "She definitely was ill at ease. The entire meeting changed when she arrived, did you notice? Was she always like that?"

"No," Jorge considered for a moment. "Well, maybe somewhat but there's something different now. I can't put my finger on it."

"Maybe I make her uncomfortable because of what I know," Paige suggested and turned more toward Jorge as she spoke. "Next meeting, I won't be there and you can see if she still is acting weird. It might be because she finds me unsettling or something."

Jorge was doubtful but he agreed to consider it. He was thinking about having some of his people watch her for a few days, perhaps check into who she's communicating with in case there is a conflict.

"She's been acting a little different since I shot Maggie," Jorge commented and then questioned his own judgment; perhaps he was unfairly assuming the worst of her. "I think."

"You don't think the police approached her?" Paige asked. "She's probably your weakest link."

"No," Jorge replied but was hesitant. He suspected if her back was against the wall, Jolene would worry about saving herself first and fuck the rest of them. "But I'm definitely going to have someone watch her. I want to be certain."

Neither of them spoke about what would happen if she were working with the police. It wasn't necessary.

"Considering her past," Paige added. "It seems highly unlikely. She seemed nervous today and why was she late?"

"Traffic, she claimed," Jorge replied.

"Wouldn't she come here with Diego?"

"She was at the office, he was at the club with Chase."

Paige didn't reply but appeared to be thinking about this fact. She finally nodded.

"I will have her watched and will watch her carefully in the next meeting," Jorge replied and pulled a cigarette out of a pack sitting on the coffee table and lit it up. "Although, if you aren't at the next meeting, Diego will be very disappointed."

Paige grinned.

"I think he has a bit of a crush on you," Jorge commented and watched her reaction. She shrugged.

"He's gay."

"Sometimes I wonder," Jorge commented. "The way he flirts with women and you, he seems infatuated with you."

"Did you see his eyes when Chase took off his shirt," Paige commented. "I think that's probably the person he's infatuated with."

"Oh, without a doubt," Jorge agreed, placing the cigarette to his lips, he inhaled and blew the smoke away from Paige. "That is common knowledge. Maybe he's interested in both."

"I don't think so," She commented and started to gather the coffee cups on the table in front of them. "I think he just wants a friend."

"He's always asking about you," Jorge grinned and took another puff off his cigarette.

"Is he? You never told me that," Paige commented as she walked to the garbage, putting the paper cups inside.

"You know me, I don't like mixing business with socializing."

"It wouldn't be you socializing with him," Paige reminded Jorge as she returned and picked up the donut box, offering him the last, plain donut left in the box.

Shaking his head, Jorge commented, "Leave it for Maria when she comes home. As for Diego, of course, if you want to spend time with him, you are free to do so."

"I know," She replied with a sly grin as took the box into the kitchen. "Why do I get the feeling you don't want me spending time with Diego?"

"It's not that I have a problem with it," Jorge shrugged. "I just figured you wouldn't want to."

"Really?"

Jorge didn't answer.

"Are you sure it's not that he's known you a long time," Paige calmly asked as she returned to the couch. "Maybe there's some dirty tidbits from your past you think he might tell me."

Jorge let out a laugh. "Baby, there are a lot of dirty tidbits from my past but I don't want his version of those stories coming out. Diego is so dramatic about everything."

"So, why don't you tell me them yourself?" Paige countered.

"Look, we were young and both did a lot of stupid things back then," Jorge shrugged. "We partied a lot. His sugar daddy was a business partner of mine at the time. This was back in the California days. Long time ago."

"I can't picture you and Diego partying together," She grinned.

"Well, it was at his 'daddy's' house and Diego was different back then," He replied. "Quieter, actually, believe it or not. He was very compliant to this man."

"Sounds controlling."

"He was," Jorge finished his cigarette and put it out in a nearby ashtray. He would have to clean it before Maria got home. "He owned Diego. Diego was a bit of a slut though and slept around on him but at the end of the day, his sugar daddy owned him. He left him everything when he died."

"Really?" Paige asked, her eyes widened in surprise. "All his money?"

"Not it all," Jorge corrected himself. "But a lot. This guy's kids were none too pleased but that's when I ran into him again, after a lot of years, at the funeral. We talked about this business he wanted to start with sex clubs and here we are now. I invested, got drugs into them and they were a hit. Diego felt the heat in California, got Jolene to start organizing parties here in Canada and the rest is history."

"That's fascinating, actually," Paige considered. "Everything came together perfectly."

"Especially for me," He replied and reached for her hand. "Who knew?"

"So in some way," Paige considered. "Diego had a part in us coming together?"

"Not unless he hired you to come to my room to kill me, probably not."

"I guess if you look at it that way," Paige grinned. "Hey, did you ever look at those emails yet?"

"No, I keep forgetting," Jorge shrugged. "If you didn't see anything then I won't."

"I'm not so sure," Paige replied as her forehead wrinkled. "I would feel better if you took a look at them."

"I will later today," Jorge replied and rose from the couch. "But we should get going."

"Where are we going?" Paige followed his lead. "I thought you just said about the wedding stuff to end the meeting."

"I did but I also think it's time we made this official," Jorge replied. "We can go get the rings, do the paperwork, that kind of thing. Whatever needs to be done."

"Are you sure?" Paige seemed hesitant. "Maybe we should wait for Maria..."

"Maria's fine," Jorge insisted. "Her father, however, wants to get this show on the road. What are we waiting for?"

She didn't reply but followed him out of the apartment.

CHAPTER 33

"But I do not wish to sell," The Korean man was defiant, regardless of the fear in his eyes as he looked across the counter at Chase and Jorge. Both of the men were larger than the convenience store owner, therefore causing Jorge to be somewhat impressed by his powerful stance but at the same time, he felt confident that he would get what he wanted. "This store, it has been my family's for years."

"Then it's time for a change," Jorge was insistent and glanced at Chase who hadn't said a word since their arrival, his eyes watching the Korean man carefully as he stood tall with both arms crossed in front of him. "Try something new, maybe? I don't know, a restaurant or perhaps take some time off, you and the wife can travel? You know, we never really appreciate the time we have with those we love."

His words sounded sincere. Jorge Hernandez knew how to talk to people, charming them was his first line of attack and when that didn't work, he would move on to the second. The third was usually when things got iffy.

"We cannot travel," The Korean man shook his head and waved his hand around the small store. "We cannot afford."

"Then why not sell the store at a rate that is more than fair, probably higher than anyone else is going to pay," Jorge pointed toward the ceiling that had a large stain in the middle. "I'm guessing this place needs a lot of work so it's no bargain. I think my offer is more than generous."

His smile was genuine, at least, as genuine as Jorge Hernandez ever got when it came to business. Shoving both hands in his pant pockets, the feel of his gun in his leather jacket pocket was noticeable to him and he suspected, the Korean man across from him. Neither said a thing for a long time but this didn't make Jorge uncomfortable as it would some people.

"How well can you possibly be doing in this store," Jorge commented with a shrug. "We've been here 10, 15 minutes already and no one has even come through those doors."

Glancing toward the exit, the door itself was old, heavy, with posters of various Korean whores stuck to the glass. He suspected they were advertisements for some form of 'entertainment' and he had been around long enough to guess the specific kind. This place didn't run on selling boxes of Chiclets and cans of Pepsi. Then again, did they even sell Chiclets anymore?

Jorge assumed this store couldn't make enough money to cover the overhead in a city like Toronto unless they had something on the side. People didn't need overpriced convenience stores in a place where large grocery chains offered more reasonable prices and locations unless of course, they were in a pinch. Parking was terrible in this neighborhood, so it wasn't exactly a convenience for customers unless they were within walking distance. The store atmosphere was anything but friendly or clean and in fact, there was barely enough products in this cramped building to even be called a store.

"We get by," The Korean man was starting to lower his defenses slightly, his eyes looking away from the two men standing in his store and Jorge could see their advantage instantly.

"It's not easy running a business these days," Jorge commented in a sincere voice as he glanced around, his eyes briefly meeting with Chase's then returned to the Korean. "So much competition, everything is expensive, power, phone, Internet, people can't afford overpriced candy and even if they can, I'm guessing it's cheaper down the road at the discount grocery stores. Those places, they have buying power, they can negotiate or dictate how much they're paying to the wholesalers and well, they got no choice but to say yes because they need to sell their product but you, you got no power."

His voice carried a certain amount of compassion and the Korean shook his head in agreement.

"I mean, unless you got something on the side," Jorge commented and grabbed a bag of kettle chips off the shelf and reached into his pocket and pulled out a Toonie, the Canadian $2 and sat it on the counter, then turned his attention to Chase. "You know, your Canadian money looks so much like our Pesos in Mexico. It's weird. I have to catch myself sometimes from giving the wrong amount to cashiers."

"Really?" Chase asked and raise an eyebrow as Jorge opened the bag and started to eat. "I didn't know that."

"You, my friend, you need to get your ass to Mexico for a visit and see what I mean," He returned his attention to the Korean man. "It's unfortunate that we must often leave our own countries to provide more opportunity for our families."

"Yes, this is true," The Korean man nodded. "That is why we come here. Now, my two daughters, they are in university."

Jorge nodded, his mind spinning in circles while on the outside, he appeared calm.

"This would be a good time for you to retire," He suggested casually. "After working in this store day in and day out for years, spend some time with your wife, your daughters."

"My daughters," The man shook his head. "They do not spend time with parents. Friends, boyfriends, but not us."

"I guess that happens," Jorge was growing bored with this conversation. "Look, I will give you a great price on this place. I don't know what you got going on behind there," He pointed toward a door behind the counter. "But I'm sure you can find a way to make it work somewhere else. Maybe a new location? A fresh start?"

Before he could reply, Jorge pushed harder, his original charm vanished as he moved closer to the counter, his eyes narrowing in on the store owner, much like an animal after its prey, slowly easing closer before the attack. "Look, we need this store for a future project. We got the club next door and this location works perfectly with some upcoming business changes that are about to take place."

"The sex club?" The man pointed toward JD Exclusive Club, his eyes grew in size. "That is yours."

"Yes," Jorge replied and tilted his head when noting the man's interest. "You are familiar with it? Maybe dropped in from time to time?"

"No, no, not me," The man glanced from Jorge to Chase and back again. "I make business there."

"*You* make business there," Jorge acted confused but continued to eat his chips and leaned against the counter. "Oh yes, how so?"

"I have girls, they go there," The man continued. "They give out business cards for massages."

Knowing the kind of massages that the man meant, it took everything in him to not grin but he remained expressionless and continued to listen. Of course, he already knew this before even entering the store. Jorge Hernandez did his homework.

"We pay," The man pointed toward the room behind him. "We pay to go, like other customers but the girls, they give a sample of their work then give out business cards at same time."

Jorge stopped for a moment to think and finally backed away from the counter.

"So that's how you make your real money," Jorge asked and realized that perhaps this Korean man and himself weren't so different. Although prostitution wasn't his thing, it was clear that the store owner wasn't opposed to less scrupulous pursuits. "And this place, covers your tracks?"

"It is a legit business," The man confessed what Jorge had suspected. Clearly, he had no pride in the shop, the place wasn't exactly well maintained or cared for but merely a cover.

"What if I can make you a deal that your girls can come in my club without hanging on to this store?" Jorge asked. "Would you sell then?"

The Korean considered it for a moment and slowly nodded. "But, I am not sure how. I do not want trouble with the government."

"Believe me," Jorge met him halfway on that one. "No one wants to deal with the fucking government. We're all in agreement on that one."

The Korean shook his head.

"Ok, leave this with me," Jorge thought for a moment. "I will figure out something for you."

A customer walked in the store for the first time since their arrival, just as Jorge and Chase headed for the door.

"We will be in contact, *amigo*, we will be in touch."

Outside, Jorge merely exchanged looks with Chase as they walked next door to the club, neither saying a word until they got inside. The place was always empty during the day, no staff necessary until about an hour before it opened and it only opened on nights when events were scheduled.

"So, he has his whores at our parties giving out cards," Jorge said as they walked toward the bar. "Normally, I wouldn't be happy about that but it does tell me that he's a man I can work with."

"I'm surprised he even told us," Chase commented as he started to make a pot of coffee.

"He was trying to tell us more than about his girls," Jorge shrugged as he sat on a stool and Chase went behind the bar. "He's trying to say 'I know you're a fucking criminal and so am I'. Maybe cause he wants to work together. I don't really blame him for sending them either, at the end of the day, they pay their fees to come in the door and probably help make the events more enticing to our customers. Maybe there is a way he can continue to do that without the hassle of that fucking store."

"I always wondered how those little stores actually made money," Chase commented as the coffee started to brew. "Especially that one, no one is ever there."

"Except, I'm guessing, horny men who want to be jerked off in the back," Jorge finished his bag of chips and leaned over the bar to throw it in the garbage before sitting back down. "He's a pimp. Probably girls new to this country or illegals hiding out. I knew girls like that when I was in California."

"Why don't they just try to immigrate here?"

"You need money, *amigo*, a lot of money," Jorge told him. "It's not cheap. Your government, they make a lot of money off people desperate to live here so that they can turn around and pay for social programs for your people who've been here for generations, but for some reason, can't seem to find a job."

"That's an interesting way to look at it." Chase grinned and nodded.

"Your people got the advantage of speaking English, being born into a rich country with so many opportunities but it's never enough for some," He waved his hand in the air. "Immigrants come here, can't speak a word of fucking English, start a business and work every day of their lives and make it work. Doesn't make sense to me, you know?"

"True but not all Canadians are like that," Chase reminded him. "There's a lot that works very hard and makes a life for themselves."

"Yes, but there are many that complain that us immigrants come here and take their jobs," Jorge reminded him. "Me, I make jobs for Canadians and our Korean friend next door, do you think he's in a business that everyone wants? How many people want to work every day just to keep a business going? I do not understand."

"I never think of immigrants taking our jobs," Chase admitted. "That's pretty negative."

"That's cause you're not a racist," Jorge commented and raised his eyebrows. "The other day, when Paige and I were registering for our marriage license, it should've been easy. We bring in our paperwork, we show identification, that is all. We did so but the woman behind the counter looked at me suspiciously when she read the form. It has one section asking your previous province or address and of course, mine is Mexico and I haven't been here long."

"But it wouldn't matter because marrying here doesn't automatically make you a citizen," Chase pointed out. "So it's not like you are faking the marriage to get into the country."

"No but people, they still see it that way," Jorge pointed out as the aroma of coffee filled the room. "They do not believe that love happens fast because they perhaps have never felt real love at all."

"I can see that," Chase agreed as he patiently watched the coffee pot as it filled to the top and quickly poured them each a cup. Passing Jorge his, Chase reached into the mini fridge under the counter and sat a carton of cream on the bar. "We live in a cynical world."

"There is certainly a lot of reasons to be cynical these days," Jorge commented and poured some cream into his coffee, grabbing a straw from behind the counter, he slowly stirred it. "But it is important that we do not allow this to be our focus. There are a lot of beautiful things in the world and *that* should be our focus. For me, I have Paige, I have a daughter, I have money and success. That is all I think about. That is my focus. It's very simple."

"I struggle with it," Chase admitted as he poured cream in his own coffee, he reached for a straw to mix it. "Especially this time of the year."

"Chase, the death of your son," Jorge shook his head and attempted to pick the right words even though nothing felt suitable. "It will always be a hole in your heart, I'm afraid, it will not go away. Every day, it will be there and this time of year, it will be a reminder of that day. That terrible day when you received the news. But you cannot, you should not, let it be your focus. You have two healthy sons, no?"

Chase quietly nodded, his eyes downcast.

"That should be your focus," Jorge insisted. "Don't get me wrong, if anything ever happened to either Paige or Maria, my life, it would be destroyed but I would want my friends to remind me of what I still have. I would want you, *amigo*, to remind me what I have left. After, of course, I find the person responsible and cut them up into tiny pieces, in the most painful way humanly possible."

Chase almost choked on his coffee and it took a minute for Jorge to realize that he was laughing.

"You would do that? You wouldn't just kill them?" Chase appeared intrigued, his eyes gentle and soft, his naïvety shining through.

"Indeed, I would," Jorge admitted. "I would find great pleasure in torturing anyone who ever took my family away. Fortunately, I have two very street savvy, smart women in my life, so I find some comfort in that, of course. Maria, although she is only ten, has much of her father's wisdom and Paige, well, I feel comfortable she can look after herself. Not that I don't worry but again, I cannot let this be at the forefront of my mind."

"When did you decide you would help with Luke Prince," Chase asked and took a drink of his coffee. "I mean, when did you decide that you would help Diego and Jolene?"

"Diego," Jorge started and pulled his cigarettes out of his pocket and removed one from the pack. "He told me your story. He told me what happened, about his trip with you to Hennessey and about Luke Prince. And there was something inside of me, a little fire sparked as soon as he started to speak and by the time our conversation had ended, I could not say no. I wanted to, of course, meet with you but I already knew what had to be done. I've rarely had Diego ask me to help him with anything that was more of a personal matter. Not in all the years I have known him, has he ever come to me with such desperation so when he did, I must say yes."

"Of course, I did not know you then like I do now," Jorge hesitated to light up his cigarette after inhaling, his body immediately relaxing, he continued. "I am glad I said yes. As Diego would say, we are family."

Chase didn't reply but his face filled with appreciation, so it was not necessary.

CHAPTER 34

Jorge got the store. Not that he ever thought he wouldn't but he assumed that it might get a bit messy along the way. Fortunately, the Korean wasn't much interested in customer service and grew tired of the headaches that came with owning a business. The word retirement had a ring to it, especially when offered an exceptional amount of money in exchange.

"His wife probably told him to take the deal and run," Jorge commented over dinner with Chase and Diego a few days later. Jolene was 'unavailable' and although Jorge said nothing when told this, his suspicions continued to mount. He had another idea on how to learn what was going on with her.

"It was the smart thing to do," Chase commented as he glanced over his menu and sat it down. "You certainly offered him a lot of money."

"Plus the man was as old as balls," Jorge informed Diego, who was squinting over his menu. "Although I'm guessing he still had better eyesight than you, Diego."

"My eyesight is fine," Diego commented as he held the menu away from him. "They just make the print on these things so small and with all the colors on the menu, I don't know." He shook his head as though it were the menu's fault. "I guess I'll get the BLT and a salad."

"Don't tell me," Jorge shrugged and narrowed his eyes. "I'm not your fucking waitress."

"I'm just saying," Diego glared at him as he pushed his menu aside. "I don't see much that appeals to me."

"It's a family restaurant," Chase commented and glanced toward their waitress, who was taking an order at another table. "They have a bit of everything on the menu."

"Yes, some Italian, some Chinese and some Mexican," Jorge commented as the waitress finished at the other table and started over. "I can't wait to see what my taco bowl looks like."

After the waitress took their orders and left, Jorge continued to discuss business before the food arrived and everyone got off track.

"I spoke with my contacts in BC and they are very excited about this business venture with us," Jorge commented as he glanced around the bland restaurant on a quiet Tuesday evening. "When I told them how lucrative my other businesses were here in the city, they were quite happy to get involved. We have different ideas on how we will go ahead but I'm still not certain if I want to carry the edibles as well as the various strains. This here is surprisingly a new world to me. I spent almost 20 years dealing mostly with cocaine. I mean, not exclusively, things change throughout the years but for the most part, that has been my main concentration."

"So are you not dealing with that at all anymore?" Chase asked as the waitress approached with their drinks. Chase had a cup of coffee while Jorge and Diego each had a glass of wine. After thanking the waitress, Jorge had hoped to answer Chase's question but instead waited for Diego to flirt with the waitress, who oddly seemed intrigued by his attention. After she was out of earshot, Jorge turned to Diego with a skeptical expression.

"Why do you do that?" Jorge shrugged. "Are you just gay sometimes or are you bisexual? What's the deal with all the flirting you do with women?"

"*Amigo*, we've known each other for years," Diego narrowed his eyes and took a drink of wine. "You *know* I'm gay."

"Then why?"

"It's fun," He shrugged and twisted his lips into an odd shape. "It's nice. People feel nice when you flirt with them."

"You obviously do not understand why people flirt, Diego," Jorge shook his head and focused his attention back on Chase. "To answer your question, yes, I am still involved but not in the day-to-day stuff. There's a man who has taken over so I can concentrate on marijuana. My boss has invested greatly in this BC operation, enabling them to expand even more and of course, pay off the right government officials to make sure we don't have any trouble. In a way, we give them peace of mind as much as money. They, in turn, have some Mexicans working for them, it's a good arrangement. Jesús is there now to learn the process."

"So the store, when are we taking it over?" Diego asked and tapped his finger on the table.

"It will take some time," Jorge shrugged. "Meanwhile, it gives me time to figure out exactly how we should proceed. Chase is doing some research for me to help us decide on the best approach."

Diego nodded and turned to watch the waitress as she approached with their food. Chase got a salad and chicken, Diego a sandwich and salad whereas Jorge thanked the waitress and looked down at his taco bowl. Nodding his head and raising his eyebrows, he grinned as he looked at the restaurant's version of Mexican food. "Interesting," his comment was dismissive while beside him, Diego grinned.

Jorge focused on his drink and wondered how he could find out where Jolene was that evening but then again, he suspected that if he asked Diego that he wouldn't know either. Also, he didn't want to seem too obvious.

"How are things at the office, Diego?" Jorge decided on this approach and see where it led. "Everything running smoothly?"

"Ah, you know, the usual," Diego spoke and shrugged. "Bickering with the staff, it's like working with a group of children sometimes but Jolene doesn't put up with it. Neither do I, but she's more tactful."

"Is the work getting done?" Jorge reluctantly dug into his food, surprised that he found it enjoyable although, not even comparable to *real* Mexican food.

"Yes."

"That is the main thing," Jorge commented and thought for a moment. "You mentioned hiring another party planner. If you do, it is very important to be careful and research their background. We do not want to get the wrong person at the office."

"I research them all," Diego commented casually as he took a bite out of his sandwich. "Chase does the usual, reference checks and that kind of thing, I go a little deeper into things with more thorough background checks.

Jorge nodded and thought as he continued to eat his food. Three bites in and he was already getting heartburn.

"We must continue to be careful," Jorge reminded him. "Never lower our defenses. If anything seems suspicious to either of you, come to me first. I want to know."

The waitress returned to see how the food was and Jorge lied and said great. It was just ok. However, the waitress earned minimum wage and didn't care and at the end of the day, neither did Jorge.

After she left, he turned his attention to Chase and asked him the same question as Diego and he also talked about the usual employee issues but didn't seem to have any major concerns. Jorge continued to think how he could bring up Jolene's name but, as it turns out, he didn't have to because Diego did it for him.

"I'm sorry Jolene couldn't be bothered to show up tonight," His comment was full of frustration but it was one that only Diego seemed to allow himself to use. If anyone else were to speak poorly of Jolene he would grow defensive and protective. It was best to just listen and ask the right questions. "She's been tied up lately. I think maybe a new boyfriend."

"Oh really?" Jorge asked with a serious expression on his face. "Too busy getting dick to bother with us now?"

"I don't know," Diego shook his head. "She's being rather secretive."

"Isn't Jolene always secretive?" Chase asked and Jorge simply followed along in the discussion.

"Yeah, this is true," Diego agreed. "Even I, her brother, doesn't always know what is going on with her life. She hides everything from me too."

"Really?" Jorge was careful not to push. "I just assumed you two were always close. No?"

Diego shrugged and seemed to consider the question as he chewed his food. "Not really actually, she doesn't tell anything."

"Maybe she's afraid you will tell everyone," Jorge calmly observed, knowing that Diego enjoyed gossiping. "You're like one of those old women that used to sit in my village as a child, watching everyone in the neighborhood and then getting together to talk about it."

Chase laughed. Diego gave him a dirty look.

"Ok, I'm not that bad," Diego insisted. "I wouldn't gossip about her but she doesn't tell me anything. She likes to hide her whole life. She could be married with three kids for all I know."

"Oh really?" Jorge acted uninterested.

"Yes, since she was younger," Diego commented and stopped eating for a moment. "She had a troubled past in Colombia so I guess that makes her not talk so much. I don't know. I was already in America at that time. We didn't talk much back then. She was still in good with our parents and they had nothing to do with me."

"I think we all had trouble in our past," Jorge observed.

"True," Diego tilted his head back and forth, followed by a shrug. "I think she got mixed up with the wrong people, you know?"

"Are we not the *wrong* people?" Jorge asked and took a drink of his wine.

"Different kind of wrong people," Diego commented. "I'm not really sure of all the details but she was really anxious to get out of Colombia and at the time, I asked a lot of questions but she wasn't telling me anything."

Jorge considered who, in Colombia would be considered the wrong people. The answers he found were definitely unsavory but he didn't reply.

"Anyway, as for now," Diego returned to the present in his story. "I don't know. I do think she has a boyfriend but I don't know who or the details."

"What makes you think she has a boyfriend?" Jorge continued to show little interest as if he was humoring Diego during the conversation.

"I don't know, I guess I just have that sense that she's seeing someone," Diego shrugged. "She seems different lately. I guess I assumed that's why."

Glancing toward Chase, Jorge noted that he was avoiding the conversation altogether, something that made him more suspicious.

Either he was the boyfriend or he knew something. Jorge hated the idea that he couldn't direct the questions he wanted to ask at either of them but to do so would be like walking on eggshells. He would work on Chase alone, at another time.

"Where's Paige tonight?" Diego suddenly changed the topic. "Why didn't she join us?"

"Cause she doesn't work with us," Jorge commented as if it were the most obvious answer. "She took Maria to see a movie. That child is so busy with school lately that I insisted that she had a fun night to do something besides school work or all the extra curricular activities that she does."

"We have a coffee date next week," Diego blurted out with excitement in his voice. "Paige and me, we are going on a coffee date."

"You do realize that a date is something between two people who have a romantic relationship, not so much friends," Jorge felt himself losing grip when Diego so casually spoke about spending time with Paige. It wasn't that he had an issue with it but he was starting to resent any attention his fiancée received from other men. He knew that it wasn't logical to feel that way but his love for her made him feel so incredibly vulnerable as if it could, at any moment, be ripped away. He wasn't used to being insecure.

"No, there are dates that are much more innocent in nature," Diego insisted as if he were teaching him the Canadian ways. "Right, Chase?"

"I'm not getting into this," Chase immediately answered and continued to concentrate on his food.

"It's just coffee," Diego insisted and continued to work on his last nerve. "It's not like she's going to fall in love with me, beg me to be straight and have my children."

Jorge scratched his face and attempted to hide his frustration. If he was this angry with Diego, a gay man who only wanted Paige's friendship, how would he ever handle other men who lusted after her? Love; it brought out a man's best and worst sides. A beautiful light that shined even in cloudy skies and an unmistakable vulnerability that could shake up your world and show you a side of yourself, you had never expected to find.

CHAPTER 35

"This is a lot of money," Marco looked uncertain as he glanced in the envelope before looking back across the table at Jorge. The aroma of bacon filled the air while the clatter of dishes and chatter in the restaurant almost made Marco's low voice inaudible. Glancing side to side, as if to make sure that no one saw him receiving this much cash, he carefully slid it into his pocket. Of course, there was nobody near them at the back booth, Jorge had made sure of it. "Are you sure Mr. Hernandez?"

"I am sure," Jorge glanced up from the menu and took a drink of his coffee as he recognized appreciation in Marco's eyes. There was something about rewarding someone who actually showed gratitude that always delighted him, especially after spending so many years dealing with people who expected and demanded, it was a nice change of pace. There was a certain innocence in this man reminding him a bit of Chase, which in turn made him trustworthy. "You helped me out."

"Oh, but sir, I wasn't much help at all I'm afraid," Marco appeared troubled. "I try to find more but I was not successful."

"You were a help and deserve a reward," He shifted his attention toward the approaching waitress. After taking their orders and she walked away, Jorge quickly continued. "The thing is, I might need you for something else. I have another person's email that might need hacking."

"Ok, I can try, is it personal or business?"

"I have both, actually," Jorge reached into his pocket and pulled out a piece of paper with Jolene's email addresses on it. "The top one is work, the second is personal."

"Ok, I can try but what would you like me to look for?" Marco replied as he glanced at the piece of paper. "Is there anything specific?"

"In her personal emails, send me everything but not say, her latest Amazon order or daily newsletter for anything. Work wise, I think maybe everything, just to be on the safe side, from June forward," Jorge thought for a moment. "But, I'm wondering if there's a better solution. You're an IT expert and this business here," Jorge pointed toward the piece of paper, "I'm an investor. I wonder if maybe you would be interested in a job? Help them with our website?"

"Really?" Marco looked intrigued with this suggestion. "Where is this, you are speaking of?"

"Diego and Jolene Inc," Jorge replied as he saw the waitress heading in their direction with two plates of food. His stomach instantly growled as soon as the plate of bacon, eggs, and toast was placed before him. After they both thanked the waitress, Marco having the same meal, Jorge immediately started to dig in and tried to regain his train of thought.

"I don't know if I have heard of this business," Marco commented as he picked up his fork and reached for his eggs. "What is it?"

"That's the thing," Jorge replied as he chewed his food and after swallowing, he answered. "They are party planners. Specifically, they plan sex parties."

Marco's eyes widened but he didn't say anything.

"Don't worry, the site, it is legal," Jorge answered the question that was most likely on Marco's mind. "It's not like a porn site or anything, just a basic site where you can sign up to go to one of their parties or request a private party, that kind of thing."

"I think I have heard of this company," Marco commented and showed no sign of judgment. "It is, maybe in the newspaper?"

"Yes, a lot of religious groups are always trying to shut them down," He pulled out his iPhone and looked up the site and reconsidered his last comment. "Not that they can, the business is stable and growing but they're supposedly concerned with the morals and whatever religious people care about."

"Modern religion," Marco commented. "It is often focused on the wrong things, I feel. It should be about kindness and love but it is often about attacking others and this, I do not believe in."

"I'm with you there," Jorge commented and turned his phone around so that Marco could see the site.

"Oh yes, ok, I see," Marco slid his finger over the screen. "This could be so much better, I think."

"That's what I want," Jorge commented as he placed the phone on the table and reached for his toast. "Would you be interested in working for us? I can promise that whatever you make now, it will be better."

"In my true profession?" Marco asked with excitement in his eyes. "Oh yes, I would love. I have tried to find a job here since we move but the best I can do is at the hotel. My English at first, it was not good so that made it more difficult."

"Well, you would be working with two Colombians and this lady," Jorge pointed toward the scribblings on the piece of paper. "Her English is broken. So this, it would not be an issue with us. I will talk to them today and see what they think. I know that they have a freelancer for IT but we need a more consistent person available to us."

"I can do that sir, no problem," Marco spoke excitedly. "Day or night, I can be there anytime."

"Nighttime, only if the site crashes or whatever," Jorge commented as he waved his hand in the air, unsure of the terminology. He could use the Internet and a computer but he wasn't exactly savvy in the area. "But we will need to update and maybe you can see a better way to do things than we can."

"I will," Marco continued to smile, no longer touching his food. "I can do anything you need."

"What I need is for you to hack Jolene's account," Jorge said and raised his eyebrows before biting into his toast. "I'm assuming it would be easier if you work with her."

"Exceptionally so," Marco confirmed and slowly started to eat again, almost as if he was still in shock over the job offer. "Most companies, people do not know but their management spy on their emails to make sure their employees are trustworthy and handling company business properly. So this will be easy, I can check any emails you wish at that company."

"*Perfecto!*" Jorge replied with a laugh. "That's exactly what I want to hear, Marco. Spy the fuck out of them and I basically bought and paid for those offices so, at the end of the day, you work for me."

Marco began to laugh and started to choke on a slice of bacon and quickly took a drink of his water. "Whatever you say, boss."

"Also, you will be helping with the website for the nightclub we own, where most of these parties take place," Jorge added and reached for his phone, looking up the website for JD Exclusive Club and turned the phone around for him to see. "It could probably use some work too. Chase Jacobs runs this place and he also has bands a couple of times a week, that kind of thing."

"I see, yes, that is fine," Marco nodded as he gave it a quick look. "Whatever you wish for me to do."

Jorge nodded with a grin on his face. Perfect.

The meeting ended on a good note and Jorge promised to get back to Marco later that day, the following day at the latest, once he had time to talk to Jolene, Chase, and Diego. Unfortunately, catching up to all three appeared to be a challenge. He texted them all with the news that he found someone who would be perfect for the IT and only Chase responded. That somehow didn't surprise him. Eventually, Jolene did as well and the three agreed to meet late afternoon at the club. Frustrated that Diego wasn't replying, Jorge sent him one last text telling him to meet them at 4 to discuss important work business.

Jolene and Jorge were sitting down across from Chase at his desk later that afternoon when Diego came flying in the room, a small, white box in his hand.

"I'm here!" He announced with great triumph as if the world had stopped without him, causing Jorge to shoot him a dirty look. "But, I brought us a treat."

He sat the white box on the desk and opened it up to show a box of pastries. "I was at this quaint little coffee shop with Paige earlier and when I noticed your text, I thought you guys had to try these. They are *divine*." He pointed toward the box, his lips curled up in a pucker.

"You were with Paige," Jorge asked, feeling his anger build up.

"Yes, we had our coffee *date*," Diego seemed to emphasize the last word and Jorge immediately knew it was to antagonize him. "I didn't see the message because I think it's rude to check your phone when you're out with a *friend* having coffee. So I didn't look until we were finishing up."

"Even when it's work related and has to do with your business?" Jolene snapped, much to Jorge's surprise. "Diego, I am sure she would not care if you check your messages."

He didn't reply, merely shrugging as he reached into the box for a pastry and Chase soon followed.

"Whatever, can we just start," Jorge snapped and reluctantly reached for a pastry, as did Jolene. He hated to admit it, even to himself, but it was quite delicious. "Look, I got an IT guy that would be perfect for both the website. I know you have someone adding information to the sites now but we need someone who can fix things, update stuff, whatever the fuck they do to make it look nice."

"We just got The Italian adding to the site but she doesn't know IT," Diego offered. "She is hardly an expert."

"Sylvana," Jolene corrected him. "Her name is Sylvana and she is our marketing department, she does not have time for this website stuff."

"Whatever," Diego spoke dismissively and waved his left hand in the air, while his right held the pastry. "I agree, we need someone who we can rely on to take care of issues that keep coming up, change things, you know, techy stuff."

"Well, we are in luck, I found someone who can do *techy stuff*," Jorge attempted to mock Diego but it seemed to go over his head. "He can do it all. I have checked him out, his references are great, he wants to work, I think it's perfect. I told him I would let him know today, tomorrow."

"What is his name?" Jolene asked and turned toward Jorge.

"Marco Rodel Cruz."

"Español?" Jolene asked in a hoarse voice that was actually quite sexy.

"No, he's from the Philippines," Jorge replied.

"Immigrant?" She continued to purr and at this point, he was sensing it was on purpose. Was she trying to seduce him? Her eyes were innocently roaming over his face and although he hated to admit it, his dick wasn't immune to this attention.

"Yes," Jorge replied and looked away. This wasn't good. It wasn't good at all, Jolene was very sexy but he wasn't about to break his commitment to Paige to have an affair. What started off with arousal quickly turned to anger when he realized that she was attempting to manipulate him, once again proving that she was guilty of something.

"Look, Jolene," He snapped and she immediately shifted gears, her look of seduction quickly turned to one of shock. "What difference where the fuck he's from? He can do the job and we need him."

"Ok, you do not have to bite my head off," Jolene snapped back. "I just ask a question."

"And Diego is right, your English is terrible," He complained, feeling the need to send her a strong message. "It's not professional."

"Right?" Diego shot out on the other side of Jolene, his head popped out from around the lone woman in the room, his eyes bugged out as he looked in Jorge's direction. "That's what I keep telling her."

"You guys, you do not have to be mean," Jolene complained and looked as if she was fighting back tears.

"Just forget it," Jorge insisted and jumped up. "I gotta go, my daughter is getting home from school and I need to talk to her about something. You guys, I will tell him he has the job and Diego, I will have him contact you and you can set things up."

Diego nodded and finished his pastry.

Jorge pointed toward Chase, who hadn't said anything throughout the meeting.

"Do you have anything to add, Chase?"

"Nope."

"Anyone else?" Jorge glanced at them all, Jolene's face was full of anger as she shook her head and Diego, on the other side of her appeared more casual.

"Diego, thanks for the pastries, they were…. good." He started toward the door.

"*Divine,*" Diego corrected him.

"Whatever, Diego," Jorge called back on his way out as he dug in his pocket for a cigarette. "Divine."

Outside, he felt his head swirl and for a moment, he thought it was just the stress of the meeting until he realized that everything was spinning. Closing his eyes, he rested a hand against the side of the building and waited for it to pass.

CHAPTER 36

One minute he was talking to his daughter about her day and the next, Jorge was attempting to steady himself as the entire room went black. It only lasted a few seconds but both Maria and Paige were insistent that he go to the hospital. Jorge attempted to brush it off but it wasn't a battle he would win and so, with much reluctance, he agreed to spend his evening sitting in a waiting room full of patients. If there was a doctor working, he certainly wasn't working too fast.

"I thought Canada had one of the best medical systems in the world," Jorge grumbled after the second hour of waiting, his eyes fixated on the television across the room, as a terrible all-news channel repeated the same stories over and over. Glancing around at all the other miserable faces, he quickly observed that this program wasn't exactly bringing much comfort to anyone else either.

"We do," Paige quietly commented. Placing her hand on his arm as if to subdue him. Jorge turned to his other side to see Maria staring at him with her big, brown eyes and it broke his heart. She thought he was really sick. He was fine. "You got to wait your turn."

"I don't understand," Jorge complained. "Why can't I just pay someone and get through faster? Don't you have that here?"

"Papa, you must be patient," His daughter seemed unusually calm. "They take care of emergencies first."

He briefly considered faking a heart attack to get immediate service but not wanting to scare his daughter, pushed the idea out of his head.

"I feel fine now," Jorge insisted. "In fact, I've felt fine for the last hour and forty-five minutes, so let's go home."

"You looked terrible at the apartment," Paige reminded him. "You should get checked out."

"Papa, Paige is right," Maria quickly backed her up. "You did not look well. You can't die too."

Her last comment tore a piece out of his heart and he immediately leaned over and kissed her on the head. "I'll be fine, come on. I was probably just dehydrated or something. I remember one time...»

That's when they called his number. He had never jumped out of a chair so fast! Following a young woman to a small room, she proceeded to ask his symptoms.

"Look, I just had a couple of dizzy spells but my fiancée and daughter were worried," He attempted to brush it off, hoping she would tell him that they were both being irrational but she didn't appear convinced and instead insisted on taking his blood pressure.

"I've never had any health issues before..." He insisted while removing his jacket and rolling up his sleeve.

"You're 44, Mr. Hernandez?" She asked and he cringed a little when she repeated his age and nodded. "Then there's a chance it could be something developing. Sometimes we don't have issues when we are young and things start showing up in our 40s and 50s."

"I'm in great shape," Jorge insisted as the nurse wrapped a blood pressure contraption around his arm. "I'm not overweight. I go to the gym a few times a week, lift weights."

"That helps," She started to take his blood pressure and he remained silent. "It's a little high."

"I've been sitting in a waiting room for a while getting anxious, that's probably why." He commented with a casual shrug.

"It could be," The nurse replied and jotted something in his chart. "Do you smoke?"

"Yes, but I'm trying to quit."

"How is that going?"

"Not well," He replied sheepishly. "I'm only doing it cause my daughter wants me too."

"Drink?"

"Yes."

"How often and appropriately how much?"

"Most days, I probably have a drink," Jorge commented with a shrug.

"Drugs?"

"No," He wasn't about to tell her about his cocaine fuelled past.

"Your weight seems good, how is your diet?"

"I don't know," Jorge replied. "I eat everything."

"Sugar? salt?"

"Yes."

"So, for example, what did you eat today?"

Jorge thought a moment. It had been such a long day but he remembered it started with a meeting with Marco. "Bacon, 3 eggs, toast and hash browns for breakfast. I think I skipped lunch because breakfast was late since I had to rush my daughter to school because she overslept and so then I had a pastry at a meeting. I think that was late in the afternoon and when I got home, I was having a beer and thinking about cooking a steak for dinner."

"Do you eat vegetables?"

"Sure, sometimes," Jorge shrugged. "Potato, that's a vegetable, right? I eat the fried kind."

"I mean, like salads, tomatoes, that kind of thing?"

"Sometimes."

"You might want to add them to your diet," She commented. "Do you have much stress? It sounds like you are quite busy."

"I'm up early and I'm usually going all day," Jorge commented and was starting to enjoy all this attention. He hadn't however, considered his lifestyle until that moment. "Look, I invest in businesses and have a lot of meetings and problems to figure out. I just moved to Canada and got engaged. My daughter's mother recently died, followed by her grandparents and she just switched schools after getting caught bringing a knife to school and I don't know what day it is today, other than it is a weekday. So yeah, I guess I might be stressed."

He hadn't added that he was almost killed a few weeks earlier but judging by the nurse's expression, she got the picture.

"I would say," She nodded and jotted something in his file before closing it. "The doctor will be here shortly."

Walking out of the room, she placed the file outside the door. He was curious what the nurse had written on his chart and was about to go look when the doctor walked in. An older white man, probably close to 60 with little hair and tired eyes smiled as he entered the room with the file in his hand.

"Mr. Hernandez," He glanced at the papers inside. "I see you're having some dizziness."

"Not a lot, just some," Jorge replied as the doctor sat down and glanced at his file. "And your blood pressure is elevated and looks like you have a great deal of stress, smoking…oh, that's not good. There are a few factors here that concern me. I would like you to get some blood work done to be safe."

"So, I'm fine?"

"I wouldn't go that far," The doctor closed his folder and glanced at him. "The problem is that things like smoking, drinking, our choices of food, they don't affect us so much when we are young but as we age, our body starts to grow weary of all the sugar, the salt, it can't handle the smoking and drinking as it did before."

"I'm trying to quit smoking."

"When did you start?"

"When I was 12," Jorge replied.

"That's a lot of years of smoking," The doctor commented. "That along with everything else isn't doing your body any favors. Our bodies are like cars. When they are brand new, the salt on the road doesn't hurt them, skipping regular maintenance isn't such a big deal but as they age, all the things we've neglected over time start to work against them. Suddenly rust develops, damages due to neglect, that kind of thing. I would recommend you quit smoking as soon as possible. Do you tend to smoke more at certain times? When you're stressed?"

"Definitely when I'm stressed," Jorge replied. "The second things get stressful, I'm craving a cigarette."

"The thing is that you feel it relaxes you but it's actually doing your body more harm than good," The older man commented. "I will send you for some tests and meanwhile, maybe it's time you take a closer look at your lifestyle. There's a chance you might have to be on medication if you don't change some of your habits or even worse, you will develop some serious conditions. High blood pressure can lead to a heart attack if left."

Jorge nodded and sighed. He knew he was right.

"Ok then," The doctor scribbled something on a piece of paper and handed it to him. "Have a good night, Mr. Hernandez."

Then he was gone. Jorge stood up and suddenly felt helpless. What if he had developed an illness, right when his life was getting better? A great love, a great daughter, a new country? It was certainly a wake-up call.

Paige and Maria immediately jumped up when they saw him returning to the waiting room. He waved the sheet around.

"I have to get some tests in the morning."

"What did the doctor say?" Paige asked.

"That I have to quit smoking," He glanced toward his daughter who gave him a look. "I know, Maria, you've been telling me that forever but he made me see what could happen if I don't quit. My blood pressure is a little high but I think that's from sitting here waiting all night. Anyway, he said I have too much stress and might have to change my diet."

"You do eat a lot of...everything," Paige commented.

"But I don't understand," Jorge commented, tapping a hand on his belly as they walked toward the exit. "I'm in shape. I'm not fat."

"That doesn't mean you are healthy, Papa," Maria reached up and held his hand as they walked toward his SUV. "We've been learning about this kind of thing in health class. Sugar, it is really bad and so is salt. I was telling the class how you ate all this bad stuff plus smoked and..."

"Wait, what?" Jorge stopped in the middle of the parking lot. "Maria! You cannot talk about your family in class. That is private matters. How many times must we have this discussion?"

"But Papa, we had to use real examples from our life," His daughter was insistent. "I didn't say your name or anything."

"You make sure of that," Jorge commented and still didn't feel comfortable with what she had shared. "Our lives, we must keep private."

"I know," Maria gloomily replied and yawned. "I'm hungry, can we get something on the way home?"

"Ah yes, I could use a burger and fries now," He replied as his stomach rumbled.

"Do you need to be fasting before your test in the morning."

Jorge glanced at the piece of paper in his hand.

"Fuck!" He immediately clamped his mouth shut. Paige hid her grin and Maria gave him a wide-eyed look.

"I'll fix you something at the apartment," Paige directed her comment at Maria. "I somehow don't think it would be a good idea to have the smell of food in the SUV on the way home."

"That is fine," Maria replied. "I have a salad in the fridge from yesterday that I didn't finish."

It wasn't until after they were back at the apartment and Maria was in her room finishing homework that Paige slid next to him on the couch.

"I think this is a warning sign," She spoke in a low voice. "You have to start taking better care of yourself."

"I know," Jorge replied. "It's not fair. You live a certain way for years and suddenly, you can't anymore."

"I think stress is a big factor here," Paige commented as her hand slid over his chest as if in attempts to protect his heart. "How often do you have fun?"

"Fun?" Jorge thought for a moment. "Smoking and drinking are fun to me but apparently, they aren't acceptable. I like sex, at least I'm allowed to still do that."

"Maybe not if you get high blood pressure and have to start taking a bunch of pills," Paige casually mentioned as her hand continued to sit on his chest.

"Wait, what?" Jorge suddenly was very alert when he realized she was talking about impotence. "I thought that was just something old men got. I mean, there was a one time when I was doing a lot of coke, but…"

"No, high blood pressure, various medications, smoking, a lot of these things cause it and then you'll need a pill for that."

"Ah, I don't fucking think so," Jorge commented. "Sex is all I got left and shooting people, at least I'm still allowed to do that."

Paige laughed and he joined her.

"Maybe you need to expand your hobbies," Paige commented. "Learn a new sport or something. Hey, didn't you say Chase was a boxer? Maybe take up boxing?"

"You want me to be buff like him," Jorge joked but secretly, the jealousy and fear crept in and he bit back from saying more while she laughed. "That Marco guy, he does a knife fighting martial art thing. Maybe I will look into that."

"You should, all you do is work," Paige commented.

"I think I'm going to go have my last cigarette," Jorge reached for his pack on the nearby table. "Finally, someone made a compelling argument for me to quit."

Paige nodded and a grin crossed her face. Rising from the couch, Jorge slowly walked toward the balcony with his last cigarette. Life was much more fragile than he wanted to admit.

That's when he remembered the emails he promised to check weeks earlier, but he was already depressed enough. He would check them the next day.

CHAPTER 37

Jorge was once again at the hospital but this time he was waiting to have his blood tests. Glancing around, he noted that everyone looked as depressed as he felt. Of course, the obnoxious child who was munching on a donut in front of a group of people who weren't allowed to eat that morning wasn't exactly enhancing the experience either. The moronic Chinese woman sitting across from him appeared to be the mother, blissfully ignorant to the fact that her daughter was wandering around, dropping pieces of donuts all over the floor. Didn't people look after their children anymore? Maria would not be allowed to do such things. How ignorant was this woman?

Seething and hungry, by the time it was his turn, Jorge half expected his blood to come out boiling as it poured into the clear plastic tubes. After filling about ten of them, he was permitted to leave. He thanked the unfriendly technician then headed out of the hospital and to the nearest restaurant, which turned out to be within close proximity. The businessman in him, as well as his growling stomach, were equally impressed by the location.

He reluctantly ordered an omelet and coffee. Not that he didn't like omelettes but he would've rather some bacon and hash browns dripping in grease and toast loaded up in a sugary concoction that resembled jam. The heavenly smell of fried foods filled the air and caused his stomach to rumble especially when he noticed the old man across from him digging into a huge, hearty breakfast. Bacon. Fried eggs. Grease.

Quickly looking away, he took out his phone to see text messages from both Maria and Paige; the latter warning him to not drive until he ate while his daughter wanted proof he had gone for the blood testing. He awkwardly took a picture of the cotton ball and Band-Aid on his right arm and sent it to her.

The omelet was flavorless but stopped his stomach from rumbling while the next task was to ignore his dire need for a cigarette. As he walked toward his SUV, Jorge noticed a convenience store across the street and stopped for a moment and stared at it. He was so tempted to go buy some cigarettes; how he wanted to feel the pleasure of that first cigarette of the morning. It was exhilarating and relaxing. He somehow doubted that meditating like Paige would have the same effect, regardless of what she tried to tell him.

Getting in the SUV, he felt depressed. Although he promised Paige to go home and check the hacked emails, he just wanted to sleep. He felt no initiative to do anything. Not that there was much to do. Diego would contact him later to let him know what he thought of Marco and his lawyer was taking care of the store sale. The pot from BC was in a truck heading to Toronto. His morning was free.

Back at the apartment, he lay on the couch and flipped through channels on television. Other than the news, everything else was terrible. Programs for children, shitty celebrity based talk shows and soap operas. He turned it off.

Paige texted him again to see how he was feeling.

I'm going to take a nap.

He wasn't successful. Finally, around noon, he drifted off for a few hours and woke up in time to see Paige and Maria walk into the apartment as the smell of chicken followed. Noting the bags that sat on the counter just as Maria rushed over to inspect his Band-Aid and Paige studied him from across the room.

"Have you eaten lately?" She asked while lifting a cooked chicken from the bag. "We grabbed some food on the way home."

"I'm not hungry," Jorge commented, as he gave Maria a quick hug and kiss then grabbed his vibrating phone. Three messages awaited him. "I gotta take these calls."

He slowly rose from the couch and walked into the bedroom, shutting the door behind him. Feeling weak and lifeless, he played them back. One was from Diego, reassuring him that Marco was hired and he was very pleased with the new employee. The second message was Marco, excitedly giving him the news and thanking him again; that lifted his spirits, if even briefly. The third call was from his lawyer saying that they had officially bought the store. That made him happy too, although not as happy as he thought it would.

Texting Diego, he asked Marco's start date. He then texted Marco suggesting they meet and discuss a few things before he started. Tossing the phone on the bed, he decided to take a shower. Thankfully this cramped apartment actually had a bathroom off the master bedroom, so he didn't have to deal with anyone for a few more minutes. He wasn't in the mood to talk to or listen to Paige or Maria, no matter how much he loved them.

The hot water washing over him helped relieve some of his misery. After the shower, he studied his face in the mirror. No longer the young, handsome man of years earlier, he was now starting to look his age. Salt and pepper stubble on his face, along with gray along his temples; not that this bothered him but it was just another reminder that his youth had slipped away. His eyes were tired, weary with small lines forming in the corners, he wondered if he would end up looking as terrible as his father. Of course, the man hardly took care of himself. Still, it was a depressing thought.

Jorge quickly put on some clothes including his favorite Beatles t-shirt before grabbing his phone and opening the bedroom door. Diego sat in the living room, still in his office wear with an empty plate on the table before him, he had both his legs comfortably pulled up on the couch as he had an enthusiastic chat with Paige. Maria did her homework on a nearby chair. They all looked up at him as he walked toward the kitchen.

"Ah, there's the sleepyhead," Diego shot out in his usual obnoxious manner and Jorge didn't reply as he looked in the refrigerator. "Marco is awesome! I just have to tell you."

"He is," Jorge agreed and noted that Paige was giving him a worried look. He ignored it.

"Good looking too," He leaned in toward Paige and she grinned while Maria's head popped up from her book.

"Diego, are you a homosexual?" Her question was blunt and from the kitchen, Jorge cringed as he closed the refrigerator door.

"Maria! You do not ask this kind of things," Jorge quickly corrected her while memories of the obnoxious child from the lab that morning suddenly popped in his head.

"Ah, it's fine," Diego waved his hand in the air and then turned his attention toward Maria, while Paige suppressed a grin. "Yes, I am."

"Ah," Maria appeared intrigued. "So, don't you live with Chase? Does that make him your lover? I thought he was straight or is he bisexual?"

"Maria!" Jorge snapped so loudly this time that everyone jumped. "You do not ask these things!"

"It's fine," Diego put his hand out toward Jorge to indicate for him to calm down while Paige appeared alarmed by his tone, Maria seemed unaffected.

"Papa, I was just asking a question," She innocently commented. "You are cranky because you aren't smoking."

"When was the last time you ate?" Paige stood up. "I can get you something?"

"No, I'm good," He checked his phone and thankfully had a message from Marco that he could meet anytime. "I got to meet someone. I'll get something when I'm out."

As he went back to the bedroom to grab his wallet, he heard Diego answer Maria's intrusive questions.

"No, Chase and I are just friends," He was insistent, even though everyone knew he would sell his soul to the devil to have him as a lover. "He is not gay."

Finding his wallet and shaking his head as the conversation in the next room continued, Jorge walked back through the living room, grabbing his leather jacket on the way.

"I will be back in about an hour," He called out and glumly walked into the hallway. He hadn't noticed but Paige was right behind him. Closing the door, she looked in his eyes.

"Are you ok? You're not...you," She commented carefully and touched his arm.

"I don't feel good," Jorge admitted. "Quitting smoking and avoiding all these foods, I don't know, I guess it started me off on the wrong foot."

"It's going to be fine," Her hand reached for his face and lovingly touched it, a small smile appeared on her lips. "Your body is starting to detox from sugar and cigarettes, so that's probably a big part of it."

"Probably," He shrugged and leaned in to give her a hug. "I'll be back later. I'm going to meet Marco."

"Ok," She gave him a quick kiss and he felt guilty over the concern in her eyes but he couldn't pretend he was fine.

Once in the elevator, he was surprised when a wave of emotion overwhelmed him and for a moment, he thought he was going to pass out. Depression surged through him and he felt powerless to fight against it but instead, he simply allowed it to flow through. It wasn't until he was in his SUV that he wiped his eyes with the back of his hand. It didn't make sense that avoiding cigarettes and the usual food he ate would make him so emotional. This wasn't like him at all. Was there something more serious wrong with him and he just didn't know yet?

Pushing the thought from his head, he mechanically drove to the coffee shop where he usually met Marco. Frustrated to not find a parking space close by, he was forced to walk a distance to get to the shop. Any other day, he wouldn't have cared but this was the one time he had no energy or initiative to move, let alone walk anywhere. Not that he had a choice.

Marco looked enthused to see him although the smile fell from his face when Jorge sat down across from him.

"Mr. Hernandez, you do not look well," His eyes expanded and were full of concern. "Do you want a water?"

"I'm..." Jorge glanced toward the counter and he hesitated. He wasn't fine. "I'm going to get something, I'll be right back."

After ordering a coffee and sandwich on a fancy bread, he sat back down and started to eat.

"I wasn't feeling well last night," He immediately started to explain between bites. "I went to the hospital and anyway, I had to get blood work this morning and basically have to quit salt, sugar, cigarettes and now, I feel like death. I'm not sure how eating healthy is supposed to make me feel better."

"But it will," Marco assured him. "You do not see it yet but it will. I also used to smoke and the first few days after I quit, everything, it annoyed me. My kids, people everywhere, everything piss me off."

"Oh really?" Jorge asked as he continued to bite into his sandwich, he slowly started to feel a little better.

"Oh yes!" Marco's eyes widened as he nodded. "I snap at my kids, my wife, it was bad. I was angry and sad, it was confusing."

"That's the thing, I quit before," Jorge admitted. "I never felt this bad."

"But did you *really* quit?" Marco asked. "Completely?"

"No," Jorge admitted. "I guess not."

"Yes, plus if you also are no longer eating sugar, salt, all of that," Marco repeated what Paige had commented earlier. "Your body, it detoxes from that too."

"Oh fuck!" Jorge grumbled and took a drink of his coffee. "How the hell am I going to get through this?"

"You know, some, they have said that pot helps get them over the first few days," Marco quietly commented. "I do not know if you like such things though."

"I like such things," Jorge perked up when he considered the idea. "I may have to look into that, actually."

"It is an idea," Marco commented casually as if he had no opinion one way or another. "That sandwich looks good, I may have to get one as well."

"I could get you one," Jorge offered, feeling appreciative of their talk. It actually made him feel better.

"No, you've done enough for me," Marco was shyly insistent as he jumped up from his seat and headed toward the counter. By the time he returned, Jorge had almost finished his sandwich and was starting to feel alive again.

"I met with your associate, Mr. Silva today," Marco commented upon sitting back down, he began to eat. "He was quite nice."

"That's good," Jorge nodded. "Did you happen to meet Jolene?"

"Yes, I did and the others," Marco replied wiped his mouth with a napkin. "Everyone seems very nice."

"When do you start?"

"I give the hotel two week notice," Marco replied and thought for a moment. "But I say to Diego that I can start part-time around that schedule now and he said this was ok."

"Good," Jorge nodded. "I'm going to need your help with something else."

"Of course, anything."

"I need you to watch Jolene," His comment was met with a simple nod.

CHAPTER 38

"I wasted all that time only to find out that I'm fine," Jorge griped as him and Paige walked out of the hospital a few days later. It was his third day without cigarettes and although it should've been getting easier, it wasn't. On top of that, he was constantly craving a greasy burger and sugar filled everything. He wasn't sure which was more torturous, leaving the house and passing a restaurant to smell the aroma of grease or staying home and watching television with a million food commercials. No wonder so many people were so fat. If he was able to advertise his drugs like the food pushers sold their product, he would be a billionaire.

"You're not fine," She calmly corrected him. "He said your blood pressure is high."

"Whatever," Jorge shrugged it off. "I'm sure most people's blood pressure is high from time to time."

"He also said your sugar is a bit high and your cholesterol is too." Paige reminded him. "That's *not* fine."

"It is to me," Jorge shrugged as they got in the SUV. "I'm going to start running, you know, more cardio."

"Hmm..."

"I'm not an invalid for fuck sakes," Jorge continued to complain as he started the SUV and shot out of the parking lot. "Fucking doctors, they want you to be sick. I'm not taking any pills either, so he can forget it."

"Maybe you should go to a naturopath," Paige suggested, her voice always so calm and relaxed as opposed to Jorge, who was now chomping on a piece of gum and resented it at the same time. "They don't deal with pills."

"Yeah, sure, make me an appointment," Jorge continued to be short with her even though he knew, none of this was her fault. He felt worse than when he was eating junk and smoking. Wasn't the idea to feel better?

She gave him a look and he sighed.

"I mean, you obviously know someone, that's all," He ran a hand over his face. "I wasn't trying to order you around. Honestly, I don't even care anymore. I never felt worse in my life than I do now and yet, I'm supposedly living a healthier lifestyle. Fuck, I fought a cocaine addiction and I think I felt better than this but then again, I had my junk food and cigarettes back then."

"It hasn't even been a week yet," Paige attempted to comfort him with a small smile. "It's not like you can never eat sugar or salt again it's just that you need to cut back and treat your body better. If you view all this as a punishment and not something you are doing to make yourself healthier than of course, you're going to resent it. I mean, wouldn't you rather turn 50 someday and look and feel better than most men your age?"

"Hey hey, 50!" Jorge complained as he shoved another piece of gum in his mouth. "Let's not talk 50 just yet."

"You know what I mean," Paige insisted. "The quality of your life will increase if you take better care of yourself."

"Look," Jorge began as they stopped at a red light. "If I have a normal breakfast now, are you going to be angry?"

"No, but I would recommend you don't have 3 eggs and extra bacon," She attempted to negotiate.

"Ok, I told you, I don't normally do that," Jorge commented as he eyed a nearby chain restaurant. "And you got to realize, I spent my life in a dangerous profession. The idea of taking care of my health when I could be shot at any time seemed somewhat laughable. It was always a race against time."

"Well either way," Paige quietly replied. "I don't want you to die."

"Baby, I'm not going to die," Jorge insisted. "I'm probably in less danger than ever before."

"That reminds me, did you ever read those emails?" She asked and he immediately cringed. "I didn't think so."

"I don't think there's anything in them," Jorge shrugged as he pulled into the restaurant parking lot. "And I keep forgetting."

"Please, can you check just in case," Paige coaxed as he anxiously swung into a parking space. "Humor me, please."

"I will," Jorge put the SUV into park and looked into her eyes. "Tell me to when we get back to the apartment."

"We have to stop by my place first," She reminded him. "I have a few things I need help moving. Someone is coming to buy my couch tomorrow and maybe the end tables too."

"I'm glad you're moving in soon," Jorge commented and leaned in, giving her a quick kiss before they got out of the SUV. Rushing around, he met her on the other side before heading toward the restaurant. "On Halloween, of all times."

"It seems appropriate considering how we met," Paige teased as they entered the restaurant. He ran his hand over her back as the aroma of bacon filled the air and he took great pleasure breathing it in.

Once seated and they had ordered, he grabbed a napkin and spit out his gum. Looking around the room, he saw only a few other people eating while the sound of 70s music filled the air. Briefly closing his eyes, he took a deep breath while Paige watched him from across the table.

"What are you thinking?"

"I was thinking how everything is coming together," He replied and reached out to touch her hand. "We got the marriage license, the rings, we just have to find a time and place to get married. I'm about to take over ownership of the store. The pot is here, selling like crazy already, even without the store up and running. I have Marco in place at the office to keep an eye on things. Maria's doing great in school and she's actually happy, making friends. All of this and yet, there's a part of me that's always nervous of what's around the corner."

"There's always going to be something around the corner," Paige reminded him in her usual, gentle tone while her eyes studied him carefully. "The key is riding the waves as they come."

The waitress returned with their food and they quietly ate their breakfast. Jorge couldn't remember the last time he enjoyed food so much; had he ever taken the time to notice before, instead of shovelling it in, always in a rush to get to the next thing. The taste, the texture, the smell of the food, it was more fulfilling than it ever had been before and of course, having quit smoking, he already was noticing an improvement in the flavor.

"Someday, once Maria finishes school," Jorge suddenly broke the silence. "I think we should move out of the city. Somewhere quiet. Somewhere that is a bit of a slower pace. Somewhere where no one knows us. Just be together and that's it."

"You mean to retire?"

Jorge laughed. "I guess. I would retire now if I could."

"Would you be able to?" She asked. "You have the money. All you need to do is invest in Jolene and Diego and let them do the work. You don't have to do anything except check things."

"I don't think I can," Jorge admitted. "I got out of coke but pot, it's about to become legal here, so I guess I'm kind of going legal. My boss in Mexico is heavily involved. He believes that this is going to be even more of a cash cow. Depending on how it works out, this could make Canada an even bigger tourist destination, festivals centering on pot, maybe combined with music or whatever. He has so many ideas as do the people in BC. There's much potential to make money and the government should be happy, they make a ton on taxes and it's the government, so they will have so many regulations that there will still be a market for the illegal pot. So in a way, some things will change and some won't. I mean, liquor is legal and yet, there are people who make and sell their own. There's usually an underground side of things, no matter what."

Paige nodded as she considered his words.

"I don't care about any of it anymore," Jorge commented as he finished his breakfast and watched Paige do the same. "I'm tired."

"You need to take more time to relax," Paige quietly suggested as she sipped her coffee. "You're always rushing here and there, with so much going on."

"I know."

Jorge was much more subdued when they left the restaurant. The food satisfied him and for once, he wasn't thinking about having a cigarette after eating. They drove to Paige's apartment in silence and went inside to find it almost empty, other than a few pieces of furniture pulled into the living room. Her bed had been sold the day before and everything else would soon be gone too. He reached for her hand and pulled her close and started to kiss her; gently, carefully, as if nothing else in the world mattered at that moment. The silence was beautiful, endearing and abruptly ended when his phone beeped. Tension filled his body as he moved away from her and pulled it out of his pocket.

"Diego has an emergency," Jorge complained and felt his body immediately tense up again. "Do you want to come with me? Him and Jolene need to see me right away."

"I have a few things I want to take care of here," Paige waved her hands around. "I have to finish packing up the rest of my clothes and make sure everything is clean."

"K," Jorge leaned in and gave her an abrupt kiss before turning to leave. "I will text you when I'm done.

He felt dread fill him in the elevator and by the time he got outside, he was craving a cigarette again. He managed to fight it off with another piece of gum, although barely, he did briefly consider stopping at the small store nearby but changed his mind. That wouldn't help anything.

Arriving at the office a few minutes later, Jorge didn't hide his irritation upon walking in, ignoring the secretary, he made his way directly to Diego's office. Jolene was already there, the two of them quietly talking, they both jumped when he walked in and pushed the door shut.

"What's up?" He asked as he approached and sat down beside Jolene. Diego was leaning against the desk, as usual wearing a suit and tie, his scrawny little body resembling that of a child while his face definitely looked brooding and angry.

"We're fucking being audited," Diego snapped, not attempting to hide his anger. "We just found out today."

"So the books, are they fixed or what?" Jorge asked bluntly and glanced around the room. "Was Clara here today?"

"Yes, we're clean," Diego sniffed and glanced toward Jolene. "I think it was that fucking bitch, Deborah, the one we fired? I think she contacted the government."

"I doubt she will talk after I dealt with her," Jorge commented as he recalled threatening the young woman and throwing her down a stairway a few months earlier. "She won't be talking."

"Sometimes, they do this," Jolene spoke up. "They claim it is random."

"Random, my ass," Diego shot back as his eyes blazed with anger. "We are being targeted."

"It don't matter," Jorge insisted. "If the books look clean, we're fine."

"Benjamin, he takes care of them," Jolene replied. "He say they are squeaky clean. I don't like government, hanging around here."

"No one likes the government hanging around anywhere," Diego insisted while Jorge took in everything, his mind sifting through the information.

"Ok, guys, let's just get through this," He insisted. "We can't stop it but we can make sure that they don't find anything. If Benjamin is thorough this shouldn't be a problem. They aren't going near the club are they?"

"No, just here," Jolene replied. "I do not trust."

"Worst case, they find something," Jorge commented. "But if they do, we will work around it. We got lawyers. Maybe we should call them in case."

"Good point!" Diego nodded. "I still say it's not a coincidence."

"Most things are not," Jolene added.

"When will this take place?"

"On Halloween."

"We got it covered," Jorge insisted and noticed that Diego started to calm. Glancing at Jolene, she appeared more worried. Had she somehow brought this on?

"You guys worry too much," Jorge commented and stood up. "So Benjamin, he can be trusted?"

"Yes," They replied together.

"Ok, I gotta go," Jorge pointed toward the door. "Keep me posted."

With that, he walked out of the office and almost ran into Marco as he walked down the hallway.

"Hello Mr. Hernandez."

"You and I," Jorge quietly spoke with him once they were out of earshot of Diego's office. "We gotta talk. What are you doing later?"

CHAPTER 39

"How was your first day?" Jorge asked Marco as he picked at his bland salad, pushing the sketchy pieces of lettuce aside and deciding to focus more on his sandwich. His appetite had diminished since he cut back on sugar and salt which made him wonder if sugar and salt were like the cocaine of foods; the more you had, the more you wanted. Not that quitting smoking had been a Disney vacation either but at least he had expected that misery. However, as days went by, he was slowly adjusting. Smoking was a crutch for him and the food was the pleasure.

"It was very good," Marco exclaimed with excitement in his voice.

Jorge grinned. You had to love this guy! No one had ever appreciated anything he did for them as much as Marco Rodel Cruz. Even the cup of coffee he bought him when they first arrived at the café was accepted with much gratitude. It was pleasing and gave Jorge a small lift to his otherwise dreary day.

"I talked to Diego and Jolene," Marco continued to speak, "and they have asked everyone at the office to prepare a list of things they would like to see change on the site. Improvements or issues. It was good."

"Not a very big staff, is it?" Jorge commented as he chewed his sandwich.

"No, this is true but it seems, they are good," Marco commented and nodded his head.

"Great," Jorge reluctantly dug into his salad as he watched a white girl with purple hair behind the counter chatting with her co-worker, neither of them appeared too interested in working. What was with this fucking millennial generation? It made him appreciate the fact that

Maria was in a school where they pushed their students hard; he didn't want a slacker for a daughter.

"And so, there was something you wanted to talk to me about," Marco continued as he leaned forward. "Is it with the emails? I didn't have a chance to look today but I see that finding them will not be difficult."

"What I want," Jorge swallowed his food and thought for a moment as he glanced out the window to watch people walking in both directions, traffic flowing and a bus stopping directly in front of the shop, letting out an older lady with a cane. "I want you to change all the passwords that you're currently using for the site. I'm not saying the old IT guy would try to mess with anything but we are about to fire him, so it is better to be safe than sorry. I know he was just a freelancer anyway but you know, we need to be careful."

"No problem," Marco grabbed his phone and tapped on it while Jorge continued to talk.

"Check everyone's emails. If anything seems even slightly personal or suspicious, I would like you to send it to me. Also, we already discussed Jolene's, of course."

'Of course," Marco continued to tap on his phone while nodding.

"I also need you to observe everybody," Jorge continued and tapped his finger on the table. "Give me your observations."

"I can do a little of that now," Marco stopped tapping on his phone and looked up. "I know I do not know them well, but I can try."

"Go ahead."

"I find Beverly nice and Gracie too, she talks a lot to that lady, Sylvana?" Marco wrinkled his forehead. "She is a boss, no?"

"I don't think so," Jorge replied. "Isn't she just the marketing person?"

"She tells me a lot to do," Marco replied and shrugged. "I did not want to cause trouble, so I say, I must first talk to Diego and Jolene about these matters. They are my bosses, right? But she, she seems to think she is too."

"Interesting," Jorge considered and thought for a moment. "Do nothing without Jolene and Diego's instructions first. Sylvana is not your boss."

"She seems very…aggressive," Marco seemed to pick his words carefully causing Jorge to grin.

"There is also the secretary, I cannot remember her name," Marco continued and shrugged. "There are two other party planners that I'm told aren't in the office much because they do stuff out of town."

Jorge nodded and took another bite of his sandwich.

"Benjamin, he does the accounting," Marco continued. "He is Filipino as well, so it was nice to learn about his experience moving here many years ago. He does not say much about anyone and kind of keeps away from the others, does his work."

"That reminds me," Jorge reached for his coffee, leaning forward as he spoke. "We are being audited soon. Let me know if you hear anything about that, however, I'm told Benjamin can take care of everything."

"Oh no," Marco shook his head. "He did seem…nervous today, perhaps that is why?"

"Most likely," Jorge replied and picked up the rest of his sandwich and popped it in his mouth. Thinking for a moment, he finally swallowed his food and pointed toward Marco. "See, I don't spend time there. I don't know any of these people. I only know what Diego and Jolene say but they are the bosses, they do not always hear or see everything. You, however, you will."

Marco nodded in understanding.

"I do trust you," Jorge commented. "If you come to me with something, I will not go back and tell them how I know anything. I will find a way to approach it but this is important, especially now. I do suspect something is going on."

Marco didn't reply and hesitated for a moment, as if unsure if he should say anything.

"I do, I feel that there is some tension between Jolene and this lady, Sylvana," Marco commented as he traced his fingers around the edge of his coffee cup. "I do not know how to explain, I just sensed it today."

"If you just started and you already sense it," Jorge quickly commented. "Then there's something there."

"Yes, perhaps so."

Feeling unsettled with this information, he decided to stop by Diego's place on the way home. Although he could tell that Marco was polite and wasn't about to say as much as he was most likely thinking, Diego wasn't one to hold anything back.

"Come in," Diego waved his arm dramatically with a huge wide-eyed grin on his face. "Is Paige with you?"

"What?" Jorge glanced around and shrugged. "Do you see Paige?"

"Oh," Diego's face fell when he realized it was just him and shrugged. "I wanted to borrow a meditation book that she was telling me about and thought maybe she was going to surprise me and bring it over."

"Pretty sure she's home with Maria," Jorge commented as he closed the door behind him. "Sorry to disappoint you, Diego."

"It's ok, you know," Diego puckered up his mouth in his usual weird manner and shrugged. "I can get it another time."

"You meditate?" Jorge asked as he made his way to the couch and sat down.

"No, Paige had said it might relax me," Diego commented as he went toward the kitchen. "Coffee?"

"See that, right there is probably why you never relax," Jorge commented and he stretched his arm over the back of the couch. "You drink too much fucking coffee."

"I find I'm edgier if I don't have enough coffee," Diego insisted as he poured another cup.

"Trust me, my friend, I'm learning a lot about this kind of thing lately," Jorge said as he glanced around. "Hey, you got any condos for sale in this building. This here is pretty nice."

"Do I look like a real estate man?" Diego asked as he walked toward the couch, his eyes widened in their usual menacing pose. "I thought you wanted a house anyway."

"I do but the houses here," Jorge shook his head. "I don't know. Real estate isn't what it used to be. You use to find a nice house, buy it, move in and that was it but now, real estate feels more like a game. You must fight for properties, pay more than they are worth and most of the people you are bidding against, don't even want to live in the fucking house. They want to flip it or let it sit empty. It is strange."

"It does make sense because property is valuable," Diego sat on the other end of the couch.

"I guess I'm old-fashioned," Jorge considered. "To me, a house is where you move your family in with the expectation on staying there for years and that is it. If it wasn't for Maria and school, I'm not even sure I would stay in Toronto."

"What? You just got here!" Diego's eyes widened in horror. "You can't leave already."

"Do not worry," Jorge commented. "I will not be taking Paige away if that is your concern."

Diego didn't respond but made a face instead.

"I mean, I want life to slow down," Jorge contemplated. "We aren't 25 anymore and the appeal of a big city isn't there for me. I lived a wild enough life for the last 20 years, we both did and now, it is no longer the same."

"Yes, I do agree," Diego replied and stared into his coffee cup for a moment before continuing. "The clubs, the late nights, all of that, I've done it before and although it was fun when I first moved to the city, now I would rather a quiet dinner or something more cultured like a museum."

"It is called growing up, Diego," Jorge commented. "It took us both awhile but now, we are here."

"Barely," Diego replied and took a sip of his coffee, curling his legs underneath him, he turned toward Jorge. "But sometimes, I hear the girls at work talking about their night out at the bar and I will admit, I'm a little jealous."

"Oh yeah, those were great times," Jorge commented sarcastically. "Getting fucked up and being sick the next day, waking up beside someone you don't remember, that was so much fun."

"Yeah, but you got Paige," Diego always put emphasis on her name. "What do I have?"

"Chase?" Jorge raised an eyebrow.

"Yes, a straight man," Diego glumly commented. "I don't think that is about to change."

"Hmm," Jorge considered. "One never knows."

"Oh, *I* know," Diego insisted. "He likes women. Not that he has great taste, he once had a fling with that Deborah girl, remember the one that was giving us trouble at the office, after we fired her?"

Jorge remembered.

"Anyway, I think he had a fling with the Italian from the office," Diego leaned in as if he was sharing gossip with him. "Not that he told me but I could tell, they were acting weird around one another before we put Chase at the club."

Jorge nodded, remembering how Chase had started off in the office before being asked to manage the club a few months earlier.

"Really?" He egged Diego on. "A lot of office affairs? And yet, your office is so small."

"I used to think him and Gracie too, the girl who helps arrange the parties," Diego shrugged. "I don't know but they did spend a lot of time together working on club events."

"Well, in fairness, that is her job," Jorge commented but his brain was running in circles. "Anyone else? What about Jolene and Chase?"

"Yes, I was wondering that too," Diego's eyes widened and then he shook his head. "But no, I don't think so."

"Interesting," Jorge continued to gather information. "And these people who work for you, I don't know them. What is your impression? I would like to be prepared since this audit is coming up. I want to make sure everyone is trustworthy."

"Oh, they will be trustworthy!" Diego insisted with a pout on his lips "I will make sure of that, if I have to scare the hell out of them, I will."

"Ah, Diego, I can always count on your for that," Jorge smoothly played along. "Is there anyone you will be keeping a special eye on?"

He considered the question briefly before answering.

"I don't know if I fully trust anyone," Diego appeared skeptical.

CHAPTER *40*

Stirring up Diego's paranoia wasn't exactly the most ethical approach but it always worked. It wasn't the first time Jorge had shaken his Colombian friend's cage to make sure that the office staff stayed in line but it only took a shot of suspicion to cause Diego to go apeshit. He would put a fire under everyone's asses and with an audit about to happen, it was necessary to keep everyone on their toes and a little scared. Intimidation didn't make for a pleasant work environment but Jorge wasn't looking to become Workplace of the Year either. So fuck that.

After sleeping on it, he decided to take matters into his own hands. Perhaps the staff had grown used to Diego's rants and raves so perhaps it would be a good idea if *he* paid a visit to the office. After all, he was a major investor and therefore, it wasn't unthought of that he might drop by before an audit. It was a small staff and his goal was to talk to everyone there and assess them. Sending a message to Diego about his decision, he was pleased that he agreed.

We will interview them together.

Jorge grinned and placed his phone back on the nightstand just as Paige walked out of their bathroom wearing a robe and slippers. Next door, in what Maria referred to as the 'real' bathroom, his daughter could be heard singing in the shower. It briefly crossed his mind that he could possibly entice his fiancée for a quick encounter but he knew there was no time. Instead, he rose from the bed, naked, he walked across the room.

"Should you be walking around in the nude when you have a young girl living in the apartment?" Paige quietly asked but it sounded much more like a suggestion than a question.

"I never walk around naked in front of my daughter," Jorge pointed toward the next room. "Maria's in the shower, she's not going to come in here. Also, I've been clear on the fact that she is always to knock and vice versa, it is called respect. I told her that if she barges into this room, I will do the same to her."

Paige grinned and shook her head.

"Besides, you Canadians," He gave her a quick kiss before heading toward the bathroom. "You're much too conservative and uptight about nudity." He winked just before closing the door.

While Paige took Maria to school, Jorge put on a suit and made sure to look as presentable as possible. He had an image to project and going to the office looking like a slob, without shaving or mentally preparing himself would be unacceptable. There was only one way to do this and he was going to do it right.

Of course, he brought donuts, even though his intrigue with them was greatly diminishing now that he was cutting sugar out of his diet. He considered eating one on the way but changed his mind.

The office was quiet when he arrived and although it wasn't his usual stomping ground, Jorge recognized that this probably wasn't the norm. He liked that Diego had already inserted the fear of God into his staff, even in that short time between the office opening and him arriving. It was an appreciated gesture reminding him why he enjoyed working with Diego for all these years. The man could be a lunatic but at least they were on the same page.

The receptionist was the first person he saw and therefore, the first person he interviewed. Her name was Verna and she was an older lady and although she seemed harmless, that usually didn't mean anything. Looking across the boardroom table at her while Diego sat at the end like the king of a castle, Jorge gave the same speech that he was about to giving everyone else.

"I'm not sure if you are aware," He began with a warm smile while his dark eyes watched her carefully, "but we have an audit coming up in a few short days. This morning, Diego and I are talking to everyone to see if there are any issues within the office. We have concerns since it is most unusual for an audit to take place this early, after all, this is a young business barely finding its legs. I thought as the receptionist, you may be aware of concerns from customers calling or even here, within the staff that you wished to share with us."

Verna took everything in and nodded as he spoke but was of little help. She passively shook her head and insisted that she did nothing more than answer the phone, reply to emails and kept out of office gossip.

"The customer's questions are about privacy concerns, private parties, payment options, some are unsure of how to use the site," She considered. "No complaints other than from the religious group that's constantly creating petitions against us."

Jorge nodded and made a quick note. It was highly unlikely that the religious group's complaints would incite an audit but it was something to consider. Some of these groups could be quite rigid in their views and took extreme measures to make a point.

"Yes, they have been pretty consistent from the beginning?" Jorge turned his attention to Diego who nodded.

"In the papers, all the time, with their petitions that have lies in them," Diego shook his head. "Apparently, we're backed by the Mexican cartel?"

Jorge gave a smooth grin and with an upward gaze at Verna, he innocently proclaimed. "This is so embarrassing to me. My father owned a coffee company and I was an international sales rep for years. Although coffee is like a drug to many, it is hardly a cartel."

Verna went along and laughed. He read her expression closely before ending the meeting. After finishing, he exchanged looks with Diego before the next person was sent in.

Beverly was an assistant to both Jolene and Diego, a bone thin white woman who looked like a frightened deer in headlights, Jorge immediately launched into the same story as he had with Verna and would with all the staff then waited for her response.

"I was asking a friend," Beverly slowly commented, as if unsure, "She works for the CRA and she said that it's not common for a new business to be audited unless something stands out or if there is a complaint. Sometimes that prompts an investigation."

Surprised by her candor, she was essentially saying what he had thought. Nodding, he glanced toward Diego then back at her.

"This is what we are thinking as well," Jorge spoke honestly. "Is there anyone you feel might have made a complaint?"

Beverly hesitated before shaking her head no.

"If there is, you can tell us," Jorge continued with his movie star smile. "Either myself or Diego at any time, if you hear anything. Of course, you have Diego's contact information but here, also, is mine." He reached into his pocket and pulled out a card and slid it across the table. "This is for your eyes only, I must add, but since you are an assistant, I feel you should be able to contact me if there is ever any concerns or issues and for some reason, Diego and Jolene are not available."

"Maybe ask your friend if she can, you know, maybe look into this for us," Diego commented, he immediately formed pouty lips after he said his piece.

"I don't think she can," Beverly spoke honestly. "They are closely monitored."

"It's the government, Diego," Jorge commented. "We don't want her friend in trouble."

"I will see what I can do," She promised.

Diego seemed impressed with this comment but Jorge merely nodded and asked her to send the next person in.

Gracie was a young woman who seemed harmless, if not shy, her face a bright red from the moment she stepped into the room until she left. Wearing a hippie blouse and long, flowing skirt, her hair was a faint shade of blue.

"Gracie, are you not the lady who helps Chase plan his parties?" Jorge asked, remembering Diego's suspicious of the two having an affair. "Both the sex parties and also inviting bands in to play, no?"

"Yes, that is me," She was formal with some reservations in her eyes.

"Oh good! Yes, you are doing a terrific job," Jorge confirmed. "The band idea, it is going very well, I am told."

"I follow a lot of local bands, so I kind of suggest who he should have at the club," Gracie was hesitant to comment.

"Well, you are doing well," Jorge complimented her and watched her original fear subside slightly. "So, I guess you know why we are here today."

He launched into his speech and Gracie nodded while her fingers played with two long thin ties that hung from the neckline of her shirt, perhaps it was originally tied together but fell apart? He wasn't sure. It was, however, distracting.

"I don't know anything about audits," Gracie nervously replied. "I guess the government probably does them randomly?"

"Perhaps so," Jorge commented and nodded. "Is there any other thoughts you would like to share with us today?"

She said no and went off to get the next person. Jorge once again shared a look with Diego.

Marco carried a different energy as soon as he walked in the room, however, the new man in the office, he had little to contribute. Of course, they would talk privately later. Jorge assumed that after a morning of shaking everyone's tree that something would fall out and Marco would be the man to catch it. They finished up with him and next on the chopping block was the one that Diego referred to as 'The Italian', a curvy 30-something with an attitude that could be sensed immediately when she walked through the door.

After telling her the same story as he had the others, he waited for her response but there was none.

"You have nothing to say?" Jorge asked as he weaved his fingers together. "Any thoughts? Have you heard anything? Any concerns? We would like to clear up everything if there are issues."

"My only issue," Sylvana shot back, leaning forward on the table, "Is that I have a lot of work to do and you guys won't provide me with an assistant but yet, you hire a new IT guy? Seriously, what is that about?"

Intrigued, if not humored by her directness, Jorge managed to suppress his grin and instead gave her a condescending look.

"Marco is here to help you too," Diego shot back at her from the end of the table. "You always complain about not having time for the website now you don't need to even go on it, I would think that's a help. I'm sure Marco will be able to help you more too."

"Right now, our focus is on Marco revamping both our sites," Jorge cut in and gave Sylvana an icy stare while his voice was relaxed, almost casual in nature. "That is our top priority, fixing glitches on the sites then after that, maybe he will be able to help you out."

"I've been hearing that since day one," Sylvana complained. "This company wouldn't exist without the marketing and I continue to get more and more business and yet, my requests for an assistant are constantly ignored."

"It is a new business, we have to plan carefully," Jorge replied. "We cannot over extend ourselves or we might not have a business."

"Right, so you and him," She abruptly pointed toward Diego, "Come in here in your expensive suits and try to tell me that the company doesn't have enough money to hire another person."

"If you feel that you need help, then you asked Gracie, you ask Diego, you ask Jolene, you ask Beverly," Jorge pointed out, he continued to stay calm. "We're a team and I'm sure someone would help you out with your day-to-day tasks but at this time, no, we cannot hire you an assistant."

"This meeting isn't about that," Diego piped up, looking completely frustrated as if he wanted to reach across the table and grab her by the throat. This made Jorge grin, which apparently mightn't have been an ideal reaction at that particular moment because suddenly Sylvana was on her feet and pointing in his direction.

"Look, maybe you're some kind of prince back in Mexico but it doesn't mean you can come in here and intimidate everyone over this audit," Her eyes snapped in anger, her stance powerful as if she were fearless, unconcerned with who Jorge was or his role in the company. "We have nothing to do with it and if you guys have nothing to hide, then what's the problem?"

She challenged them both before turning on her heels and walking out the door.

Diego looked as though his head was about to fly off his shoulders and he pointed toward the exit.

"See what I have to put up with every day!" Diego snapped and reached for another donut. So far, most took one upon leaving but others did not. This was something else Jorge was noticing. The guilty rarely accepted a donut. There was a part of them that felt they didn't deserve it. This is why Jorge purchased the most eye-catching donuts he could find because they were harder to say no to; it was as much of a test as anything else.

"Replace her."

"Her work is too good," Diego fumed. "How dare she talk to you, an investor that way!"

Jorge merely grinned. "She wasn't wrong. I did come in to intimidate people and I also liked to consider myself somewhat of a prince back in Mexico."

This made Diego laugh even though his face still appeared angry. Only Diego could look happy and furious at the same time.

"The most important thing is what she said about the intimidation," Jorge commented. "Perhaps we've already shaken the tree more than we realize."

The next person to arrive was Benjamin. It was the first time Jorge met their accountant and he was left with a very pleasant impression. He explained how some of the 'excess' money had been added to the books in the form of fake accounts, often when a 'client' paid large amounts for very detailed, 'private' parties as a legal approach to carefully filtering money through. Although he didn't ask a lot of questions, it didn't seem to concern Benjamin that he was helping to launder money. He was highly confident that nothing would grab the auditors attention when they arrived on Halloween.

"What a day to have them arrive," Jorge commented as Benjamin reached for a donut, a huge grin on his face. "Seems appropriate though."

"Do we know the name of the auditor?" Diego asked.

"I forget his name," Benjamin commented. "It's on my desk if you want me to get it."

"No, that is fine," Jorge waved his hand. "Maybe we can persuade Jolene to show some cleavage that day."

"That would be different from every other day because?" Diego asked and the three men laughed.

"This is true," Jorge commented as he reached for a donut.

"I thought you couldn't eat those anymore," Diego commented with a raised eyebrow.

"Ah but my friend," Jorge waved his hand in the air. "We must occasionally take risks in this life, no?"

CHAPTER 41

"I would like to come," Jorge bluntly insisted. Determined, his eyes fixated on Paige, who appeared surprised by his candor even though it was hardly a new outfit for him to try on but more of a regular ensemble. When she didn't respond, Jorge sat on the end of the couch and studied her face. Was she hiding something from him? "What? Is that not ok for me to do?"

"Well, it's my work," Paige was hesitant, her eyes softened as she watched him in stunned silence, almost as if she weren't sure of how to handle his request. "I have to consider a few factors, obviously."

"I understand," Jorge shrugged and pulled a piece of gum out of his pocket and carefully started to unwrap it then stopped and looked into her eyes. "Unless you don't want me there?"

"It's not that I don't want you there," Paige spoke with more confidence. "I just have to be careful about this situation. It might be a little dicey closing in on this guy and I…I have to think about it, Jorge. That's all I'm saying."

Popping the piece of gum in his mouth, he watched her nervously turn and walk toward the kitchen, where a fresh pot of coffee awaited. Without saying a word, she poured them each a cup and Jorge felt his heart drop as he watched. She was hiding something from him but rather than making him angry, it made him feel weak.

"Paige," He said her name with much more emotion than he intended as he stood up and crossed the floor. Her blue eyes searched his face as he approached, ignoring the cup of coffee that awaited him on the counter, his focus was only on her. "What's going on here? Why aren't you telling me anything? Who's this guy you're….. who's the assignment? Tell me."

"It's not that I'm trying to be secretive," Paige replied with sincerity in her eyes combined with a kindness in her voice which gave him some relief as she turned slightly, facing him. "It's because it's work, I can't talk about it a lot and to be honest, I don't want to put you in any kind of danger. I just…I haven't even thought about how or when I will do it. When I do, I will let you know if you can come but, I…"

"You would rather I didn't," Jorge attempted to finish her sentence and suddenly grabbed a nearby paper towel and spit out his gum. It was sweet and disgusting.

"It's not that I don't want you there," She reached across the counter and gently touched his arm. "I have to be extra careful with this one."

Jorge stared into her eyes for a moment in silence.

"Are *you* in danger?"

"No," She answered after a slight hesitation, just long enough to make him question her sincerity. This worried him more than his original fear that she simply didn't want him to join her.

"I don't want you in danger," He pushed. "It's not worth it. We don't need the money and I…look, it's not worth it. Let someone else do it."

"I have to do this one," She spoke quietly and he immediately sensed that this was more personal.

"Why?"

"I can't tell you," She whispered, "at least, not yet."

They didn't discuss the subject again until a few days later when she reluctantly agreed.

Meanwhile, Jorge was tied up with finalizing details for the store, as well as a few other meetings about the pot shop. It was looking like the best solution was to start a simple medicinal marijuana store and depending on how laws changed, expand in the future. People would need their physician to complete the proper documentation and if they didn't have one, Jorge had a doctor in his pocket. Again, he raved to Chase about how Canadians were so 'accommodating'.

"Everyone wants to help," He mocked sincerity as the two walked through the empty club a few days later, after having a productive business lunch. Everyone was happy with the arrangement and although the store hadn't officially opened yet, the supplies continued to sell fast through various club events and beyond. Chase had even arranged a 'smoke room' in the basement for those who chose to light up during an event. The previous owner had rented out the lowest level as a dingy, little apartment so technically, it was a private residence, therefore making it legal to smoke unless the landlord stated otherwise. Jorge was the landlord. He didn't care.

"We definitely try," Chase countered and Jorge let out a laugh as they headed for the office, where they were to meet with Diego and Jolene a few minutes later. The two sat down and Jorge ran a hand over his face.

"Oh, speaking of which," Jorge suddenly remembered the conversation he had with Paige before leaving that morning. "Would it be possible to ask you a small favor? Next week, Juliana is coming from Mexico for a couple of days to look after Maria while Paige and I go out of town. Since she is not familiar with the city, would it be possible for you to give Maria a drive to and from school?"

"Of course," Chase shrugged as if it were no big deal.

"I don't like to ask but she isn't familiar with the city," He waved his hand toward the door. "Although, she must try to learn it. I think she's coming here to work for me."

"To look after Maria?"

"That and to help at the store," Jorge commented, "I need someone I can trust. Juliana and her boyfriend broke up so she might want to stay. Also, Jesús will run the store for me, at least, at first. We need someone intimidating and he's it."

They heard the main door open and both fell silent. Diego walked into the room a few seconds later, the keys still in his hand. His eyes bounced between the two men.

"Well, you look like the cat that just ate the canary," His comment directed toward Jorge, who was vaguely familiar with the expression and merely laughed.

"I eat a lot of canaries, Diego," He commented as he watched the Colombian sit beside him. "And Jolene? Where is she today?"

"She had to stay back at the office, we had a little *situation* this morning," Diego reported, his eyes bugged out as he spoke.

"What kind of situation are we talking about?" Jorge immediately asked while focusing carefully on Diego.

"Clara found a listening device in Jolene's office," Diego replied as his nostrils flared out and he silently continued to make eye contact with Jorge for a long, silent moment. Eventually looking away from Diego, he slowly nodded and didn't reply.

"We swept the place and didn't find anything else but one, to me, is too many," Diego commented and twisted his lips in a tight pucker.

"Last time, back in Calgary, it was also Jolene's office."

"That was Maggie who put it there that time," Diego referred to the woman who was spying for the RCMP, the woman Jorge had killed for the crime. "We are going through the video to see who's been in the office since Clara was in earlier this week. Fortunately, we haven't talked about anything delicate in there. We rarely do at the office unless we're sure it's clean."

Jorge remained silent as he thought.

"Didn't you just have a meeting with everyone there?" Chase piped up while leaning back in his chair. Besides Jorge, Diego nodded vigorously.

"It's no coincidence, *amigo*," He replied and shook his head. "Someone is feeling the heat."

"The boardroom is always locked, right?" Jorge asked and Diego nodded. "And that only leaves your office and Jolene's to be a target."

"Beverly is almost always in my office," Diego insisted. "So no one can get past her. Jolene is usually by herself so if she leaves the office for a minute…"

Jorge nodded as he continued to think.

"Someone slipped in."

"It would have to be since Jolene watches people so carefully," Chase insisted. "She has to, we always did even back in our Calgary office."

"There is a camera in the hallway," Diego reminded them both. "Jolene is going through the footage now. She said there's not a lot of people in and out so it shouldn't be difficult to figure it out."

"It's not a big staff and Clara is there every couple of days, right?" Chase asked as he continued to lean back in his chair. "Did Jolene have any meetings with anyone from outside the office? Had, I don't know, did someone fix something in the office? A delivery guy in? A friend?"

"Jolene doesn't have friends," Diego insisted and made a face. "Come on!"

"I don't know, just trying to think outside of the box," Chase shrugged and let out a laugh. "It's a short time period and not many people, I'm sure she will have it figured out soon."

"Tell her," Jorge cut in, his eyes fixated on a random spot on the floor as if locked in a trance. "To let me know by the end of the day. Even if she doesn't have it completely narrowed down yet."

"Will do," Diego insisted. "I already told her you will want to know."

Jorge simply nodded but didn't reply. He didn't want to say it out loud but secretly wondered if it was actually her that planted the listening device but it wouldn't make sense. No meetings ever occurred in Jolene's office. Regardless of both Chase and Diego's blind faith in Jolene, he wasn't as convinced that they could trust her. Something was off.

Putting it on the back burner, he instead told Diego about the meeting him and Chase had earlier that day and finally, they went on to discuss the audit coming up the following morning.

"Everything is set?"

"Benjamin went over everything with a fine tooth comb," Diego insisted. "He's ready for anything."

"*Perfecto!*"

"I'll be glad when this fucking audit is *terminado*," Diego loudly insisted as he fixed his tie. "And it was someone who tipped off the CRA, I also found that out this morning. Beverly's friend did some snooping."

"We have to give that girl a raise," Jorge commented and reached in his pocket for some gum. His craving for cigarettes seemed more aggressive than it had when first quitting but he chose to control it not allow it to control him.

"I'm already on top of it," Diego insisted. "We need more people like Beverly and less like Sylvana," He sniffed, wiggling his nose in an exaggerated manner. "Maybe it was her."

Jorge didn't respond. He was once again lost in his own thoughts. When he saw that Diego was waiting for a response, he simply shrugged and gave an uncommitted 'maybe' but didn't add anything more.

"We left the device there," Diego suddenly added and although Chase looked surprised by this comment, Jorge merely nodded. "It will be normal business as usual and that is that."

"Wait, what?" Chase sat forward in his chair, leaning on his desk. "You're going to leave it?"

"Someone's working hard to bring us down," Jorge replied. "We will show them that there is nothing to know. That, along with the audit, we come out clean and when we find out who did this, that person is going to talk to the *policia* and tell them a very convincing story about why there is nothing to report and that they don't feel comfortable spying on us. If it's not the police, then we take care of that person ourselves."

"That's it?" Chase made eye contact with him.

"We gotta be smart here," Jorge insisted and continued to vigorously chomp on his gum. "If it's the police and things look clean then they got nothing. Not to suggest we aren't going to be keeping a close of an eye on things but it looks like discrimination on their part if they continue to harass us."

"Discrimination?" Chase asked.

"Yes, the Mexican and Colombians, racism could be the centre of this or maybe because of the kind of business we run, perhaps the police are unfairly targeting us. There are so many factors here that make it look like they are making a lot of unfair and unjustified assumptions about us. We could feel harassed and it might be interrupting our business."

"We will take a picture of the device with a date and time in a few days," Jorge continued. "And if ever needed, our lawyer can report that we found it... but of course, we will make it look like we didn't notice it for a few days when the cleaning lady will deactivate it while washing the desk."

Chase leaned back as a grin crossed his lips.

Jorge smiled and nodded. "Meanwhile, I will be talking to my contacts in government. This nonsense has to stop."

CHAPTER 42

"Thank God that fucking audit is over," Diego dramatically commented as he entered Jorge's apartment with an exhausted Chase not far behind. Both headed directly toward the couch while Jorge glanced into the hallway and shook his head.

"What? No Jolene, again?" Jorge made no attempt to hide his hostility. Her absence was becoming too common. Closing the door, he noticed that Diego was glancing toward the kitchen, probably after noticing the aroma of coffee throughout the apartment. "Where the fuck is she this time?"

"She's on her way," Chase commented and shook his head. "She's got a good reason for being late."

"Ah fuck, what a crazy day!" Diego ran a hand over his face while shaking his head. In truth, both looked as if they were ready for a stiff drink not a cup of coffee. Chase was loosening his tie as if it were strangling him while Diego pointed toward the kitchen and before he could say anything, Jorge nodded.

"Help yourself to the coffee, Diego."

The words were barely out of his mouth and the Colombian was bouncing off the couch and heading into the next room, leaving Chase behind.

"Do you want a coffee?" Jorge asked him and watched him shake his head. "I take it, you were at the office today too?"

"Yup," Chase replied. "I didn't have anything at the club so I thought I would go in case they needed me for anything. The place was a fucking madhouse."

"And the audit?" Jorge asked, slightly concerned by the energy that was filling the room. "Should I be concerned?"

"Ah, the audit," Diego's voice boomed behind him as he returned with a cup of coffee in his hand. Shaking his head, he sat down on the couch and took a sip while beside him, Chase looked defeated. "It was fine."

Silence.

"Wait, what?" Jorge was confused. "So, the audit, we passed?"

"Oh yes, with flying colors," Diego's eyes doubled in size when he replied and put his hand up in the air. "It was a hell of a fucking day getting there, *amigo*, but we *did* pass."

"Then why the fuck are you guys acting like you were both ran over by a truck?" Jorge shrugged, his eyes jumping between the two. "I do not understand."

"It's the government," Diego attempted to explain and made a face. "We had everything together but of course, they wanted something more and they ask a million questions. Trying to fuck you up but thank God for Benjamin, that man is a genius."

"He deserves a raise," Chase suddenly piped up. "I would've cracked under the pressure."

"I would've cracked and shot the fucker," Diego commented casually and made a face. "But they would've just sent someone else, so, what difference."

Chase grinned and exchanged smiles with Jorge.

"I gotta say," Chase shook his head and ran his fingers over his buzz cut. "I'm not prone to violence but I was starting to feel the same way."

"I know, right?" Diego let out a laugh and playfully slapped Chase on the arm. "Especially when he asked for that one, like really specific thing on the fourth fucking hour. It was like, are you kidding me? It was like the asshole was *looking* to find a problem."

"Are we sure he was really who he said he was?" Jorge asked suspiciously and headed toward the kitchen.

"Yes, he had ID," Diego insisted.

"And everything, it is good?" Jorge reaffirmed as he poured a cup of coffee for himself. "We are finished with the government?"

"It looks that way," Chase replied. "And Diego is right, they definitely were there on a mission. But they failed. We were clean."

Jorge smiled as he stirred cream into his coffee. "If they are trying to get us, they aren't going to get us that way. Tell Benjamin tomorrow that he has a raise, a bonus, whatever he wants."

"That's the plan," Diego crossed his legs and leaned back on the couch, loosening his tie and making a face. "I would kiss that man's feet right now."

"Let's keep the kissing to a minimum," Jorge teased as he returned to the living room and sat across from them. "And Jolene?"

"She had to stay back and talk to an employee," Diego grinned and exchanged looks with Chase.

"Ok guys, what the fuck is going on here?" Jorge asked as he sat his coffee down on the nearby table that separate them.

"Jolene will tell you," Diego insisted as he began to shake his foot around with a nervous twitch. "It's her story to tell."

"We got the person who put the listening device in her office," Chase let him know. "Diego and Jolene crucified her after the auditor left and…yeah, Jolene will tell you the rest. She'll be mad if we tell you everything."

"Then who the fuck is she talking to now?

"Marco," Diego replied. "She needs him to shift his energies a bit. You know that guy has a really broad background. He could probably run our company. In fact, we suspected someone and he was able to put the final nail in the coffin for us. He found something in an email."

"Yes," Jorge nodded. "IT is his specialty but he's a smart guy. He could do anything."

"That's what we need," Diego insisted and glanced toward the bedrooms. "Where's Paige and Maria?"

"They're out," Jorge replied. "They're having some Halloween event at the school."

"Oh that's right, its' Halloween," Diego replied and uncrossed his legs. "This fucking audit consumed my day."

"No party at the club tonight?" Jorge shifted his attention to Chase.

"No, all private parties," Chase replied. "It's kind of better. I'm not crazy about Halloween events. Anyone can walk in wearing a costume whether they are underage or on the most wanted list, you know?"

"Good point," Jorge nodded. "This is true."

"I've seen it when I worked in a bar in Hennessey and at one of our parties too," Chase sighed. "I'm not comfortable with it."

"I trust your instincts," Jorge replied and thought about Chase's hometown. "Hey, did you talk to your kids today?"

"Yeah," Chase replied, a smile lit up his face. "The twins were dressed up and ready to go out when I talked to them on FaceTime earlier."

Jorge laughed. "What did they dress up as?"

"I think they were supposed to be superheroes of some kind but I never got a straight answer," Chase replied. "I'm thinking of going back to Hennessey for Christmas this year."

"You should," Jorge insisted and thought about the son Chase lost the year before and looked away. "The twins, they are around 5 now? That's a good age. It's still fun."

"What did Maria dress up as?" Diego's eyes lit up.

"A prison inmate," Jorge replied and when met with silence, he shrugged. "*Orange is the New Black*. She's a fan."

Both men grinned and Chase nodded.

"She wanted to chain her legs together and Paige reminded her that this might be a little awkward."

The buzzer interrupted. It was Jolene.

"I am so sorry," She rushed into the apartment moments later and Diego's eyes lit up when he saw her carrying a box of donuts. "I actually finish earlier but was tied up in traffic."

"So you decided to stop and get donuts?" Jorge asked as everyone made a leap for the box; including him.

"No, I got before but after, traffic was bad," Jolene insisted. "Did they tell you?"

"They only said you found out who put the listening device in your office, that's it."

Jolene plunked down on the couch between Chase and Diego while Jorge returned to his own seat.

"It was Gracie, can you believe?" Jolene looked shocked but Jorge wasn't surprised. That was his guess after the brief interviews he had with the staff. Her body language was the biggest giveaway but also, she was the only person who didn't take a donut. Even Sylvana slinked back later and took one.

"I still can't believe it," Chase spoke up. "I never would've thought..."

"It was," Jolene interrupted. "I did not think either although, it does make sense now. She was close with Deborah so they must be alike."

"Wait, what?" Jorge asked as he moved forward in his chair. "Was she behind calling the CRA?"

"No, she say no," Jolene replied and bit into a plain donut. "Gracie say she was approached by the police and of course, she's soft so she help them."

"It explains everything," Diego insisted. "The sudden audit, I mean, they want to catch us on something."

"Well, they're not going to," Jorge insisted. "I got someone in government I've been meaning to call. This is enough bullshit. I got to find out where this is coming from."

"We put the fear of God in that little girl," Jolene was suddenly full of fire as she spoke and beside her, Diego let out a laugh. "She won't be a problem again."

"The two of you," Jorge glanced between Jolene and Diego and grinned. "I can only imagine how that conversation went down."

"It did not go well for her," Diego confirmed. "We raked her over the coals. She won't come anywhere near the office."

"And what did she do there?"

"She helped me organize parties," Chase replied quietly. He appeared sad by this turn of events. "I had no idea. I keep racking my brain and I can't think of anything that would've made me suspicious."

"It is always the one you least suspect," Diego insisted.

"So, she confessed to everything and you guys scared the fuck out of her," Jorge confirmed.

"Yes, I tell her to keep far away, we don't want to see her again," Jolene's face hardened, her eyes were small and dark as she took another bite from her donut while beside her, Diego finished his and shook his head.

"That little bitch was shaking in her boots by the time she left the office," Diego confirmed. "I made it very clear that we aren't fucking around with her and if the police continue to hang around, it's her ass on the line."

"We say that this was our one and only conversation with her," Jolene insisted. "The next time, there will be *no* conversation."

Chase continued to look disappointed but it was clear he understood what this meant and hesitantly agreed.

"I wonder how long this was going on?"

"Not long," Jolene replied to Chase's question. "I knew too, I knew something was wrong at the office and it made me nervous but I didn't know why I feel this way. Now I know."

"Now you know," Diego repeated.

"I trust too easily," Jolene complained and pointed toward her left breast. "I think too much here."

Jorge's eyes followed her hand and he fell silent along with Chase on the other side of the room, whom also noted where Jolene pointed.

"Guys, she means her heart," Diego spoke up with some frustration in his voice.

"Yes, of course, what else?" Jolene gave Diego a dirty look before turning her attention back to Jorge. "No Mrs. Nice guy for me, from now on, I don't trust anyone."

"It's always good to be suspicious," Jorge agreed. "Didn't we do a background check on this girl?"

"It was clean, nothing made us think that she could've done this to us," Diego insisted. "Nothing."

"So will she go away quietly?"

Both Diego and Jolene started to laugh.

"Yes, she practically pee her pants before she left the office today," Jolene insisted. "I probably should remind her again very soon."

"So Marco is going to help out with her job for now," Diego spoke up and reached for another donut. "Until we find someone else."

"I got someone," Jorge spoke up. "Juliana. She is moving here to help out some with Maria and I was also going to have her sometimes at the shop when it opens. She could help Chase some too."

"I only really need someone part-time so yeah, that would work," Chase agreed and nodded. He appeared satisfied.

"Can we trust her?" Diego asked.

"Yes," Jorge insisted. "She worked for me for years in Mexico, in different capacities. She's one of us."

Everyone appeared content with the answer.

"She will be here in a few days," Jorge commented. "I will talk to her at that time."

CHAPTER 43

"So who's this guy we're taking care of tomorrow?" Jorge whispered in the dead of the night as he lay naked beside Paige, the sweet scent of her hair filled his lungs as his fingers gently grazed her stomach and he pulled her closer. He kissed her naked shoulder and closed his eyes.

"*I'm* taking care of him," Paige gently corrected him and started to turn around, causing Jorge to open his eyes, his hand sliding over her back and pulling her closer. "I'm the one shooting him. Your job is to keep back, remember?"

"I know, I know," Jorge said as his face formed a lazy smile and he leaned forward, giving her a quick kiss. "I will stay out of the way. I just want to see you…in action."

"Why do you want to watch me kill this guy?" She asked as her head sunk down into the pillow, her eyes looking up at him. "What's the big deal? It's not like you haven't shot people yourself or probably seen other people shooting, for that matter."

"It's not the same," He insisted. "There's something about you being dangerous that turns me on. Like the night we met, in the hotel? When you had the gun to my head?"

"I've never met or even heard of anyone who thought having a gun pointed at them was sexy," Paige commented with a serious tone, followed by a giggle. "You might want to explore what that's about."

It was Jorge's turn to laugh. "Wonder what Freud would say?"

"You might not want to know," Paige calmly replied, which made him laugh again. "Have you ever had a woman point a gun at you before me?"

"No baby, you were the first," Jorge let out a mischievous laugh. "Even if any other woman had pointed a gun at me, it wasn't *you* pointing a gun at me. You had this sexy, calm voice and when I caught a look, a nice ass and I don't know, I guess maybe there was something about you being powerful that turned me on. I'm used to meeting weak women, women who are naïve. I'm not used to women who are so…. Independent, strong, I guess that's why I had never wanted to marry before. You amaze me. No one ever amazes me."

She smiled and didn't reply.

"I was thinking," He continued to speak, this time with a certain amount of vulnerability in his voice. "I was thinking when we're in Niagara Falls tomorrow, maybe we could get married?"

"What?" Paige's eyes widened then quickly softened as her hand reached out to touch his face, gently caressing the stubble before sliding her fingers into his hair. "But…. we can't. Maria wants to be at the wedding and we would have to make the arrangements long in advance especially in Niagara Falls, I'm sure lots of people get married there every day."

"Ok, so," He spoke slowly, tilting his head down, Jorge gave her an upward gaze. "I kind of went ahead and made the arrangements as a surprise." He hesitated and noted that she definitely looked surprised, her hand no longer moving but frozen as if she was too stunned by this news and so he quickly continued. "I thought, this, it should be special, just you and me. Not anyone else and then later, we can marry again with family and friends, whatever you wish. I feel that this…our relationship, it is just with us and I don't want to share that moment with anyone else. Does that make sense?"

"But wouldn't Maria be upset?" She spoke softly, her voice full of hesitation. "She would be so hurt if we didn't include her."

"We do not have to tell her," He replied and pulled her closer. "It's not necessary. It will only be for us, no one else. We plan another wedding after we return and not tell anyone."

Paige blinked rapidly, her long eyelashes moved so quickly that it took a moment for him to realize that she was fighting back tears. He instinctively pulled her closer. "Unless you don't feel we should…"

"No, I don't know what to say," Paige sniffed and wiped a stray tear from her cheek. "When did you, I mean, what made you decide to do this? How? It's still pretty short notice…"

"As soon as you said we were going to Niagara Falls, I made the arrangements," Jorge confessed. "I figured, the worst you could say is no and if that happens, I would cancel but it was my wish that you would say yes. As I said, we do not have to tell anyone. This is just between us."

"Just between us," She repeated.

"Exactly," He whispered and pulled her a little closer, giving her a quick kiss. "So, does that sound good? Are you ready to become Paige Hernandez?"

"Paige Noël Hernandez and yes," Her eyes lit up and he started to laugh.

"Ok, yes, you can keep your Noël, whatever makes you happy," He confirmed as his smile relaxed. "It will be *perfecto.*"

"*Perfecto*," She repeated and moved closer. "I love you so much."

"I love *you* so much too." He whispered.

"I still can't believe you did this but I'm happy you did," Paige leaned her head against his chest, her finger ran over his collarbone and toward his back. "There was actually an opening somewhere on such short notice?"

"I made an opening," He replied.

"Do I want to know?"

Jorge let out a short laugh. "Don't worry, no one was hurt or killed. The story is less dramatic. Chase helped me to find someone who would meet us there. He will be paid well and that is that. We get married at the hotel just after lunch."

"And after that, we take care of business," Paige referred to the man she was set to kill. "Busy day."

"And an even busier night," He spoke seductively and kissed her on top of her head.

The following morning was quite rushed between getting Maria to school and picking Juliana up at the airport. With a fresh haircut and wearing both a dress and heels, Jorge had to look twice because Maria's babysitter didn't look the same as a single woman as she did while in a relationship.

"New woman with a new attitude," Paige commented as they walked toward her. "That's what a breakup tends to do."

"Had she done this before, maybe she'd still have her boyfriend," Jorge muttered without thinking as Paige smiled towards Juliana while grabbing his arm and giving a tight squeeze and he laughed. "Well, it's true."

"It goes both ways," Paige muttered as Juliana got closer. "I've seen her boyfriend, remember?"

After both of them told her how lovely she looked, they quickly rushed her out of the airport and back to the apartment before jumping on the highway and heading toward Niagara Falls. It wasn't until they were in the SUV and well on their way, that Jorge asked Paige about the impending victim that night.

"So this guy, what did he do?" Jorge asked as a sprinkle of rain hit the windshield. "The assignment, what did he do?"

"He.... crossed the wrong people," Paige's answer was vague and he immediately didn't like that she was holding something back from him.

"Come on, I think you can tell me more than that," He insisted. "What was he involved in? What kind of business?"

She seemed to think for a moment. "I don't want to talk about that, it's so depressing. Can we talk about the wedding? You didn't tell me all the details like who's marrying us? Chase found him?"

"Yes, he knows a guy at the gym who performs marriages and he agreed to do ours," Jorge replied. "We will pay him well of course because he is also traveling to meet us."

"So, Chase is the only person who knows?"

"Yes, well he is the only person I could trust to not talk."

"Are you sure? If he tells Diego, he'll be crushed."

Jorge let out a laugh. "Diego will survive but Chase, he won't tell anyone. He has a lot of secrets under his hat."

"He certainly doesn't talk much," Paige commented as she looked out the window.

"That is why he's perfect for our line of work."

"I feel terrible that I didn't have time to shop for anything nice to wear today," Paige commented and glanced down at her outfit. She wore a fitted, rose colored dress that was simple but yet highlighted the blue in her eyes and her curves. Jorge didn't care what she wore and personally hadn't thought about his own outfit, wearing one of his regular suits.

"You look beautiful and who cares," Jorge shrugged. "Whether you wear a $10 000 gown or a dress you buy at a second-hand store for $2, this is not about the dress or what I wear, it's about love. Too many people they worry about such silly things and it does not matter."

Paige grinned and nodded. "You're right. I guess as a woman I'm trained to look perfect on my wedding day. As if me looking perfect will mean a perfect marriage. Isn't that weird we think that way?"

"Not really, we live in a superficial, ridiculous world," Jorge replied casually as he turned off the wipers, the rain quickly passing. "People want everything to look perfect on the outside to satisfy others and not to satisfy themselves. We could get married naked, it wouldn't matter. We are marrying for the right reasons and I suspect, that makes us the minority."

Traffic was heavy but they managed to get to the hotel shortly after lunchtime and although Jorge was starving, Paige insisted that they didn't have enough time to eat. So he chewed on some disgusting, sugary gum instead and drank a cup of coffee.

It felt surreal that he was about to get married. It was not something he ever considered for a moment in his life. Not with any ex-girlfriends, not even his first love in high school, the woman who was too old for him and probably laughed at his naïvety. He had never even uttered the word 'marriage' to Maria's mother nor had he considered it once before meeting Paige. In fact, he kind of laughed at other people getting married as if they were merely falling into society's norm, mindlessly, like a bunch of sheep.

Now, however, he felt differently and yet, he couldn't properly express himself when looking into Paige's eyes. The words, they just weren't there for him. He couldn't take what was in his heart and express it and perhaps, there were no words for such things. How do you communicate how deep your love was for another human being, how they lifted your heart, made you hopeful and excited about living in a way you hadn't even been aware was possible? It was too big to put into words. It wasn't impossible but it was impossible to him. In both English and Spanish, words were difficult. They never seemed to capture a feeling properly and perhaps, it was the way the rest of the world watered them down. How love was a casual way to express everything from how much you appreciated a new car to a deep, spiritual connection with another human being.

It wasn't until minutes before the ceremony that he felt nervous. He was *never* nervous. Butterflies in his stomach would've been cute, tickled his soul but instead, he felt encompassing fear, like nothing he had ever felt before; was this a mistake? Had he acted too quickly? He hadn't even known Paige for long and yet, he felt like he knew her forever. The logical and emotional side was so vastly different and which one did you follow? Was he being gullible? Was he turning into a love-struck teenager, caught up in lust?

It was fine. He was fine. Once the wedding actually started, the mere moments it took, it was as if he were lost in a trance. It was like he was on earth and at the same time, floating above himself watching, like this couldn't actually be happening. His body felt weak like a feather could knock him over and yet, enlightened as an electrical shock flowed through him, setting his soul on fire as he broke out in a cold sweat. He couldn't hear Paige speak but he saw her lips move, her eyes water and the next thing he knew, she was kissing him as his heart pounded erratically and his whole body shook when he suddenly came back to earth.

Glancing around, it suddenly hit him that he was a married man. It wasn't a dream. It was perfect. Completely perfect.

CHAPTER 44

He used to laugh at people who got married. Not that he hadn't taken marriage seriously but because it seemed so exaggerated; the entire event was a spectacular show meant to touch everyone's heart and yet, it was him who slipped out of the church during those ceremonies to enjoy a cigarette. Now, he recognized that there was something about watching two people say their vows that he couldn't face. It made him feel uncomfortable and awkward in a way that simply wasn't natural. Perhaps it was the pressure his family put on him to marry from such a young age. It was almost like an expectation rather than a hope for him and like most things that Jorge felt pressured to do, he resented it.

Verónic had wanted them to get married when she learned that she was pregnant with Maria. To that, Jorge laughed before snorting another line of coke and walking out of the room as if she had suggested that they move to Mars and build a house made of chocolate. In truth, Jorge knew he had broken her heart a million times and it started on that day and went on and on until her death. He assumed that's why she resumed doing cocaine after Maria was born; his constant insistence that he didn't love her and that he never would. In fact, up until his daughter was born, Jorge believed that he had no love in his heart. He had no connection to his family, his friends, he felt nothing for anyone.

Maria changed that because the second he looked into her eyes, he knew that his heart did exist. She was it. And so he tolerated Verónic for his daughter's sake. For the first few years, he truly believed that his daughter needed her mother, which in itself, was enough reason to keep her around but when that aspect started to fade and her coke addiction became clear, he knew it was time to get her the hell out of his life as well as Maria's. Except, of course, she wouldn't leave. Verónic was stupid enough to think that she could threaten him and live to talk about it.

His love for Paige, it was very real. No one could've been more surprised than him that a night of passion after a woman held a gun to his head could've translated to love but yet, it happened without him even seeing it coming. It stopped him in his tracks faster than that bullet ever would've been able to as his eyes opened to a whole new world. It was something he wished for everyone, even his enemy, if only for a day.

After the wedding, he briefly forgot why they were in Niagara Falls in the first place, his head in the clouds as they kissed; slowly, gently, as if the world had stopped and was waiting for them to catch up. He fell silent, unsure of what to say but at the same time, feeling as if words weren't necessary.

"I have to change," She whispered and Jorge felt as if he was falling back to earth as he shook his head, his eyes still transfixed on her face. "I'm sorry but I've tricked this guy into meeting me at an abandoned warehouse just outside of Niagara Falls. It's a bit of a drive so…I'm sorry, Jorge."

"That's fine," He smiled and briefly held her hand. "I'm coming with you."

"You don't have to…"

"You know I want to."

She didn't argue but he saw something in her eyes that made him wonder about the missing piece of the puzzle, what wasn't she telling him? He had blind faith in her and would follow her lead, regardless of where it would take him.

They drove mostly in silence as he fought back the urge to tell everyone that they had just married but thought of Maria's disappointment and held back. Paige was also quiet, her mind clearly preoccupied with details about the hit she was about to make. He wanted to know what she was thinking but knew what it was like to be in that stage before murdering someone; you were running through every possible scenario or potential problem, mentally preparing for anything and everything that could go wrong. It didn't appear that Paige had many hits go wrong so he had to trust her process and wait.

They eventually arrived at a dingy warehouse that seemed hidden from the rest of the world. Paige removed a gun from her purse and put on her gloves, her eyes carried some sadness when she looked in his, causing him to feel an invisible hand reach up and grasp the back of his neck as a chill ran up his spine. There was something she wasn't telling him. She glanced toward his bulging pocket that held his gun and quietly asked, "Are you ready?"

"Yes," He replied with some hesitation but followed her out of the SUV and headed toward the building. She stopped him just as they were about to go inside, her gloved hand gently touching his arm.

"Follow my lead," She insisted and shook her head. "Don't take over no matter what."

Jorge wasn't sure he could agree but followed her inside the dark, bleak building. Paige's comfort level as she slowly walked through indicated that she was familiar with the setting, her shoes barely touching the ground, she moved like a cat stalking its prey and put her hand up to indicate he stay back as she turned a corner. That's when he heard the voice. It sounded familiar but he wasn't sure why.

"You got him?"

Jorge reached for his gun but Paige's hand stopped him. Her eyes connected with his and for a moment, he felt a sense of calmness. She wanted him to follow her lead. He had to trust her but trust, it wasn't exactly something that came easily to him. She reached for his arm and roughly pulled him into the next room and he weakly allowed it, her gun suddenly out and pressed beside his head as her left arm grasped around his neck. He briefly closed his eyes, praying that he hadn't been wrong about her all along but feeling an odd sense of serenity that he shouldn't have expected at that moment. If it was his time to die, he would have to accept it.

"I do," Paige replied calmly and Jorge opened his eyes and stared at the man across the room. He was a white man, average height, in his early 50s but yet, there was nothing distinguishing about him. He wasn't familiar. "And you wouldn't believe what I had to do to get him here so you better have the money."

Jorge's body suddenly felt weak and he let out an involuntary whimper.

"Ma'am, I've got your money," The man reached forward for a duffel bag that was on the floor nearby and it was at that precise moment that everything started to pick up the pace.

Paige tightened the grip around Jorge's neck, pulling him back while her arm extended and she shot the man in the head; literally blowing the top off his head. Blood was everywhere; on the wall behind where the man had stood, running on the floor toward them, he felt her arm loosen as he stood in stunned silence.

"We should go," Her voice was suddenly back to normal as if nothing had just taken place. Jorge found his feet and began to walk then stopped.

"Wait, the money?"

"It's not real," She shook her head and glanced toward the man then back at Jorge as if there were nothing out of the ordinary about this scene. Her eyes were cold. "Besides, do you really want to dig through bits of brain to get to it?"

Shaking his head no, he followed her outside.

"Cameras?" His arm felt heavy when lifting it to point back toward the warehouse. Not a car was in sight, the SUV parked in a dark corner, unnoticeable from the highway. Suddenly, his brain switched to high gear as his heart began to race. "You sure no one else is here? Why did he want you to kill me? Does he know who I am? I don't understand what the fuck is going on."

"No cameras, I already checked it out last week," Paige calmly assured him and hesitated for a moment and reached for Jorge's hand. "He's alone and I will explain everything else when we get on the road. We shouldn't stick around here for long."

Following her orders, he silently sat in the passenger seat and attempted to put everything together. This man wanted to kill him. That's why she had been so secretive. Had he not insisted on coming with her, would Paige have told him about this at all? Had there been anyone else she had killed to protect him?

Beside him, she looked calm, as if she hadn't just killed someone and suddenly it hit him; she was him. Jorge was probably looking at her the same way Chase had him after he killed Maggie Telips a few months earlier. At the time, he assumed it was his naïvety kicking in but now, he saw things differently. They were completely desensitized. At least, he had been before that day. Why was this murder affecting him?

"I don't understand," He managed to say as they got back on the highway leaving the dead body far behind as they drove toward Niagara Falls. "That man wanted me dead? Who was he? I didn't know him."

She hesitated for a moment before speaking. "Sometimes it's the enemies we don't recognize that are the biggest threat," Paige commented as she reached over to turn the heat up but it wasn't killing the chill in the SUV.

"That guy is with the church. His name is Don Warrens." Paige calmly started to explain. "He's part of the church group that wanted the other Hernandez dead but he's also part of the group that wants the sex clubs shut down. When he found out that the suite was originally supposed to be yours and you were involved with the clubs, he apparently saw it as a sign from God that you should die too. He thought it was too much of a coincidence to ignore."

"Fuck," Jorge finally found his voice. "So those religious people who start petitions against us…"

"He's one of them," Paige commented as she continued to focus on the road. "He's probably their loudest protester…or *was*, their loudest protester." Her lips formed into a small grin. "He recently contacted my boss to have you killed."

"But it's fake money?" Jorge began to unravel everything. "How do you know?"

"The man has nothing, I checked out his assets because I figured he was bluffing and then worried that he might get the idea to kill you himself. I wanted to know what I was dealing with and well, I figured out that he planned to put a few real bills on top and fake ones on the bottom since he had been Googling repeatedly for the last couple of weeks," She let out a laugh. "It's a super 'bad movie of the week' idea and any assassin would see through it and killed him for wasting their time."

"Wow," Jorge continued to feel stunned, his heart still racing as he glanced at the traffic beside the SUV. As he began to calm down, he felt a familiar sense of desire overwhelm him as he replayed those moments of her shooting Don Warrens. Her power, her strength as she took charge of the situation and got him; it was so fast, so precise, with not even a second of doubt, she killed him instantly before the man even knew what was happening. He bit his lower lip as his temptations grew with each passing second.

"So, this guy has an interesting history," Paige continued as Jorge mentally calculated how far they were from the hotel. He wanted to devour her. "He made a botched attempt to kill an abortion doctor once, years ago and the church somehow got him out of it. He also stalked another abortion doctor for years and made her life hell but yet, a restraining order doesn't do much. Then he got wind of the sex club and immediately gathered people together to protest them and when he recently found out you were involved, he decided you should die. He's been obsessed with you for weeks."

"How did you…." Jorge couldn't finish his question; his brain was half on the conversation, half in another magical place, a fantasy land that he wished to soon become reality as he searched for signals that they were about to return to Niagara Falls and even more importantly, their hotel.

"The person who organizes my hits got a call about you. He claimed to be representing the church. We knew it wasn't true because there's only one person from the church that we deal with and it's not him. It didn't take me long to put it all together after that point."

Paige briefly glanced at him and somehow seemed to miss the bulge in his pants as Jorge glanced toward the road signs indicating that they were almost in Niagara Falls.

"Of course, I was told immediately," Paige continued as her eyes watched the road. "I did some research on him and I guess you know the rest of the story."

"You're amazing, Mrs. Hernandez," Jorge replied in a quiet voice. "Absolutely amazing."

"Noël Hernandez," She gently corrected as her eyes glanced at his crotch. "And we're almost there."

CHAPTER 45

It had started in the SUV as they returned to Niagara Falls. It was merely a look between Paige and Jorge that would've meant nothing to anyone else but to them, it carried a hidden meaning that was more powerful than words. They were able to communicate without speaking, something Jorge hadn't experienced before in his life; the ability to read each other's thoughts, know each other in a way that was beyond logical explanation. It was beautiful.

By the time they reached the elevator of the hotel, it took a lot to suppress his desires that were simmering below the surface. He knew there was something incredibly twisted about being turned on by a woman who had just brutally murdered a man in front of him but he had long given up on understanding what churned his longings. Perhaps it was because she killed the religious fanatic in his honor, a powerful gesture symbolic of how deep her feelings ran for him. Loyalty was everything to him.

Then again, he had just married. It already felt like a lot of time had passed when in fact, it was only mere hours. So much had transpired and yet, his only focus as they walked into the hotel room was devouring her. The door barely closed when Jorge playfully pushed Paige against the wall, his lips immediately found her neck, the dingy smell from the warehouse filled his lungs, as he tasted her flesh. Letting out an involuntary moan, his breath immediately increased and as his tongue reached out to touch Paige's earlobe causing her to let out a short gasp as her arms tightly wrapped around his neck. Without a second thought, Jorge slid his hands over her hips and immediately pulled her up, her legs suddenly wrapped around his waist, he wasted no time getting her to the bed.

Moving away from his wife, he quickly ripped off his shirt and tie, throwing both on the floor as she lay back and quietly watched him.

"Do I have to do everything here?" Jorge teased as he moved forward and started to remove her boots, which seemed to take forever, as she giggled at his frustration. "You know you could help me out, come on."

Without replying, she sat up and began to gently kiss him, which he met with a hungry response, easing her back on the bed, his tongue slid into her mouth as his hand moved under her shirt and he quickly unclasped her bra. His fingers reached for her breast while his other hand eagerly worked to unbutton the jeans she put on before they headed out of town, causing him to suddenly wish that she still was wearing the dress from earlier that afternoon. Recognizing his struggle, she reached forward and opened the excruciating button as Jorge's head ducked under her shirt, he felt her wiggle under him, a soft moan left her throat as his tongue slid over her pink nipple, the skin becoming tighter with each passing second as his hand drifted inside her pants, finding the warm place between her legs, his fingers slid inside Paige causing her hips to lift while her hand opened the button on his pants and finally slid into his underwear.

Laying his head on her chest, Jorge thought he would lose his mind as her hand slowly, oh so slowly, squeezed his dick, only to let it go. He quickly moved away and removed his pants, underwear while she, fortunately, was following his lead. Women's clothing was so much more complicated, so many buttons and clasps, he returned to the bed and laid down as he watched her work. Her top and bra were already on the floor, as he stared at her smooth stomach, Paige struggled to remove her jeans, which made him grin when she finally did so, followed by her socks but for some reason, she left her skimpy little panties on.

Crawling on top of him, she leaned down with her ass in the air and he thought he was going to lose his mind as the gentle curve of her hips peeked out of the top of her panties, Jorge's hand immediately landing on her ass with a loud slap as her lips hungrily met with his and he squeezed her ass and roughly pulled her against him then rolled on top of her. Crushing his body against hers, Jorge continued to grasp her ass as he panted like a wild animal, his teeth sank into the skin just below the back of her neck, he noted the dark patch on the other side from where he did the same a few night's earlier. Had someone viewed his wife's naked body, they would think he abused her she was full of bite marks, bruises while his own body resembled one attacked by a vicious wild cat. Of course, no one could see. They hid it well.

Paige gasped loudly as his teeth sank into her soft flesh, her body jerked as he thrust his hips forward, feeling pleasure as he rubbed against her, knowing that her desires were mounting, he could tell by her reaction as her legs enclosed him, pulling him closer. Although he was tempted to tease her, to drive her crazy as he normally did, there was simply no way he could wait for another second longer as he spread her legs and slide inside.

She was so wet as he pushed deep inside and began to thrust roughly as she wrapped both her arms and legs tightly around him, her fingernails jabbing into his back as his breath became completely erratic, pleasure increased until he was on the edge, he struggled to keep it together as his teeth once again sunk into the flesh of her neck, Paige let out a loud, animal-like moan and instructed him to push harder, which he did as beads of sweat formed on his forehead, his lips moved away from her neck, unable to control the noises coming from the back of his throat as she cried out so freely, the bed rattling against the wall, she let out that last, squeal that was unmistakably his cue as he finally exploded inside of her as intense pleasure rang through his body and as he finally collapsed on top of his wife.

His heart was pounding furiously, sweat was pouring off his body, even his hair was wet as Paige's hand gently slid down his back as she relaxed beneath him. He rested his head on her shoulder and felt unexpected emotions spring inside of him, as he closed his eyes a tear slid out of his eye. It had been an intense day for so many reasons and although it would've been Jorge's preference to hide these emotions, Paige recognized the difference between sweat and a trickling tear.

"Are you ok?" She whispered in her usual relaxed tone as he reluctantly lifted his head, wiping his face with the back of his hand.

He looked into her eyes and opened his mouth but was unable to speak. His tongue felt twisted and he simply shook his head.

One of her hands ran over his back while the other slid through his hair. Pulling him close, their lips met, their kiss this time was gentle, serene, silent. When it ended, neither spoke as he rose from the bed and walked into the bathroom. Staring straight in the mirror, he wondered what was wrong with him; he felt broken in a way that didn't make sense. Did love make you soft? He didn't feel like the same person he had been only a few weeks earlier and this concerned him. Turning on the water, he splashed it on his face and leaned up against the sink for another minute before returning to the bedroom.

Paige had moved to the other side of the bed and he smirked knowing that it was probably slightly more comfortable, all things considered, he got on the bed and crawled over to her side. She had the blanket pulled over her breasts, in a conservative way that made him laugh since he had no intentions of wearing clothes again until they left the hotel, he grinned and got under the covers beside her.

"What are you thinking now?" She asked in a casual tone even though her eyes appeared to be searching his face in an analytical manner as she turned toward him.

"Honestly," Jorge spoke quietly, his voice cutting out, he cleared his throat. "I'm thinking that I need a drink of water." He put his finger up as if to indicate for her to wait for a second as he reached on the nightstand and grabbed his bottle left there earlier in the day and took a drink. He sat it back on the nightstand and returned his attention to her. "I'm thinking that I would fucking love a cigarette now."

She let out a laugh and looked away.

"Such deep thoughts," She teased.

"Yeah, well, the blood is just returning to my brain after being gone for longer than is probably healthy," Jorge joked. "That's the best you're going to get at this point."

"Please don't smoke," She quietly requested and he leaned in and gave her a quick kiss.

"Don't worry," He replied. "I'm not going to especially since you told me about the impotence thing. Fuck, I can live without a cigarette, I can't live without sex. Just put a fucking knife through my heart."

"I will put a knife through someone else's heart *for* you but I won't put one in you," Paige confirmed and began to laugh. He quickly joined her.

"Deal," He grinned. "So, this guy today, he hates the sex club thing so much he actually wanted me dead? I've had a lot of people want me dead over the years but never because I was involved in a sex club. That's fucked up."

Continuing to sit up, Paige did the same, still holding the blanket over her chest as if she were too shy to show him her body and he grinned but didn't say anything. It was actually kind of cute for some reason.

"He did," Paige confirmed. "These religious fanatics can be very dangerous. They think nothing of killing to prove their dedication to the church. They think they're the Lord's soldier."

Jorge let out a laugh and rubbed his eyes. "Some fucking soldier," He commented as he thought back to the warehouse. "So he thought you were going to kill me for a bag of money."

"Yes," Paige confirmed, her eyes were suddenly full of emotion. "I hated not telling you what was going on but I knew I had to play along to get this guy. I had to send a message to that community."

"That's why you didn't want me to come with you," Jorge observed and glanced at her as she fought back tears.

"I didn't want you to know," Paige quietly admitted. "I wasn't sure if I should tell you. After the emails that Marco sent us, I couldn't shake the feeling that there was something more going on. As it turns out, the answer came to me."

"But when they find this guy…"

"That's the beauty of it," Paige said with a grin. "It's a cop's gun."

"What the fuck? Are you serious?"

"Just as some extra insurance, we use guns we steal from cops," Paige confirmed. "Not so much steal as a switch. That way if the gun is found, they'll most likely drop the case in order to cover up any wrongdoing in their department."

Jorge's eyes widened and a smile crept on his face. "Holy fuck! That's brilliant. And what, they don't even realize is it's not their gun?"

"Nope," Paige let out a laugh. "We're talking the young, inexperienced ones. We always get them early and well, the rest is obvious, police departments quietly let them go and push everything under the rug."

"Oh that's fucking incredible," Jorge laughed. "I love it. That's perfect."

"It works for me," Paige confirmed. "Although I considered making his death look like a suicide or an accident, something inside of me wanted to shoot this man and make his death brutal. He deserved it for wanting to kill you," She mused for a moment. "Hopefully these people get the message."

Her last words were cold, smooth and yet, so enticing to him. He found pleasure in the fact that her love for him ran so deep that she was willing to murder someone to prove her dedication. This was rare. No one had ever loved him that much before and in fact, he doubted many had loved him at all, especially in comparison. To some, it would possibly be considered sadistic but to him, it was a beautiful gesture. It was a powerful sign of dedication. He would never doubt her.

"Paige, if anyone ever even thought of hurting you," He turned toward her, his eyes widened as an inner rage combined with unmistakable lust rose inside of him. "I would kill them in the most brutal way imaginable. I would make them suffer and beg to die and then I would torture them more without a second thought. I wouldn't leave them alone until the last drop of blood poured out of their body. And I would have no regret. That's how much I love you."

Her eyes filled with tears as he spoke and she stared at him as if under a spell, her lips parting slightly but she didn't speak.

CHAPTER 46

"It feels weird wearing clothes again," Jorge teased Paige as they drove back to Toronto after a couple of days in Niagara Falls for both work and pleasure. After taking care of Don Warrens, they essentially stayed in their hotel room, uninterested in hearing anything about the outside world. It was only on their way home that a radio announcer mentioned the murder in her newscast, simply stating that the police felt it was a 'random shooting' that they were still investigating but there were no leads. Exchanging knowing looks, neither commented on it.

"I would think you'd appreciate your clothes after you walked outside this morning," Paige replied from the passenger side as she briefly glanced to her right then back at Jorge. "Winter is coming."

"Yes, I was thinking the same," His reply was tense and they immediately ended their conversation. For the rest of the drive, Paige was on her iPhone, occasionally making comments about various current events but for the most part, not talking at all. It wasn't until they were back in Toronto and met in Clara's parking lot that they both breathed a little easier.

The three shared a smile with the 'cleaning lady' before she went to work going through the vehicle with a fine tooth comb but much to their surprise, she didn't find anything.

"*Estás seguro?*" Jorge asked and watched the older lady nodding her head.

"*Si.*"

Tired, Jorge thanked her, gave her some cash and got back into the SUV and after giving Clara a quick hug, Paige did the same.

"I was afraid that someone might've left us a wedding present while we were enjoying our honeymoon," Jorge finally spoke after they were inside the vehicle and both fastening their seatbelt. Feeling stressed, he reached for a pack of gum and shoved two pieces in his mouth. "I guess paranoia has taken over."

"Considering your lifestyle, I think it's smart to stay vigilant," Paige commented as they got back on the road and headed toward Diego and Jolene Inc. for a meeting. "You know, I don't have to come with you to the office. If you need me to do something else?"

"No, you should come," Jorge commented and reached out to gently touch her hand for a moment. "You are as much a part of all of this as anyone. I want you there."

Everyone was waiting for them in the boardroom when they arrived. A box of donuts sat on the table with a couple of empty, greasy spots where two were taken; Jorge's stomach gurgled when offered one but he shook his head. He did, however, accept a cup of Diego's coffee as did Paige.

Sitting beside his wife and across from Jolene and Chase, no one said a word at first, an obvious tension in the room, they waited for Diego to return with their coffee. Finally, looking ill at ease, Chase spoke.

"How was Niagara Falls?" He asked as Jolene grimaced beside him and Paige glanced toward Jorge, who answered.

"Nice," He nodded. "Have you been?"

"No," Chase replied. "I hear it's pretty."

Jorge opened his mouth to reply but just then, Diego flew in the door with two cups of coffee; cream and sugar were already on the table. His attention, of course, was on Paige, something that didn't feel as threatening to Jorge as it once had and he wasn't sure why.

"*Paige*," Diego said her name with great emphasis as if he were reaffirming her identity. "Do you have pictures? Did you do any shopping? I heard that the stores in Niagara Fall and…"

"Diego, can we leave the girl talk for another time, we got a meeting to conduct," Jorge asked with a shrug.

"It's not *girl* talk, it's just normal conversation," Diego quickly corrected him. "I'm her friend, I care."

"We'll talk about it later," Paige shared a smile with Diego, who appeared satisfied and returned to his seat at the end of the table. "This coffee is perfect, Diego, thank you."

"Someday, I will show you my secret," He puckered his lips, nodding his head.

"You will not show me your secret but you show her?" Jolene didn't attempt to hide her irritation. "I am your sister!"

"Ok, enough fighting boys and girls," Jorge snapped at Jolene. "We're here to have a meeting not discuss fucking coffee."

Jolene's eyes grew dark as she clasped her mouth shut.

"So, some important things happened that we need to discuss," Jorge jumped right in as he poured some cream in his coffee and carefully stirred it. "There was a threat recently made against me by a guy named Don Warrens. I won't get into the details with you but the important point is that this guy is no longer a concern, however, we know he was connected to a religious group."

"Specifically," Paige suddenly took over, allowing Jorge to gratefully take a drink of his coffee and slowly reach for a donut, despite the look she was giving him as he did. "The same religious group that is always complaining to the media about this business, the same group that starts petitions and complain about how the sex parties are ruining the moral fiber…" She drifted off, her eyes moving from person to person and finally back at her husband.

"Diego," Jorge briefly allowed his train of thought drift off topic. "This coffee *is* really good."

"Thank you," Diego spoke with pride as Jorge turned to Paige.

"You definitely got to learn how he does this," He spoke gently. "Cause I'm going to fuck it up if I try."

"I thought we were to discuss important issues," Jolene spoke loudly with clear irritation in her voice. "This is not it, no?"

"You're right, Jolene," Jorge continued. "As Paige was saying, we know that these religious fanatics are more dangerous than we originally thought. I used to think they were just a pain in the ass but now I take them very seriously."

"But what do we do?" Jolene asked. "Will they try to hurt us?"

"I say we wait and watch," Paige suggested and directed her next comment to Jorge. "I think we sent a strong message. Let's see how they react."

There was a silent acknowledgment around the room.

"Should we be monitoring them for the next few days?" Chase suggested. "Maybe they will step back. Let's see if there are any letters in the paper or protesters outside the club, that kind of thing."

"Any protesters lately?" Jorge asked Chase, knowing that it was rare that this happened but it had occurred a few times, as a way to intimidate their guests. It hadn't worked.

"Not since the summer," Chase replied. "I didn't see anything in the paper today either."

"No, there was nothing," Jolene confirmed and opened her MacBook. "Let us see about the petition."

"Petition's gone," Diego spoke up before she had a chance. At the end of the table, he was tapping on his phone. "At least, I can't find it."

"Should we be encouraged or does this mean they are looking for a different way?" Jolene asked. "Do you think...*we* are in danger here?"

"Not if they know who they're fucking dealing with," Jorge answered with some anger in his voice. "I'm not playing around with these holier than thou types, I can fucking tell you that much. If we didn't send a strong message already then we are going to have to figure out who's at the top."

"It might not be what we think," Chase cut in and waved his hand around. "We assume that it's coming from a religious group but what if they are actually working for someone else? Our competition?"

"Well," Jorge sat up a bit straighter and exchanged looks with everyone at the table. "I'm not fucking around with whoever it is. When I find out who is behind all this, I'm taking care of it myself, personally."

He made a point of glaring at Jolene, making eye contact long enough to send a message because regardless of what had taken place, he didn't trust her.

"Which reminds me, what's the latest with this Gracie girl?" He directed his question at Jolene. "Where the fuck is she?"

"She decide that the city life, it is not for her," Jolene commented gently in her usual broken English as she slid her fingers over her coffee cup. "We had a serious discussion and she see that she is not happy here and that the city, is dangerous for little girls from small town. She return home."

"How do we know she won't return home and talk?" Jorge pushed as he continued to size up Jolene from across the table.

"I suspect because she will be too busy talking about how she was mugged at the bus stop late one night," Jolene commented in a soft voice, her eyes innocently glancing around the room. "She has such bad bruises, it's unfortunate, such a pretty girl. They threaten to shoot her and she was so upset, she does not know what the man looked like."

"The man?" Jorge asked with a smirk on his face.

"Of course, isn't it always a man that is the violent one?" Jolene replied with a shrug. "We know men are far more violent than women. We have wars because of it."

Jorge grinned and looked toward Paige, who nodded. Chase was expressionless and Diego was quickly jumping in.

"That's cause men know that it's all about power, Jolene. You have to send a message to your enemy."

"I believe she got the message," Jolene confirmed with confidence in her voice. "I do not think she will ever want to talk about any of this to anyone. Also, I know where she lives. I know her family and I also know where her sister lives here in Toronto. If we have any issue, then so will she."

"Sounds reasonable," Jorge commented casually as he reached for a second donut and then stopped, looking back at Paige who merely shrugged.

"You know the possible consequences," She muttered and with quick flashes of his last two days of sexual euphoria, he decided against the donut.

"So, we got that covered," Diego asked. "I personally don't think we should've let her go with just a few bruises."

"There were more than a few," Jolene quickly corrected him. "She could barely move to get on the plane home. They put her in a wheelchair, I am told."

"She's young," Paige commented. "It's easier when they are young."

"And a party girl," Diego added. "Party girls are always easy."

Chase grinned and avoided Diego's eyes.

"I didn't mean that way," Diego corrected himself at the end of the table. "I mean, they scare easily."

"Like a kitten," Paige gently added.

"Ok, enough of that," Jorge curtly ended the conversation. "So the store, I'm hoping to have it opened next week. My associate Jesús is in town and him and I will discuss the details probably later today. Once it's opened, we think our business is only going to grow stronger."

"The cocaine, it is still selling a lot at parties," Jolene added.

"Cocaine never goes out of style," Jorge insisted.

"So," Diego cut in, "what about the girl, this Juliana lady? She can help us with the parties?"

"Yes," Jorge replied. "I have spoken with her. She will do whatever you need. She's smart, been to college, all of that and Maria does not need as much attention now that she's got me and Paige around. I feel that Juliana is capable of more and occasionally, she will also help at the store too. There are times, I may need you there," He pointed at Chase. "Pop over and check things out."

Chase nodded and his eyes softened.

"You can teach Juliana everything you know," He commented and then added in a seductive tone. "Or perhaps the other way around, you know she is single now, Chase."

Chase didn't comment just grinned and shook his head while at the end of the table, a dark cloud formed over Diego while Jolene simply looked disgusted.

"She is not hired to be his plaything," She snapped and that was when Jorge once again suspected something was going on between them, however, he was smart enough to hide his instincts. Merely grinning, he avoided eye contact with them all; for various reasons.

"It was a joke, Jolene," Jorge commented even though his eyes were quickly switched to Diego who looked more sad than angry and he immediately felt bad. "We got too much work to do without having dramatic office affairs." This time he raised his eyebrows at Jolene who looked away.

"Ok, so we covered the store, we covered Gracie and her replacement," Jorge rushed ahead, suddenly feeling antsy to get out of the office. How did all these people stay stuffed in this place all day? It seemed so unnatural.

"The wedding?" Diego spoke up.

"That's not work related," Jorge quickly cut him off.

"Want me to do some research on this religious group we were talking about earlier?" Chase asked. "See if I can find anything?"

"That would be perfect," Jorge replied and nodded. "I think Paige has already done some research so maybe you two keep in contact about this one?"

Paige nodded and watched Chase, who looked instead at Jorge and said a quick, "Yes."

"The office, it is fine since Gracie left?" Jorge glanced around. "No questions? Gossip?"

"They say she got attacked at the bus stop and that is all," Jolene commented. "It is quiet here."

"Even Sylvana is quiet," Diego insisted. "And that woman is never quiet."

"It is true," Jolene confirmed. "She not say much now. But her work, it is good."

"Beverly?" Jorge asked.

"Her friend cannot find who sent in request to investigate us but it is fine," Jolene insisted. "We pass."

"Nothing more?" Jorge glanced around the table and everyone remained tight-lipped and Diego made a face and shook his head.

"Then we must go," Jorge stood up and quickly finished his coffee.

Everyone left the room. Once out of the office, him and Paige exchanged silent looks.

CHAPTER 47

"*Buenos días*, Marco," Jorge sat across from the Filipino man who appeared unusually tired, with dark circles under his eyes, he still, however, remained friendly with a bright smile. Granted it was shortly after 7 in the morning, so it was understandable. He definitely wasn't feeling overzealous either.

"Good morning, Mr. Hernandez," He spoke with a gentle enthusiasm as he took a drink of his coffee. "How are you this morning?"

"Fucking tired," Jorge answered honestly and Marco laughed. "I'm sorry to have a meeting at such an early hour but I wanted to talk to you before you went to the office."

"Of course, sir," Marco replied, his eyes widened as he spoke. "I am happy to meet with you."

"Are you still working the other job?" Jorge asked while watching Marco carefully, knowing that this was probably the reason he appeared so exhausted. "I know you wanted to finish your two weeks at the hotel. That must be almost finished?"

"Yes, it finished last Thursday."

"Still catching up on your sleep?" Jorge asked with a grin. "Or did your wife keep you up late last night?"

Marco giggled and briefly looked away, showing a touch of shyness that Jorge hadn't expected, followed by him shaking his head.

"No, I am not sleeping because of my neighbors," Marco admitted hesitantly. "Loud music, people in and out at all hours and they have a loud dog. One of those, very scary dogs that frightens my children."

Jorge knew the signs of a drug dealer. He knew it all too well and immediately started to nod in understanding. "You got to get out of there, my friend."

"I know, we are looking," Marco admitted. "It is not easy to find a place."

"Tell me about it," Jorge related. "We are trying to find a house that doesn't cost a fucking fortune and isn't a dump."

"Exactly!" Marco replied. "Us too, but we need an apartment and it is difficult."

"If you need anything," Jorge commented and leaned forward. "*Anything*, you let me know. If you ever find yourself in a sticky situation with these neighbors, call me. I'm really good at solving problems."

Marco nodded slowly in understanding. "I will, thank you."

"So, the office," Jorge commented and took another drink of his coffee while making a mental note of looking into these neighbors when he had a chance. "How are things lately? Since my meetings with everyone, Gracie leaving, that kind of thing?"

"It has been good," Marco seemed to think. "I have forwarded you any possible suspicious emails but things are quiet, especially since Gracie left."

"And you," Jorge asked and leaned back in his chair. "Are you helping Sylvana?"

"Yes, sir."

"What is she like to work with?" Jorge asked.

"At first, I thought she was going to be difficult," Marco admitted, his forehead wrinkled and then relaxed as he shrugged and shook his head. "But now, she is fine. We actually work well together. It is nice."

"Good," Jorge nodded. "And the office, notice anything strange? Maybe with Jolene?"

"I did notice something I wanted to say," Marco commented and lowered his voice. "I notice that she and Sylvana argue often but maybe I have already mentioned this…"

"I think so," Jorge commented and was suddenly alert. "Do you know why?"

"I do not know," Marco answered honestly. "I see them in the boardroom recently and it appeared they were arguing. I tried to see if Benjamin knew but he did not. The secretary, she does not get involved and Beverly, I don't feel I can ask her. She's usually with Diego anyway."

Jorge didn't reply but nodded as he finished his coffee.

"Sorry, I am not able to tell you anything," Marco continued and frowned. "It is a secretive office. I will continue to watch though."

When he later returned to an empty apartment, Jorge suddenly had an urge to look at the emails that Marco had originally hacked for him, the same ones that Paige constantly asked him to check but he hadn't. With some apprehension, he opened up the file and began to go through them. As he suspected, there was nothing that stood out as he scanned through, quickly growing bored, he was about to delete them when something caught his eye. It was so small that he almost missed it.

When Paige arrived home, he was lying on the couch, flipping through the channels. Blinking rapidly, she crossed the room with a surprised expression on her face.

"Are you ok?" She asked as he turned off the television, throwing the remote on a nearby table. "Is something wrong?"

"Nothing you can't fix," He extended his hand which she took and proceeded to lie down with him. Wrapping his arms around her, he fought anger from his heart and instead enjoyed that moment with her. Face to face, he knew that she could see right through him and at first, he honestly had no intention of saying anything. "I checked the emails today."

"Really?" Paige said with a smooth grin. "The same ones I've asked you to check for weeks?"

"I know, I know," He replied and pulled her closer. "I'm a terrible husband who doesn't listen."

"I didn't say you were terrible," She softly replied and leaned forward to gently kiss his lips. "I'm saying you don't obey."

Jorge laughed while his hands kneaded her back and he briefly closed his eyes.

"So what's wrong?" Paige coaxed him. "I can tell you found something. I went through them carefully and didn't see anything."

"That's cause there's nothing in the content," He whispered and suddenly didn't want to deal with any of this and wasn't even sure of what to do. Opening his eyes again, Jorge recognized the concern in Paige's eyes. "When Jolene was sending an email to Chase to let him know that I would be in town the night, the same night you came to my hotel to shoot the other Hernandez? She sent a blind carbon copy to someone else and I almost didn't notice who."

Paige's eyes widened and her mouth fell open slightly.

"Now, I have to have a conversation with Jolene about it," Jorge said and hesitated. "And it won't be a pleasant one."

"Do you need me...to do anything?" Paige was hesitant to finish her sentence. "Maybe you should...wait before you talk to her?"

"I'm going to her apartment tonight," Jorge replied and bit his lower lip. "I can't talk to her at the office about this and I want to surprise her."

"Do you want me to come along?" Paige looked nervous. "I don't know if I want you to go there alone."

Jorge looked into her eyes and leaned forward and whispered, "No, I'm fine *señora*, I can handle her."

"I'm coming," She insisted. "I will be downstairs or somewhere but I just.."

"Im fine," Jorge insisted. "I love you for worrying though."

"Of course I'm worried," Paige was insistent. "What are you going to do?"

He didn't reply. It wasn't a question he had the answer to yet and it would be on his mind for the rest of the day. Paige went back and checked the emails again and saw what he was referring to; it was just one email, simple in content but Don Warrens was in the BCC, meaning Jolene had tipped him off. A solemn mood hung over the apartment as Jorge attempted to understand but the truth was that there was no explanation that could be justified.

That evening, Paige insisted on going with him, even if it meant waiting outside in the SUV. She wasn't about to allow him to go to Jolene's alone. Her eyes reflected the dismal reaction in his own just before he got out of the vehicle and approached the main door. Buzzing her apartment, Jolene sounded apprehensive when she found out he was downstairs causing Jorge to automatically reach in his pocket to grasp his gun, preparing for anything once he got inside.

He was surprised when she opened the door wearing a sheer nightdress. Giving her the once over, it was hard to not be distracted by ample cleavage, the material clinging to her body, showing every curve but he was stronger than perhaps she had guessed.

"This here," Jolene pointed toward her body. "This is not for you if that is what you think."

Blinking rapidly, his eyes jumped past her into an empty apartment and to what he guessed was her bedroom door, which was closed. Feeling powerless in this situation caused anger to rise in him. "Look, I don't care who you fuck Jolene and I'm not here to seduce you. I need to talk to you and I need to talk to you now."

"Come by the office tomorrow," Jolene snapped. "This is my private life."

"Really?" Jorge asked with a syrupy sweet voice, he muttered. "You think you're in the position to make the rules, are you? We need to talk about Don Warrens."

Jolene's expression automatically changed, her eyes full of fear. She turned and walked toward the couch where she sat down. Jorge entered the apartment and closed the door behind him. He sat in a nearby chair, his eyes once again drifted toward the closed bedroom door. Perking up his ears, Jorge was certain he could hear someone else in the apartment.

"So what's the occasion?" He boldly asked and his eyes challenged hers as he gestured toward her outfit.

"I have a friend coming here," Jolene abruptly commented. "Maybe I have a life too, do you not think?"

"You're very secretive," Jorge replied as his hand eased into his leather jacket and caressed the gun while his eyes scanned the room for clues. "For example, I didn't know you were friends with the man who wanted to have me killed."

Tears formed in her eyes and she attempted to blink them away. Her body suddenly appeared tense as she leaned forward, her eyes drifted toward the bulge in his jacket. "We are not friends. When he protests our business, we get more customers and when I see this, I decide it was a good idea to use it to our advantage."

Jorge was expressionless but played along.

"Then why didn't you tell me the truth?"

"When I learn that he was dangerous, I was scared you would think I was involved," Jolene weakly admitted, sitting up straighter, she pushed her breasts out. "I did not see that the religious were crazy people. I wanted them to protest us to get more business and he thought I was helping him because I also did not approve of the clubs. He said that when you came to town, he wanted to protest at the hotel."

"Oh, like that's any better?" Jorge replied with gentle sarcasm. If nothing else, he found this story to be entertaining. "Having them protesting at my hotel? Do you think I'm believing any of this, Jolene?"

"You do not believe me? Go to the hotel, ask them about the protesters that were there that night," Jolene insisted. "They were immediately removed because it is a private business. They didn't want the attention. You were late, no?"

"Jolene, I'm not a fucking moron," Jorge insisted. "You expect me to believe that you went behind everyone's back to arrange for these religious nuts to protest at the hotel because I was there and this would somehow bring in more business?"

"I thought it would bring more attention," Jolene spoke desperately. "Diego, he would kill me if he knows I did this."

"Finally! Something me and Diego can agree on," Jorge spoke sternly and removed his gun from the jacket. "Jolene, give me one good fucking reason why I don't kill you right now."

"My friend is coming..." She pointed toward the bedroom, her eyes filled with tears.

"I can kill both of you without a second thought and you know it," He spoke calmly as if they were having a civil conversation. "You know me, I'm impulsive sometimes."

"No, you would get *her*," Jolene gestured toward the door. "She, Paige, you will get *her*. She will do your dirty work."

"I can do my own dirty work," Jorge spoke sternly.

"You do not think that she will not kill you someday too?" Jolene began to cry. "She's an assassin and if she want, she can make you look like a suicide too. She will."

Jolene was trying to throw him off track. She wanted to cause doubt in the one vulnerable area of his life but instead of making him upset, it infuriated him. Jumping up from his seat, he pointed the gun at Jolene as she quietly cried.

"You have to believe me, I swear," Jolene moaned in desperation "I did not want him to kill you. I did not have anything to do with that, please. I swear." She stood up. "I do anything, just tell me."

"Anything? Kill the person who's coming to see you," Jorge glanced toward the bedroom door. "Or is he already here?"

Panic filled Jolene's face.

"You want to prove your loyalty? You want to show me that I can trust you?" Jorge spoke with ease. "Kill him."

"I barely know."

"Perfect," Jorge insisted. "Then it shouldn't be too difficult, should it?"

"I cannot do," Jolene seemed to lose her voice, now she spoke in a whisper as tears continued to pour out of her eyes.

"I'm not in a fucking charitable mood, Jolene," Jorge insisted. "You've got to give me something cause I can guarantee you one thing, someone is going to die tonight."

Jolene wiped away one stray tear, her eyes full of terror, her voice was hoarse as she spoke. "I know who. He works with that man, that Don Warrens. I know where we can find him."

"Right now."

"Now?"

"Tell the friend you're hiding in the bedroom that you have to go out for a couple of hours." Jorge calmly shrugged, "For a work thing."

"But, I...."

"You're horny?" Jorge spoke in a condescending tone and pointed toward the bedroom. "So am I, but work comes first. Go put some clothes on unless you plan to go out like that. I'll be waiting here and Paige is downstairs, so don't get any ideas Jolene."

Stunned, she silently turned and headed toward her room.

Chapter 48

Dressed in jeans and a form-fitting sweater, Jolene slunk out of the room a couple of minutes later and walked toward him. Her makeup removed, the lines around her eyes and lips suddenly more prominent as she approached him. Giving Jolene a quick once over, he demanded her to stop and patted her down to make certain she wasn't carrying a gun.

"What about him?" Jorge pointed toward the closed bedroom door. "He got a gun? Am I going to be shot in the head when I turn around?"

"No, nobody is in there," Jolene confirmed. "I text that I will be late."

"Hmm…" Jorge thought for a moment and pointed the gun toward the door and watched Jolene carefully. "Well, just in case, maybe I should-

"No!" Jolene's eyes doubled in size as she put her hand up in the air to indicate he stop. "No one is there! Look, I show you!"

"Do it," Jorge spoke calmly, finding some sick pleasure in witnessing her fear.

Following close behind with his gun pointed toward the bedroom, he was ready to shoot the first thing that moved but instead, she opened the door to an empty room. Not fully trusting her, Jorge went inside and searched everything, opening the closet door and even looked under the bed. There wasn't anyone in the room.

"See, I told you that there was no one here," Jolene said as she dramatically waved her hands in the air. "When you arrive, I thought it was my guest here early, that is why I was surprised to learn you were at my door."

Jorge didn't show any emotion but definitely felt incredibly stupid, something he quickly covered with hostility. "I guess you were telling the truth. That's good because if found out you lied to me, the person in this room would be dead right now."

"I was telling truth," She gently closed the door and continued to whisper, a sense of relief filled her face. "I am telling you the truth on this man too. It is the person who helped out Don Warrens. I take you to him. I know where to find him."

Jorge didn't reply, tilting his head toward the door to let her know they were on their way out. She obediently walked ahead as Jorge shoved the gun back in his pocket and followed her. It wasn't until they were outside in the SUV that anyone spoke again. This time it was Paige.

"I see we have a guest?" She said pleasantly even though it was clear she had summed up the situation quickly. "Where are we going?"

In a weak voice, Jolene gave an address. Paige pulled onto the road and Jorge turned in his seat to watch Jolene carefully.

"Where the fuck is this, Jolene?"

"It is a church," Jolene quietly replied as she avoided eye contact with Jorge. "This man, he work with Don Warrens. Together, they protest the sex clubs but I do not know if he had anything to do with wanting you killed."

"Someone knows," Jorge replied. "And it's your job to convince me it wasn't you."

"How am I supposed to do?" Jolene cried. "He will not tell me!"

"You tell him the cops saw an email and are poking around," Paige calmly cut into their conversation, her eyes briefly looking in the rearview mirror at Jolene.

"Come on, Jolene!" Jorge snapped. "Is this your first fucking day as a criminal? You know how this is done and the bottom line is that you resolve this and resolve it now or your head is next on the chopping block cause right now, I don't think I can trust you."

"I swear, I did not know," Jolene insisted. "Are you crazy? We work together, I am not going to go behind your back."

"Unless you thought someone else was going to do the dirty work and never trace it to you," Paige commented from the front seat.

"Don't ever think we aren't watching," Jorge warned. "We know everything."

"Then you know that I did not do this," Jolene insisted. "I will do anything. Please, I beg, I am not disloyal."

Jorge didn't reply but shared a look with Paige.

When they arrived at the church, Jolene was hesitant to get out of the SUV. Paige was quickly by her side, passing the keys to Jorge as he pulled on a pair of leather gloves. He noted that she was already wearing hers.

"So this is what's going to happen," Paige spoke in her usual soft, emotionless voice. "We are going to go inside and you're going to get the truth."

"This man is a priest," Jolene spoke hesitantly.

"Then I'm sure he's going to be honest," Paige replied without as much as blinking her eyes.

Jorge stood back as the two women walked toward the church. He trailed behind, planning to watch from a distance. He waited until they both were inside before slipping in the door and listening for some sound. He didn't want to be far away in case Paige needed him. Seeing no one in sight, he walked through, ignoring all the religious statues that were staring down at him from both sides. They had no meaning. Since the day his brother died, there was no God.

Once at the back, he heard Jolene's muffled voice as she quickly shifted gears. No longer the victim begging for her life, it was as if reality suddenly hit her. From outside the door, Jorge could hear everything. Jolene was not holding back, fury rang through her voice as she demanded.

"Why? Why was there a policeman at my door asking me about Don Warrens," She screamed and there was some shuffling inside the office, "Why am I being questioned about this murder, as if I know anything? I only help you because I was hoping that the business would move away and me, I would finally be free! Instead, he wanted to kill Jorge Hernandez? Did he not think this man would not find out?"

She was certainly convincing but then again, which story should he believe? Her story about getting publicity was so far-fetched that he was unable to believe it but at the same time, what reason would make her want him dead? It didn't make sense.

"I don't know anything about it," He heard the panic in a man's voice. "I know that Don was a bit erratic because of his past but I didn't think he would really go after this Hernandez man. He talked about it but I tried to calm him…"

A gun clicked and Paige spoke. "Let's try the truth this time."

Silence.

"Don came to me with this notion of killing Jorge Hernandez," The man's voice was shaky as he spoke. "I said that the church could not help him with this matter. Only one person is allowed to approve such things and this wasn't one of those cases. He wanted to do it himself and I insisted it was the work of the devil. He wouldn't listen. He insisted on getting our contact that…takes care of these matters for us. He said he would fund it himself."

"So you gave him the name of someone who would do this for him?" Jolene snapped, her voice growing louder. "Now we have a man dead and the police, they are coming around at my business asking questions and next, they will be here doing the same to you. Do you not see why this is a problem?"

"My understanding at the time was that the person who does this work is careful and makes it look like an accident and that's what I thought would happen," The man's voice continued to be shaky. "And the more I thought about it, the more I realized that this man, Hernandez, he *is* the devil. He thrives on selling sex, I'm told he's part of the drug cartel that kills so many, he's probably committed heinous crimes too, so maybe Don wasn't wrong. Maybe this man should be dead. I don't know what happened, he must've found out and killed Don first."

Jorge suddenly pushed the door open and walked in, much to everyone's surprise. Jolene was standing with her arms folded over her breasts while a middle-aged man wearing a priest collar sat behind a desk with his hands in the air. Paige was pointing a gun toward the priest.

"Oh, he found out," Jorge pulled a gun out of his pocket. "You fucking hypocrites, every last one of you. Here you are saying that it's okay to kill me because I'm evil but what the fuck are you? Putting hits on your own people? Allowing a crazy man that's a part of your church to target me? To hurt people? Do you think you are God? At least I know what the fuck I am. I know that I'm evil and yes, I'm probably the devil to someone like you but at least I'm honest with myself."

"Please, I misspoke," The priest shook his head and raised his hands even higher into the air. "You're right, I do not know you at all. Obviously, you have a lot of pain inside your heart, young man..."

"Oh fuck you," Jorge snapped and pulled the trigger, shooting the man in the forehead. His heart pounded erratically, for a minute he thought he was going to pass out but after closing his eyes for a second he felt himself begin to calm. Beside him, Jolene showed no remorse and Paige merely moved closer to inspect the body before nodding.

"We should get out of here," She calmly commented and the three of them left the office and Jorge stopped them both outside the door, closing it gently he glanced around and made eye contact with Jolene.

"You better be telling me the truth, Jolene," His comment was stern and direct. "Cause next time, I'm not fucking asking questions."

"I promise, I do whatever you say," She insisted. "I promise, I did not know any of this."

Paige remained silent but he was curious what she was thinking. Something in her eyes told him to let it go.

He didn't respond but started to walk toward the door. Suddenly he felt as if his body was being swept away and for a split second, it was as though he had entered into a peaceful state of grace, where nothing could hurt him. Where life didn't matter. Then everything went black.

CHAPTER 49

It took him a minute to realize what had happened. Everything was blurry as a cold draft drifted across his face, slowly alerting his attention as he began to focus once again. Paige's blue eyes were full of fear as he felt a leather gloved hand on the side of his face. Heavy feet were running in the distance as Jolene's panicked voice echoed through the room.

"Where do I find water?" Her voice moved closer as he started to regain consciousness just as Jolene suddenly stopped and looked down at him, her eyes expanded as she leaned in closer. "It is a panic attack, maybe? Chase has them sometimes, this is how he is too. We need water."

"Jolene, please be calm," Paige spoke evenly although her face was full of anxiety. "Do me a favor, go watch the door that no one comes in before we can get out."

"I will do," Jolene said in little more than a whisper, rushing toward the exit.

Paige leaned in as her hand ran over his face and Jorge started to move.

"Wait, are you experiencing any chest pains? Does your arm feel funny?" Paige spoke slowly as if he were lacking the neurological skills to comprehend her questions.

Suddenly remembering the dead body in the next room, Jorge sat up quickly causing the room to spin for a moment, he closed his eyes and shook his head. "No, Paige, I'm fine. My arm, no chest pain, nothing, I'm fine, Paige. I promise you, I'm ok. We gotta get out of here."

She helped him up in silence but her eyes continued to carry concern.

"You need to go back to the doctor," She whispered.

"I'm fine," Jorge insisted as they began to walk out of the church. Glancing down, he suddenly stopped. "My gun?"

"I got it," Paige insisted and they started to walk again.

"Did I fall on the floor?" Jorge was suddenly confused. "I don't remember what happened."

"You started to fall and Jolene and I grabbed you," Paige explained. "We helped you on the floor. You were only out for a few seconds. You scared us both."

"Do you think she's..." Jorge didn't finish his sentence as they got closer to the door. Jolene was just outside.

"I think we're fine," Paige nodded and that was all she needed to say.

Outside, Jolene looked nervous as the three of them got in the SUV. Jorge insisted that he didn't need help and that he could drive, Paige reluctantly agreed.

"It's a panic attack," Jolene insisted once again as they started to drive away. Jorge glanced around to see if anyone was nearby but the street was quiet. Ignoring what Jolene was saying, his brain quickly went into defense mode.

"If for any reason, anyone saw us here tonight," Jorge commented while glancing between the two women. "We were looking for a place for Paige and me to get married."

Paige snickered but quickly nodded in understanding.

"This, it does seem reasonable," Jolene commented from the backseat. "We went in and no one was there so we decide to return another time. He must be doing a confession or some private conversation."

Paige nodded in agreement and then returned to Jolene's original comment. "You know, maybe you are having panic attacks."

"I don't know," Jorge shrugged. "I haven't eaten much today, that's probably it but I'm not worried. I'm eating better than I ever was, I stopped smoking and started running. Let's just forget about it."

"Chase, he gets panic attacks," Jolene repeated her earlier comment and at that point, this wasn't a concern to Jorge. "He passes out too. I have seen a couple of times but Diego, he said he see it a lot especially after Chase, his son die."

Everyone fell silent as they made their way back to Jolene's apartment building.

To Jorge, any form of illness was a sign of weakness and he hated that anyone had seen him that way, let alone Jolene. The last thing he wanted was for her to feel like she had any power in this situation. The fact that he was letting her live had more to do with her being Diego's sister than it had to do with him trusting her. He was going to keep a close eye on Jolene Silva in the upcoming weeks. One false move and she would have an accident. However, he wasn't going to give her any indication, one way or another, where she stood with him.

Back at her apartment, Jolene nervously said good-bye and Paige turned and nodded as she got out of the SUV but Jorge said nothing. He remained silent until they got back on the road again.

"I don't trust her," Jorge commented. "If it weren't for Diego…"

"We should talk to him," Paige insisted. "I'm sure he knows nothing about any of this. He confides a lot to me and I'm certain this is something he would tell me about."

"He confides in you?" Jorge asked, his attention suddenly shifted. "Like what?"

"Confides," Paige grinned and reached out to touch his arm. "It means it's a secret."

"Him and Chase?"

"I'm not talking about that," Paige replied mysteriously as her lips curved into a smile. "I won't betray his trust."

"I'm your husband," Jorge insisted. "You're supposed to tell me everything."

"Why are you so interested in his relationship with Chase?" Paige countered as her hand slid up his arm.

"Come on," Jorge said and laughed. "Diego wants him. Everyone knows that. It's not a secret, Paige."

She didn't reply and shook her head and changed the subject. "How are you feeling, really? Tell me the truth."

"I am telling you the truth," Jorge commented and sniffed. "What? You don't believe me?"

"I know you hate going to the doctor so there's always a chance you aren't telling me everything," Paige replied as they sat in traffic.

"I am fine," Jorge confirmed and removed his gloves, his hands now hot and sticky. "Life, it is beautiful. I just felt funny for a minute and now that minute has passed."

Traffic was slow but they eventually arrived at Diego's condo. Fortunately, Chase wasn't around, which was ideal because Jorge didn't really want to discuss anything in front of him.

Unlike Jolene, Diego didn't seem suspicious of their visit, which in itself, was a good sign. Although Jorge briefly wondered if Jolene had filled her brother in on everything, if she had, Diego wouldn't have been able to hide it. His face was often an opened book.

"We need to discuss something with you," Jorge commented after they all sat down, him across from Diego and Paige on the couch, almost directly facing the huge lime tree by the window. "It's of great importance."

Diego looked surprised and briefly turned his attention to Paige. "I would love to give you away at the wedding, is that why you're here, to talk about the wedding?"

"What?" Jorge asked and couldn't help but to laugh. "No, Diego this is not about the wedding. Although yes, that is important too, this has to do with business and it's urgent that we talk to you about it now."

"Have you talked to Jolene tonight?" Paige asked Diego who looked at them both skeptically and shook his head.

"What's going on with Jolene?" He looked puzzled. "She's been kind of a bitch lately, I don't know what is her problem is."

"We might know," Jorge commented and after exchanging looks with Paige, launched into the story. He told Diego everything from the night he met Paige at the hotel, about the Don Warrens, the emails and finally, he ended the story with everything that had taken place that night. Diego appeared to take everything in stride until they arrived at the end of the story and specifically, Jolene's part in everything.

"Wait! What?" Diego asked as he abruptly jumped up from the couch, his eyes expanded in size while his lips twisted together in an angry pout. "Jolene wanted to have you killed? What the hell is going on?"

"We aren't sure of that," Paige responded and stood up, her hand touched Diego's and a hint of sadness crossed his face as their eyes met. He quickly switched his attention to Jorge and shook his head. "I didn't know anything about this, Jorge."

"*Amigo*," Jorge put his hand in the air. "Calm down. We are not suggesting you knew anything and we aren't even sure about Jolene. All we know is what we told you. She may have been just trying to create a controversy, however, doing so without telling us, that in itself makes me...not happy."

Paige managed to get Diego to sit back down, his face distraught as if everything was slowly sinking in. Shaking his head, he remained silent.

"She knows that this is not acceptable," Jorge continued. "I have made this extremely clear to her. Now what we must do is make sure that no one else is going to give us trouble although, I suspect that these recent deaths might send out a very strong message to this community."

Diego nodded and Paige gave him a sad smile.

"We know this must be shocking for you to hear," Paige spoke softly to Diego. "But we wanted you to know the truth."

"I feel like an idiot!" Diego spoke emotionally. "I work with Jolene, she's my sister and all this was going on and I didn't know."

"She wasn't exactly going to share this with you," Jorge commented with a shrug. It was clear to him that Diego knew nothing of this deception.

"I should've known," Diego was insistent as he turned his attention back to Paige. "I trusted her!"

"I know," Paige spoke sympathetically. "She's your sister, of course, you would."

Anger crossed his face and he turned to Jorge. "She must go. We can't have her at the office anymore if this is the case."

Jorge was surprised by this suggestion. He hadn't actually thought that far ahead but perhaps he was right, maybe it was time for her to go.

"Let's wait and see," Jorge replied and moved ahead in his seat as if he were about to rise. "I believe that if she is guilty of anything, we will soon know. I have her being watched closely. This is the time the truth will come out. We must make her feel that she is safe but tell me something, Diego, are you sure your loyalty is not to her? She is family, after all."

Glancing at Paige then back at Jorge, Diego shook his head. "My loyalty is with the both of you. I gave Jolene a chance when she wanted to get out of Colombia after having no relationship with her for years. I trusted her. But you, Jorge, we go far back."

"Yes, we do," Jorge nodded. "Back to our time in California, at least 20 years."

"Those years, Jolene wasn't a part of my life," Diego shared this comment with Paige. "But us, we worked together for many years."

"On and off, yes," Jorge commented with another nod. "This is true."

"And you know that in all those years, I've been very loyal," Diego sternly remarked. "I am sorry to bring Jolene into the picture but I had no reason to ever believe she would betray you, that she would betray us."

"We don't know for sure she did," Paige reminded them both. "Let's not put her on the stake just yet. Let's see what happens the next couple of days. We will be vigilant and Diego, you didn't have this conversation with us. If anything, maybe suggest Jorge came over and asked you a lot of questions about the religious protestors but you weren't sure why."

"You got a camera here too, right?" Jorge asked as he glanced around.

"Yes, it's in the lime tree," Diego commented, causing both Paige and Jorge to laugh. Neither looked at it though.

"Can she see in here, now?" Jorge asked.

"Privacy, I don't see in her place and she can't see in mine," Diego spoke sternly. "We agreed on that long ago. The cameras are for us to monitor our own homes for safety reasons."

"Can that be changed?" Jorge asked and shared a look with Paige.

"Yes, but only I.." Diego suddenly stopped and jumped up and rushed out of the room, quickly returning with his laptop. "I can change it. She will never know."

"That is what I was hoping you would say," Jorge commented as he stood up from his chair and Paige did the same. "We have another person to visit but you, Diego, must keep an eye on her. That is your job and I am trusting you to let us know if she has a visitor tonight. She seemed to be dressed for a *date* when I arrived."

Diego looked surprised by this comment but quickly tapped the keys and sat back. "No one's there yet."

"Keep us posted," Jorge commented as him and Paige made their way to the door. "We will talk later."

"Sorry, Diego," Paige gave him a heartfelt look as they reached the door and Jorge gently touched her arm to usher her out, while across the room Diego shot her a sad smile.

Jorge sent a quick text message before they rushed out of the building and headed for the SUV. Their next stop was across town and they drove in silence. Jorge attempted to process everything while Paige, on the passenger side, appeared to be doing the same although her face carried some sadness. She sent a couple of text messages, which he assumed was to Diego, her face in a frown when they finally arrived at the next stop.

Standing outside an apartment door, Jorge had barely knocked when the door swung open and Sylvana stood on the other side. With a grin on her face, she gestured for them to come inside the apartment.

"I figured I would hear from you soon, Jorge," She commented with humor in her voice as she pointed toward the table and chairs that barely fit into her kitchen. Before he had a chance to reply, she extended her hand to Paige. "I don't think we've officially met. I'm Sylvana. I'm Jorge's cousin."

CHAPTER 50

Life is a series of beautiful moments and yet, we never know when it will end. Although we are fragile, most of us refuse to acknowledge this in our youth. We live recklessly, as if challenging fate, as if daring God and perhaps, even the devil. There's something glorious about living each moment as if it were your last and yet, ignorantly assuming that the last moment is never going to come.

Jorge Hernandez was fortunate. There were so many times in his life that he could've died and yet, he was still alive. Had Maria not been his full-time responsibility, if Verónic had been a good mother and a miracle named Paige Noël hadn't come into his life, perhaps he would've continued to live ignorantly with little care about what happened to him. A man needed a reason to get up in the morning and when those reasons started to fade away then, unfortunately, so did he.

No one knew how much his younger brother's death still haunted him. Thirty years later, a man in his forties, he could still see that child on the ground with his eyes wide opened and blood pouring out of his head. Miguel had always been so skinny, so small for his age, much like his own daughter now, his brother was fragile. Had it been one of his friends or another kid from the neighborhood that fell off the bike that day, chances are they would've survived.

It was Jorge's fault. No one had ever told him otherwise. His father blamed him, beat him with a mixture of fury and grief, showing no remorse for doing so and it was during that horrendous, excruciating lashing that Jorge first wished for his own death. He deserved it. His father had been right. He forced his brother on the dirt bike that day.

It was never Miguel's idea; he was always slightly delicate, avoiding activities that other boys were drawn to, instead he enjoyed spending time with their mother. He preferred playing with girls, he didn't like toy guns or anything that Jorge played with as a child but instead seemed reluctant. It wasn't in his nature.

Without a doubt, Miguel was a homosexual. It was so obvious to Jorge now as an adult but as a child, he was conditioned to believe that his little brother wasn't 'normal' and therefore, he felt compelled to force him to be more masculine. Had their father ever suspected that Miguel was what he referred to as a *maricón,* a 'faggot', Jorge's brother would've been beaten and forced out of the family home. It had been Jorge's job to protect him and in attempting to do so, he killed him instead.

Diego Silva was about the same age as Miguel would've been, had he lived. He reminded Jorge of Miguel. Perhaps that is why the two had been friends and business associates for over 20 years, why a part of him was protective of the man who once admitted to him that his own father had cast him away at a young age, after learning he was gay. Had Miguel lived, this would've been his fate too. It was in part, for this reason, that he hadn't killed Jolene that night. He certainly would've shot her had she not been Diego's sister.

It wasn't that he was sure that Jolene wanted him killed but it was undeniable that something wasn't making sense. Jorge had learned long ago that when things didn't add up, you didn't fuck around and wait until your head was on the chopping block, you took care of your enemy immediately and asked questions later. But why would she want him dead? What had he ever done to Jolene other than help her become a Canadian citizen, give her a job and try to improve her life? Was he missing something?

Diego didn't understand either; the information was still percolating and unfortunately, later that night a phone call to Paige only managed to complicate the situation even further. She was clearly comforting a troubled friend, her voice soft and loving as she listened more than talked, her eyes full of sadness, a frown formed on her face as she looked down, avoiding eye contact with Jorge.

The call didn't last long but ended with a promise to meet the following day. When it concluded, her eyes flickered to Jorge who was lying naked under the sheets, as he quietly thought. There was too much to process and she was about to add something else to the mix.

"Diego is upset," She finally spoke, her voice little more than a whisper as she lay against her pillow and moved close to Jorge, the smell of her shampoo was enticing as he reached out and moved a strand of hair from her face. "He was watching Jolene's apartment through the security camera and…he saw Chase arriving there. He said that Chase and Jolene were kissing…then he closed the laptop because he couldn't look anymore."

Jorge nodded. Regardless of the fact that Chase had never given any indication of being gay, there had been a part of Diego that held out hope and although it was easy to brush it off as being delusional, perhaps he knew something that others did not. Still, suspecting that someone you loved didn't feel the same way and seeing it with your own eyes was a whole other thing. Especially when the person they were with was with your sister.

"He's devastated," Paige continued and hesitated for a moment, "I think I might invite him over if you don't mind. I'm a little worried. He feels betrayed because Jolene knows how he feels about Chase and…. I don't know, it's such a mess."

Jorge didn't hesitate to reply with a shrug. "Yes, please, go ahead."

Paige grabbed her phone off the nightstand and tapped abruptly and waited.

"He's on his way."

Jorge didn't say anything but nodded.

"I know you probably think this is silly," Paige continued. "I know they weren't together or anything I just, I think he had valid reasons to feel that maybe there was something there. And I'm not saying he's right but it doesn't matter because he *felt* it was right. What we believe is powerful."

Jorge knew that all too well. He suddenly thought of Miguel and nodded.

He had greatly underestimated how upset Diego would be when he arrived. Although Jorge knew the man for over 20 years, he had never seen this side of his friend. Always tough, hardly someone to back down from a fight, he never would've expected to see Diego completely broken before his eyes. Not that Jorge blamed Chase because it simply wasn't in his nature to do what didn't feel right and he was young, a naïve boy of 25, what did he know about love? He knew lust only and Jolene knew how to manipulate with her attractiveness. The honeypot was wide open.

"I couldn't believe it," Diego sniffed as Paige attempted to comfort him, handing him a box of Kleenex and placing a cup of camomile tea on the nearby table. Diego hadn't even been this upset when his sugar daddy died a few year's earlier. Then again, he had never loved that man. "I mean, I don't know what I thought would happen or who Jolene was expecting in her apartment but I never thought…"

Paige nodded with compassion in her eyes while Jorge sat across from them, silently watching, listening…thinking.

"I did," Jorge spoke up and Paige gave him a warning look as if to suggest it wasn't a good time to comment. "I mean, I suspected that maybe…I don't know, what do I know?" He quickly back peddled. "I thought maybe there was a little flirtation."

"But Jolene, she flirts with everyone," Diego commented with a shrug, he twisted his lips at the same time and then fell back to his original gloominess. "I didn't think, you know, they were working together for a long time. If something were to happen, why now?"

Jorge decided to not answer this question and he didn't need Paige's warning glance this time.

"Here, have some tea," Paige encouraged Diego. "It will make you feel better."

"Tea is not going to make him feel better," Jorge insisted. "A joint, maybe? A drink? Some tequila? Yes? What do you say, Diego?"

"Liquor is not a good idea," Paige commented and gave him another look. "It's a depressant."

"She is right," Jorge replied. "This is true. I have a joint. It's been a long day, maybe we all need to share it."

They were in agreement and Jorge grabbed it out of his jacket pocket and met them on the patio, where Diego continued to pour his heart out to Paige while she attempted to comfort him. But nothing she could say or do would help a broken heart, as far as Jorge was concerned, it was just about getting through the night.

Lighting it up, they passed it around, each taking a hit. Diego was the first to react.

"This is it? This is what we are selling now?" His eyes were full of excitement. "This is good."

"Only the best," Jorge replied. "Why do you think this is now my focus? It's about to go crazy once it becomes legal. We're going to cash in."

"This is the best," Diego insisted. "Although, I did have some in California once that was pretty close."

"BC Bud," Jorge commented. "How could you not know that? Its reputation precedes it."

"It wasn't exactly on the citizen test," Diego said with a shrug, his usual disposition slowly returning.

"Perhaps it should be," Jorge insisted. "It is soon to be one of the things Canada will be known for throughout the world and we're here, we'll be a part of it."

Diego seemed to enjoy this and took the remark on a deeper level.

They were silent. Sharing the joint, looking out over the city of Toronto, no words were necessary.

After they finished and went back inside, Jorge ignored Paige's comments on tequila and poured them each a shot.

"But only one," He insisted and they each reached for their glass. "To the three of us. We are more powerful than anyone that tries to take us down or breaks our hearts," He made brief eye contact with Diego and then turned his attention to Paige. "We must remember that we are indestructible and our loyalty to each other, more powerful than our enemy."

Tapping their glasses together, they sank the shots then sat in silence.

"Diego, I must be honest with you about something," Jorge felt compelled to share the truth. "Marco, he is a spy in the office."

"Well, I figured that," Diego's voice returned to its usually arrogant level, his eyes expanding in size. "You're the one who sent him. He's obviously a hacker."

"True," Jorge agreed. "But what you don't know is that Sylvana, the one who drives you *loco,* she is my cousin."

"No fucking way!" Diego's voice was louder than expected which caused Paige to hit his arm and point toward Maria's bedroom door. He immediately looked regretful but continued to speak. "I should've known! She's obnoxious like you."

Jorge laughed at this remark and Paige joined him.

"But she's Italian?" Diego commented. "She doesn't look Mexican."

"Well, her mother is Mexican," Jorge gently explained. "Her father is Italian. Sometimes us Mexicans, we like to try new things." He gave a sanctimonious smile toward Paige who shook her head and laughed. "That's how the Italian got into the picture and now, we have Sylvana."

"Mind you, Sylvana was a baby when I was a teenager, so I barely knew her when they immigrated to Canada. We saw each other occasionally in passing over the years. When you were looking for people for the office, why do you think I wanted to see the resumes. I knew she was applying. I wanted to have someone keeping an eye on things and well, that has served us well. She keeps me informed."

"Wow," Diego continued to look surprised. "I never would've guessed that."

"I know," Jorge countered. "That is why she was perfect."

"All the times I've told you she was a bitch…"

"Oh and yes, that is true," Jorge laughed. "She's feisty. How could she not be when she's half Italian and half Latina? The woman is doomed to marry a man that she makes crazy both in and out of the bedroom. That is how it is, you know?"

Appearing relaxed but still preoccupied, Diego seemed to slip away to another place and sensing his sadness, Jorge quickly kicked in.

"Diego, Paige and I were discussing it," He gave her a quick glance and knew she would be on board with whatever he said at this point. "We would like to have a wedding soon. Something small, very intimate with only a few people but neither of us want to plan it. You know, we aren't that good at this kind of thing."

"I'll do it!" Diego instantly perked up. "I would love to plan your wedding."

He instantly looked at Paige then back at Jorge. "I…. I don't want to sound rude, I couldn't picture the two of you planning a wedding," The smug expression returned to his face and he instantly shot Paige an innocent look. "No offense."

"Oh, none was taken," She insisted and shared a brief, relieved look with Jorge.

"None here either, my friend," He directed his comment at Diego. "If you do not mind helping us?"

"No," Diego looked at him as if he were insane. "Are you kidding? This is my thing. It will be low-key but classy." He assured them.

"Yes, please, nothing tacky like doves flying everywhere," Jorge wrinkled his nose. "My cousin did that years ago and there was bird shit everywhere."

"But Diego," Jorge insisted. "Small, no big wedding. Nothing over the top."

"I promise you."

The sound of a door clicking interrupted them as Maria entered the room wearing her pink nightdress, she carried an empty glass with her. "I needed more water." She immediately gave the excuse without being asked. "What's going on?"

Jorge noted that she didn't get more water but instead walked over to the couch and sat down beside Paige. "Did I hear something about the wedding?"

"Diego has graciously agreed to help us plan our wedding," Jorge replied with a nod.

"Can I help?" She directed her question at Diego.

"Sure," Diego agreed with a nod. "I definitely need your help. These two, they are useless when it comes to this kind of thing."

"It's true," Maria agreed with a yawn. "Plus, you're a homosexual, so this is your forte."

"Maria!" Jorge snapped at her. "You do not say these things."

"It's fine," Diego insisted. "In this case, it's kind of true."

Jorge grinned and he made brief eye contact with Paige before glancing at his phone.

"Maria, it is late," He insisted. "Back to bed."

"Ok," She agreed with another yawn. "I will text you later this week Diego and we will discuss the wedding plans."

With that, she rose from the couch and walked back to her room, closing the door behind her. Glancing at the empty glass sitting on the coffee table, Jorge raised his eyebrow and shook his head.

"She's her father's daughter," Diego quietly commented.

"And this, is it a bad thing?" Jorge asked and glanced at his phone again, noting that he had a missed call and a voicemail "This is the day that will never end, I must check something," He commented and walked into the bedroom, leaving Diego and Paige to talk privately. Neither questioned what he was doing and for that, he was grateful.

The message was brief, to the point and with it, everything changed. Glancing back into the living room, Diego appeared to perk up as he excitedly spoke to Paige about the upcoming wedding and Jorge decided to wait. This was not news he had to share yet. At this moment, his family was having a joyous moment and he wasn't about to take that away. The news would wait until the morning. But until then, Jorge watched them and he smiled. Life was beautiful.

Love the book? Write a review! Want to learn more about Jorge, Diego, Chase and Jolene? Check out *Always be a Wolf* and *We're All Animals* by Mima!

To keep updated on the sequel to *The Devil is Smooth Like Honey*, please go to <u>www.mimaonfire.com</u> and sign up for the newsletter!

Printed in the United States
By Bookmasters